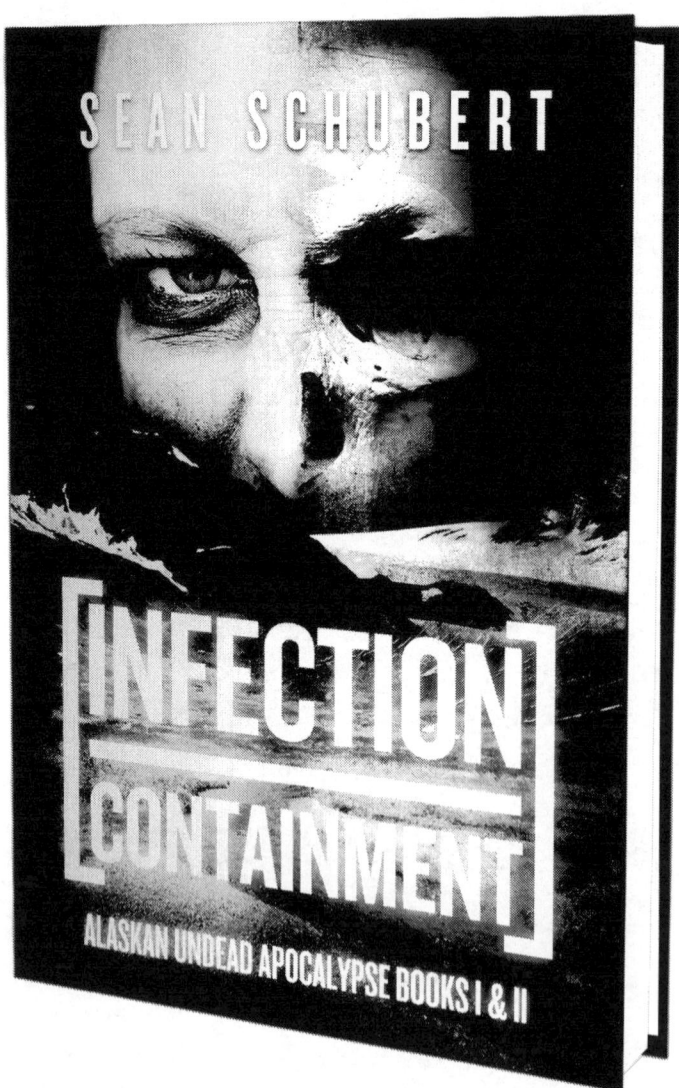

[MITIGATION]

ALASKAN UNDEAD APOCALYPSE BOOK III

SEAN SCHUBERT

A PERMUTED PRESS book

ISBN (trade paperback): 978-1-61868-0-679
ISBN (eBook): 978-1-61868-0-686

Mitigation: Alaskan Undead Apocalypse copyright © 2013
by Sean Schubert
All Rights Reserved.
Cover art by Dean Samed, Conzpiracy Digital

**PERMUTED
PRESS**

[PART I]

1

[PROLOGUE]

The cold, unrelenting and worsening, forced them from their lonely trek into the cave. Without fire, the cave was equal parts dark and cold, though it provided some shelter from the remorseless winds. Anything was better than being out in the weather, even their prehistoric brains knew that. Though largely still, the air in the cave remained bitterly cold. The walls and dirt floor boasted glistening patches of ice like jeweled adornments. The trio hunkered down under a large animal skin to warm themselves. Absently they lifted pinches of frozen earth from beneath them and stuffed it clumsily into their mouths. The ice, the water anyway, they needed, and the dirt went into their empty bellies attempting in vain to fill the greedy and protesting void.

It had been days since they had eaten, so he parted company with his two huddled companions in search of anything he could find. If he could happen upon a sleeping animal, perhaps he could plunge his crude spear into the beast. With one aggressive stroke he could have a warm coat and food. They would be saved and then he would mate with the female. He had tried before but she was with the other male, which only led to challenges and fighting and painful bruises. If he were to bring back food, she would certainly present herself to him. Her strong scent was maddening to him, and watching the other male take her time and time again didn't help matters.

The darkness was an enveloping mouth closing in behind him and snuffing out the dim light. His large, hairy hands groped in front of him like a curious cat's whiskers, seeking changes in the air and the encroaching walls to either side of him. Until his eyes could adjust, his hands would lead him.

The path grew more and more narrow, like he was walking down the narrowing throat of a predator. Thankfully, both the walls and ceiling had been eroded to largely smooth surfaces after centuries of water and air movement through the tunnel. He soon found himself standing at the threshold of a larger cavern.

Suddenly the air became warm and moist. The echo of his labored breathing changed as well, wandering into the higher corners and ceiling only to bounce back to him. He took two steps into the cavern and stopped suddenly, instinctively lowering his already stooped posture into a much tighter and defensive stance. A pungent odor, a tantalizing and threatening blend of life and death...growth and rot, tickled his nose and set his senses on alert. It was a den. Instead of opportunity, he felt alarm. He should not be there.

Blind and terrified, he started to back out of the cavern, painfully aware of every echoing sound he made. Leaping silently from the darkness, the faceless beast latched onto his shoulder just below his neck. His tough, weather-beaten skin with its thick coat of dark hair was torn by the beast's ruthless gnashing teeth.

The beast reeked with a foulness he'd never encountered. The pain, anguishing and sudden, was completely unexpected. His senses, feral and unrefined, were overwhelmed. He tried to throw his attacker off but its teeth were too deep and its jaw too strong. His flight response forcefully aborted, primal fear elbowed its noisy self to the forefront and demanded attention.

His scream, so seemingly distant and foreign to him, echoed in the dark while the pain reverberated through his chest. Once again, instinct guided his response. His left arm was useless, tightly clutched in the beast's ruthless maw, but his right arm was free and eager to fight for his survival. With one forceful jab, the heavy wooden spear, nothing more than a strong rock-sharpened stick, penetrated both darkness and the beast. His attacker, which looked like nothing more than jagged teeth and darkness, spilled its lifeblood in a sticky, warm surge covering his hand and arm.

The grinding jaws, holding tight to his violated flesh, released him and retreated into the gloom. Not waiting even a second, he spun around and stumbled his way back to his companions. His entire left flank was painted red with his blood, as were the cave walls he had used to steady himself along the way. The blood loss was starting to take a toll on his senses. He felt like he was walking through a fog that wrapped itself tightly around his head, restricting his vision and his hearing. And yet, the open wounds that had been splashed with the more viscous fluid of the creature felt...different. It felt as if they bubbled and burned, but it wasn't necessarily raw pain like he felt from the other gashes in his flesh. The tissue was changing rapidly.

He was doing little more than staggering and struggling for breath when he reemerged from the cave's depths. Despite the absence of light, the other two could sense both his wounds and his fading life. He reeked of death...salty and rotten. With a series of primal grunts and gestures, he communicated that danger lurked deeper in the cave and that they should leave at once. Looking out at the howling winds and blistering snow, they knew they had to at least wait for the darkness to pass and the light to return.

Empty-handed and now bloodied, his hope to mate with the female faded and strangely, so did his desire. The burning and the pain could not be ignored despite his best efforts. He wanted to surrender to his anguish and wail, but he stubbornly resisted any sign of weakness. All he could think to do was rest. Maybe the pain would diminish if he slept. As his blood continued to seep and flow mercilessly, his energy and his consciousness began to fade so that sleep could not be eluded.

Sometime shortly before dawn, his breathing shallowed out to nothing and his heart stopped. This would have been the end for him except that his brain, primitive as it was, continued to function. Some new organism, introduced through the bite wound on his shoulder, had invaded his brain, changing its chemistry.

His frontal lobe, the part of the brain that controlled reasoning—however limited it may have been for him—stopped working, but other segments continued to fire off electrical currents to nerve endings controlling muscles. The limbic system, the center of his emotions, flared violently with current until every synapse for every emotion was silent and dead; every emotion, that is, except for rage, which found all the unspent energy for every other feeling funneled into it. His temperature, thirst, and fatigue, all answering to the hypothalamus, found themselves things of the past, but his hunger, also a hypothalamic function, surged to insatiable levels. It was the hunger and rage that roused him.

When he opened his eyes that following morning, the world had changed for him. His eyes saw everything only in hints of red and his former companions nearly glowed, as if on fire.

The nagging hunger in his stomach from the night before had multiplied to an overpowering driving force compelling him to seek out the only meal to be found. And they were right there in the cave with him.

He rose from beneath his thick animal hide covering and fell upon his still sleeping companions.

He grabbed the female first, her scent once so sexually arousing now only calling to his suffering, hungry brain. He bit the back of her neck, tearing away chewy bits of hairy flesh. His teeth fell again and again rending tissue from her as she screamed and struggled beneath him. He didn't pause to even chew as he swallowed the warm chunks into his belly. Soon, the whitish bones of her neck were peeking up through the swelling, red morass. His face was streaked with warm crimson blood and dangling bits of skin and tissue. His biting was sometimes too aggressive to allow his chewing to keep pace, resulting in pulpy morsels of flesh falling from his mouth in awful and partially chewed wads.

His male companion rolled away and found a spear. The larger male came at him, screaming and threatening as any frightened and threatened animal would. Still feeding on the struggling but weakening female, his infected brain told him that this victim was too weak to escape and that he should now attack this other prey before it escaped.

He stood just in time for the spear to be thrust into his chest. He felt nothing, the wound having no effect on him or his own attack. He leapt forward, spear and all, and grabbed the other male by his shoulders. They wrestled one another to the floor of the cave. Though the other male was bigger than him, the infection, which limited and focused his energy and his strength by shutting off certain functions of his body, poured unused resources into his arms and his legs, infusing him with unlimited stamina and unequaled power. The hunger drove his attack, which surprised and unsettled his victim all the more.

He bit down onto cheek, then cheekbone, and finally onto an eye. The soft, wet tissue surrendered itself to his bite with a delicious sucking ooze of salty fluid. When his victim tried to bite him back, he simply used that opportunity to instead chew off the other man's lower lip and tongue. The battle was vicious, bloody, and horribly one-sided. Despite the spear and his superior size, the other man could not compete with the infection.

The feasting on the two corpses didn't last much longer than the fighting had. No matter how much he ate, he never seemed able to quench the hunger. The bodies had been picked clean to the bone and still he needed more.

His hunger took him back into the cold, where he wandered aimlessly for countless days seeking sustenance. His skin, whipped gruesomely by the wind, began to crack and peel. He lost toes and tips of finger as they froze and simply fell off. His hair continued to grow, though it also began to fall from his body in clumps. His eyes too eventually froze and burst from their sockets, but he didn't need eyes when he had the hunger to propel him forward. With his muscles deteriorating and his limbs failing, he walked until his legs could no longer move. He didn't fall though. He simply stopped walking. He was a living statue, standing still as snow and ice slowly but steadily tightened their grip around him. The frigid elements of the advancing Ice Age devoured him much the way he had devoured his companions. He was wrapped in ice, locked in its seemingly eternal white embrace.

And within the cold stillness of his unforgiving prison, the hunger persisted. His flesh, though mostly preserved by its icy confines, continued to rot and decay and his senses faded into an oblivion of white. Still, when the rest of the world had withered into a gray malaise, the hunger called to him, nagging, festering, torturing.

* * *

Centuries later, on a planet that was gradually warming, his frosty tomb slowly began to release its grip. It started with cracks and pops in the ice, running through the glacier like seismic jolts along tectonic plates. Fissures filled with running water and long absent scents and tastes from a forgotten world. The process took centuries, but still he and the infection waited.

Partially exposed, he had forgotten how to move despite the freedom to do so again. Thousands of years embedded in the glacial grip had taken its toll on his body, most of which was bone with only the barest of tissue remaining. His eyes had long ago rotted in their sockets, but he found his olfactory and auditory senses still served him.

Then one day, a familiar aroma roused him. *Prey.* It was close and coming closer. It was right on top of him, just below his nose and, more importantly, his mouth. The infection, never dormant but always waiting, sparked long quiet nerves back to life which found willing, if seriously atrophied, muscles starting to once again respond. At first his body resisted his efforts to move, having been motionless for an Age. However, the infection wouldn't be denied.

Starting with a single tic, which split the resistant tissue at the corners of his mouth, his lifeless face reanimated. The hunger, sensing its quarry so close, directed his nearly toothless mouth forward until it landed on something warm, something that awakened in him the awful rage that had awaited this moment for tens of thousands of years.

His first bite came down on something foreign—not flesh and not animal hide, but something different. His second blind but determined attempt found its mark. One of his few jagged teeth sank itself into something soft and fleshy. It tasted of youth, so sweet and fatty. But a taste was all that he was granted. There was screaming and then there was quiet.

That quiet lasted a bit, but to him, time no longer had any meaning. Once, long ago, before the infection and its eternal night, he had measured time by the coming and going of the light of day. During his multi-millennial torment in the glacier, when time was not measured but was instead endured, there was no sleep and no rest. There was always the hunger and now that hunger, teased maliciously by the single morsel, was rippling electrically through his still-partially ice-encased torso.

His convulsing, a near constant tremor through the ice, delivered exactly what the infection craved: freedom. As the ice separated in front of him, he fell forward awkwardly. Behind him, the bottom third or more of both of his legs were still embedded in the receding glacier, the rotten gray stumps protruding ever so slightly higher than the ice that still held them in place. His dismemberment caused not the slightest pain or distress.

Legs or no, the hunger called to him and he was powerless against its beckoning. Using his arms to pull himself along the stream bank, he slithered and crawled toward the faint but undeniable scent of prey.

He grunted and moaned slightly as he moved, the temptation of the kill exciting him. Sometime later, the air changed slightly, his senses recognizing the shift as the approach of food. It was coming to him.

And all at once, there was a roar such that he'd never heard and then his body was rocked with a violent impact. There was another violent noise, this one more organic...alive...a voice...his kill...his meal. Another barking clap of sound and another punching pressure against and through his back and then his chest.

Laboriously, he rolled onto his back so that he was facing from a sitting position whatever was behind him. Sensing that it was his prey, he reached blindly toward the sound as it echoed again. His hand disintegrated painlessly. He was aware that it was gone but it was of no consequence. The loss of the limb was less important than feeding the hunger. Had he known that he was being pelted with bullets, it likely wouldn't have mattered. He reached out with his obliterated stump and absorbed two more of the blasts in his upper chest. His bones splintered and more of his already inadequate flesh holding his frame together disappeared in a hail of buckshot. Soon there wouldn't be enough of him to continue to move. The anguish and the hunger, however, would never quit.

So, he turned himself around and, with his one good hand, belly crawled the other direction after his now retreating prey who smelled like the other one tasted.

[PART II]

2

Leached of color and life, the gray sky seemed a fitting companion for Dr. Caldwell. He leaned back in the white plastic chair, fear and pain coupling themselves with the infection in his veins. As soon as his friends had dropped out of sight, he began to doubt his resolve and his decision to separate himself from the ragged group of survivors that he had come to think of as family over the past few months.

A ripple of pain from the bite wound on his hand sent another jolt seemingly through every nerve in his body at once. He held his breath and closed his eyes, hoping to hold onto the moment for just a few seconds more. He could feel his body's chemistry begin to change. His thirst was unquenchable and yet, every time he cracked his mouth a sea of saliva spilled from its corners and onto his chin. He'd stopped wiping away the excess quite a while ago. There was no one left to impress and he could care less, so he left it to dangle in lazy strands from his chin.

The surge of pain subsided, though it never actually stopped. Just like the ebb and flow of a river, sometimes a torrent and sometimes a trickle, the burning ache was always there. Realizing his eyes were closed, he jerked forward, opening them in fear that his life would end in total darkness.

How long had he been sitting there alone? He had no way of knowing. Was there any real value in time at the end of the world? Yet, time was what he wanted; a few more hours, a few more days, a few more weeks. He wanted whatever he could get but he wasn't likely to get any of it.

He couldn't feel his feet or his legs anymore. The pins and needles sensation had long since faded, leaving his lower limbs cold and lifeless. Had he wanted to chase after his friends who had left him at his own urging, he couldn't. He'd chosen his lonely fate and now he regretted it.

Dr. Caldwell was sitting in the desolate parking lot of a ruined convenience store along an abandoned stretch of the Seward Highway which led south out of Anchorage, Alaska. The destruction, so complete, suggested that perhaps a tornado had ravaged the little highway pit stop. A large semi-trailer was on its side behind the devastated station building and its contents, like its entrails, were spilled across the pavement. There were cars too, most with doors open and some scorched and melted from long extinguished flames. There didn't seem to be anything left. His world had unraveled, leaving in its wake only hopelessness and fear... and a very big mess.

He looked down at the swollen tissue on his hand. The skin around the still seeping wound was festering with infection, changing color and texture with each passing minute. His arm too, with its hardening and darkening veins, was starting to show signs of the mysterious malady's spread. What was it that had taken so many lives and ended the civilization to which they had all grown so accustomed?

How many weeks had it been since that little boy was brought into the Providence Hospital Emergency Room by his terrified parents? His name was Martin and he had a similar bite on his hand, though the child's wound was seemingly far less threatening; not much more than a scratch really.

His parents told the hospital staff that he'd been bitten by something in the woods. They insisted that it was some kind of a rabid animal, but the children who had been with little Martin reported that it had been something else. Martin's sister, Jules, said that it was a caveman who'd bitten the boy. No one listened. They were all too busy fighting a losing battle to the mysterious infection.

Try as they might, the doctors and nurses were helpless in fighting the aggressive illness. After a brief battle, the boy was declared dead. If that had been all, then the boy's tragic death would have been filed with eminent epidemiologists and studied. That wasn't all though.

Death wasn't the end for little Martin. He arose from his death slumber as a maniacal predator, killing and maiming all those around him. And those who fell due to his attacks rose as well, adding to the bedlam. The uncontrolled chaos spread throughout Providence and then across Anchorage. With each new victim, there arose a new monster. In a matter of hours, the chaos had reached every corner of Anchorage and rendered the city a wasteland.

Safe refuge was sought by those fortunate few who had not fallen victim to the undead plague in its opening stages. While legions of the walking dead roamed the otherwise deserted city streets, the terrified and confused survivors had hidden, hoped, and waited.

Dr. Caldwell had been amongst a group of souls brought together out of necessity. Partially by design and partially out of luck, they had managed to stay one step ahead of the undead curse.

By default as much as anything else, a younger man named Neil had assumed the mantle of leadership for their group. And for that, Dr. Caldwell was both thankful and perhaps a little resentful. Dr. Caldwell was older and more experienced than Neil, but the circumstances under which they had become a clan of sorts were well outside his realm of expertise.

Dr. Caldwell was, as his title suggested, a man of science...of hard practicality rooted in scientific principles. When he witnessed the dead reanimating in a homicidal rage and start to perform atrocities that defied imagination, the foundations on which he had based his many years were shaken to the core. The world was no longer the predictable, consistent place that it had once been. And while everyone else, Dr. Caldwell included, had nothing but doubts and fears, Neil seemed to have answers and ideas.

The rest of their group were as different from one another as the day was long. There was Jerry, who had been a nurse's aide at Providence, and the two children, Jules and Danny, whom he had rescued and had been protecting ever since.

Jules and Danny were placed in Jerry's care at Providence Hospital at the outset of the calamity. It had been Jules' brother and Danny's best friend Martin with whom the undead holocaust had originated. Their Alaskan family vacation became a living nightmare without end.

The three women in the group were Emma, Meghan, and Claire. Emma had been an administrative employee at Providence, and had been with Dr. Caldwell since their terrifying flight from the hospital. Over the months, Dr. Caldwell and Emma developed a relationship that had always flirted with romance but never went so far as to be romantic. Dr. Caldwell, out of a sense of fidelity to his likely dead wife, never allowed any sort of physical intimacy to arise between them, a fact he presently regretted.

Meghan was with Neil, Jerry, and a small group of survivors hiding out in a bunkered suburban home in South Anchorage. She was as strong as she was beautiful. She was pragmatic and thoughtful, typically listening more than speaking. She was young but she didn't allow that to handicap her in any way. She was also perpetually at Neil's side both physically and during discussions, supporting his ideas and strategies to keep them all safe.

Claire was younger still and acted like it. She had been a college student without any real direction and not much had changed. She was far from intellectually challenged but her impetuous youth oftentimes led her to speak without having heard all of a story. More and more, she and Jerry had become an inseparable pair, their mutual "twitterpation" encouraging smiles on everyone around them.

These souls and a few others who had come and gone became his "family of the apocalypse". He loved them all. And, at present, he wished that he had their company again. In the short while since they'd left him, he was already missing them as if he hadn't seen them in a lifetime.

3

Through the disorientation of his delirium, Dr. Caldwell detected a distinct sound standing out from all else around. At first, he doubted his own senses. He could have sworn that it was the sound of an automobile's engine. It resembled the lower choke of a small diesel engine...a European car perhaps.

Gradually, the decidedly mechanical hum's volume grew enough for him to suspect that it was indeed a car approaching him. Was it a hallucination? Could this be the buzzing that the younger members of the party were able to hear whenever the undead were near?

If it was the horde of zombies, or zekes as they decided to call them, he only hoped that he would be dead before they reached him. Dying was bad enough; he didn't need to be dismembered and devoured in the process.

And then he wondered if he would be on the menu at all. Would his infected flesh not attract the undeads' attention? It likely wouldn't matter anyway. He'd probably succumb before then. An immense sadness followed his last thought.

He thought of his wife, Val, who had died just as alone as he was destined to do. When his thoughts turned to his children, Laura and Jacob, both hopefully safe in the "lower forty-eight" states, he felt regret and concern. He couldn't begin to guess what fates awaited them and everyone else...everywhere. What would become of all of them and the world in which they lived? Would they be able to outlast this tragedy?

And finally he thought about another woman with whom he'd fallen in love. Emma's face was burned indelibly into his memory. He was concerned for her future as well. He wanted her and everyone else in their family of survivors to continue to see tomorrows for as long as they were able. He dreaded the possibility that, assuming he did reanimate as a monster, he would hunt them.

He had neither the strength nor the coordination to run, so whatever was coming would catch him. There was no denying that. He looked around quickly, trying to find anywhere that he might hide. The simple motion of looking about was enough to invite more dizziness and nausea.

He closed his eyes and found himself doing something that hadn't crossed his mind in years. He prayed. He solicited the Lord Almighty's help in his time of need. He didn't pray for salvation or for deliverance. No, he prayed for a quick death. He prayed that he would be spared the violent end that so many others had endured, including his wife. He prayed that perhaps he would draw his final breath before the cold, gray claws of the undead could lay themselves upon his flesh.

And when he opened his eyes, he was surprised to see a small car heading south down the Seward Highway. He squinted his eyes against the fading light of the day, inviting his headache to further tighten its hold on his senses.

Despite the distance and the discomfort, Dr. Caldwell was able to see that it was a small black sedan. The little car moved along at a good pace, ignoring the posted warning signs declaring that section of highway had been designated a safety corridor. Patrolling State Troopers would likely have taken exception to the utter disregard for the signs or the laws. If, of course, there were still State Troopers around to enforce such rules.

He thought for a moment that he recognized the little black car. Perhaps it was just an illusion created by the unfortunate cooperation between the infection killing him and the emerging evening light.

As it neared him, however, he was convinced that he did know that car. It looked like a black Volkswagen Passat. And if it was that car, he already knew who was at the wheel.

For the first time since his friends had left him, he regretted not having a gun. Several weeks before, when the calamity that had laid low Anchorage and its population was still in its early stages, they had run across another survivor.

Her name was Maggie. On the surface, she appeared to be an eccentric but relatively harmless older woman. With a trunk full of Bibles and not a single weapon with which to defend herself, she seemed the least threatening person in the city. That assumption had cost them dearly.

Although they were never able to determine for certain, they all suspected that she was a sociopath bent on helping people toward holy salvation by turning them into hot meals for the undead.

She recited the Lord's words from the Bible, but tended to share only those words about vengeance and redemption through death. They should have been more on their guard with her, but who would have guessed that someone with a car full of Bibles could be so...sick?

Nevertheless, sick she definitely was. She hadn't actually led them to their deaths at the hands of the walking dead, but she had tried. When they ran across Maggie and her little black car, they had the advantage of traveling in the comfort and relative safety of a minivan. They could keep on the go and haul around with them more supplies than they would have been able to carry otherwise. It was their deluxe life raft in the flood and she took all of that away from them with a single, malicious stroke.

Maggie had sabotaged the van's engine in the middle of the night and then fled, but not before she took most of their stores of food. She also propped open the doors of their temporary sanctuary and all but invited in any zombies who might have happened by them. She rang the proverbial dinner bell and then left. Dr. Caldwell suspected that she was likely just searching the area for some of the abominations to lead back to them, but he couldn't be certain. Luckily, it didn't come to that.

As a result of her rendering their transportation useless, she forced them back onto their feet, making their search for safety both longer and more dangerous. Several people were lost due to those circumstances, Dr. Caldwell himself merely being the most recent.

Despite the fog of his infection, he struggled to think of any options. Perhaps he could throw something in the road or force her to crash somehow. Looking around though, he couldn't find anything that he would be able to lift and throw that could possibly bring such a wish to fruition.

His focus on the task helped him to find a little clarity in his thoughts and a small reserve of strength in his limbs. She was getting closer and still nothing presented itself to him. Desperate, he did the only thing he could.

4

Behind the wheel of the black Passat, Maggie was humming a hymn to herself and enjoying the relatively clear weather. The rain had stopped and the road was open. It had been a good several days and the Lord was smiling on her.

After leaving those blaspheming fools stranded and hopeless with their damaged minivan, she'd wandered Anchorage for more than a week without seeing any other souls to save. She was beginning to think that her work was done. Maybe all of God's children had been delivered to His Kingdom.

She wasn't quite sure what her next step should be. Was she to give herself over to the Lord's instrument of salvation so that she too could be delivered?

And then in East Anchorage, she found a thriving community of survivors who had found refuge in a Costco. The giant store's walls were strong with very few windows and its shelves and storeroom were filled to overflowing with food stuffs and other necessities. The conditions couldn't be more ideal for a long wait.

Many of those survivors had started that first morning of the catastrophe at the Bear Valley Fire Station in South Anchorage. With no hope of help arriving any time soon, those willing had loaded onto one of the large fire engines and tried to make their escape. Before too long, it became apparent that their diesel-powered ark would not be able to get them through the snarling tangles of traffic on Anchorage's roads. They decided instead to find another refuge and settled on the East Anchorage Costco by virtue of the fact that they were close to it and it promised both supplies and safety; maybe enough of both to help them subsist until help did finally arrive.

Since that time, they had been joined by families lucky enough or smart enough to happen upon their haven. All had been welcomed to share in their bounty and their security.

There were dozens of people there who were eager to hear God's words. Maggie was more than willing to share His message and her own testimony. They welcomed her work and His words with open arms and willing hearts. It was more than she could ask and decidedly more than she had expected.

She lived with them for several days, enjoying company but always waiting for her opportunity to perform her true work. Her purpose was clear in her mind and free from her thoughts was any sense of guilt or doubt. She was, after all, performing His work. How could doing such great things create either guilt or doubt for her or anyone else for that matter?

Early one morning, Maggie awoke to hear His voice instructing her. He told her that it was time and that he would show her the way. She found, with his guidance, an unattended emergency exit. She knew what she had to do. On foot, she ventured into the adjoining neighborhoods and found what she sought.

They may have been His instrument, but that made them no less frightening. There was a large group of ashen-colored devils near a school nestled back in the neighborhood. It was as if He had gathered them there for her. There wasn't much enticement needed. All that was required was for them to see her and they were immediately fast on her heels, shuffling hungrily after her. She moved just fast enough to stay ahead of them but not so fast as to lose them. Their festering ranks swelled steadily as more and more of them joined the horrible procession.

She led them back to the same Costco exit that she'd left propped slightly open. Following the scent of prey, they piled through the door to pounce on the unsuspecting families still rising for the day. The chaos that followed was horrible and redeeming. Men, women, and children, largely defenseless and totally unprepared, were ruthlessly butchered. The Costco floor became a torrential sea of red. There was nowhere to run for any of them. Their walls, once protecting them, had been used to trap and, ultimately, doom them all.

Maggie once again managed to get herself out and back on the road to continue to perform the Lord's bidding. There had been a handful more people here and there, smaller groups mostly, who had been delivered as well. With each new victory, she felt reinvigorated and inspired and ready to do more of the same. These were truly wonderful days and could never have come to pass without His intervention. She thanked Him for the wonderful opportunity with each waking day.

It had been days since she had seen anyone though, so she suspected perhaps all of Anchorage's souls had been harvested. With her car's fuel tank full of pilfered gasoline, she decided that it was high time to move to more fertile grounds.

She was unable to get out of Anchorage on the northbound Glenn Highway, so she decided to try her luck heading south. Once again, the Lord showed her the way.

She found her way onto the southbound Seward Highway and decided that was the path for her to follow. The unknown was again before her, but her faith in God carried her forward.

There she was heading south with nothing but possibilities and opportunities in her thoughts. So wrapped up in her thoughts was she that she didn't see the man crawling into the road ahead of her.

5

Dr. Caldwell was more or less spent when he finally was able to get himself out of the parking lot and into the road. His legs were of little use to him, so he pulled himself along the abrasive pavement with his hands and sheer will, looking like a six foot serpent.

His fading, opaque skin glistened with the deluge of sweat that poured from his forehead down to his chin. The salty fluid dampened his hair, his neck and his clothing. He could feel it course down his chest and his back in torrents. It appeared as if he was crawling through a fog, as his deep exhaled breaths gathered in front of him. Every muscle in his body that continued to respond to his requests was struggling to propel him forward.

It would all be worth it though if he could....

Now that he was in the road, he wasn't certain *what* his next move should be. He doubted his ability to get himself there, so he hadn't entirely fleshed out his next steps. He figured that he would likely collapse before ever arriving.

With the black car barreling down on him, he thought it only fitting to fight fire with fire. He got himself into the middle of the road, steadied himself on his numb haunches, folded his hands in front of his face, and continued the prayers that he had already started. His prayers were for peace for his wife and safety for his children. In those last seconds, he asked God to grant sanctuary and life for his friends, who were even then fleeing south on the highway. He raised his head and opened his eyes in time to see the black car only a handful of car lengths away from him and he asked God for one more small favor: justice.

6

Maggie didn't see the praying figure until it was almost too late. Her screams in tune with those of her protesting tires, she jerked her steering wheel hard as she pressed her brake pedal to the floor.

The little black car tried to maintain its composure, but it was not to be. The car lurched right and then left before pitching itself into a glass-shattering roll. Bits of plastic, chunks of metal, and shards of glass all took to flight in a swirling storm of destruction.

The Passat came to a gradual rest beneath a settling cloud of smoke and dust, its final living gasp escaping in the form of a series of metallic clanks as its motor died. And much like the car, Dr. Caldwell too was no longer breathing. He was lying face down in the road, his hands still clutched in prayer in front of him. With his forehead pressed into the pavement, the doctor's corpse remained motionless for several moments.

Though his breathing had ceased, there was still activity in his brain. Confused neural synapses and cerebral tissue, continued to send rudimentary signals, slightly altering functions and delivering new instructions. With a couple of twitches, his body accepted its new chemistry and began to reawaken some of his dead flesh and nerves.

When his eyes reopened, any kindness or understanding of the former man were replaced with confusion and anger... and hunger. The doctor remained there on his knees for a handful of seconds, not certain what this new life held in store for him. He flexed his fingers and clawed at the pavement, shredding most of his fingernails.

A faint voice roused him from somewhere behind him. The words no longer held any meaning for him, but the sounds themselves communicated one thing to him which led to the single thought, the single impulse that his preternatural mind could formulate: prey.

With the agility and urgency of a predatory cat, he leapt to his feet. He listened again and heard the voice once more. A short distance away sat a black object, ticking and popping and wreathed in a swirl of slowly rising smoke. He looked at the object and waited until he heard the voice again. It was faint and a little desperate, but was definitely coming from the black, smoky object.

Excitement, like electricity through a wire, filled his veins and charged his actions. He ran to the black object and looked in through a large opening which once held a windshield.

Maggie, still dazed from the accident, looked up and saw the doctor standing there. His wound, largely superficial and out of sight, did not immediately betray the transformation. She recognized him and forced an awkward smile, not sure if he still harbored any ill will toward her. As he approached and she could see more clearly his eyes, she realized her mistake. There was, however, neither time nor hope for her to react.

He dived across her hood and slid in through the opening where the windshield had once been. With his jaw snapping shut as hard and as fast as a machine, he lunged at her again and again trying to find purchase. She tried unsuccessfully to fend him off with her hands, but he brushed aside her flailing arms and brought his gaping maw to her neck and ear. As he sunk his teeth into her hanging lobe, Maggie stopped struggling for the briefest of moments, her terror trading places with her utter disbelief and shock. The creature ground his teeth together over her flesh like a pair of jagged saws until he withdrew, her outer ear in his mouth. He chewed the tough cartilage and skin like the appetizer that it was. There was much more to be eaten. And eat he would.

Shaken from her momentary disbelief-laden stupor, Maggie tried to fight back. She pushed him away with one hand and pulled at the stuck seatbelt latch with the other. The belt refused to release her from her restraints. Unable to extricate herself from her seat and her ability to fight back ebbing with her blood as it flowed down her neck, she was forced to sit and watch him swallow chunks of her flesh from her face and neck as he set about satiating his hunger. When she brought her hands back up to push him away, he merely bit off fingers and devoured them instead. Her death came slowly and painfully, and her screams were heard by no one.

7

Shortly after parting ways with Dr. Caldwell, the sun decided to call it a day, making room for the burnt hues of evening. Neil Jordan, through his exhaustion and internal anguish, still forced enough emotion to be amazed by the brevity and beauty of Alaska's autumn. The golds and reds of the season, like spilled paint, splashed onto the trees in mellow autumnal smiles.

There was no smile for Neil though. He wasn't certain that he would ever find it in himself to ever smile again. He tried to remind himself that the melodrama would not please Dr. Caldwell but he couldn't help his pain. When Dr. Caldwell, who had been bitten, demanded that Neil lead away their small clan of survivors, he obeyed. He did so without thinking or, more importantly and perhaps more tragically, without feeling. The acute ache starting in his chest and then spreading like a miserable disease to his extremities and back again was a powerful force of self-doubt and loathing, but it didn't rear its poisonous head until it was too late.

He didn't doubt the logic of leaving the doctor to his unavoidable fate, but turning their backs on him and leaving him to face it alone seemed a cruel measure. It didn't matter that he'd asked them to do exactly that. Dr. Caldwell was as much a brother to Neil as anyone in the world, including his actual brother living in Middle America somewhere. Neil felt nothing but guilt and a profound sense of loss, though his faculties were not functioning well enough for him to be able to frame such a rational thought. The cold burn in his chest would not allow it, and he was forced to remember what he wanted to forget

He regretted their stoic departure. He regretted not having said so many things to his friend. Maybe that was just how it was with loss. He'd never really lost anyone that close to him and was not prepared for the emotional ice pick lodged to the handle in his chest.

It had only been a few months, not even a season, since they had all come together as desperate survivors. Their experiences bonded them each to the other as tight or tighter than the prototypical nuclear family. Neil had come to depend upon the good doctor's steadfast rationality and strength, maybe more than anyone else in the group. There wasn't a single decision or action taken that the doctor had not in some way helped to shape. Whenever Neil faltered, Dr. Caldwell was always willing to hold the reins until Neil regained his direction.

Neil thought back on his last conversation with Dr. Caldwell and the days leading up to their parting. They'd been fighting for their lives for so long and seeing all hope slowly slip further and further from view. If it wasn't for the doctor, Neil doubted if they would ever have made it as far as they had. He, as much as anyone, was responsible for keeping them all going. He didn't deserve the end that he surely faced. No one did, but especially Dr. Caldwell. He was a good man; something of a dying breed. Neil hoped that the doctor's final moments were at least peaceful.

Neil wasn't the only one suffering. They all were. But Emma, she was in a completely different dimension of pain from everyone else. When she finally allowed herself to be pulled away from Dr. Caldwell, she felt a spark of light, tiny and struggling in the deepest recesses of her being, snuffed out and sent away. That beacon's demise didn't prevent the sobbing or the explosion of pain and loss from grabbing hold of her chest and squeezing with its chill, heartless grip. But she quickly realized that she would likely not allow herself to love again. She doubted she would be able to survive a loss like that again. She couldn't and wouldn't allow the possibility of that kind of pain ever again.

When she looked at Meghan and Neil, she felt a slight resentment for their happiness, but she also felt a rising foreboding for them as well. Both emotions were newly emerging and somewhat surprising to her, although when she thought about it, neither was that much of a surprise. She didn't wish her suffering on anyone else. It was unrequited love at its worst. She also suspected that, had her relationship with the doctor become as deep or as manifest as theirs, she would likely be more than just upset.

She'd refused to get close to anyone since her last break-up, which was more than a few years ago. Her present sorrow was proof enough for her that her decision so long ago was well founded. Romance just wasn't worth the potential devastation of heartache.

Normally chatty and eager during camp preparations for the night, Emma was, instead, the proverbial bump on the log. Most of the necessary tasks fell to Claire, Jerry, and Meghan. Even Jules and Danny helped dig the fire pit and gather kindling. She, like Neil, was too deep in mourning to be of much use doing anything. If the thought had surfaced, they both would have expressed their gratitude to the others for their care and their efforts. As it was though, grief temporarily consumed their thoughts and limited their actions. It seemed that every action, every thought, every breath was brimming with sorrow.

The fire brought them neither warmth nor comfort. Had it been allowed to be anything more than embers, Neil doubted it would have made any difference.

8

As slow and reluctant as dawn was in rising, Neil still barely registered it. The transition from dark to light was barely noticed. His soul wallowing in a toxic mix of self-pity and self-loathing, Neil felt.... Well, that was the problem really. Neil wasn't certain what he felt, if anything. He was, however, sure that he'd never felt its equal.

Meghan's sudden presence at his side raised his spirits slightly. He tilted his head and rested it on her shoulder. "You ever lose anyone close to you?"

The question caught her more than a little off guard as it was the first thing he said to her. She knew what he wanted, but also knew that she couldn't give it to him.

She said, "Neil, honey, of course I have. Most recently I lost my fiancé. Remember?" She lifted his head and turned to face him. Quiet tears escaped from the corners of her eyes, so she hugged him and said in a whisper, "Neil, I can tell you a dozen times that it wasn't your fault. I can tell you a hundred times that doing what we did was the right thing. But not a bit of any of that would matter if you're not telling yourself the same thing.

"I'm not a priest; not that I could have been one anyway. I can't offer you absolution. And even if I was, I'd tell you the same thing. You've got to work through this. All of what you're feeling is natural. What is important is that you understand that what's done is done. You can't go back and change what's happened. And for the record, what you did was right. Once again, you made the right call and, as a result, we're still moving. Dr. Caldwell knew that too and that's why he sent us away. There was really nothing more that we could have done. The quicker you accept that, the quicker you'll be able to do what you've been doing: keeping us alive."

She pulled back from the embrace, looked him in the eyes. "It's up to you.

You're the only one who can forgive yourself. You're the only one who can realize for yourself that some things, especially now, are just beyond your control. You don't get to choose who lives and who dies. You're not Sophie, this isn't your choice. When all is said and done, it's just not up to you. But, again, it's all a matter of accepting that and not beating yourself up over it. I'm amazed that we've made it as far as we have, as intact as we have. Jesus, Neil, the cards are really stacked against us but somehow we keep coming out on top, and you're the largest part of that. Honey, no one holds you responsible for anyone's death, but we all do owe you our lives. It's time you understand and accept that."

She kissed him on both cheeks and then softly on his chapped lips. Without another word, she stood up and walked away from him. All he could think to himself was *easier said than done.*

The air was already moist, so when the drizzle started, Neil wasn't surprised. He did, however, think to himself that the rain was an apt reflection of his mood. The temperatures once again plummeted with the wet air, transforming his exhalations into small, white clouds that dissipated as quickly as they formed.

He thought to himself, in a somewhat mocking fashion, that maybe he should stop getting up so early and alone. Then perhaps he wouldn't have the same opportunities for self-persecution. He knew that Dr. Caldwell, had he still been with them, would have told him that Neil could ill afford such doubt. Of course, Neil knew that, but knowing and accepting are two completely different states of mind. He still needed to make that journey between the two. For the time being, he felt like he could occupy himself with all the day-to-day and could possibly put his worries on the back burner to simmer and await his return later.

Shortly thereafter, the camp came to life. Each of them piled around the slight campfire, seeking whatever limited warmth it had to offer. When they ate, everyone's mood, including Neil's, picked up slightly. They chewed their granola bars and washed them down with the last of their sports drinks.

Jerry and Meghan were conducting an animated if quiet discussion about something. He had his backpack and she had hers. They pointed at the bags and spoke and pointed again. Neil spied the conversation and tried to ignore it, but in the end he was forced to inquire.

"What's the matter?" he asked them both.

Jerry looked at Meghan for direction. They'd been trying to avoid laying any more worries on Neil, but there was no avoiding it now. Jerry could see that in Meghan's eyes.

Meghan said, "We're almost out of food. We might have another couple of meals...sparse meals at best, and then we're out of supplies. We're already out of water."

Neil smiled and said to himself as much as to the others, "*Neil, I think we got a problem.*"

Jerry and Meghan looked puzzled. To which Neil continued, "I kind of got accustomed to hearing that whenever I got news like this. So, we gotta find food."

Meghan, her voice heavy with apology, said, "I don't think it's as simple as that."

"What is it then?"

Jerry stepped into the discussion. "We've been on the go without a moment's rest for days. We stop at nights, but there's no real rest. If any of us sleep, it's in fits and starts, we get up feeling more tired than when we laid down to begin with. We're on the ragged edge, Neil and there's no denying it. We gotta find some hope again. We gotta find a reason to keep going. We need that more than food."

Neil knew that Jerry was right, but he doubted that he would ever have been able to detect it. Hope was an intangible that oftentimes didn't register on Neil's radar. He was impressed with the younger man's observations and the way in which he communicated them.

"We've still got Whittier," he said. "It's just down the road a bit. Maybe once we get there—"

"It's not enough," Meghan cut in. "Not this time. We all need something more. We need something we can hold; something that can keep us going. We need something that will get us down the road in the first place."

Neil's face was as empty and bare as his thoughts. He kept waiting for some kind of revelation or an epiphany like he was a character in a book or movie, but none were forthcoming. Apparently, those pages still needed to be typed. He was doomed to wait. Realizing and readily accepting that he wasn't wired to be a fugitive mastermind with all the answers, he asked them , "So, any ideas?"

9

With the discussion about food behind them, it was apparent to Neil that Jerry wasn't done.

"What's on your mind?" he asked.

Jerry looked back over his shoulder at the road behind them and then at the highway still in front of them. "It might be better if we get off the highway. If there are any of those things around, I think this is where they'll be. Maybe it would be better if we didn't run into them...at least head on I mean. If we could just, well, slip by as many of those things as we can, well, I guess, I just...."

Neil nodded. There was no denying the logic, but there were limited options. "I agree. What do you suggest?" .

Meghan, who was still standing there said as she pointed, "What about over there? On the railroad tracks? They pretty much follow the road but are a bit off the main path. We could walk along the tracks and stay out of sight. Maybe if we do come upon any of them, they won't even know that we're here. Maybe."

Neil and Jerry looked at the tracks and agreed with her. The railroad tracks ran parallel to the Seward Highway but were, for as far as they could see, some distance further in from the coastline and in many places separated by water and increased elevation. It wasn't a bad idea, and to make it even more appealing, much of the track hugged tightly to the mountain's rock wall, which might serve as a barrier to some of the increasingly bad weather they could expect.

Neil said, "Yeah. I think we should get everyone over to the tracks before we start getting too comfortable over here. Look. Just a way up a bit there's that pool of water between the road and the tracks. That looks like a good place for us to rest a bit."

He paused for a second but both Jerry and Meghan could tell there was more. He finally said, "Thanks guys. I can't do this on my own. Any time you see anything like this or have any ideas at all, please share. I need your help more than ever."

Meghan put her arms around Neil's waist and kissed him on his mouth tenderly. "All you ever had to do was ask."

10

Claire asked doubtfully, "Are we sure this is safe?"

Some slight humor returning despite the pain that lurked, Emma answered, "If it were, we wouldn't be taking along these." She lifted the Remington .410 shotgun and pointed to the more impressive twelve-gauge variety in Neil's hands.

Meghan still doubted whether it made the most sense to send Neil and Emma on this errand, but she understood the importance to all of them to show solidarity. She nodded her head to Claire but said nothing. She was too afraid she would surrender to the apprehensive tears that were threatening to spill or to the acrimonious anger that was threatening to scream.

She hugged Neil, kissed his cheek, and whispered into his ear so that her voice tickled the soft contours inside his ear, "See you in a bit."

Her voice as much as her words produced an opiate-tinged euphoria that kissed his every nerve at once. So sweet was the sensation that he found he was holding his breath. He let the smile bloom across his face. He whispered back to her, "This will be good. It'll help us focus on something else. We need something to do."

Earlier, while eating their meager meal, they discussed their options. With their spirits and their energy ebbing to new lows, they all agreed that wandering into the unknown was not in their better interests. The likelihood the devastation had preceded them was a foregone conclusion, but how that devastation manifested itself in the surroundings was worth knowing. Their larger group was not likely capable of moving suddenly or quickly until they'd gotten some rest, but a pair of them might be able to move fast enough to avoid...well, whatever might be out there.

Neil summed up the discussion and ended the debate with a simple, "So, who's gonna come along with me to look on down the road?"

Emma eagerly jumped at the chance, and so it was decided that the two of them would venture down the road while others rested and regained their strength.

The two of them were to travel light, carrying only weapons, ammunition, and whatever else they could easily fit in pockets. With their collective food supplies dwindling, they decided that a single package of sweet, gummy fruit snacks was all the food each of them carried.

Meghan was present for the discussion and remembered nodding her head along with everyone else, but that certainly didn't make her like the plan. She was about to say as much when she felt her hand tugged. She looked down and saw a pair of tired but beatific blue eyes looking up at her. Jules smiled, looked at Neil and Emma who were already walking away from their camp, and asked, "Will you read with me?"

"Read?"

"Yeah. Danny has some comic books in his pack. They're mostly icky boy comics, but I don't mind much."

"Do you like reading, Jules?"

"Yeah. Mommy used to tell me that I was a good reader but that I needed to practice."

Smiling for herself as much as for Jules, Meghan said, "Yeah sweetie, I'll read with you. What comics do we have?"

Jerry and Claire, while not on the move at present, could ill afford to be idle. They needed to put together the camp, collect firewood, and, of course, be watching for any of the monsters potentially following them from Girdwood. Jerry was especially concerned that amongst the zekes to be coming down the road could be their friend Dr. Caldwell. His death hadn't been any easier for him than it had been for Neil, Emma, or anyone else for that matter. He'd known the good doctor much longer than anyone else and knew that he was a good man apart from their present circumstances. Jerry dreaded the possibility of having to shoot the man. He hoped that it wouldn't come to that.

To his credit, Neil had chosen a good campsite. There was a creek and a bridge that separated them from Girdwood, funneling anything that might be following them through one location. It made keeping vigil much easier. They were camping in the immediate shadow of a high, steep cliff and in front of a small pond—really nothing more than an overzealous drainage pool. They were about a hundred yards from the highway with the pool separating them from the roadway. Between the railroad tracks and the cliff face, the gravelly ground dipped slightly, helping to hide the glow of any fire they decided to make. Overall, it was a good spot to rest, and at the same time, feel somewhat secure. Still, Jerry and Claire wandered a little ways north away from everyone else so that they could have a better view of the bridge and the ground behind them. No point in being complacent.

The two of them sat amidst and upon a pile of large stones and small boulders that had fallen or been pulled from the cliff behind them. From there, they could better see back up the road from where they had come, were well shielded from the wind and weather still, but were more or less out of sight from the others while they rested. This, of course, afforded the two of them some time alone and the sleeping bags upon which they sat provided an added element of privacy.

They hadn't sat quietly for very long before they exchanged their first passionate kiss, which led to another and another. Jerry couldn't deny the physical response his body had to her delicate but aggressive touch, but his guilt at his pleasure was palpable. It was a more than a little distracting. With Claire's cold fingers struggling to open the zipper on his pants, Jerry withdrew slightly but suddenly and took her hands away from his waist.

"It's okay," she said, her breath hot and inviting upon his neck. "No one's watching. They don't care anyway. It's not like our parents are back there or anything."

"It's not that."

"Not in the mood?" she asked, rubbing the front of his jeans with the palm of her hand.

Jerry smiled and shook his head. "I think you can tell that isn't the case."

"Yeah. I didn't think that was a roll of quarters in your pocket."

Jerry leaned his head back and fought back the lump in his throat. He confessed, "It just doesn't feel right is all. It hasn't even been twenty-four hours since we left Doc Caldwell back there. I don't know. I guess I'm just feeling a little guilty is all. I just..."

Where her breath had been warming his neck, she placed her lips and then her tongue. She spoke as much into him as to him, "We each deal with our grief differently. At least that's what I used to hear on daytime TV. It's okay to feel sad if you have to. I guess, I just like to forget...at least for the moment."

Jerry said wistfully, "I don't think I can."

Her lips now on a southward course down the salty slope of his neck, she said confidently, "I bet I can help with that," and smiled.

11

"Thanks."

The voice, if not the word, caught Neil by surprise. He and Emma had been walking for at least an hour without so much as a syllable exchanged between the two of them. He was glad for the break in the silence. Counting railroad ties and keeping an eye on the broken path between each wooden stripe of the tracks only went so far as a distraction—not that they needed to be distracted.

He asked, "For what?"

"Well, everything really, but I guess especially for the last few...well, since we, you know, left.... I know there really wasn't much of an option back there with him, but I still don't think that I'd have been strong enough to walk away."

"Well, I don't know if...."

"Shut up dammit! Let me finish. It was the right decision. If we would have brought him along, he would've died and he would've come back. I think dealing with him then would've been a helluva lot harder than just walking away. It's what he wanted anyway, for the exact same reasons. He knew, just like you, what would happen. Someone had to take responsibility for the decision, so thank you.

"And last night, you and everyone else just gave me the space that I needed. Sometimes misery doesn't love company and I needed some time to come to grips with, well, with all of it.

"It's funny, but it felt like he and I had been together for a lifetime. Hell, it hadn't even been a full season and we weren't ever really together. Not like you and Meghan. The pain in my belly and the emptiness in my chest tell me otherwise though. But it's the same with everyone. We've seen so much in so little time that.... aren't you afraid that...?"

She stopped short of finishing her thought. He knew where she was headed with her question and, yes, he did fear all she was thinking. How could he not? It was sheer delusion for any of them to think for even a moment that loss and pain was behind them.

Despite that, Neil could not deny his affection for Meghan any more than he could the same for everyone else in their dwindling ad hoc family. Emma was right in another of her observations and this one, when Neil acknowledged it, was very unsettling. The carnage that had forced them all together and into survival mode had started in August and, to the best of his knowledge, it was now only October or early November. So much had been lost in such a brief stretch of time. It was staggering when he paused to consider it. The world, at least the world immediately around them, was set on its head and it seemed like nothing was ever going to restore life to how it had been.

He looked at the road to their right and thought to himself that the cracks and the breaks in the pavement would likely never be fixed. The partially burned gas station where they had left their stricken friend Dr. Caldwell would likely never be rebuilt. If he allowed it, the sense of permanence with their current state would be overwhelming. As it was, their immediate needs and his concern for those who were counting on him were pressing enough to push any other thoughts from his present considerations. Quite simply, he had too much to worry about today to give much thought to how things will or wouldn't be tomorrow. After all, if every day was a fight for survival, what did it matter that the Department of Transportation wasn't repairing potholes on the Seward Highway?

In front of them, the railroad tracks entered a much larger staging area where tourists had once boarded passenger cars en route to Whittier and Seward. Everything seemed so gray to Neil. The tracks sat in a sea of cinder-colored fine gravel. There were patches of grass and weeds fighting for space here and there, but it was evident the struggle was futile. The sulky ashen color was determined to set the mood. The small building seemingly floating atop the gravel tried its level best to add a splash of color but it too failed miserably. The sky, the ground, their path, the imposing mountain faces immediately to the left and the water of the Cook Inlet off to the right all seemed eager to embrace melancholy.

Maybe the two of them wandering off like this wasn't such a good idea after all. He was decidedly unable to focus and Emma was too busy coming to terms with recent events to be watching their surroundings. Neil was about to say as much when Emma stopped dead in her tracks. Neil's breath rushed out of his chest as fast as adolescents escaping from school at the end of a very long Friday. His feet were forced to make room for his stomach in his shoes as well. He stopped too, trying to determine where she was looking, although there weren't a whole lot of options.

He looked at the station building and tried to see what she was seeing. Parked out front were three cars, all of which appeared to be abandoned and in fairly bad shape. There didn't seem to be an intact windshield on any of them.

"Either my eyes are playing tricks on me," she said, "or I just saw someone duck around the back of that building."

"Duck around? You mean like they're hiding?"

"I guess."

Neil was as confused as ever. "But zekes don't hide."

"Well, that's the theory anyway. What do we do?" Emma asked, never taking her eyes off of the building and its surroundings.

Neil said bluntly, "Shit, I don't know. I'm still trying to figure out zombies and now I gotta work on.... If you said someone, then that might mean we've got a live person down there."

"Remember Claire's story," Emma warned. "There might be bad people still out there who wouldn't think twice about robbing us or maybe even worse."

"But if they think the same about us and run off... Okay. I'm gonna keep going forward. We can't let them just leave. I want you to wait about twenty paces and then follow," said Neil as he began to walk. He didn't want to appear threatening but he wasn't a fool either. He un-slung the shotgun from his shoulder and had the firearm in his hands. He looked over his shoulder to verify that Emma had done the same and she had.

Neil felt like he was a rat dropped into a snake pit. His sense of vulnerability was close to incapacitating, but somehow he continued walking. He tried to walk without letting his unease affect his gait but each step showed his apprehension. He could very well be walking into an ambush. For the briefest of seconds the thought occurred to him that he would prefer to be shot than chewed to death. He had to admit, though, he wasn't *really* interested in either.

With his hand, he signaled for Emma to start arcing to his left so that she could cover that side of the house-like building. After a couple more steps, he decided that he'd moved close enough.

"We saw you over there," he yelled. "C'mon out before someone gets hurt. We don't mean anyone any harm. We were just looking around for food for the two of us. Like I said, c'mon out. If someone's hiding over there and we get spooked, someone might get hurt and we don't want that. Please show yourselves."

Perhaps it was the tone of his voice or maybe that he'd said please, regardless, it had worked. Showing both of his hands from behind the building first, a man slightly stooped with age and a lifetime of hard work emerged. His brown Carhartt coveralls were filthy and looked to be wet from his thighs down to his feet. They obviously were not ordinarily his because the ragged, frayed cuffs hung well-lower than his boots. He looked cold and hungry and, above all else, desperate. Emma, coming over closer to Neil, thought to herself that he resembled the souls that motorists would typically see on Anchorage street corners in days gone by. Then, as now, the first emotion that arose in her was pity.

The bent old man stammered, "You folks just watch your step. My man has his rifle aimed at your chests. One wrong move and we'll leave your bones to be picked over by the ravens."

Emma sniped, "I think most of the ravens are dead by now. You see any of them around lately?"

Neil shot her a look, slowing his pace but continuing forward. There was something less than threatening about this man. The crowbar dangling from the man's right hand seemed almost benign, a harmless prosthetic of utility. There was no danger about him. Of course, they had all thought the same about Maggie, so Neil remained somewhat on guard.

A mere handful paces away from the man, Neil stopped to consider him. From there, Neil could see much more. The wispy strands of white across his scalp barely constituted a comb-over. The stubble on his cheeks and chin was thicker but equally as light as the hair on the top of his head. His eyes were dark beneath his glasses and the whites were more yellow than white from decades of coffee and tobacco use. He had the hard edges of working class living etched into the contours of his face. Neil was reminded of a latter day Robert Duvall when he looked at the man.

Neil suggested to all of them, "I think we can all just settle down a bit here. I don't think anyone wants any problems. There's no need for anyone to get hurt."

Adjusting his grip on the crowbar as the tool became heavier at the end of his arm, the man said, "You don't go tellin' us what needs we have. Ain't no one gonna tell me what I want. You make one wrong move and there'll be trouble. You can count on that."

Neil asked him, "Is that what you want? By the looks of you, I'd say that you have a lot of needs. Maybe you were thinking that you could get the drop on some travelers. Maybe you were thinking that you could ambush some folks and take all that they had...maybe even take their lives while you were at it."

Neil looked at the Robert Duvall character in front of him and asked, "Is that what you want?"

The old man slumped his shoulders forward and protested, "We ain't bandits. We ain't like the other folk still out here. How we know you ain't neither? For all we know, that's what you had on your mind too. We was just...."

Neil suggested, "It's hard to have this conversation with a rifle aimed at our chests. You think you can at least have 'your man' come out in the open?"

"You tryin' to get the drop on us? You askin' for us to lower our guard? Maybe make us easier targets for the two of you?"

Neil smiled, put the shotgun back on his shoulder, and said as he extended his hand, "No. I'm just asking for a little faith in each other."

The other man looked puzzled as he pondered what to do next. He clearly was conflicted. He looked beyond Neil at Emma and the rifle she was sporting. The man wore doubt on his face like some women wore blush. His decision was preempted when a large window on the front of the building shattered with a crash of exploding, cascading glass. Echoing loudly in every direction, the sudden disturbance startled all of them to silence. On the heels of the clamor, like insult added to still unfolding injury, several gray-green arms reached hungrily through the new opening.

Startled by the unexpected development, Neil very nearly fell over backward as he jumped away from the sound. The old man too was caught off guard and did fall. Unable to regain his footing fast enough, the man, like an intoxicated crab, scooted awkwardly away from the building without having gotten back to his feet.

Neil could see that the ghoulish arms were protruding through several tightly packed postcard racks. They weren't going to be coming through the window any time soon, which presented itself as much as a curse as a blessing. As it stood, if Neil and Emma were to deal with the beasts, they were required to open the front door and let them out. That, of course, would require one of them to ascend the short flight of wooden stairs to the patio and then open the door. Neither of them was too quick to volunteer to do that.

The creatures' tortured chorus was anything but music to all of their ears. The horrible hymn the beasts moaned was enough to curdle milk and wilt flowers. Emma looked at Neil for some sign of what to do. Lacking any firm directive from him, she raised her firearm. Neil stopped her before she could to shoot.

"No! Wait! We don't know if there are more in the area or not. A single gunshot could attract all of them for miles the way sound travels around here."

Emma asked doubtfully, "You suggesting we just leave them in there?"

"No. Remember Jerry's suspicion about their moans working like homing signals for other zekes? We gotta deal with 'em but I think we need to be more...discreet."

By then, the old man was on his feet and had gotten closer to Neil and Emma. He looked over his shoulder to the rear of one of the parked cars and called, "Ricky. You come on out now."

From behind the metallic blue tail of a Honda Accord appeared a teenager still very much in the early years of adolescence. He couldn't have been older than sixteen and was likely not that old yet. He was holding a small caliber rifle not very different than that which Neil carried. He lowered his head to his right and then swept it back to his left to adjust the long bangs on his forehead.

Emma said, her humor shaping her words like a sculptor's hands manipulates clay, "This is "your man"? Jesus, is he even old enough to have a driver's license?"

Nodding to the boy and pointing at the monsters still reaching through the empty window pane, the man said, "He's old enough to pull a trigger and that was what was important; not his age."

Neil's eyes were glued to the phantom arms which were clawing hungrily at the air. He said, "Let's stay focused here. I guess we need to open the door."

"Yeah?" Emma said without moving her feet. "And how exactly is that going to happen? Maybe we should just shoot them and be done with it."

Neil shook his head and said doubtfully, "What if we draw more to us? Maybe we should—"

Emma wasn't waiting any longer as she saw the shiny metal and plastic souvenir display rack start to bend and break, letting the arms reach a little further. "Fuck this!" She pulled the trigger on her gun. The bullet obviously hit one of them since a pair of arms disappeared after she shot.

Neil growled, "Emma! For Christ's sake!"

Emma pumped another round into the firing chamber. "Someone had to do something and I sure as hell wasn't going to go up there to open the door. Stop whining and help out a little, will ya?"

Neil pivoted around so that he could see more clearly into the window opening. There were at least three of them inside and one of them was most certainly a child...or a former child anyway. The one Emma shot was back up and just returning to its post.

Neil realized the shooting may not be the best course of action but he couldn't argue with its efficiency or its range. Following Emma's lead, he got his shotgun back into his hands, found a fairly static target, and shot. It was that easy and that quick. In just seconds, the moaning coming from within had stopped, as had any signs of movement.

Almost ignoring the man and the boy named Ricky with him, Emma and Neil mounted the stairs and were standing to either side of the front door. The door was locked from the inside and refused to even budge when Emma tried to force it open with her shoulder. Neil stood back, sizing up the door. It looked like a standard front door for any house. It probably had a solid deadbolt in a semi-solid door frame. If they were lucky, the deadbolt would have required an absent key to engage and wouldn't pose any real obstacle. There would likely be other items placed against the door as additional insurance, Neil surmised.

He ran all of this through his head as he stormed, shoulder first, into the door just above the handle. When the door flung itself open much easier than he had anticipated, he fell in a heap of aching and bruised muscles and limbs. He landed just inches from the lifeless jaw of one of the dispatched zombies lying in the little shop, the rancid foulness that was once its breath still escaping from its dark mouth.

Emma followed him in closely, wincing as Neil thudded to a stop. Not the most graceful of actions. Seeing him there on the floor amidst the carnage, Emma said, "Aren't you glad we went with my plan instead? Think what Meghan would've done to me if I hadn't come back with you. Look at you. You woulda landed right at their feet. Talk about servin' yourself up to—"

"Okay, okay, enough. Jesus. I almost pissed myself and you're not helping."

"Just sayin'."

There had been three of the undead in the building. Neil figured they were a mother, father, and a child. One had been bitten before they'd successfully fled Anchorage. They stopped here when whoever it was who'd been bitten got too sick to travel. The rest of the story was there on the floor in front of them.

Neil looked into the parking lot, remembering there had been more than one car out there. There were three cars in front of the building. Three cars... He started to back toward the open door slowly, bumping Emma in that direction as he went.

Emma could see his alarm but asked, "What's going on, Neil?"

His eyes wide and alert, Neil answered, "Too many cars and not enough drivers."

"What?"

As he started to reply, they could both hear the scratching and thumping of fists against walls and a door.

Emma said, "Bathroom I bet."

"Yeah. Do we leave it in there or roll the dice again?"

"You're the one who's in charge here. You're supposed to have all the answers. Why you askin' me?"

Neil bit back the string of profanity that threatened to break at any moment. Instead he looked up at the old man who was now standing in the open doorway behind them.

"You folks do this before or something?" the man asked.

Emma and Neil looked at him with both answers and questions in their eyes. The man then said as a way of explanation, "You just seem...I don't know...good at it, is all. No disrespect intended."

Neil suggested, "Maybe we could at least go back outside to talk."

"Sure. I'm DB by the way."

Neil smiled. "I'm Neil and this lovely lady is Emma."

12

Neil's strained smile relaxed into a genuine grin. "DB, it's really good to see people...living people still about. It's been a long time."

Curious now, DB asked, "How needy do I look anyway?"

"What?"

DB said, "You said it looked like I had some pretty tall needs."

Embarrassed by his observation, Neil was at first hesitant. He did, however, finally say, "You looked...desperate...on the brink...maybe willing to do anything to get by. Sorry."

DB started to protest and then said honestly, "We are. Well, I was anyway. We ain't eaten in probably three days now. And our last meal wasn't much. Just some uncooked pasta noodles and sugar packets. I'd be lying if I said I wasn't hungry 'nough to kill for my next meal."

Neil raised his hands. "I'll spare you the suspense. We're outta food too. Haven't seen any for some time. We were kinda hoping...."

DB nodded. "Yeah. I 'spect most things have been picked pretty clean by now."

Emma asked them both, "So what now? We gotta eat. Where we gonna find food?"

Neil didn't know. They still had Whittier down the road a bit where they could likely find food, but they needed food now and not down the road. And now, they had two more mouths to fill. There was still daylight in which to search, so Neil felt comfortable continuing south for a bit before turning back to the others.

The decision as to when to return was still a matter for Neil to decide. DB and Ricky seemed harmless enough, but Neil didn't want to reveal the others just yet. He wasn't going to be as willing to trust people since their encounter with Maggie back in Anchorage. She'd taken their transportation. Neil was loath to learn what more could be taken from them by ruthless, selfish people. DB appeared worthy of trust, but Neil was still withholding.

The four of them started walking south together, and Neil asked, "So is Ricky your son? Or...?"

Obviously a practiced habit, DB spat a mouthful of saliva onto the ground, a few droplets of spittle clung to the longer hairs just below his lower lip. He walked with a slight but noticeable limp and kept his hands in the pockets of his worn jacket. Neil thought that perhaps the man hadn't heard his question but decided not to press. Then all at once, DB said, "No. I found Ricky walking along the road down in Soldotna. We decided to team up and help each other out. I don't know if either of us would still be here if we weren't watchin' out for each other. He don't say much." And as a way of answering the question differently, DB finished with, "My boy moved to the Lower Forty-eight a few years back. Down to Arizona. I don't hear from him much no more."

"So, you came up from the Kenai Peninsula then?" Neil asked.

"Yeah."

"How bad was it down there?"

"As compared to what?" DB asked. He wasn't trying to be difficult but it seemed kind of a relative question. Neil immediately recognized that his seeking clarification wasn't strictly rhetorical.

"You guys must know something happened," Emma asked DB and Ricky, "but do you know what? Do you know the scope of what's happened?"

Spitting again, DB said, "I was a handyman. I can fix damned near anything...always been able to really. When work was good and bountiful, so was life. Lately, it's been nothing but struggles. A little borrowing from Peter to pay Paul and sometimes not even that. So when I had work, I had to go.

"That mornin', when all this started, I got a call about a water leak at a church in Sterling. I had just about enough gas in my truck to get to the job and back home. I usually get paid in cash, so I just planned on filling the tank after the job and probably getting a new can of Kodiak and some beer. But I had to work to get paid.

"Well, 'bout halfway between here and there the radio started talkin' 'bout somethin' goin' on in Anchorage. It sounded bad. Bad enough to have the Governor call up the Guard. Sounded like Anchorage was burnin' and people was dyin' and no one had the first clue who was in charge. They kept saying that people were dyin' by the dozens and that it was just ordinary folk who were doin' the killin'. The folks on the radio was tellin' folks to stay inside and out of sight. Sounded like a real shit storm.

"All at once the road started to fill up with trucks and SUVs, most was pulling boats and campers. I got no wife and my dog was with me, so I just kept goin'. 'Sides, there was still that water leak and maybe a paycheck at the end of it. Anchorage is a long way off from Kenai so I just didn't see the point of panicking. I thought those folks were just overreacting. Remember everybody getting all worked up over the New Year in Two Thousand, and then what happened? Nothin'. So I didn't pay it no mind.

"The Fred Meyer parking lot in Soldotna, right there at the highway heading out of town, was nuts. I never seen so many people there. They was runnin' every which way. I think I may have heard some shootin' but it coulda just been some good ole boy's truck backfirin'. I didn't pay them much mind cause I didn't have no money anyway. No use worryin' 'bout somethin' that don't concern me."

"A few minutes and I was in Sterling. That place looked like it had already emptied out. Course, Sterling always looked a little deserted if you ask me. The church was a little off the main drag. And when we got there, everyone was gone. Doors were still open, but the offices, the classrooms, the little cafeteria, everything was empty. Well, not everything.

"There was a lunch all made and ready for the eatin' left right there on the counter. A couple dozen corndogs, a small mountain of tater tots, an open can of peaches, and a jug of Gatorade or juice or Kool-Aid. Me and Duke, Duke's my dog, we had ourselves a bit of a feast and stuffed our pockets full too. I found some canned food and dry milk in one of the pantries. Me and Duke wandered around and then found a TV. I thought it might be a good idea to get us some news. All the Anchorage channels were just test patterns. Fox News had some story on it about unconfirmed reports of a terrorist attack in Anchorage, but there were no details, only aerial shots of burning buildings and groups of people runnin' on the streets. I even decided to check out CNN to see what the Libs were talking about. Their mornin' people had some video taken by some amateur reporter or something like that in Anchorage. Well, they said it was Anchorage anyway."

DB stalled for a breath as those first images resurfaced in his memory. The video had been unsteady, bouncing and moving in every direction. The camera could have been a cell phone or maybe a small digital number with limited capabilities. The images it captured, though, were breathtaking and perhaps a little unbelievable. Even the host, a pretty woman with dark hair and warm olive skin, expressed her doubt about the authenticity of the video, suggesting that they looked more like the scenes from George Romero's latest.

DB wasn't sure what he thought after seeing the video. It looked like it had been shot from a balcony overlooking a street. The pavement was filled with screaming, fleeing people. He was reminded of a video he'd seen of the Running of the Bulls in Pamplona, Spain. There were adults and kids; men and women; people from all walks of life. They looked more like stampeding cattle than people. After a few seconds, he could see intermingled with the terrified people a few others who looked enraged. It was quite clear that it was from these few that the others were running. He saw one of them grab a pretty lady wearing a nice business suit and drag her to the ground by her pretty hair that he had wrapped around his hand. He then set about assaulting her. At first, DB thought he was trying to rape her. He could feel his anger rise as he watched others, including men, just run by her as she struggled. He cursed them for their cowardice. When a second person kneeled beside the still struggling woman and started to chew off her fingers, he knew that there was more happening than what appeared on the surface. Seconds later, the video image abruptly stopped though sound feed continued. CNN put a dialogue box on the side of the screen as a man's voice cried, *"Oh Jesus. Oh Jesus. I hope CNN gets this in time. [Screaming]. On no! We're trapped."*

There was just the one video, but they showed it over and over. The pretty anchor said that the President was consulting his cabinet. He would likely declare a state of emergency and deploy additional troops to help contain the violence and restore order. The anchor noted that the opposition party's response to the President's action would follow after the break.

After reliving those first minutes, DB continued, "I musta' dozed off because the next thing I remember was waking up to a test pattern on that channel too. In fact, it was on every channel. Me and Duke loaded the extra clothes, the few blankets and all the food we'd found into the truck. We was all set to leave when we heard a commotion up the road."

Emma asked, "How soon was this after you'd left your house?"

Ignoring her, DB continued, "It was people, wide-eyed and full of fear. They were coming to the church for...well for whatever they thought the church might be able to give them. When they got there and saw only me and ole Duke, I guess you could say that they was a bit disappointed. Poor folks. I guess seein' the two of us when you're expectin' salvation was probably quite a letdown. I tried not to take it too personal. I think it mighta' hurt Duke's feelings though.

"They talked for a bit. A few prayed. I don't know for sure how long they stuck around. They may still be there for all I know. I've never favored crowds, so I just left when I figured out they really didn't know any more than me.

"Some of the folks had talked to others back in Anchorage before their phones stopped working. Anchorage was burning and people was killing other folks. And then someone said that the dead...the dead weren't stayin' dead. It was the dead that was causin' all the troubles. The dead was coming back and killing folks...maybe even eating them. What kind of crazy talk was that? Who'd ever heard such a story before. I mean, we all thought it was nuts.

"Well, that spooked everyone pretty good. Me too I guess. I didn't seen any point in stickin' around there. I had everything the place had to offer and I wasn't tellin' no one what I had neither. Me and Duke left. The people at the church were still debatin' and I don't think they even knew we left.

"Not sure what else to do, so me and ole Duke just went home. My truck was sputtering on fumes by the time we got down my driveway, but we made it. My house is just a trailer on a wooded lot, but it was out of the way and felt sort safe in a 'outta sight outta mind' kinda way.

"I stayed there a coupla' days and then I guess curiosity got the better of me because I decided to go on out and take a look around. I lived alone mosta' my life, but I ain't never felt so...isolated. There was no one around. And when I say no one, I mean no one. If we woulda had tumbleweed in Soldotna, it woulda been too lonely to blow.

"I took my Honda out. My four-wheeler, ya know. It had gas still, so I fired it up and took a ride around town. Ain't nothin' was open. None of the shops or restaurants or hotels. They all was dark and closed up for business. The roads was empty and the radio was dead. If I was the sentimental type, I guess I mighta said that I was lonely but I ain't so I didn't.

"I was down in California with my wife and my son years ago, before they both left me, and we visited a movie company. We got a tour an' everything. We went to a authentic movie set. It looked like a town...a town waitin' for people to come and give it life. That's how it felt there in Soldotna. It didn't feel much like a town no more. I guess I know the answer to that question about what makes a community—its buildings or its people. Well, there was plenty of buildings but it sure didn't feel like no...community.

"I didn't have much gas, so I knew that was the first thing I needed to find. Turns out, it wasn't so hard to get. The gas pumps mighta' been workin' but I didn't have no way of gettin' gas from those, that didn't seem to matter much. When people left, they only took one car. D'you know how many homes had more than one car in the driveway? Hell, I coulda' found enough gas to last the rest of my life given the chance. It only took a coupla' days before Duke and me was first class gas bandits. We'd just roll on up, empty the tank of the van or wagon or little rice burner that was sittin' in the driveway and then we just roll on. That was a good few days there. We had us some food and some gas and some quiet. No phone ringin'. No mailman with no bills come a callin'. It was just me and ole Duke. It coulda' been like that forever...for the rest of my days anyway, and I woulda' been one happy soul."

DB paused again, taken suddenly by a memory with much rougher edges. Neil and Emma looked at one another during the respite, not sure if the story had come to a close. Hoping to rekindle the narrative, Emma asked, "When did you find Ricky?"

DB nodded his head, remembering the day. "I guess it was about a week later. Me an' Duke had a full tank and a full reserve, so we was livin' high on the hog. We had the run of the town for the most part too. The big stores were pretty well emptied by then, but there were lots of places to look for food and other things too. We didn't take much more than what we needed...typically. I ain't never been one too fond of fancy things. Seems like all you do is fret over this or that gettin' broke is all. Never seemed worth the headache to me.

"We'd been foraging a little further into town. I guess we was just feelin' a little cocky. We was driving through a neighborhood and I thought I saw someone standin' in the road down to my right...at a cross street. I hit the brakes and backed up and sure enough. This guy was just standin' there. I guess it was a guy anyway. I yelled out to, ya know, see if he was all right. I shoulda' known he wasn't right just by the way he was standin'. It didn't look...natural, I guess. When he looked up, I could see, even from that distance, he was one of those things that killed that pretty lady in the CNN video. He was one of them. He started to run, but he was all over the place...'bout as coordinated as a baby moose. He built steam though and was runnin' right at us.

"I didn't need no more encouragement. We just drove on until we saw another one. This one was a little girl with pigtails and all. Her skin was the same color as the thin trees in the yards around her. She was the scariest thing I ever did see. There's just somethin' chillin' about seein' a little kid that's been turned into a demon.

"We shot outta the neighborhood but ended up in another. I didn't think about it at the time but I guess I shoulda'. But how could I...how could anyone've known? We drove close enough to be able to see the hospital, but that was too close. If I thought that little girl and the man was bad, man was I in for it. Like they was waitin' for me, there were...I don't know...a hundred, maybe more of those damned things standing around in the street. They saw us and like we was the rabbit at the track and they was greyhounds, they took off after us. Some of 'em ran pretty damned fast. I was afraid that maybe we was gonna get caught. And then they just kept running. They never get tired, do they? They can just go and go and will unless something else gets their attention."

Emma interjected, "Yeah, or they catch you."

Neil said, "That's a theory that we've developed anyway."

DB raised one of his thick, gray eyebrows. "Looks like you two have worked on more than theories."

"We can get to that," Neil said. "But tell us about finding Ricky."

Neil really just wanted to get more information about the Peninsula. It was an option in front of them. He had hoped that perhaps the undead hadn't become a presence on the Peninsula yet. It made sense that there would be zombies near the hospital, if anywhere. People, bitten and infected, could have been transported south before everyone knew how it spread. Those people would have died at the hospital just like Jules' brother Martin had. The terror in Anchorage would have been repeated here and probably in Seward too. Neil wondered though, if DB's account of events was true, then maybe the majority of residents managed to escape. Maybe there was some hope that the number of zombies away from Anchorage was significantly smaller. That was at least some good news.

DB continued, "We put a little distance between those things and us and were heading back out onto the highway when we saw this skinny kid walking along the road. He had his head down and was carrying a rifle. When we came to a stop, he looked up and I could see that he was just a kid. Hungry and dirty to the bone, but a normal kid. He looked lost. I asked him where he was headed and he pointed to the sign that said hospital. I told him what was waiting for him at the hospital and offered him a warm spot at my trailer. I guess the trailer was more his speed 'cause he hopped in the truck and we took off. He and Duke hit it off right away.

"He ain't never said a word. I started calling him Ricky and he hasn't complained once about that. He don't eat much more than he says but I guess I like his company. He does what I tell him to do and don't make no fuss. He's a good kid. I guess he musta' lost his family or somethin'. "We been scavenging but keepin' a low profile ever since. We wanted to get our hands on every scrap of food we could get. We knew that whatever was out there was it for what looked like would be a long time. Soon we knew that we weren't alone on the Peninsula, so gettin' the cans and boxes and bags of food and batteries and whatever else was still lyin' around was our top priority. There were others around, and not more of those monsters either. Just others who was lookin' out for their own and not lookin' to share with no one."

The last comment rang in both Emma's and Neil's ears. They wondered what he meant by "others". Neil's encounters with "others" so far hadn't been too encouraging. His first thought was of Maggie and her treachery. Neil could hear the alarm bells ringing in his head. Subtly, he started to look around for anything that might catch his eye as a waiting threat, an ambush ready to pounce. Emma too could feel the foreboding. The hairs on her arms and the back of her neck stood on end to get their own look around, wanting to contribute their vigilance to the greater good. Both of them, almost casually, slipped their shotguns from their shoulders and couched them in their arms instead.

Neil stopped dead in his tracks. "DB, where are you taking us?"

DB too stopped. He had been doing his own sizing up, trying to maintain caution without venturing into paranoia. He said finally, "We're not monsters. Not Cannibals, rapists or plunderers. We've seen a lot of that sort and I am hoping that the two of you aren't that sort either. We're...I'm puttin' a lot of faith in that hope and I guess it's too late if you two aren't what you appear to be. Just up the road a spell is a van. That's where we've all been holed up the past few days."

"So there are others then?" Neil asked expectantly.

DB looked at him again, wondering if perhaps he had both trusted and said too much.

Reading the look, Neil said, trying to reassure, "It's just exciting to learn that we aren't the last of us. Sometimes it started to feel that way. I guess we went looking for hope and found you."

DB smiled and nodded his head. He looked over at Ricky and smiled some reassurance, though Ricky's deadpan expression did little more than acknowledge his own understanding.

13

Hope can be a funny thing. She's the pretty sister of reckless Luck and the mother of Possibility. The progeny of idealistic parents, Hope can appear under the most random of circumstances or never show her welcome face. Fickle and unpredictable, Hope was always welcome by those who sought her.

Now walking along the highway at DB's direction, Neil was discovering a newfound respect for Hope and her euphoric elixir as the four of them approached a seemingly abandoned touring van, a blue and gray Ford Econoline. The van looked like any other vehicle stalled along any stretch of rural highway awaiting its owner's eventual return. To look at it, one would never guess that it was now a home to an endangered species. Which was, Neil surmised, the desired intent. If it looked abandoned, maybe it would be passed by without a second look back. A gamble borne of Hope but kept alive by Luck.

Neil's first thought was that it was unrealistic and perhaps a bit naive to believe that the ruse would work long-term. He wondered if DB had any plans because Neil would like to hear them. Most pressing upon his thoughts, though, was to learn why DB was this far north. If he had come from Kenai, he would have passed by the Portage and Whittier access road. Why? As seasoned as DB appeared, the prospect of Whittier being a safe haven from the infection had to have occurred to him. With its lone access through a tunnel cut through a mountain and the city's ability to close that tunnel, it seemed to him that Whittier was as likely a place as any to find safety.

Neil was almost too afraid to ask when his mouth involuntarily spilled, "What about Whittier? Why didn't you...?"

DB turned around, screwed his face into a doubtful question, and then continued on. "Della!" he shouted. "It's just us. C'mon out."

To Neil's surprise, a matronly woman with skin so dark it shined, emerged from the opposite side of the road. She forced her large frame up the side of the ditch, stopping as she got her feet onto the pavement. In tow, she had two children, neither of which appeared to be hers, and an old Golden Retriever who wagged his entire body at the sight of DB. The dog yelped with excitement and ran across the road toward its human. Their reunion was enough to make both Emma and Neil smile. DB's rough exterior softened somewhat as he showered the dog with affection, rubbing his ears and patting his head.

Though malnourished and wearing threadbare rags for clothes, the woman and two children didn't look wide-eyed with fear. With the calm, searching eyes of the Sphynx, the woman DB called Della scanned her surroundings and the new faces with DB. The whites of her eyes flashed like neon bulbs against the contrast of her flesh. Neil knew immediately that, though she possessed the appearance of a kindly motherly figure, this was not a woman with whom to trifle. She exuded strength and wisdom and caution.

Behind her, like a pair of needy ducklings, were the two children. The older of the two was a white boy who appeared to be about as old as Jules perhaps. The other child was barely more than a toddler. She had the skin tone and facial features of an Asian, maybe of Korean descent.

Neil couldn't conceal his pleasure. He said warmly, hoping not to offend, "Well DB, you've got yourself quite a family here. Who would've thought?"

DB tried to hide his smile by spitting and looking away, though his body language betrayed his more austere veneer. There was little reason or attempt to do so though when he looked back at Neil.

"I ain't never really had one really; a family that is. I wasn't home enough when my ex-wife and boy lived with me. I was always workin' on the Slope and then doin' jobs around town when I was home. I mostly just paid the bills until I came home one day and they was gone. Duke was the closest thing I ever had to a family and he's just a dog."

Duke didn't seem to be insulted by the comment as he made his way over to Neil. The dog sniffed and wagged and wagged and sniffed. Neil was all too eager to scratch the grateful dog behind his ears and pat his side with a friendly hand.

DB continued, "I don't know if what I got now could be called a family or not, but I can say that I'm feelin' more and more protective of them every day. Della there, she don't need no protectin' from nobody. She's hard as nails but don't let her kid you though. When it comes to those kids and even Ricky here, she's all mama.

"Me, Ricky and Duke found the three of them back in Soldotna. She said she was working at a hotel...the Aspen I think. She found both of those kids at the hotel. Can you imagine? I always wondered what happened to their parents and Della ain't never said. I guess I pretty much figured out what happened to their folks but I never got how them kids stayed alive. They're just so little."

Neil answered, "Without her and then you, they wouldn't have. They couldn't have. You're what's kept them alive."

Emma asked, "How long have you been on the road? And where's your truck?"

DB shrugged, doing little else to answer. Instead, he said to Della, "We got visitors," as if he was coming home from work with company for dinner. Della was not as casual with introductions. She was as deliberate as a glacier in her movements, always careful to keep the children shielded behind her ample frame. She measured the newcomers, trying to divine their intentions. Her expression was guarded, her eyes filled to their bright yellow corners with questions and calculated assumptions.

Neil felt completely disarmed by her eyes. There was little to no discernible distinction between her irises and her pupils, which appeared be swirling, dark eddies in small but consuming seas of yellowish-white. Neil found it impossible to guess her age. She appeared neither overly young nor old and frail. Her face, though, bore the wisdom of experience arrived at only after several decades of hard decisions and toil.

She neither extended her hand nor shared her name. She merely watched and waited as she walked slowly across the pavement toward the van. Without so much as a look over her shoulder, she said, "We ain't got much, but what we have we can share."

"Likewise. I'm Neil. This is Emma."

"Okay, Steve."

"No, I said my name is Neil."

"Yeah, I heard you the first time, Steve."

Neil looked at Emma and was all set to ask a question when DB said, "I've been with her for a few weeks now and she still calls me Steve. I don't think it's an accident and I don't know why she does it, but I don't see any point in fightin' it."

Neil knew that DB was right, but Della's seeming disregard for his identity bothered him nonetheless. He watched Della walk away and wondered to himself if her attitude was a product of their current circumstances or if it originated sometime in the past. Had she been hurt by some man or a series of men who had melded into a single amalgam of personalities all with the common title of "Steve"? Who was "Steve"?

What a weird day it had become.

14

Reunited.

It took some convincing on Neil's part and some trusting on DB's and Della's parts, but finally it was decided that they would all venture up the railroad track and join the others at Neil's and Emma's camp.

Neil offered to help with carrying supplies only to learn that there were no supplies to be carried. There was nothing. Well, not precisely nothing. There were five more mouths to feed...six if you counted Duke. What was the sense of adding more? More mouths? More children needing care and protection? More responsibility? Despite any misgivings or hesitation, he knew that it was the right thing to do. They would simply figure a way to make it all work. And by *they*, Neil always assumed it meant *he* would figure a way.

Figuring was just what he'd been forced to do these past several weeks and it didn't appear to be slackening any. Dr. Caldwell had been right. Neil needed to accept his role, regardless of how uncomfortable it made him feel. He knew this to be true and yet he found himself, on occasion, trekking further and further from that reality.

The biggest challenge to Neil accepting his role as a leader was that he had always gone the direction of the Beta male; rarely first but never last in sports, academics, and with girls. He was usually good at most things but he was never the best at anything. He never considered himself leader material. Bureaucrat, middle manager, crew leader at the fry station, but never head manager and certainly never leader. It wasn't hard to understand Neil's present reluctance.

And yet, he'd just successfully rationalized himself into leading a larger tribe. Sometimes he was his own worst enemy.

Jerry spotted the approaching group and immediately recognized Neil at its head. He was relieved to see that both Emma and Neil were still armed and smiling. Without taking his eye from his hunting scope, Jerry said, "They're baaacckkkk! And they've got friends with 'em."

Meghan leapt up and ran for her own rifle, fearing that Neil's friends may not be friendly. "Does everything look...? Is he...?"

Jerry nodded and said with a smile, "Relax. It's okay. Couple adults. Couple of kids. And a dog. Danny, it's a Golden. D'ya think your dog followed you up here? What was his name again?"

Danny answered from somewhere out of Jerry's limited vision, "Roman. Romie. Do they really have a dog with them?" Danny's reaction to that piece of news was especially excited. There was just something uplifting to him to have a dog around.

Standing next to Jerry, Meghan could see all of them now without the aid of a scope. Claire was there too. She could see the emotion starting to color Meghan's cheeks. She touched Meghan's shoulder and rubbed it gently.

There was no point trying to deny her feelings. Meghan was always so excited when he returned from his excursions, of which there were entirely too many. Truth be told, she was always relieved and pleased to see everyone return from any jaunt whether long or short. But with Neil it was something different...something special.

She knew that she loved him but was surprised at her increasing dependence on him. She had loved Brian, her former fiancé, but was far more independent and self-reliant. Of course, to be fair, times were significantly different then. She had a job and an apartment then. She slept inside then and wasn't a potential nightly special on the menu back then. She wondered how Brian would have done in Neil's position. Would he have ever found himself in Neil's position?

The thinking and remembering and wondering touched off a tinge, a lone peppercorn of guilt, that revealed itself unexpectedly in her misting eyes. She hadn't gone looking, but the tears found her anyway. There were neither sobs nor sniffles. The tears were quiet and few. They filled the corners of her eyes and left semi-clean streaks on her cheeks as they went south.

Jerry looked at her and, thinking they were tears of relief, said out of the corner of his mouth, "Jeez. He wasn't gone that long."

To which Claire nudged him with her elbow. "Shut the hell up. Lady's entitled."

Meghan merely smiled and nodded, preferring the simple assumption over the complicated truth.

Just moments later and with much fanfare, the travelers were back within the warmth of their camp. Introductions and handshakes were shared, as were a few scraps of food. There were smiles all around when Jules looked up in disbelief and said, "Alec?"

15

The boy DB had taken to calling Ricky was, in fact, Jules' older brother Alec. He hadn't said a word since joining DB, leaving the other man to guess about the boy's origins, his family, and even his name. Although, truth be told, DB wasn't much of a guessing man, so the farthest he had gotten in solving those mysteries was bestowing upon the boy the random moniker Ricky.

In all actuality it wasn't a random name at all, despite what he may have tried to tell himself. It was the name that he wanted to name his son, but his wife was having none of that. She'd said that Ricky wasn't a name worthy of her son. It just wasn't dignified enough. She named him after her father, Edward, and it was to him that she'd run while DB was on one of his two week stints working the oil fields of the North Slope.

She always appreciated the fine things that his large paychecks could buy, but she never seemed to appreciate the man who delivered those checks to her. Theirs was a fiery romance at best and an utter disaster at worst. She made him feel like an unwanted and over-stayed houseguest while he was home and completely ignored him when he was gone. And he wasn't without blame. As often as he could, just to get under her skin, DB would refer to young Edward as Eddie.

When he came home to an empty house and divorce papers awaiting his signature, he wasn't surprised but he was hurt all the same. Maybe he figured being unhappy was better than being alone and hoped that perhaps she was of the same mind. DB had spent the last couple of decades and then some mostly alone. Duke was his lone companion until recently.

When the mute boy came into his life by climbing in his truck that afternoon, it was only natural that the name Ricky was the first to surface. So the mute Alec had become the mute Ricky with no fuss and no filing of irritating documents at the courthouse.

That was all in the process of changing however. At first, Alec's recognition of Jules was as absent as his voice. His eyes, as alert and coherent as a lobotomy patient, panned across the little girl. There was nothing at first but then he hesitated. Perhaps a hint of recall. Just enough to fire some neural engine that had been put into a hibernating state after he'd seen and shot the thing that bit Martin.

He was remembering more. The family had driven away in a rush to take Martin to the hospital, which left him at the cabin alone. He'd already seen the rifle on the dish cabinet earlier and thought that perhaps he would take a look around. The bite on Martin's hand didn't look that bad, so how dangerous could the animal be? He doubted he would see anything in the first place; the thing would have likely run off. He needed a distraction and this adventure sounded like it would do nicely to kill the time.

When he found the shallow glacial creek and cool air using the creek bed like a bobsled track, he was reminded of the last time his family had journeyed to Alaska. He and Martin had run up and down the creek bank every day. The creek in his memory was much more robust and full. It seemed like a raging torrent. Back then, the same crisp edge was on the air but now there was something more. A lively, rank foulness gave the air's shallow coolness an unwelcome dimension that twisted his nose unpleasantly.

He was still on the bank when he saw something crawling, slithering like a lizard really, on the gravel of the creek bed. He knew that it couldn't be, but it kind of looked like it was a human without legs. When it moved again, he replayed in his mind what Jules and Danny had said. They said that a caveman had bitten Martin. Alec was looking at their caveman. But to think about the abomination in terms of being a man was really stretching his imagination. He could see its head and its shoulders fairly clearly, but beyond that the thing was formless and largely colorless.

He wanted to throw something at it when he remembered the rifle in his hands. It looked and felt so much heavier before, like some ancient, powerful weapon. Would it be enough? He lifted it to his shoulder, looked down the barrel to the sight on the end, and squeezed off a quick round. To his astonishment, the bullet hit the creature on its back. And to his equal astonishment, it appeared to have had no effect at all. He shot it again, shouting curses at it. When it turned over, he shot it again and again, but nothing seemed to be able to stop it.

Confused and more than a little scared now, Alec sprinted back to the cabin. He locked the doors and hid in the loft for hours. It became dark and no word had arrived from his parents. He wasn't sure how they would contact him because his cell phone wasn't working and the cabin didn't have a phone. He had no idea when they would be coming back and only hoped that it would be soon.

The next morning, he looked out the window and saw no sign of the thing from the creek. He couldn't have known that the creek bank was too steep and the Ice Age zombie with only one hand was unable to pull himself out. His ignorance of this fact was causing him to turn the cabin into both a refuge and a prison.

When he turned on the television, his day went from bad to worse. He was certain that his parents had gone to Anchorage, and it was there that some unknown tragedy was unfolding. His parents had unfortunately ended up right in the middle of an emergency that would likely delay them. When the television stopped broadcasting, he chose to watch some of the movies that were in the cabin. He'd seen most of them before, the good ones anyway, but he was willing to sit through them again. Of course, every sound outside solicited immediate but cautious glances out every window which made watching movies quite a challenge. Summer was just beginning its sprint into fall, and the Alaska wilderness all around the cabin was buzzing with wildlife trying to take full advantage of the waning days.

After several days and having eaten most of the food in the cabin, Alec made the terrifying realization that he might need to go find help. If something happened to his family or something happened that would simply delay their return, there was no one who knew that he was at the cabin. He was all alone out there...well, not entirely alone. That *thing* was still out there somewhere.

He hadn't seen any evidence of the creature so his worry was starting to center on his belly. There was still some food left in the cabin, but he decided that maybe he needed to ration it. With his time, he started to dig through the cabin, looking for anything he could find that would be useful. Actually, he'd gone looking for more bullets for the rifle. He found a partial box of small twenty-two caliber shells in a locked drawer that the cabin front door key conveniently fit. It was several of those that he used to shoot the thing. He was left with a handful of little bronze bullets that he kept in his jacket pocket at all times. He also found a couple of flashlights, some matches and a lighter, and next to the dwindling woodpile in the cabin was a small hatchet. With the exception of the rifle, all of this was pretty standard for most cabins.

Alec had no idea that the rifle was something that typically would not be an item that was so easily accessible in a rented cabin. The owners would have been mortified and concerned about possible legal ramifications of having a weapon in a rental property. Vaughn Beckett, one of the owners, brought the rife with him to share shooting a gun with his two young grandchildren. He was doing this despite his wife Dottie's objection, so he brought in the gun clandestinely and hid it on the china cabinet out of little hands' reach. The opportunity never presented itself during their very short visit primarily because the weather had soured, becoming cool and very wet. He didn't usually have that particular rifle with him and so, when it came time to depart, he simply forgot about it. The rifle sat where it was left for just shy of two weeks before Alec spied it.

As the days passed, the malaise of sleeplessness and hunger began to take its toll. He felt like a spectator in someone else's dream, disconnected and powerless. His bad thoughts began to crowd the oversized cabin like unwelcome guests. He tried desperately to distract himself again and again, but there really was no point. The thoughts were borne of the lingering remnants of his juvenile imagination which hadn't been corrupted and suppressed by his emerging adulthood. The imaginary specters and phantoms lurking in the dark corners of the cabin or just out of sight in the surrounding trees were enough to convince him that he needed to find help.

He didn't remember making the decision to leave the cabin. He could only recall suddenly walking along a lonely stretch of highway heading back the way from which his family had come on the first day of their vacation. He didn't have a full grasp of where he was heading; he only knew that he was on the move putting the cabin and the creature in the woods behind him. He had some essential supplies in his backpack and the rifle in his hand.

Outside and still alone, the quiet seemed so much more...absolute. He was walking north, at least that was the direction in which he thought he was walking, and not entirely certain what awaited him at the end of his journey. He only hoped that he would eventually be amongst people again, and he could let them worry about his safety. He complained to his parents about not being trusted to take care of himself and now he regretted ever having suggested it.

Walking along that highway was nothing like walking along a road back home. There was nothing for as far as he could see that would suggest people had ever been there other than the road itself. There were no billboards, no rest areas, no McDonald's, and no gas stations. There were only trees and rocks, rocks and trees. The sky overhead, which had been threatening rain for a couple of days, finally made good on that threat and spilled a cool rain on him after he had been walking only a couple of hours. The weather never cleared, though there were occasional dry spells.

He was shivering, cold and miserable, his stomach was growling, and his legs were tired, but he forced himself to keep walking. His first night away from the cabin, he spent along the side of the highway at a vehicle turnoff. There was a wooden picnic table there under which he slept.

The next morning, he awoke to dry, but gray skies. If he were a tourist, he would have been awed by the scenery. The road and the vehicle turnoff sat on the precipice of an incline which gave way to a beautiful valley of gray slate and green grass. On the far side of the great opening in the earth, the mountain rose to an impressive height, the top of which was already white with snow. The dark stone appeared smooth, almost polished from this distance. It looked like a broad, steep slide that ended in a lush, soft bed of grass. Such an impressive sight which could be beheld on the side of a highway. Simply amazing. He wasn't a tourist though, and the only thing the great space next to the road made him feel was claustrophobic. He couldn't run down the steep slope if he were chased, so his options were seriously limited by the expanse. He had less room in which to run.

Early the next day, he came to a road sign that let him know should he turn he would reach a place called Soldotna in less than half the miles that he had to travel to get to Anchorage, and his bone weariness decided for him to change his course. He marched down the winding road, passing a long stretch of water on his left. He passed several road signs but none of them registered in his exhausted eyes. There were likely names for the waterway, littering warnings, speed limit changes, and all the other usual instructions found on a rural highway. To him they were all a blur. He hadn't slept much the night before under his picnic table accommodations and his legs were already begging to him to stop. He wanted to stop but there just weren't any reasonable options in which to do it. Weary and miserable, he pressed forward hoping to reach civilization.

He finally came to a small town. Cooper something, he thought he read. The buildings and few cars here and there were empty. There was no one around. The shops and restaurants were boarded shut, as were the handful of homes he passed. As the day began to wane toward evening, he luckily found an unlocked car in which he could rest for the night. But try as he might, he couldn't bring himself to sleep. He rose from the car the next morning feeling no more rested or refreshed than he had the night before, and in front of him was more highway.

After a couple hazy days of walking, with little to no recollection of the journey, he came to the edge of another small community. There was no one to be found, as before. Again, business doors and windows were boarded, as were the few homes along the main stretch of road. He began to wonder if he was the last person alive on the earth. He thought about that movie with Will Smith and the Night Stalkers that hunted him. Could he be all that was left of the human race?

Alec wasn't certain when the last time it was that he had spoken, but it had been days and perhaps weeks. He tried to invoke his voice a few times but found that he could not will any words from his mouth. Given that he was still alone, his becoming a mute was a problem that would have to be dealt with later. For the moment, all that he cared to remedy was the growling in his stomach.

He broke into a small convenience store for some food and found bags of chips, candy bars, and sports drinks. He ate until he couldn't eat anymore, leaving a fluttering, plastic carpet under his feet when he'd finished. He was stuffing the last bag of stale Gummi Bears into his pack when he heard a noise outside.

He could feel the chill tighten his jaw and tease his arm hairs on end. Quietly, he picked his way through his Frito Lay floor covering and chanced a glance out the window. Coming up the driveway to the parking lot out front was a man. Well, he looked like he used to be a man. Alec wasn't quite sure what he would call him at present.

He was wearing some kind of uniform. Alec thought he saw the logo 2Go on the chest of the man's royal blue shirt. He was limping and not doing that very well. Alec could see that his leg was broken horribly below the knee and bent backward impossibly. The man's skin appeared faded, with almost an opaque translucence to it. At first Alec thought the man must have fallen into something because the man's left side from ear down to knee was stained darker than the rest of him. The man's dangling, empty, swaying sleeve convinced Alec that the dark stains was the dried remnants of the man's blood. Like his arm, part of it at least, the man's ear had been gnawed from his body.

The man's pace was stilted and slow due to his ruined leg, but determined. Looking out the window at him, Alec realized that the man was coming for him and looking at him just the way the eyeless creature back at the cabin had. He felt so much like cornered prey. Alec knew that he needed to act fast. He grabbed his backpack and headed toward the back of the store. He passed the bathrooms and came to another door with an exit sign above it. He pushed the door hard and almost fell into the store's back parking lot. He stumbled to his feet and ran as fast as his legs would carry him. In his running, he saw more people, all of whom looked like the man at the shop. None of them looked right to him and none of them certainly acted right either. They all seemed to be coming at him...*for* him.

Luckily, none of them were able to move very fast so he managed to get down the highway and leave them well behind him. However, he was now more worried than he ever had been at the cabin. He thought he wanted to be around people again, but when he finally found some, all they wanted to do was eat him. Back at the cabin, there was one monster stalking him from the shadows. Out here, he was being chased by monsters at every corner. He had jumped from the proverbial frying pan straight into the fire.

A day or two later and after several similar close encounters with more of the monsters, Alec found himself hiding in a restaurant near a big grocery store called Fred Meyer. He found his hiding spot almost by accident. He saw five or six of those things walking around the grocery store parking lot. He went around the back of the building trying not to be detected. Once out back, he found the back door had been left slightly ajar. As quietly as possible, he opened the door and crawled inside.

He found that he was in a big kitchen. A restaurant kitchen. The stench of rotting food filled the air with its toxic foulness. Flies, as big and slow as Winnebagos, twisted and swirled as he inched inside. Other bugs and critters scurried into corners and out of sight, not appreciating Alec's intrusion into their ongoing feast. The room, especially there at the floor where Alec was crawling, was dark, the meager light peeking in through the high windows barely reaching below the countertops. The floor below him, though dry, retained some of its slippery greasiness of its years of culinary activity.

Thankfully, there was no sound in the diner. He peeked over the counter and into the dining area. The chairs and tables were all neatly stacked and waiting for the next breakfast rush. The white and red checkered plastic table covers reminded him of every small town diner in which he'd had a meal with his family.

Then, despite the reeking odor and the disgusting image of the flies in the kitchen, he remembered his hunger. He turned back into the kitchen and found the storage area. There were buckets of pickles still in their aromatic brine. Some bread and some buns were still holding off the clutches of mold.

There were also a number of cans of fruit and beans and chili and.... He realized he'd hit the food jackpot.

He was so pleased with his find that he completely forgot about the nightmare that awaited him outside across the street. He forgot about his missing family. He forgot about everything that didn't involve opening the next can or swallowing the next salty, delicious bite. He went from one thing to the next and to the next over the course of more than an hour, never pausing or slowing his consumption. He ate so much that he made himself sick.

He vomited twice in the still clean toilet bowl of the men's bathroom. The nausea likely resulted from his eating too quickly and possibly eating something that was no longer edible. He always hated throwing up. He cried afterward, and even a little during the act itself. The tears, of course, made him miss his mother and her comfort.

Quietly, mostly to himself, he cried in a dark corner of the restaurant's dining room. He dozed off, still weeping, with his head on one of the plastic table covers. The flies and other bugs, sensing that the intruder had moved on, returned to their own feast on the moldy, rotting remnants of once fresh fruit and vegetables on the prep line.

Alec awoke the next day with a start. He didn't immediately recognize his surroundings which sent him into a temporary panic. He jolted up, grabbing his rifle, and spun around. In so doing, he knocked a chair from its perch on a table which hit another and another. The resulting crash of furniture helped to remind him of where he was. He stopped circling and went to one of the restaurant's dark tinted windows.

Just as he feared, the ruckus, however brief, had drawn the attention of those loitering monsters in the parking lot across the street. Their rigid limbs all at once began to quake and shiver as the infection sensed Alec's presence. Jerking and twisting, the ghouls slithered into the road and then waited. They waited for the next noise, the next smell, the next clue as to where Alec was hiding. He figured rightly that there were far more of those things than just the ten he could see immediately in front of the restaurant. He also figured that it was just a matter of time before the demons located him.

He decided that he didn't want to wait around to figure out what happened next. He wasn't much of one for planning though, he just grabbed his backpack and the rifle, and ran out the back door. He cut across some open fields and had to pick his way to the opposite side of a small creek, but soon he was on the go again. He felt better, rested and fed, but his fear was on the rise.

He was back on a main road when he saw a sign with an arrow pointing him toward the hospital. In a matter of minutes, he joined DB and Duke in their truck and then back at their trailer.

The memories of his first days alone and the fears that he would never see his family again exiled his voice. He was afraid that he would never have a reason to speak again, but really it wasn't as if he was not speaking by choice. His voice had abandoned him.

Of course, that all changed when he finally realized and accepted that the little blonde girl with the pigtails and dirty face was indeed his sister. With tears pouring down his cheeks, Alec knelt down to his sister and, through his emotions, said only, "Jules?"

16

Alec, kneeling by his sister, blurted out as he pulled her close to him and hugged the breath right out of both of them, "Jules! I never thought.... I can't believe....Oh God!" His words were washed away by the flood of emotions which swept over everyone in the small camp.

It was nothing short of miraculous. Danny too joined in the embrace, the three of them holding one another as tightly as their arms would allow, their joyous sobs muffled by each other's shoulders.

Meghan covered her mouth with her hand and refused to fight the tears. Warm and satisfied, her smile emerged from around the barrier of fingers in front of it. Standing next to Neil, she could no longer contain herself. She wrapped her arms around him and buried her face against his chest. She was quiet for several seconds while she reveled in his touch, his smell, and his presence. She was not surprised when her tears changed flavor from those of satisfaction for Danny and Jules to relief for Neil's return. She shuddered as the feelings completely overtook her. Her legs felt weak, so she leaned even more forcefully against him, hoping to hold the moment.

She peeked over at Emma and her relief was slightly tempered with guilt. She wondered to herself how Emma was doing. Dr. Caldwell's death was still so fresh and unresolved for all of them, but especially for Emma. Despite the overwhelming happiness that was warming her chest, Meghan couldn't help but wonder, if even for a moment, how she would be doing if their roles were reversed and it was Neil that they had left back at the gas station instead of Dr. Caldwell. The thought came very close to dousing her good mood, but she fought back the fear with another deep breath filled with Neil's presence.

For the moment, however, the amazing and unlikely appearance of Alec was enough to put smiles on all of their faces. Maybe, just maybe, there still was that outside possibility that more good news would find them somehow.

Meghan pulled herself away from Neil and gave Emma a long, warm hug as well, ending it with a gentle kiss on her cheek. To Meghan's surprise, Emma was as warm and reciprocating as a town square statue of some long forgotten historical figure.

Emma did manage to say, "Thanks. It's good to be back. Did we miss anything exciting?"

Jerry answered, "We heard some shots a bit ago. Got nerves a little frayed for a bit, but..."

"Maybe you should introduce us to your friends," Meghan said. "I understand this young man is Alec, but how about everyone else?"

Neil stepped aside and, motioning to the people still standing behind him, said, "This is DB, Della, and...well, I don't know the kids' names."

DB nodded to the others while Della just stared at all of them in turn. The awkward silence that followed raised everyone's discomfort. Della wasn't seeing people or a warm fire, she was only seeing strangers and a lot of guns.

When she looked at Jerry, he said to her, "Why don't we go over to the fire? We can talk and you guys can warm up a little."

Everyone but Della heeded his suggestion. But while everyone else wandered toward the glowing coals of the fire, she stood and watched and waited.

Jerry suggested, "Della, if you'd like—"

"I heard you the first time, Steve."

Jerry started to correct her when Neil caught him by the sleeve and shook his head. Taking the hint, Jerry turned himself around and opened his palms to the warmth, hoping that perhaps he could make her comfortable enough to join them. But still she waited.

17

There were many questions, and there were stories to tell and experiences to relive, but knowing what was behind and in front of them on the road was the most pressing concern for all of them.

Neil said, "So, we're headed for Whittier. What was the road like between here and there?"

DB stirred the small fire with the long, brittle stick in his hand, finally burying enough of the tip in the red coals to have it stand of its own accord. He spoke slowly, "Whittier, huh?"

"Yeah. We heard that maybe the tunnel was closed in time, that maybe the infection didn't make it there. Lots of people headed that way I guess."

"Ain't no real point in going to Whittier. Bunch...maybe hundreds of those things between you and that tunnel."

"Is the tunnel closed then?"

"What difference does it make? If it is, then you're shut out. And if it ain't, well, it won't be no different than everywhere else. Might as well be the moon where you're headed. Whittier's not worth the effort."

Neil felt his stomach, already growling in protest, start to do rebellious back flips. He thought to himself, *now what*? DB was obviously coming up from Kenai, and they wouldn't have left if circumstance hadn't dictated it. And behind Neil was Girdwood and then Anchorage beyond and both were crawling with the undead. What options did they have?

He found going over the same questions with the same doubts and the same necessities to be nothing but tiresome. Much of the positive energy created by finding DB was sapped by the dark thoughts tormenting his mind. Neil kept his thoughts to himself for the time being however. Meghan was, of course, intuitive enough to see the trouble in Neil's eyes, so she took hold of his cold hand in her warm one.

Jerry asked DB, "Where were you guys headed?"

DB didn't look away from the fire. He, like many, enjoyed watching a fire tend to its own business. He always found it ironic that it was fire's basic nature to eat itself to death. Fire consumed everything within its reach until there was nothing left to burn, killing itself with each greedy mouthful. He answered Jerry, "We was just headed. Nowhere in particular. Just trying to stay off of everyone's radar. Runnin' into you was a bit of a happy accident."

Jerry nodded. "Yeah. I know what you mean. The longer I go without seein' one of those things, the better I feel."

DB spit into the fire and wiped his chin absently. "Those things ain't the only bad guys out there."

Neil was suddenly interested again. "What do you mean by that?"

"Let's just say not everyone out on the road is as friendly as you all."

Meghan looked disgusted, "You mean, even with all that's happened...?"

Claire interjected reproachfully, "See, I told you. Those bastards I ran from back in Anchorage weren't my imagination. Just cowardly shits taking advantage."

DB wanted to spit again but thought better of it. *No point in being rude after all.* "Yeah. I don't know that I ever seen one of them things do nothin' bad or aggressive to another one. They just kinda hover and wait. Kinda funny that those things treat each other better than we treat ourselves."

Claire nodded her agreement and firsthand understanding, while she carefully used her teeth to remove every sticky morsel of granola bar clinging to her fingers. This might be her last meal and she didn't want to waste a single nibble.

Cradling his forehead in his palm, Jerry commented, "Yeah. A laugh riot."

DB measured Jerry with his eyes. He would have guessed that Jerry was young, maybe not much beyond twenty-one. Jerry didn't fit the mold if he was as young as DB suspected now that he had been able to more closely observe him. DB searched the pool of his memory trying to stir his vocabulary. The agitated, undulating caps of adjectives seemed so common and ill-fitting. And then he seized upon a word riding the others: poised. Yes, the man...the boy was poised. DB was satisfied with his quick assessment and moved on.

"There are folks all around. I mean, you know, the kind that don't eat people. I seen'em around, here and there. Small groups and sometimes just loners. They just lookin' to stay alive. No different than me or any of us. Mostly, them folks keep to themselves. But there's others marauding the

Peninsula, from Cooper Landing all the way down to Homer. If it ain't them things out to get you then it's those bastards followin' behind to finish you off. Crazies that banded together and just want to stir the pot until it spills onto the floor. Got no regard for nothin', not even themselves. Drunk or stoned and riding around on motorcycles creating havoc amidst the chaos. About as bad a mix as it could be.

"But that ain't all. Down outside Soldotna, some of them citizen militia people got organized in a hurry. Hell, this was kind of what some of them had been predicting and preparing for for years. I'm sure that to some of them, this was just Christmas come early. I ain't had much to do with none of them, but what I seen ain't been too complimentary.

"Me and Duke and Ricky...I mean Alec, I guess, we was on foot on the highway. This was about a day or so before we found Della and the kids. Well, my truck...let's just say it wasn't going to be driving us nowhere. So, like I said, we was walking the highway when I heard something comin' up the road. It sounded like an NRA parade salutin' the history of the gunshot. But then I heard the engine sound too. Motorcycles. We dropped out of sight, hopin' they'd just pass us on by. There wasn't much in the way of hiding spots to choose from. We was near Kenai Central. Ya know that high school there on the highway? We just got as small and still as we could in the shallow ditch that ran along the side of the road.

"When I peeked back onto the road, I realized there was more to it. There were a couple people on bicycles that were being chased by whoever was on the motorcycles, who were still a little off in the distance but closing fast. It was going to be a short chase. I could tell the bike riders, a man and a woman, were already at their limit and the motorcycles were doin' nothin' but gainin' on 'em. It was just a matter of minutes...seconds and maybe not even that long.

"The fellas on the motorcycles, when they came into view, were wearin' uniforms. Like full on military uniforms with the yellow yarn on their shoulders and everything. The militia boys ran them other two folks off the road. They sent 'em crashin' ass over tit onto the road. They couldn't a been more 'n twenty, maybe twenty-five yards away from where we was hidin'.

"The man from the bike got up first. He looked over his shoulder at the woman who wasn't movin'. He tried to get away on foot, but his leg was broke. He was facing right at us. I think he may have even seen us, but I can't be certain. He yelped like a wounded animal when he fell. He tried to crawl but the angle of his broke leg made it impossible to move. It was terrible. One of them uniformed boys walked over to the man and said something like, 'In the name of the new order of law' or something, and shot the man in his back. Then the militia boy nudged the man with his boot until he groaned. So the boy shot him again, and laughed when he seen the man's legs twitch a little. It ain't never easy to see a man die.

"About then, a big, black Humvee pulled up on the street. More of the uniformed boys piled out and stood around waitin' for something to happen, but the man in the passenger seat of the SUV stayed where he was. He was the boss, so he didn't have to get up for no one. At least that's how it looked to me. He sat in his comfy, padded seat and told everyone else what to do.

"I heard them talk about what happened. I guess the two bike riders were suspected of, get this, *looting*. The militia, being the new authority in town, was enforcin' the laws that seemed important I guess and looting is now a capital offense, but when they searched the dead bodies they didn't find nothin' on either of them. D'you know what the son of a bitch sitting in the Humvee said then? He zipped up his coat until the metal teeth almost pinched his neck skin and he said, *'Well, let that serve as a lesson to anyone who might be thinking about looting then.'*

"I see a couple of them uniformed boys goin' through a couple cars on the road and lo and behold they found themselves some beer in a cooler in the back of a truck. Another one of 'em had a woman's garter around his forehead. Ya know, the kind of garter that guys get at a wedding and hang around their mirrors. They just rummaged around the cars grabbin' anything they could get their hands on. *Looting*? I guess not much changed with the changin' of the guard. The ins are always sticking it to the rest of us.

"Pretty soon, all the noise them fellas was making got the attention of a bunch of those things. Probably twenty or so of the monsters started to come at them from the high school across the street. Remember how I said them boys had been preparing for all of this? Well, they showed me just how thorough they had trained. It was just a few seconds and a lot of shooting before all those things were piled in the middle of the road. There was more of them off to either side of the road and some more still comin' from around both sides of the school. I was afraid to look over my shoulder to see if there was any behind us. Hell, I didn't know what we would do if there were. We had Ricky's gun but if we shot or even stood up to run, them militia boys woulda' filled the three of us full o' holes too."

It must have been time for a commercial break in the action, because DB paused his story as he stirred the fire again. Darkness was falling all around them, making the small fire glow all the more.

Meghan sighed incredulously. "Jesus."

Della, whose eyes shimmered with the fire's reflection, said from behind them, "I think we can leave Him outta this," and then finally sat down, joining the others around the warming flame. She opened her hands above the fire, letting the heat circulate through her body like a boiler filling pipes and radiators with scalding water to warm its host. She almost betrayed the soothing sensation with a smile, but stopped just short of actually doing that.

Della realized that all the eyes around the campfire were on her and waiting for her to speak again, however, she felt no need to rush into saying anything more. She was not one of those people who felt that every quiet moment needed words or sounds to fill it. Sometimes silence was enough to fill the void in and of itself.

Della's hands warmed significantly; she held her palms to the back of her neck and felt the comfort trickle both up and down her spine, resisting the urge to shudder with the simple pleasure of shaking away the cold.

In their van on the side of the road, they had decided to forego having a fire for fear that it would attract others to them. Inside the van, the cold was not so extreme at nights, but it was never warm. She accepted things for the way that they were at all times, but there was something to be said for not being cold. She sat silent for a few moments more, realizing that the quiet was waiting for her to break it.

She began, "It was them militia people or the marauders or maybe both that set me and these kids on the path to all y'all. Some damn fools came along to the hotel where we was hidin' lookin' for...well, they was looking for whatever they could find.

"I was a housekeeper at the hotel. I was workin' when the TV in the lobby started to jabber on 'bout something happenin' in Anchorage. I 'spose I saw the same news that DB saw. Them news people were guessing and talking, having experts from the CDC and Homeland Security and who knows what else come on the show to give their two cents worth. Nobody knew what was goin' on.

"The last thing I saw before the TV went dead was a woman talking about how there were some new reports about this thing spreading to Fairbanks and maybe even to Vancouver and Seattle. By that time, most of the folks in the hotel decided it was time to leave. Some came down to the front desk to check out, but most just left. The parking lot went from full to empty in about an hour. Most just ran off without any place to go or plans to get there. They was just runnin'. All them folks from outta town...from the Lower Forty–eight took off but where was they gonna go? Not like they could just drive to home or safety or nothin'. I didn't know where they was headed and they prob'ly didn't know neither. It was just good enough for them to be headed and so that's what they did. They all just disappeared. A few families stuck around the hotel. I guess when they got to thinkin' about where to run, they realized that there wasn't much runnin' to be done. Maybe they was hopin' that all the troubles would stay in Anchorage or that maybe someone would swoop on down to save 'em.

"All the ladies that worked the front desk was gone too. The last to go was the manager. He was some young guy...just a kid who had a degree and a connection through his family to get the job. Least, that's what everyone say 'bout him. He was nice enough. I ain't never seen him sweat until that day. Well, I guess before some big time manager was up from the Lower Forty-eight, he was a little worked up but nothin' like that morning. This was somethin' different and I could see it in his face. He was scared and wasn't puttin' no effort into hiding it.

"He took me aside and gave me his keys. You know, the ones that open every door. I had a master key that opened all the guest rooms and the utility and laundry rooms, but his keys opened every door. He said that I could stay at the hotel with the guests who was stayin' too. He told me to take care of things, but I could tell he didn't care one way or t'other. He just wanted to be gone. It was hard for Steve to be so young and so scared at the same time. He was so used to being invincible and powerful. I think maybe he was thinkin' his fear was making him less of a man or something, but that didn't stop him from runnin' out to his little black car and drivin' hisself on outta that parking lot without ever lookin' back.

"By the end of the day, it was just me and a few families. They was all from somewhere out East, travelin' together... the typical dream vacation to Alaska."

Neil and Meghan gazed sympathetically at Jules and Danny, who had come into their company in much the same way.

Under her breath, Della's thought found her voice and she said, "Dyin' together too I guess. Them poor folks."

Della felt all the eyes back on her again. She chewed her lip, revealing for the first time any hints of frailty. She scratched her neck lightly and rubbed her chin. "At the hotel, we got ourselves comfortable. We had lotsa food...mostly breakfast sausage and muffins and such. We just waited. A few nights into it, the lights went out. We knew it was coming, but it took us all by surprise. The hotel's got a generator but we decided we would wait until the morning to turn it on. Turned out to be a good idea. I guess them things started to come into Soldotna. We heard a buncha' screaming and then some shootin'. The hotel was dark, so it all just passed us by but it sounded horrible. By the time it was to full steam, when all them folks was screaming and shootin' and dyin', and no matter how far we went into that hotel, we couldn't seem to get away from it. The noise shook the whole hotel. It was like we was in a earthquake or somethin'. I ain't never heard nothing like it and hope I never do again.

"We blocked off the front doors and the windows, but they was big doors with thick glass. We thought they would hold most everything out, so we wasn't worried. We had lights when everything was dark. We had food. And we had security, we thought. We was such fools.

"A few of them things came around. They made a mess of the glass on the front doors but that was about it. We hung some sheets over the glass so that the things couldn't see us and we couldn't see them. There was a buncha kids with us, I think nine in all, and they didn't need to be lookin' at those demons. I ain't never seen nothin' like it. Like I said though, we didn't pay them no mind. If that was as bad as it was going to get, well...it wasn't.

"About a week later, we heard some motors comin' up the road toward us. We'd heard motors before, but always during the day. This was a little bit after sunset. A coupla' the moms thought that maybe it was all over and help had finally come. I knew better. I tole' 'em all that them motors didn't sound like the type of thing the military or government would be using. Those motors only sounded like trouble to me. None of 'em listened to me though, like I was some kind of a fool or somethin'. I just went and found me a place to hide. I didn't want no part of whatever was comin'."

The grisly conclusion of her tale was halted when Della gazed over at the two young children in her charge and thought better of it. Her face was as rigid and warm as stone, but her eyes glistened with soft, tender kindness. She continued more quietly, seemingly carrying on the conversation directly with the fire in front of her, "I don't know fo' sure what happened. From my spot in the luggage closet, it sounded a lot like the way it did on the road in front of the hotel those first few days. I heard runnin' and screamin' and shootin' and even some beggin'. It sounded like them nice folks was goin' through hell. I guess it don't take much imagination to figure what happened. It was done and over so quick.

"Whoever they was didn't leave much behind. I think I heard a few of the younger moms and maybe some of the kids being taken along. When it got quiet enough for long enough and I thought it was safe, I took a look around.

The food was all gone. What they didn't take was scattered all over the floor and on some of the furniture in the lounge area. They took all the diesel for the generator too. They left behind quite a mess though, and the food on the couches was just the start. Windows and doors were smashed and someone had sprayed a fire extinguisher down the hallway. They even sprayed some graffiti on the walls. I understand the food and the fuel but the rest of it, especially the graffiti.... I guess I just don't get some folks is all. Things weren't messy enough already?

"There was a coupla' bodies floating in the little pool. Their skin was as white as a linen sheet. Whatever little bit of color bleached right out of 'em by the chlorine in the water. There was three or four more bodies out in the parking lot. Their hands were tied behind their backs and they had plastic shopping bags over their heads. I didn't look close enough to tell if they'd been shot and the bags were just their version of an executioner's blindfold, or if they had been smothered by the tight plastic. Don't matter much no how.

"In a room on the main floor, I found two moms in beds. I don't even want to tell you how I found them poor ladies. God rest their souls. I decided I was gonna leave the next day as early as I could. I just planned to go to my trailer and see what happened next. I looked around for anything that them others might have left behind by accident. I wasn't never comin' back to the hotel, so I wanted to make sure that I grabbed whatever I could. I found me some chips and cookies hidden in the break room by one of the desk girls. In the locked manager's desk drawer, I found me some canned breakfast drinks and some energy drinks too. Never much took to either of those, but I knew that it would come in handy down the road.

"I went into the laundry room to see if anything in there might be helpful. I wasn't plannin' on gettin' anything useful from in there but I looked anyway. I mean, what would I possibly need with clean sheets?"

Claire interrupted with a prolonged sigh of longing, "Cleannnnnn sheeeeeets."

Della continued without losing pace. "I opened the door and these two little heads popped up from inside one of the laundry carts." In a rare moment of levity, Della smiled through a slight chuckle. "Looked to me like a coupla' prairie dogs, I swear they did. I grabbed 'em and found a quiet room upstairs that wasn't too bad where we could sleep for the night."

Della's eyes expelled any humor and became serious and grave. "The next mornin' was cold and wet on the other side of the window. I was thinkin' maybe we could wait one more day. No point in leavin' if it was goin' to be nasty outside, especially since it was dry and not so cold in the hotel still. The little boy though, he said that he was hearing somethin' that was making his head hurt and then the little girl said the same thing. And then I thought that maybe I heard it too. I don't know how to explain it."

"It's okay," Neil said. "We've all been through it too. We think that it, whatever *it* is, tends to affect younger ears much more than older ears."

Della considered Neil's assessment before she spoke. "I didn't have as much time to figure that sort of thing out right then because all of a sudden there was some banging on the door and that sound got worse. Don't know that I ever been so scared. I didn't know what to do. The kids were cryin' and I might've been too; I don't know fo' sure. If it was one of them bastards come back to finish the job, I wasn't gonna give him the satisfaction. And if it was one of the things that was out in the street, well I wasn't quite sure what I was gonna do. I didn't have no weapons and I was afraid that if we tried to jump out the window...well, look at me and you know what I was worried about tryin' to do that and them kids couldn't drop that far without hurtin' their selves neither.

"The thing at the door was gettin' a little more serious about it and was gettin' louder and louder. I didn't think we could out last it, so I had to do somethin'."

Meghan wondered, "What did you do?"

Stretching her arms high over her head, Della paused, letting the difficult memories settle before speaking again. "I did the only thing I could think to do. I opened the door. The only thing I had in that room that I could use to protect myself was a fire extinguisher. So I locked the kids in the bathroom, got that extinguisher in my hands, and opened the door. The thing looked as surprised as I was that I'd done a fool thing like that. But that was what I was hopin' for. I sprayed its face and knocked it back into the hallway. Then I swung that heavy, metal son of a bitch and hit the thing on his head. He just fell down, gurgled a bit, and then went limp. There wasn't no other things in the hall but I knew that we didn't have much time.

"I ran back in the room, got them kids outta the bathroom, and we ran out one of the side exits. There was more of them things in the Carrs parking lot across the street, but they didn't see us. A little bit later, the kids started to complain that they could hear that noise again. We was movin' slow, tryin' to stay outta sight as much as possible, so we just waited.

"Coupla' seconds later, we saw 'em. There was maybe four or five of 'em lookin' in the windows of a service station. And then they started to get all...agitated and excited. They started to bang on the glass until I heard a scream from inside. All of a sudden a woman ran out the back of the building and down the direction we just come from and them things take off after her. A few seconds later, we heard another scream and then nothing else. Lucky for us, all those things chased after her, so we could get movin' again.

"We spent the next few days just movin' from place to place. We ate when we could, but mostly we just wanted to hide. We just laid low. Movin' like that, from hiding spot to hiding spot, until we found DB."

Della looked up at the darkening skies. "One of those days after we left the hotel, we saw some cycles that looked like maybe they coulda' made the kind of noise I heard on the night that the hotel was attacked. They was big and shiny and, I bet, loud. The bikes was just sittin' there in the middle of the road on their kick stands like they was horses waiting outside the saloon for their cowboy riders to return. They wasn't abandoned though. They looked too particular and neat. They certainly looked out of place, like they didn't belong. Lookin' at them, I kinda' hoped that maybe God still had enough vengeance left in hisself to visit a little on some of those evil men. Maybe they had to answer for their sins after all. Truth be told though, them bikes coulda' been sittin' there since the beginning of all this hell on earth. It was fun to think that maybe there was still some justice left in this big, ole, broke world."

"Back then, we seen some other folks still around. Normal folks, ya know. They was lookin' around for food and such just like us. Some looked okay but I wasn't chancin' nothin', so like I said, we just laid low."

The story wasn't anything new to any of them, other than the specific details. They had, unfortunately, lived through similar events recently and would hopefully continue to live through the harrowing times in front of them. Neil did have one question for her. He waited patiently until he was certain she was done speaking, and then inquired, "After all those days and all the other people, why DB? What was it about him that was different?"

Della sidestepped the question at first, letting it bounce away like an errant ball hit out of bounds. She wasn't sure if she had an answer that would either satisfy his question or her own curiosity. If she were honest with herself, she would have to admit that there wasn't a single factor that led her to trust the old man, but if there was one thing that she could name it would have to be the man's eyes. There was no malice in the fading blue orbs. The wrinkles to either side of the light blue pools were honest and harbored no spite. They were eyes worthy of trust and so she had done that. She felt no compulsion to immediately answer Neil's question, and decided in the end to leave it unanswered. She simply stirred the fire with another of the longer sticks and let the inquiry slip away from the conversation and disappear into the encroaching night.

But what did it really matter? She and those two kids were cold, hungry, and desperate for salvation when they happened upon the man, the boy and that old dog. She had thrown caution to the wind and put her faith in a complete stranger. By the grace of God, it had worked out and there she sat amongst these strangers as living proof of her successful gamble.

Finally, when everyone else had given up on hearing an answer, Della spoke defiantly, "Steve, if I knew I guess I'd tell ya. As it is, we here because we went with them two. That's all. Nothin' mystical or profound really. Steve just done his job and got us here."

Emma's eyes betrayed her exhaustion, despite the air of excitement around the camp. She said, "We all got stories about how we got here. Maybe we should put off any more of this until tomorrow. I don't know about the rest of you, but I could sure use some sleep."

Her suggestion was met with nodding heads, stretching arms, and yawning mouths.

Jerry stood with his rifle balanced across both of his shoulders. "You folks have been on the move all day. Maybe you should get some shut eye. Me and Claire and Meghan can keep first watch. We'll get you up in a few hours to take over."

"You don't have to tell me twice," Neil said gratefully. "Thanks. I could use the rest." He was exhausted and the spell of sitting had only made him understand that reality that much more clearly. His legs ached, and it felt as if he was wearing cement shoes.

He scanned the campsite and found his sleeping bag still rolled tight and anything but ready. He decided it was too much effort and so elected to simply zip his coat closed and cross his arms across his chest. He closed his eyes and let the calmness of the moment tempt him to sleep. When he felt his legs being lifted and moved slightly, he barely cracked his eyes to inspect the source.

It was Meghan. She was coaxing him as gently as possible into his sleeping bag. He complied, and was soon wrapped in down-filled comfort. Inside his warm cocoon, he was once again isolated with his thoughts. He thought about the day now behind them. He missed his friend Dr. Caldwell's company and judgment, but, for a change, things seemed to be on an upward swing.

18

"Neil. Neil."

He was being shaken awake, but he resisted. Neil had been dreaming, or maybe more accurately described as *remembering*, in his sleep where memories weren't forced to parade themselves through the filter of his conscious reality. He was revisiting his wedding day. The marriage notwithstanding, the actual wedding ceremony and, more specifically, reception were pretty good.

His recollection lacked clarity, coming to him as familiar yet hazy forms. It was like looking at a picture from a distance and through flowing water. All around him in a happy swirl were smiles and laughter, music and dancing, and, of course, the prospect of a lifetime of happiness and love. He relived his brother's rambling but sincere toast, though the specific words, like the images, defied coherence. His parents' approval, evident in the warmth of their presence, was perhaps the most fulfilling memory that graced his dream. And his bride...she was gorgeous. There was no other way to describe her. Her dark, elegant curls and soft, feminine features were enough to take his breath away on that day so long ago and were still stirring to him in his dream. He couldn't have been more in love.

His dreamy reality, perfect and pristine, was interrupted by a voice, then by shaking and finally by a face floating above him. At first, the face was foreign and accompanied by a staccato beat resembling the sound of a thousand out of sync woodpeckers banging out a thousand confused rhythms all at once. This was not a face he remembered from his wedding and the noise wasn't even a part of his hangover the morning after. The face was young but lacked naiveté and had hints of dirt and grime over its splotchy red cheeks. Recollection was slow, but when he finally recognized Jerry, his wariness raged to pure terror in an instant.

The near absolute darkness and the roaring cacophony all around further fueled his disorientation driving him nearly to a panic. The air kissed Neil's cheeks with its cool, salty wetness forcing his breath deeper into his lungs. He could smell the moisture and realized that the woodpeckers were actually raindrops hitting upon the tarp that had been laid over him to keep him dry. Neil started to shuffle and move under the tarp, making a bit of noise in the process.

Jerry touched Neil's shoulder to get his attention. He held his finger over his pursed lips to quiet Neil as he awoke. The younger man leaned closely and whispered into Neil's ear, "We got company over on the road. I don't think they know we're here, but I think we should get the others up."

From his semi-dry blue plastic cocoon, Neil couldn't see anything other than Jerry's shadow-enshrouded face. He fought back the urge to retreat further from the waking world into his current sensory-deprived surroundings.

Neil rose slowly, as if the heavy world would have it no other way. His weariness had hidden from him the hard uneven surface of his makeshift bed, but the resulting aches and pains were all too eager to point themselves out. He was thankful he wasn't already on the run, allowing him the opportunity to stretch. Neil eased himself out from under the tarp, careful not to make any more noise than was unavoidable.

He realized he was the last adult to be roused. The others were already kneeling in various intervals around the camp. In the modest moonlight, Neil was only able to discern the most basic shapes and forms of individuals, but defining features and characteristics were absent. Della was hovering near the still sleeping children. She didn't have a firearm, but she was sporting a baseball bat that cast a bit of a metallic glint against the darkness. DB and Alec, an honorary adult, were the furthest away and were both now armed with rifles given to them by Neil. Emma and Claire were a little closer but still several feet away. They too were armed and ready, looking out toward the highway beyond.

Finally, Meghan, waiting patiently next to Jerry, handed Neil his shotgun and then fell against him. Her cheeks were wet with rain, but he could tell that the rain was doing its level best to conceal the warm tears that were also present. With her fragile vulnerability pleading from her eyes, Meghan could not possibly have looked more beautiful or precious to Neil. Despite her matted, dripping hair and the filth of living on the go and largely in the wild clinging to her, Meghan was every bit as beautiful as the still fading dream image of his long ago bride.

It didn't seem to matter that the world was dying in violent convulsions all around them when he looked at her. He begged for the power or the insight to make things better for her. Neil did the only thing he could think to do. He wrapped his arms around her and tried to hug away the fear and the accompanying tears. He kissed her forehead and professed his love with a knowing look and a second kiss on her lips.

She tried to smile, but Meghan was nearing her limit, that much was clear to Neil. And like his past failed attempts at resolving problems in relationships, he was at a loss as to what to do. It wasn't as simple as stopping smoking, remembering to take out the trash, or taking constructive criticism and advice more seriously. Try as he might, he couldn't seem to figure a way to stave off the horrors of the world for Meghan.

For the moment, all he could do was help them all to see another sunrise. That would be something at least. To that end, he leaned against the dark, wet curtain of thick slate slabs screening them from the passing horde.

Jerry motioned toward the road with a head nod and whispered, "There's a big group over there...on the road. I think they're moving north. That's how it sounds anyway. With any luck, they'll pass us on by."

To Neil, that wasn't necessarily a sound gamble. He worried aloud, "I hope we're not counting too much on our luck. Last time I checked, our luck wasn't serving us too well." Neil paused for a thoughtful moment and then said quietly, "Why are they on the move?"

Jerry considered Neil's question and then answered with a whisper, "Maybe your shooting down the road? If I were to venture a guess, I'd have to say that's as likely a cause as anything."

Neil felt the frustration in Jerry's words. He was, after all, more than likely right in both his assessment as well as his irritability. Neil could easily have pointed out that it was Emma who started the shooting in the first place, but stopped himself before the juvenile excuse of *she started it* was given voice. Instead, he asked, "So where are they going then?"

Jerry shrugged his shoulders. "They probably don't even know. They heard the gunshots and their brains told them to follow the sound to find food. Once they get going, it's really just one of Newton's Laws of Motion. They'll keep heading in that direction until some other force causes them to stop or turn around. They'll just go and go...probably right off a cliff if something doesn't stop them first."

"Do you really think it could be that simple?"

Shaking his head in doubt, Jerry replied, "I really don't know. So long as they keep passing us by, what does it matter? If they're not in front of us, isn't that a good thing? Rather them in the rearview mirror than the headlights, know what I mean?"

"Yeah. I guess you're right."

Jerry's judgment was logical and entirely possible. It was also something that they might be able to use to their benefit in dealing with the undead in the future. Despite this possibility, Neil was finding it hard to be comfortable. Regardless of the direction in which they were heading, there were still scores and perhaps more of the walking corpses passing them a mere handful of yards away. He was worried that he and the others would never be granted the opportunity to explore Jerry's suppositions. The peril of their situation was staggering.

Neil was right too. The dragging shuffle of feet on pavement and the occasional tortured grunt or moan emerging from the darkness was unnerving to say the least. Some of the sounds were coming from disturbingly close and led many of them to start, chewing on fingers already gnawed to the quick.

He wondered to himself if there was anything he could do to improve the odds. He imagined, for a moment, running headlong into the pack. He'd have his guns blazing and when they were all emptied, he would start swinging his bat. In a heartbeat, he envisioned him successfully bludgeoning enough of the fiends to rally support from the others until they had killed them all. And then, in the same instance, he imagined him swinging the bat a few times until his exhaustion and the sheer numbers of the ghouls overwhelmed him beneath a pile of decaying, but still clawing flesh. That's just how it was with Neil and even the end of the world hadn't changed his self-defeating nature from emerging during his own redemption fantasies. He was, instead, frightened to inaction once again, choosing to allow circumstance and chance to determine his fate. He was the master of passivity.

Meanwhile, the rain and the dark worked hand in hand as unwitting allies to the small band's survival gambit. They hunkered down beneath blue tarpaulins and waterproof tent vinyl. Their hands and feet threatening to lose feeling in the damp cold, they each reminded the other to flex fingers and wiggle toes as much as possible. The waiting and the wondering created frustration and anxiety all night as each new sound sent off alarm bells in their heads. It promised to be a sleepless and restless night once again.

19

The cold wet night passed into a cold wet morning with the zombie migration finally starting to show signs of waning. The torrential river of undead was fast becoming a trickling stream. Despite the numbers seeming manageable enough to force a confrontation, Neil knew that it was a bad idea. If the beasts were simply allowed to pass without ever knowing that Neil and the other survivors had been there all along, that seemed to be the best option.

It seemed that with the dawning of a new morning, perhaps they would for once enjoy a little good luck. The children were all awake by then but still sitting out of the rain beneath and on top of a tarp. Della had stirred them from their sleep but forbade them from coming from beneath the plastic cover.

Things were really looking good. Neil counted perhaps ten of the foul creatures still on the road. Most were sporting injuries to their legs which slightly inhibited their walking, causing them to straggle far behind the main pack, but straggle and continue forward they did.

These few barely constituted a threat, given the numbers Neil had faced in the past. It felt like maybe things were starting to get better. He knew he shouldn't tempt fate with his optimism, but it was hard to resist. So little had gone their way that he couldn't help but feel somewhat contented with the current turn of events.

He turned back away from the road and looked down toward DB and Alec, who were the farthest south of their group. Beyond where they hunched behind some larger, round rocks, Neil thought he spied some movement. He was still sitting down, so much of the distant area to the south of them was obscured. Still, he thought he saw something. It could just be his eyes playing tricks on him but he couldn't tell for sure. He'd been staring so intently into the darkness through most of the early morning hours, he could have just strained his eyes.

No. He was certain he saw it that time. There was something coming toward them up the tracks. *Something?* There was no doubt in his mind what it was.

He grabbed Jerry's arm and pointed down the tracks. He needn't do more as the ghouls' heads were slowly coming into view. At precisely the same time, Jerry's and Neil's stomachs rolled themselves over into nauseating knots. Now something had to be done. Ignoring the problem and hoping that it would merely go away was not an option. The problem was coming straight at them.

This was one of those moments in which Neil would have been thankful for someone else to make the decisions. They could easily take the three nearest to them but would also more than likely attract the attention of the monsters still on the highway. Neil was fairly confident they could even kill the ten or so zombies on the road handily, although it would require the use of firearms. This eventuality would in all likelihood be the force about which Jerry had spoken responsible for turning the horde back on its heels and straight at them in the first place.

All of this raced through Neil's thoughts as he watched Della rise up from her roost like an agitated bear. Neil didn't realize the ghouls were as close as they were. She was upon them with such fierce suddenness she set all three of the creatures off balance. She wielded her bat with the deft skill of a ninja but the brute power of a Viking.

She struck the first one's rotting skull so hard, she very nearly severed it from its similarly decaying body. The impact created a hollow, wet thump of a sound, followed by the beast crumpling lifelessly to the ground. She squared off with the other two still coming at her. One must have noticed the children and recognized them as easier prey because it bypassed Della and started toward them instead.

From Della emerged a scream that would have rattled both heaven and hell. The fearsome spawn of primal rage and maternal instincts, it was a ferocious growl with all the subtlety of an atomic shockwave. Like a linebacker, Della stormed right over the beast in front of her and, in the same motion, swung the bat in a high, air-cutting arc. The bat struck its target with a bone-crunching thwack between its shoulder blades.

The zombie collapsed onto its belly and tried to get back to its feet, but to no avail. Della had crushed its spinal column and broken its back. She took one step and finished it off as it tried to claw its way closer to the children.

The third ghoul was just getting to its feet from Della's rush. She wasn't apparently in the mood to give it a moment's reprieve. This time, she swung the bat in a low, wide sweep, hitting it squarely in the legs. The blow broke at least one of its legs and sent it too sprawling to the ground.

Neil looked at Jerry and then back at Della as she stood amidst the carnage. Jerry said flatly, "Well, I guess we'll just have to see how this turns out."

Neil cracked a humorless smile and agreed with a nod. And as Neil had suspected, Della's assault did draw the attention of the undead octet on the highway. Luckily, there were just the eight and no more of the larger group in sight. Neil stood, ready to wade into battle with his bat, but stopped when he heard the gunshots.

It was DB and Alec. They were shooting wildly at the advancing zombies, both wasting ammunition and creating exactly the kind of ruckus Neil wanted to avoid. Realizing it was too late to avert disaster, Neil nodded to Jerry who fired off three successive shots, bringing down three different targets.

By then, the fiends were less than twenty feet away, so Neil leveled his shotgun against his shoulder and let loose a deafening blast which brought down another. DB had also claimed one, leaving just three more still coming at them.

The hideous wretches started to gain speed the closer they drew to their prey. They were a trio of nightmares. All three would have to gain weight to be considered wraiths, but that was not the worst of their appearance. Their flesh was ripe with open, festering sores and pulled tightly across the protruding bones of their hands and arms and was starting to pull back away from their eye sockets and mouths revealing brittle, weather-beaten bone. Their heads sagged and bobbed with all the muscle control of newborns, but the hunger animating their expressions belied any suggestion of innocence.

Emma and Maggie were no longer content to watch. The two of them, closest to their assailants, leaned against the slate slabs and fired their own firearms. Meghan was using a smaller caliber shotgun, while Emma was sporting a pair of semi-automatic pistols. They created a field of leaden punishment that spread out before them. Neil too fired his weapon, as did Alec. It was a triangulation of fiery death into which the three monsters charged and never emerged. Their shattered bodies rested in horrible twisted heaps beneath the still settling smoke.

Neil, with a look over his shoulder, confirmed that Della was still okay and then did the same with everyone else. His breathing was coming fast and shallow, trying to keep pace with his rapid heartbeat. There was something more though. He felt satisfaction and a little bit of lingering adrenaline that bordered on blood lust.

Looking out over the bodies scattered across the road, Neil wondered if he was feeling the same emotions as guerrilla warriors after a successful ambush. Could they, he and the other survivors, exist in this manner? And for how long? There were guerrilla movements all over the world that had faced overwhelming government forces and materiel for years and had somehow successfully emerged time and time again victorious. Could his group be as lucky?

There was very little time for consideration at the moment. They needed to get themselves going before the horde turned about and started heading back toward them. The tarps were folded into tight but still wet rolls and lashed to backpacks. That was all the packing needed before they were back on the path heading south.

20

The junction for the Portage Highway was a short way south on the railroad tracks. Typically a bustling crossroads of vehicles coming and going from the scenic Portage Glacier Park and the city of Whittier, today it looked like the busiest intersection on Venus.

Actually, defining Whittier as a city was only possible in the village and small town dominated nature of Alaska. Whittier sat in a sheltered bay and became a stopover for large and small water craft in days gone by. The community that grew up around the anchorage was a hodgepodge of small and large commercial ventures ranging in interests from simple tourist trade, to fishing guides and processors, to government services. The largest structure in the community was the monstrous and largely vacant Buckner Building which was a relic from, first, World War II and then the Cold War. There were a few houses, hotels, and even some multiplex apartment buildings. To refer to Whittier as a city would have been insulting to the smallest of traditional cities in most other places in the world, especially given the fact that the arrival of a single cruise ship to the port was enough to have a significant growth impact on the city's population for the day.

Despite all of this, Whittier had one remarkable feature that set it apart from all of the communities on the road system in Alaska: it had a single land route entrance that could be closed off by a gate which resembled the impregnable gates of medieval castles. To get to Whittier, a passage had been cut through a mountain which was part of a range walling off Whittier from all other approaches. The passage had been created intentionally narrow and limited with the intention that the gate would be opened and closed to help control the flow of traffic, both vehicular and rail, in either direction. No moat had ever as effectively guarded its palace walls as did Mother Nature's contributions on the Kenai Peninsula.

Whittier, if the gate had been closed in time, could be safe and free of the infection that had wreaked so much havoc on the rest of the state. Whittier could be a safe haven, if...

It was that hope which propelled Neil on his way that morning. They were so close. It was only a few short miles up the road. His enthusiasm was, however, tempered by their recent experiences. They had been running from safe haven to safe haven since that first morning so many weeks ago, and every refuge they found was short-lived. They had been temporary due to glaring flaws. Whittier might be something different. There were a lot of ifs and maybes standing between them and this next possibility.

Scanning the highway, Neil saw, scattered both on and off the road, a few abandoned vehicles; cars, vans, and trucks left by their owners when it seemed like there was no other option. Many of the bones of those owners were left to rot not far from their abandoned automobiles, the zekes close on their heels having overcome them. There were also the rotting, stiff carcasses of ravens who had picked the contaminated flesh from the bodies only to succumb to the same fate.

Dark and damp, the slick pavement of the highway stretched itself defiantly into the scant tones and grim moods of the late autumnal weather. If Neil didn't know better, he would have guessed that they were at the crossroads of Hell and Purgatory. The trees themselves, leafless and seemingly lifeless, appeared to claw at the sky, angry for having ever sprung from the sorry earth.

To make matters worse, the weather had soured. The misting rain was becoming more aggressive, manifesting itself in heavy, colder droplets threatening to freeze upon impact. Coats, gloves, pants, and boots were all starting to soak through. Their discomfort increased with each passing, miserable moment. With chattering teeth and shivering lips, they made their way across the road to the Visitor Center to take a short rest. The building and its contents had been gutted, but its walls were still standing and the roof provided some respite from the rain.

Thankfully, there were no surprises waiting for them in or around the building, so they got inside without incident. From the floor, Jerry gathered discarded brochures of activities that visitors to the state could enjoy ranging all up and down the Kenai Peninsula. Thinking the paper might make good kindling for a much needed fire, he began to twist some into tight rolls. Neil and DB, meanwhile, looked for ways to hang their blue tarpaulins in the gaping windows, trying anything to limit the cold's entrance into the building.

Della and Meghan helped the four children out of their wet clothes, again trying to mitigate the effects of the cold on their little bodies. The two women wrung gloves and pants of as much water as possible while the children scrambled to put on drier clothes from their backpacks. Most of the adults did not have the luxury of putting on dry clothes and were forced to suffer into the chilling grips of the onset of hypothermia.

They worked quietly, trying to keep their presence a secret to all but themselves. Dealing with the cold alone was bad enough. To have to do so while fighting off the walking dead would have been a grim prospect at best.

The undead had been thankfully absent since the skirmish earlier in the day. The shooting from the battle would likely draw the horde back toward them, so the break in the storm was very welcome.

For Emma, the respite allowed her to retreat into the stormy domain of her thoughts. She was so desperately confused. Like a fresh scab eager to be picked, the pain of having lost Dr. Caldwell was ever present, surging on occasion and feeling like a punch to the stomach. Her loss and its accompanying agony manifested itself completely differently during the melee however.

Her typical anxiety was replaced with fiery rage, an anger so absolute and so raw she was barely able to contain it. She channeled her fury into the pistols in her hands and allowed them to speak for her. The sleek handguns' voices were sharp and direct, slicing through reanimated tissue as easily as the air. She lacked composure and control, pulling the triggers wildly. It was through sheer volume alone that she managed to hit anything, but hit the targets she did. She gritted her teeth with each shot but reveled in each wounding. Her bullets punched holes and shattered bone. Through her clenched jaw, a smile full of venom and bleak satisfaction slithered to her lips and spread itself across her face.

She pulled the triggers until there were no more bullets left to fire. Her hands were pulsating with echoes of the shooting reverberating in her palms. In her chest, her heart tried desperately to keep pace with the throb in her hands. Emma would swear that there were rodents whose hearts didn't beat as fast as hers was.

Since then, her heart may have slowed a little, but her hands still harbored hints of the violent kick of her pistols and the smile hadn't retreated one step. It wasn't a smile that held any warmth or joy. It was the smile of the jack-o-lantern. It was the smile of the madman. It was fiddling Nero's smile as he watched Rome burn. If the others had stopped and paid attention, her smile would have left them unsettled and worried.

Standing there in the back doorway of the small building, Emma watched the others working so hard to scrape together an existence that, at present, barely seemed worth it. Even with the tarps hanging in the windows, dry clothes on their backs and a small, smoky fire burning in the trash can, they were still all going to be cold. The other thing that occurred to her that no one was talking about was that they were out of food. To her knowledge, they had finished whatever scraps each of them had been able to hide and hold. That last reserve ration was now gone, so the growling protests from their stomachs would simply continue.

She pivoted from one foot to the other and was starting out the door when Neil asked her from over his shoulder, "You goin' somewhere?"

She wasn't sure and her hesitation betrayed this fact to both Neil and herself. She shook her head and said with that same twisted smile splayed about her face, "Just gonna go look around is all. Maybe find some wood to burn or..."

"I don't think you should be goin' off anywhere by yourself."

"Don't worry. I've got plenty of company," and she patted the two pistols on her hips. She didn't wait for him to formulate a reply, which likely would have been an objection. She bounced down the narrow wooden stairs and walked out on the dark cinder back parking lot. There was a big, heavily used Dodge truck parked across a few of the very limited parking spots.

Emma thought to herself as she considered the parking job, *asshole*. Crossing the lot to the truck, she was careful to look both ways. She didn't want to be surprised. The truck's doors were all shut, but she could see through the windows that there was no one inside. She walked over and pulled the truck handle. Locked. Her first thought was to just move on to some other distraction, but all at once she spun about and made one of her pistols into a hammer, shattering the window with a loud, cascading pop. Standing on her tiptoes, she reached into the cab and unlocked the door.

In another time and as a self that she had come close to completely forgetting, she would have been horrified by the dismaying tableau across the seat. The decaying remains of a man and a small child, a father and son perhaps, were lying next to one another across the long bench seat. Both bore head wounds, likely inflicted by the large silver revolver on the seat next to the man. Emma paused for a moment and decided on a course of action.

She went around to the opposite, now unlocked, door and opened it. She then simply pushed the man's body out until it fell out the other side. The carcass didn't have much weight, as most of his body mass had long since shriveled and withered. Just as the body started to slide out, she spied in his front pocket a nearly full pack of cigarettes. Her eyes widened and she got hold of the package as the body slid to the ground.

She was exhaling her first long drag when Neil appeared in the doorway of the Visitor Center. At first she felt anxiety akin to being caught smoking in the bathroom in high school. When the nicotine rush hit her senses however, she would have been able to ignore the Pope and possibly even her mother. She quit smoking years ago. It was a pain in her ass, but she'd done it. She was never a serious smoker anyway. She mostly smoked when she went out with her friends, so it could have been much worse. There was no denying the appeal of that first drag though. It was like a welcome visit from a long absent friend. It was damned near euphoric.

As he walked his way across the lot, Neil joked, "You know, those things will kill you."

"According to my mother, they're also very unladylike. It's why I never found a husband." Then she added, "Look what else I found." She then held up the heavy, polished, silver pistol she took from the truck.

"Nice find. Any shells?"

She opened the pistol's revolving chamber. "Four in here and I bet...." She leaned over and opened the glove compartment but didn't find anything. She considered her options for a moment and then looked in the rear seat, seeing a light jacket. She hoisted it, noticing the large front pockets sagged with weight. Triumphantly, she pulled from one of the pockets two boxes of shells. The other pocket held another pack of cigarettes and a bunch of keys on an assortment of key rings.

She leaned forward again clutching the handful of keys. There was one set of keys sporting a Dodge key fob remote opener. She pressed one of the buttons on the fob and the doors confirmed they were unlocked. She met Neil's curious eyes with her own. Her hands were almost shaking as she slowly inserted the key into the ignition. She held her breath when she turned the key and, to her own amazement, the truck's engine started. It had approximately a half a tank of gasoline and a bunch of room for all of them. Of course, some of their group would have to ride in the back, but it was a far cry better than walking. They could cover themselves with a tarp to stay as warm and as dry as possible.

Meghan was the next to appear in the open door. Her eyes were as wide as saucers. Neil yelled to her, "Tell everyone to get out here. We're putting some distance between us and them. When they come back this way, we'll be someplace else."

She enthusiastically nodded. "On it."

Neil looked back at Emma and smiled. He said, "You may have just saved all our lives."

She smiled back at him, but this smile was genuine and warm. She said coyly, "All in a day's work."

21

Merely sitting in the warm air of the heated truck cab was almost enough for Neil. The goose bumps on his skin felt as if they were enjoying the peak moments of a dance competition. Every hair on his body was standing on end in pleasure. He couldn't help the shiver from crawling down his spine. He breathed deeply into his lungs the deliciously warm air and that was when the smile appeared. He couldn't contain it. And the smile produced a little chuckle that grew into a full laugh.

The really wonderful thing about an infectious, spontaneous laugh is its ability to sweep through a crowd and lift the collective mood of the group. Neil's laugh, full and unexpected, lured smiles from all of his compatriots and laughs from a few.

In the open bed of the truck, they fashioned a bit of a canopy using a blue tarp. With the aid of zip ties and bungee cords, the tarp was anchored against the cab of the truck. The back window was open, allowing some of the heat to migrate into the makeshift camper mockup. It wasn't as comfortable as inside the car, but it definitely was a better option than walking in the cold and the rain.

Neil lowered his hands to the steering wheel and felt the vibrating pulse of the large truck. To Neil, it felt as alive and as hopeful as anything that he had encountered in quite some time. That was what he was thinking when Meghan, sitting next to him, put her hand on his leg and squeezed very gently. He could see a message in her eyes and rightly surmised its meaning.

Meghan was ready to be on the move again. She didn't like staying in one place for too long, but it wasn't some primal nomadic nature bubbling to the surface. For her, it was simple practicality. Every time their group had gotten comfortable somewhere and had started to settle in, *they* had found them. It had been slightly more than an hour since their arrival at the visitor center, but she was already sensing that they were there on borrowed time. They needed to get moving again.

Emma, sitting on the far side of Meghan and nearest the passenger side door, was exactly the opposite. She was calm but vigilant. She watched her side of the truck, her eyes scanning the entire area, careful to look at everything without getting distracted by any one stimulus. She didn't want to get caught missing the forest by staring at the trees, to reverse a familiar adage. It wasn't that she was immune to the fear; she just found it to be adding fuel to a different kind of fire. If she hadn't crossed the precarious rope bridge into the state of not caring, well then, she was at least staring at the precipice the bridge spanned.

Emma was aware of a change in her disposition. She was most curious in considering whether this was a permanent or temporary change and if she might slip further into this existential funk. The shift in her mood, despite its suddenness, did not worry her at all. In fact, she welcomed the change. She felt less like a victim. An impartial observer might also suggest that she felt less compassion for those around her as well, but this fact was merely background for her. Her sense of liberation simply felt, well, liberating. She felt like a completely new person. And why not? There was nothing of the world left in which she had become so comfortable and complacent. Never in her life had she even contemplated the rigors under which she now lived every day.

Behind them, on the narrow bench seat in the rear of the cab, sat Jules and Danny and next to them, as silent as always, sat Paul and Nikki, the other two children. While Paul and Nikki were not mute, it was quite clear that they restricted their words to quiet exchanges with Della and, on rare occasion, with DB. They had the thousand yard stare of shell-shocked combat veterans most of the time. Their little brains had blown several neural fuses which had yet to be repaired. Luckily, they didn't seem to eat much more than they said and they seemed to be willing to walk themselves wherever they needed to go.

Everyone else was in the bed of the truck under the tarp trying to stay warm. It wasn't a perfect setup but it was passable. Della and DB were sitting on one side and Claire and Jerry sat on the other. They sat atop camping pads and sleeping bags to make the Rhino lined truck bed a little more comfortable. And in the middle of them were huddled Alec and Duke, holding tight to one another to minimize their sliding back and forth. Duke was the picture of calm, trying to continue his afternoon nap despite all the activity and movement. Between his outstretched front paws was a thick stick DB had given to him as a distraction for later.

While adjusting the rearview mirror, Neil caught a glimpse of Jules entertaining the two younger children. She was showing off a string trick Jerry had shown her. Her movements were meticulous and slow, while she remembered each step in the right order. Concentrating intently, she worked her teeth with her tongue like it was a polishing cloth on a fine gem. In an instant, Neil's breath caught behind the emotional knot building in his chest.

How could there be even a lingering remnant, a fading memory of innocence left in any of them? And yet, there was Jules in a seemingly suspended state just being a kid.

Neil put the truck into gear and as it began to roll forward, he said to Meghan, "I think we're gonna be okay. I know it sounds awfully optimistic...especially for me. But I think we may be getting this thing behind us."

Meghan kissed him lightly on his unshaven cheek. "Let's just get outta here and start with that."

"I'm already on it."

22

The Portage Glacier Highway was a lazy, loopy road that, on a map, looked like someone had just discarded a length of string that happened to connect one terminus with the other. Seeing that both ends of the string were connected, the state of the central coil of the winding snake of a road didn't seem to matter.

If asked, most Alaskans would admit that they eagerly anticipate the first snowfall of the season during the waning days and long nights of autumn. It really has little to do with recreational activities such as skiing, snowboarding, or enjoying the horsepower-fueled excitement of riding a snow machine. In fact, the coming of snow means something very different for most Alaskan residents.

Autumn in Alaska was more than shorter nights and cooler temperatures. Fall also was that period of time in which the land itself began to come to terms with the fact that the impending winter season was upon it. Animals ate heartily from the sparse, extant vegetation, preparing themselves in their different ways for the upcoming hunger days of the cold. Plants, and even the ground itself, seemed to retreat from the press of decay of the fall. Soil hardened with the cold, restraining water from roots, which in turn starved leaves and blooms. Trees and other flora wilted then sagged, and finally appeared to die, their leaves drying into twisted husks and falling to the ground. Water, left to fester in small pools on the surface, collected the detritus of the season into sucking, stinking puddles that provided neither sustenance nor comfort to anything. *Fall* was definitely the best way to describe the mood of the season.

With the coming of snow, however, the desolation of the season was buried beneath a clean carpet of white, as if the slate had been wiped clean leaving behind a pure white canvas on which nature was able to create a new reality. The white of snow also chased away the brooding darkness, even at night, as the tiny crystallized water droplets captured and reflected the remotest hints of light during all times of the day.

Looking to either side of the road and seeing the wetlands in full retreat, desperately awaiting the deliverance promised by snow, Neil felt a similar longing for winter's offering. To Neil, it was hard to imagine this place as anything other than a desolate, lifeless morass. More than landscape, it looked like the barren remains of a large animal left to rot, the bare trees and clinging brown moss appearing to be bones and withering sinew. It looked and smelled like death all around them. The absence of any wildlife for as far as the eye could see only helped to reinforce the foreboding. No amount of imagining on Neil's part could ever encourage him to see this as a thriving ecosystem. He felt like looking over his shoulder to make certain they hadn't passed a sign with Dante's ominous warning to all visitors of his inferno. Should they abandon all hope? Had they crossed the River Styx into the Underworld?

He couldn't allow himself to become overly distracted with his mood or his grim observations. They were starting to pass more abandoned vehicles, some on the shoulders of the road and others simply stopped in the middle of the lane. So far, they hadn't seen any more of the undead. For that, Neil was thankful but was also painfully aware that there was little to no possibility of sustaining that fact.

They were driving intentionally slowly, giving as much of a berth as possible to the abandoned cars and trucks stalled here and there. It felt as if they were moving along a maze path toward some golden bull that awaited them at the end. Their truck's engine purred, sending a gentle, tickling vibration through all of their bodies. The buzz raised their collective awareness and anxiety. None of them had been in a serviceable vehicle in some time.

When they did finally see the undead, it was a single, lanky-armed and confused former middle-aged man. He was wearing battered and torn Dockers and a once bright red golf shirt. His hair was silver gray but matted and greasy, looking like dirty mop strands hanging in his face. The exposed skin of his arms, neck, and face had the pallor and texture of modeling clay spread too thin over a plaster bust. His cheekbones were impossibly pronounced and his cheeks overly shallow. Above and through it all, his dark eyes burned with rage and hunger.

He was already aroused with the sound of the approaching vehicle. His body was becoming agitated, quivering with spasms and violent tics. When his cesspool eyes caught sight of the large silver truck, however, he twisted his lips into a brown, toothy snarl. With gray, sore-pocked arms raised, he began to stumble and stagger toward them.

Meghan's breath caught in her throat at first sight of the creature. "I guess I'll never get used to seeing..." she trailed off.

Jules asked, still doing stars, cups and saucers, and cat's cradles with her string, "Seeing what?"

Meghan looked up at the truck ceiling and said, "Nothin' sweetie."

"It's another one of those bad people isn't it?"

At first, Meghan wasn't quite sure what to say. She didn't know if she should try and protect her by hiding the truth. That seemed like the sensible thing to do. It's probably what her mother and father would have done for her. And in that instant of considering her parents, her breath once again caught in her throat. She tried to answer...anything, but she couldn't force any sound from within. She merely nodded a quiet, teary affirmative. "You kids keep your heads down."

Neil didn't hesitate. The engine's purr became an aggressive growl as he pushed the accelerator and steered the truck right into the zombie's path. The collision sent the rotting creature hurtling through the air and into the unforgiving side of an RV. The impact against the larger vehicle was loud and wet, the back side of his head erupting like an overripe melon. The lifeless corpse slid down slowly, leaving a streak of necrotic brownish fluid in its wake. They were all thankful for the muting effect the truck's engine noise produced.

The threat neutralized, Neil slowed the vehicle again and continued them on their way. The traffic jam was rapidly becoming more and more dense, restricting Neil's ability to thread the truck through the collapsing needle's eye. It was nearly impossible to allow for any safe room between their vehicle and others. On more than one occasion, Neil was forced to use his truck's bumper to nudge another vehicle over a bit to create enough room to pass. The sides of their truck, once pristine and polished, were soon dinged, dented, and scraped.

Jerry, Claire, DB, and Della were all up on their knees with axes, camping spades, and baseball bats in their hands as a precaution. The increasing number of motor homes, campers, tour buses, and other taller vehicles heightened the tension for all of them as their space became tighter and tighter. They looked like castle guards watching over the battlements for any evidence of their threatening foe.

It didn't take long. Around the front of a Gray Lines tour bus, they happened upon a group of four of the ghouls loitering around a couple piles of clothes that appeared to be stuck in clumps to the pavement, likely the sticky remains of the devoured former occupants.

Neil said loud enough to be heard through the rear window, "No guns. We don't want to—"

Jerry shouted back, "Way ahead of you, boss! Just keep moving. We'll get whatever you don't."

Neil actually felt a smile try to find its way on to his face. They charged headlong into the crowd, a mighty war elephant plowing into the fray of battle. Neil ran over two of the beasts, their bodies crunching and breaking beneath the weight of their war steed.

The other two zombies, who both appeared to have once been adolescent girls, moved onto Jerry and Claire's side. Jerry's bat came down with a metallic thwack twice into the first monster's head, the brittle skull imploding into the soft, gray ooze inside. With a gurgle and a grunt, the thing fell to the ground, tripping the other zombie as a result.

Unfortunately, more than just the walking shadow was caught off guard and tipped off balance. Claire was in mid-swing with the camping spade when her target suddenly disappeared from in front of her. Her swing carried through much further and harder than she was anticipating, sending her head over heels over the gunwale of the truck bed. She threw a surprisingly effective body block into the now recovering zombie, knocking it backward again, then spun away and came to rest a few feet from the off-balance undead creature. She was on her back and looking up at what should have been the roiling bruise of a sky. Instead, all she saw were stars and patterns of light exploding in her dazed vision. She reached blindly but couldn't lay her hands on her shovel some yards away. She was helpless and had the wind not been cleanly knocked from her lungs as a result of her fall she would have screamed such to all within in earshot.

Temporarily blind, breathless, and helpless, Claire likely made an appealing target. She tried to roll onto her side so she could get to her feet, but the pain in her shoulder and back was too much for her. She was terrified to feel her foot being tugged violently and instinctively kicked blindly but was unable to discourage her attacker.

Jerry and Alec, meanwhile, rolled themselves out of the back of the truck and were sprinting the several yards separating them from the fallen woman. Jerry threw his bat, hitting Claire's assailant squarely between the shoulder blades. It stalled the attack only briefly as the thing considered the threat and the interruption, but that was the only window that Jerry and, more to the point, Alec needed. The teenager, who likely wasn't any older than what the abomination had been before turning, carried only his rifle. He knew better than to shoot for fear of drawing more of the things to them, instead he changed his grip so that he was holding the rifle's barrel. His swing cut from east to west, slamming the monster in its side. It didn't dispatch it, but it did send the demonic wraith sprawling away from the still stricken Claire.

Jerry grabbed Claire's shovel and buried the stubby blade into the scabby creature's cranium. All at once, everything seemed to stop. Jerry stood with his hands holding the shovel, which was holding the zombie in apparent suspended animation. It was quiet and still, but was still standing as if waiting. Jerry let go the handle and both the tool and the zombie fell away.

There was no time to wait. Jerry ran to Claire and Alec retrieved the shovel which stood upright like some sick version of the sword in the stone. Alec was forced to use his booted foot to pry the shovel blade from the tight fissure, resulting in a wet pop. He also found Jerry's bat.

Claire was hurt, that much was certain. Jerry knew that moving someone after such an injury was unwise, but he also knew that those four wouldn't be the last walking dead they would encounter and so getting back in the truck was of tantamount importance.

Jerry kissed Claire's cheek. "Can you hear me honey?" he said calmly.

She nodded slowly.

"Can you speak?"

She clenched her jaw and answered through the pain, "Yeah, but if I don't have to, well then..."

"We need to move you. Can you tell me what's hurt? What did you hit?"

"At least my shoulder and my back. Landed pretty hard."

"Okay, then. Alec and I are going to help you up to your feet, okay?"

Rather than using her voice, which sent pain arcing through her body like an electric current, Claire smiled and blinked her eyes, which were just starting to come into focus. With Jerry on one side and Alec on the other, they helped Claire to her feet and back in the truck.

Claire's right arm hung uselessly at her side. The road rash on her shoulder throbbed and oozed, the gravel of the road and fabric of her ruined jacket mixing with her sticky blood and violated flesh. It felt as if her entire arm was on fire. Jerry was unable to detect any of the telltale signs of a fracture, but he handled her injured limb as delicately as possible.

The truck was back under way as Jerry got her into a reasonably comfortable position atop a soft pile of sleeping bags and backpacks. He leaned down and whispered to her again, "No more heroics from you. Okay? I don't think I could handle any more scares like that."

She smiled and answered coyly despite her pain, "You ain't gettin' no arguments from me. I'll just stay home and make sure there's dinner waiting for you when you get off from work, dear."

Smiling back at her but also with a few worried tears misting on the surface of his eyes, Jerry said, "I think I could get used to that."

"Oh yeah? You may change your mind after you eat my cookin'."

The kiss that followed was filled with warm emotion and relief but the tears, both his and hers, shining on her cheeks belied the fearful undercurrent of everyone's mood. Despite the fear, or maybe because of it, Jerry was suddenly more convinced than ever that he was in love with this beautiful, sassy coed.

He delicately wiped away the mixed pools of tears from her face. "You just rest here for a bit. I'll keep an eye on things while you get some rest." He kissed her again and then pulled himself away from her.

23

Neil was right to get them moving again. Their fracas had drawn the attention of several more of the walking nightmares who were stumbling down the road toward them. Like ghouls from crypts, they crawled and slithered from doors left ajar on vehicles. They also clambered up the shoulders of the road, having finally had some outside force recall them from a long ago feeding frenzy in the woods. Most, however, were simply standing, waiting, hungering in the middle of the road. Like the tickling sensations of a struggling moth to the spider in her web, the sounds of the tussle drew the attention of every zombie in the area. So far, they were out of sight, but when Jules complained to Neil that she could hear "that sound" again, Neil knew to be watching for them.

She hadn't complained in quite some time which concerned Neil. It could mean that there was a larger group waiting for them further up the road. He had no idea the reality was that the group wasn't waiting for them at all. They were converging on the unsuspecting survivors. Dozens of the scabrous, stinking wretches were closing in on them with every passing second.

"Oh shit!" Neil saw them walking stiltedly toward the group, seemingly ready and willing to eat the truck along with all of its passengers.

Emma, speaking for the first time since they had started driving, said, "Speed up." She was calm, almost serene as she checked the load on her pistols. She caught Neil's reproachful look. "Don't worry. They're only as last resorts," and she showed him the blue aluminum baseball bat stuffed into some loops on the backpack at her feet.

He tried to smile through his clenched teeth, but instead turned back to the looming targets in front of him. Using the Dodge Ram hood ornament as a targeting sight, he lined up the truck so that he would be able to plow into most of them and still stay on the road. He counted at least ten of them and if he was able to work it his way, he would be able to get most if not all of them as new grill decorations. They were packed so conveniently tight that they were presenting him with a single target.

Revving the engine and driving hard at them, he plowed into the crowd with a teeth-chattering series of grisly thuds. Scarred faces, twisted in the fury of an endless violent death, appeared and disappeared in the truck's windshield as it barreled into them. When the truck finally spun to a stop, there wasn't a single one of the creatures still posing any threats. A couple were attempting to claw themselves along the pavement, dragging behind their shattered bodies. Worse still, from beneath the gory mess smeared over the bottom third of the truck, they could also hear above the engine's settling voice some labored groans and scratching.

Jerry looked at everyone in the truck bed with the question in his eyes that everyone else had in their minds. He cautiously leaned over the side, moving with all the care of a boater peering into the depths of shark infested waters. There was a leg, well, the rotting, shattered partial remains of a leg, jutting out from the tire well. He said to no one in particular, "I think we may have a stowaway under the truck."

Neil joked over his shoulder, "I thought for sure you were gonna say, *You're gonna need a bigger boat.* Can you get it out?"

Jerry didn't answer immediately, so Neil took the hint and instead said, "Well, so far it isn't keeping the truck off the road, so we'll just deal with it later. Keep an eye out for it though. I don't want it to crawl out and surprise us."

His voice showing the first signs of excitement, DB observed, "Speakin' of surprises...," and he pointed behind them at another oncoming and slightly larger crowd of undead. It was an eclectic group of former tourists, commuters, and all varieties of uniformed service workers.

Something dawned on Emma as she watched the lumbering pack of rotten hunters. Their skin had become very homogenized, with no clear distinctions remaining between bodies of different ethnic origins. All of the walking corpses had begun their nightmare maintaining the pigment signatures of their ethnicity; albeit with a nagging suggestion of death's olive green creeping along as a slowly encroaching partner. That had changed. All of the beings on the road were simply gray of skin with only the slightest variation separating one from another. Truth be told, other than their clothes, the only thing that stood out to Emma as a way to differentiate one ghoul from the other was the pattern of darkened and still festering scar patches on their faces and visible fatal wounds on their necks, limbs, or torsos.

There was a pause, both in and out of the truck, as they all thought about what this meant and what options they had. They could run again. The new approaching mob was behind them and not lying between the survivors and their ultimate destination. Flight was likely the most prudent decision, but that was not what struck Neil as the right one. He was sick of running.

Neil took a deep breath, held it, and then pulled the truck around forcefully, spinning the tires into a belching, smoking cloud. They hurtled forward like a cruise missile, a wake of white smoke and greasy, spattering mortal remains trailing behind them. It felt to all of them as if they were riding a charging, snorting bull as it plunged into the ring.

With a stretch of open pavement beyond the crowd, Neil didn't feel the need to restrain the truck and instead punched through the group at full speed. An arm, severed from its owner, corkscrewed out of the crowd, striking the window forcefully enough to crack the glass and then coming to rest in the gap between the windshield and the hood.

Those in the bed of the truck were fully engaged in battle themselves. Jerry and DB, steadied by Alec and Della respectively, swung their weapons wildly, striking anything and everything in their paths. Like two chariot riders in a Bronze Age battle, they wielded their tools of war trying to expand the carnage.

Once through, Neil swung the truck around. There was a sizeable gap separating the truck from the reeling mob. The destruction reaped upon them seemed to only excite the few still standing. Neil fingered the wiper control, immediately regretting not triggering the washer fluid first. The grisly mist covering the windshield streaked in heavy, brownish bands, all but obstructing their view. It took three quick applications of washer fluid to clear the glass enough to be able to see through it. In that time, the zombies had already started to close the distance to the truck.

Emma said flatly but nodding her head. "Hit 'em again. This seems to be working."

Neil didn't need any other suggestions or urging. He pressed the accelerator to the floor and roared ahead again.

Meghan, sitting next to Neil, had reached her limit. She lowered her face into her hands and held her breath deep in her chest. Like the soothing voice from a dream, Jules spoke, full of calm and innocent reassurance. She said specifically to Meghan but all of them hearing and absorbing her words, "It'll be okay. We can get through this. We always do. Don't worry so much. It'll be over before you know it." All the while, she never looked up from the knotted string stretched between her hands in what was becoming a Jacob's Ladder.

The serene and absurdly simple nature of her words and her message brought tears to Meghan's eyes and stole away Emma's breath. Jules knew that the situation was precarious, but such circumstances were becoming commonplace. Of course she was worried, and more than a little scared, but she believed Neil was very capable of finding the reputed light at the end of the tunnel regardless of said tunnel's length. For her lone comfort, she leaned against Danny, who was wrapping himself tighter and tighter in his seatbelt.

For his part, Danny was more than a little bit concerned about his well-being, but he wouldn't be able to deny a rising sense of excitement either. His rifle was at his feet. Though it was unloaded, the dark object on the floor of the truck emanated the power of an enchanted talisman; and it was his!

Most recently, Danny had been given something else which had elevated his mood. Shortly after their impromptu ambush on the highway, Neil found his way to be walking next to Danny. Neil smiled at him and told him that he was proud of how brave and sensible Danny had been. He didn't use typical grownup talk in doing it. Neil used words that Danny and his friends would use. Neil could not possibly have known what his saying it or the manner in which he said it could have meant to Danny, but the boy was star struck. Neil had become a hero...no, he was more like an idol for Danny, so the praise was all the more welcome. After saying his piece, Neil took a small pistol from his pocket and gave it to him. Danny could not believe it. Now he had a pistol and a rifle. Neil explained that both weapons were of the same caliber, so it was easy to keep just one type of ammunition to keep both active. Neil told him that he felt like Danny had shown enough responsibility with his rifle and their need was such that Danny having the pistol and keeping an eye on the other kids made sense. Neil was entrusting Danny with being a last line of defense between those monsters and the kids. Neil knew that he could count on Danny to not treat the pistol as a toy because it wasn't. Danny was instructed to keep the pistol in his zippered pocket. He was to always keep it unloaded to avoid any accidents. The boy readily consented to every condition, the glow of having a pistol making it all sound like music in his ears.

Now that pistol was pulsating on his hip as if it had a heart of its own. Danny patted it confidently and pulled again on his seatbelt as they lurched forward harder just before the collision.

On the final pass, the truck's wheels lost their grip amidst the gore on the road. Neil tried to correct left but the truck instead spun right. Meghan and Emma were pressed against Neil as he fought with the steering wheel for control. It was a losing battle. In the front windshield passed a panorama of the bordering wetlands followed by a blur of stalled vehicles on the road followed by a different panorama of the opposite side of the bordering wetlands followed by a blur of empty road and back again to the bordering wetlands. They had spun a full circle and were now idling.

Neil's heart was galloping at full bore, trying its best to leap from his chest. His hands were doing their utmost to twist the steering wheel into something resembling a Twizzler. And yet, he was the only one inside the truck who wasn't screaming.

He immediately looked around to get his bearings. They were at a ninety degree angle to the road and the few remaining zombies who were closing with the truck fast. He grabbed his baseball bat from next to him and said to Meghan, "Hop on over here and get this truck turned around."

"Where the hell are you goin'?"

Neil unlatched his seatbelt and slid out the open door. He kissed her lips quickly and then shut the door. Jerry and DB climbed down from the back and Emma joined them from her side. There were only five of the zombies still in front of them, but they were an intimidating sight...much more so than from inside the truck.

None of it seemed to faze Neil at the moment. He waded into the roadway with ill intent on his mind. He fought with reckless abandon. He had already beaten to motionless piles two of the monsters and was working on his third when the others finally caught up with him.

Jerry pummeled one who was dangerously close to grabbing Neil's back while DB and Emma dispatched the last. It was quick, violent, and breathless for all of them. A few of the ghouls unable to do more than use broken arms to pull broken bodies along the dark, slick road were still trying to come at them, but Emma and DB were making quick work of them.

That wasn't to be all though. From the tighter packed vehicles on the road in front of them, a familiar moan started to resonate toward them like a brewing storm. Neil knew what they needed to do but was hesitant to suggest it. He'd grown surprisingly comfortable with his sudden change in disposition but he couldn't be certain about everyone else. He was ready. He wanted to take the fight to them for a change but what would everyone else want to do.

"Up for kicking some more ass?"

Jerry answered, "I'm in. Let's move the truck up closer to us and clear a path as we go."

24

Meghan was to stay in the truck in the driver's seat and keep the vehicle ready to go. She was also to keep an eye on the kids along with Della, who had moved to the passenger seat. Claire was trying to stay warm and comfortable on her back while Alec and Duke were there to keep her company.

Neil, Emma, Jerry, and DB were all going to wade into the tangle of vehicles on a search and destroy mission. The mix of blunt and edged melee weapons helped their ragtag group resemble a peasant army of serf conscripts marching off to fight in their lord's war.

Immediately running into trouble, the four of them split into pairs and set about their grim task. Neil finished off the first of the monsters in his path, then he and Emma switched positions, with Jerry and DB doing the same on their side of the road.

As they disappeared from view, Meghan could feel her anxiety rise and her heart rate increase. She hated it when Neil was away from her. She'd had similar responses when her former fiancé would be gone overnight on business trips, his absence compromising both her security and peace of mind. Her feelings now, however, were understandably much stronger and distracting. For a short while in the past, she used prescription medication to control the panic attacks and keep them at bay. She wondered what her therapist would have recommended to her for controlling the anxiety brought on by the coming of the apocalypse. Had Pfizer or Eli Lily developed some magical little pill to help during these extreme circumstances? She was sure that if there was money to be made, then a pill would follow, regardless of the world's end.

It didn't take long for her angst to build into nervous fidgeting, which quickly led her to get out of the truck. When she opened the door, Della shot her a direful look. Her eyes, more yellow than white, flashed a warning.

Meghan couldn't ignore the signal. She said comfortingly, "It's okay. I just want to get a better look. Maybe we should be stayin' within sight, just in case."

"I think you should just keep an eye out for the others. It'll be okay."

Alec was hanging half in and half out the rear window. Claire was asleep and under a pile of blankets and sleeping bags keeping warm, so Alec decided to do the same for himself in the warm air of the truck cabin. His athletic frame nearly filled the entire back window as he crowded himself into the warmth. The simple creature comfort was so deliciously inviting it produced a smile that tickled his body from head to toe. His comfort brought satisfaction to everyone else already in the truck.

Between Alec's presence, Meghan's distraction and their limited view, no one in the truck was paying any attention to behind them. In that yawning blind spot, there could have been a convoy of relief trucks or a regiment of Marines. As it was, there was none of that approaching from behind. There was, however, a pair of staggering, stinking terrors drifting toward them with all the intent and focus of moths to a flame, moving slowly and silently.

Meghan opened the door and hopped out, peering in the direction of the others. Because she couldn't see well enough, she decided that she would move ahead a little more. She leaned back away from the path of the door and was surprised when something touched her extended arm. She was even more surprised, stunned speechless, when she turned and looked into the face of death.

She tried to find her voice but even her breath was failing her, and she could only utter a simple, "Huh?" As she was pulled backward by another set of hands from another of the fiends, she kicked forward and shut the door. In so doing, she both set a barrier between the undead and her friends in the truck and isolated herself from them in a single stroke.

Off balanced and strong-armed, she tumbled over and was tangled with both of her attackers in the process. The beasts weren't necessarily strong, but they were relentless. Meghan was awash in their mildewy, briny pungency. She pressed away the face that was lunging at her with chomping, brown-and-yellow-teethed jaws, kicking blindly toward the other clawing at her waist. She fought desperately, but she couldn't possibly forestall their attacks indefinitely.

She cried out desperately, "Heellllllllp!"

Realizing what was happening, Della was trying to come to Meghan's assistance. Her door was locked and she couldn't for the life of her figure out how to open the damned thing. She adjusted the mirror and lowered her window, but none of the buttons she pressed seemed to have the desired effect. She pawed at the lock itself with her thick fingers, but the knob was too narrow and embedded too deeply into the door. She could feel the growl beginning to grow deep down in her chest as the frustration and helplessness continued to build.

Alec too was unable to immediately come to Meghan's rescue. He was trying to extricate himself from his position, but he was not having much more luck than Della. He wiggled right and left, but he had so wedged himself in the narrow opening that he was finding it nearly impossible to pull himself free. His struggling and squirming was in fact cutting nasty gashes into his sides as he struggled.

Claire too tried to lift herself from her position. She was having the best luck but she was also the least likely to be able to deliver Meghan any help. Claire got herself onto her aching elbows and was finding it difficult to do anything more. She could almost see Meghan but she was unfortunately of no assistance beyond being a witness.

Meghan was completely on her own for the moment, which was her worst fear. She didn't like being alone under normal circumstances before the apocalypse. She typically craved company to feel secure. Since their world had so drastically changed, Meghan made it a point of never being far from others. She hated how exposed and afraid isolation made her feel.

And lying on the ground outside the truck, she couldn't have been more alone. She was fighting for her life with little hope of anyone arriving to deliver her from the tight spot in which she found herself. Swallowing her fear, she grasped onto the reality that if she had any hope of staying alive, it was up to her to fight. Unfortunately, fighting was something in which she had neither experience nor skill. She kicked with her feet and pushed with her hands and arms, but she did so without coordination and therefore without much effect. Sometimes her foot found its target and bought her a little room to maneuver and sometimes her foot and leg became more entangled with her attackers. Meghan finally got what appeared to be a break and pushed the snapping attacker closest to her face backward and away for a moment. With the weight across her temporarily lifted, she pulled herself on her backside out of the knot of legs and arms. Her breaths were coming so rapidly and so shallowly, she was flirting with hyperventilating, but she scooted herself regardless. In her blind haste, she neglected to see the bared teeth descending toward her exposed left hand and arm.

Della was frantically pulling on the door handle when she heard the scream. Like an icy dagger, Meghan's shriek stabbed each of them sitting in the truck. Della had heard that scream many times in the past and too many times much too recently for comfort. And now she was hearing it from that pretty red-headed girl who was so nice to them kids. She didn't deserve it any more than any of them folks back at the hotel. But that was just how it was these days.

As if Meghan's painful howls were the divining rod for the lock control, she looked over and hit the right button finally. She spilled out of the truck like a dark, threatening wave and diffused around the truck toward the fatally wounded girl.

Della grunted deeply as she went to work. She had a garden hatchet in her left hand and a tire iron in her right, both of which she used to great effect. In a handful of swings, she had dispatched Meghan's assailants, removing scalps and collapsing skulls.

With the two devils no longer moving and the immediate vicinity clear of any more of them, Della was finally free to pull the motionless bodies from the young woman. Once the gray-skinned husks were moved aside, Della could see the damage they had wrought on this once vibrant young woman.

Meghan's left wrist, mangled with freshly chewed gore, pumped out a steady pool of crimson, though the current was dissipating as her heart struggled to find enough blood to fill her veins. Her face, normally as white as talc, was fading to an opaque shade of gray blue, making her eyes shimmer all the more. They looked as if they were crackling with electric charge they were so blue. Her neck and shoulder had also been chewed, but the real damage was to her wrist.

Della realized there was nothing she could do for this girl except provide her with comfort and prepare her for the final journey. Della searched her memory and found an ancient culling song she'd heard her mother sing a lifetime ago whenever the woman set about butchering a chicken or some other barnyard animal. Hearing her mother's voice from the past, Della began to hum the resonating low tune. She stroked the young woman's red hair and held her right hand.

Meghan was confused by what had happened and what was happening. Much of the attack was a blur and most of her pain had been dulled by the surge of endorphins her adrenal gland had pumped into her blood. She could guess the reason for the sadness in Della's eyes, but she couldn't be sure whether it was for her or not. She was unable or perhaps unwilling to connect

SEAN SCHUBERT

all of this to herself. She just couldn't believe that she had been...bitten.

Was that what happened? Am I going to become one of those things?

She wasn't ready to die but she certainly wasn't ready for what came next.

She looked up at Della. "Neil..." she said softly, struggling to find enough breath to form any words, but she forced herself to continue. "Neil won't be able to.... you're gonna have to.... don't let me...." Her eyes flooded with tears, choking her words to unintelligible mumbles.

A spasm shook her body as shock began to ripple through her extremities. Della held her hand and continued to hum the culling song, seeking to connect with its wisdom and its peace. Meghan's grip tightened for a few seconds and her legs began to work in feverish jerks. Her dying body was struggling to hold the scant few seconds of life still within reach. And then her legs went slack and her hand limp as her final breath escaped from between her lips.

By this time, both Alec and Danny had joined Della. Both boys were crying as they watched Meghan's life pass before them. Della sat there motionless for a breath or two, but realized she had very limited time in which to work. Some of the things were back on their feet in just minutes while others took longer, or so she had heard. There was no telling what to expect.

She said to Alec, "Steve, why don't you take the other boy on around to the other side of the truck. I gotta do somethin' she asked me to take care of."

"What...?" Danny asked through his sniffles and tears. "What are you gonna do?"

"I gots to do what I gots to do. You go on around t'other side for just a quick second. Go on now."

Once the boys were out of sight, Della removed from her boot a long, narrow, pointed instrument that resembled Satan's knitting needle. She kissed Meghan's cooling forehead and drove the stainless steel tool into the dead woman's ear. Once in significantly deep, Della gripped the rubberized handle and swiveled the pike forcefully until she was satisfied the gray matter inside would not harbor any remnants of the infection. She withdrew the slick, glistening needle from the wound, wiped it generously on one of the other body's jackets, and then put it back in her boot. She looked around with the eyes of an inmate to make sure the coast was still clear.

"Okay boys. Ya'll can come back over here."

Della looked down at the still motionless woman. The hole she created was well disguised and hidden by its placement through Meghan's ear. Most of her blood had already seeped from her body, so the new wound on Meghan's head was virtually blood free. Della was satisfied that Meghan's last wish had been granted. It was the least she could do for the dying girl and more than most could expect.

25

There was nothing that could be done by the time Neil and Jerry came running back out from their foray ahead. He didn't see Meghan lying on the ground at first, but when he did, Neil broke into a full sprint. He stopped cold about five feet from her supine form. He was having a hard time bringing himself to close the distance, both physically and emotionally.

Despite Della's best efforts at arranging the corpse to appear as natural as possible, Meghan was still just a corpse. Neil didn't say anything for a long time. He didn't appear to even breathe, and he may not have been. He scarcely had any more animation than did Meghan. The bat clutched in his right hand seemed to fall to the road of its own accord, its clanging, metallic voice punctuating the silence all the more. Neil seemed to be incapable of anything at the moment. The fact that he was still on his feet was astonishing. Every fear...every anxiety...every painful failure in his life came screaming back at him in his mind. The cacophony of accusing voices drowned out all the other stimulus around him. He focused on Meghan's legs because he couldn't force his eyes to look at her face. Perhaps, in his mind, he was trying to convince himself that if he didn't acknowledge her death, then maybe it wouldn't be real.

The periphery of Neil's vision's clouded and became opaque, as if he were gazing through a frosty, icy window. The masking distortion also impacted his hearing as well; voices muted and slowed, floating around him in an unintelligible soup. Almost blind and nearly deaf, Neil was forced to endure that moment as a statue.

Emma and DB emerged next and walked briskly toward the gathering crowd. Emma could see legs and feet on the road but nothing more. She could, however, see from Neil's slouched and defeated body language that it was someone special on the ground and she was quick to surmise who it likely was. She walked up and stood next to Neil but said nothing. She sighed deeply as she looked down on her friend's lifeless body. Meghan seemed to be at peace, though her end had been met violently.

After a few quiet moments, Emma slipped her arm around Neil's slouched shoulders and led him over to the truck.

Claire, conscious again but still lying down in the truck bed, was leaning over the side of the truck despite the pain in her back and shoulder. She was sobbing quietly. Through her sniffling she said, "I am so sorry, Neil. I just... I tried but I couldn't. I wanted to help her. I just couldn't... Oh God, I'm sorry Meghan." She looked at Meghan's cooling corpse and burst forth a loud, painful, sorrowful wail.

Neil abruptly halted and resisted Emma's efforts to move him forward. He looked at Claire's concerned, watery expression and was momentarily confused about her comment. In fact, he was struck with short-term amnesia that robbed him of any memories from the moment he climbed out of the truck. He didn't remember navigating his way through the packed automobiles or dispatching the lone zombie. He couldn't remember the scream he and Jerry had heard that had drawn them back to the others. It had all vanished from his thoughts as if none of it had happened. He was lost in the exact moment in which he stood and couldn't remember why he was standing there in the road.

In his doubt and confusion, Neil once again allowed himself to be led to the open driver's side door. He sat heavily and exhaled a long, deep breath that reached out beyond all of them. The sigh ventured blindly into the past and hopefully into the future, seeking understanding and sympathy. It sought answers to questions that had been asked thousands of times by millions of voices but never satisfied. And, just as in every case in the past, the sigh came back empty-handed but sorry.

With nothing else to do, Neil lowered his face into his hands, drew in a deep, full breath and screamed to the world a resounding and echoing, "Fuuuuuuuuuuuuuck!"

26.

Kneeling next to Meghan's body, Neil asked no one in particular, "Can someone get me the shovel?"

Anyone could have asked it, but Jerry was the first to actually say, "What?"

"I said, bring me the shovel."

Shaking his head doubtfully, DB remarked, "What are you plannin' to do, boss?"

"Well, what do ya think I'm gonna do?"

Jerry shot back at Neil, "This is a bad idea, man."

"She deserves to be buried. I gotta do it."

Jerry hated to have to argue the point with Neil, but it needed to be done. He typically trusted Neil and his instincts, but this was different. They weren't safe; not yet. Meghan's dying only illustrated that point all the more. They'd created an opportunity...a window, and now they needed to make the most of it. They needed to get away. They were so close to the end of the road and next steps; they couldn't afford to stall for even a moment.

"Neil, please," Jerry begged. "It's just not practical."

Neil's mood had remained largely flat. His voice was smooth and steady, if a little empty. Like an echo of an echo, the words were all there but there was virtually no human emotion. He said, "It's not about practicality. Not this time anyway. It's about doing what's right."

DB countered, "The ground is frozen, Neil. It's not even about what's right. It's about what's possible."

Neil considered this last point before speaking again. DB was probably right. Neil remembered in the past talking with a coworker one winter about a dying relative. He remembered her saying that they were going to have the service but would have to wait until the spring to bury the body. Regardless of the wisdom, he had to try.

"Please, someone bring me the shovel."

Emma had heard enough. She stormed the handful of steps to the truck and retrieved the spade. She spun around and threw it toward Neil, the tool's gravelly voice along the pavement causing all of them to cringe in surprise.

She shouted, "There! Take the damn thing! Go dig a goddamned hole for the both of you!"

Neil looked at her, confused and stung. Everyone else had been calm and rational, trying to help Neil see their way. He was taken slightly aback by Emma's abrupt and loud reaction. Try as he might, he wasn't able to build any steam for any emotions.

With a defeated demeanor and sad eyes, Neil protested, "It's what's right. She deserves..." He trailed off, realizing his argument was both already anticipated and pointless. He was trying to apply the morality of a world that no longer existed. He breathed deeply. "I don't expect any of you to understand, but it's just something that I gotta do."

Della had heard about all she was going to be able. She stood and walked slowly over to the truck. Her voice was low, just a decibel above a whisper. "You folks. You act like there ain't never been no sufferin' before any of this. There's some people, that's all they know. Their mother gave them a life and the world been takin' from them ever since.

"You think slaves used to sing them ol' work songs 'cause they like the melodies? They sang 'cause it was all they could do to make this cruel ol' world a little more livable. They never talked about what was right. All they talked about was what was real and what was now.

"Look at all you now. Bitchin' and cryin' 'cause the truth about what this world gots to offer is finally bein' shown to y'all. There ain't been no surprises to me since all this started. Y'all are hurtin' and that much is true. God decided he was gonna test us today is all. It's up to us how we gonna face that test."

Della fell into humming another deep, resonating tune from her chest. She flashed her luminous topaz eyes at her audience and then turned her back to them again to finish the short walk back to the truck.

Neil pleaded, "I can't just leave her here. Not like this. Not in the middle of the road. I just can't."

Jerry offered, "C'mon, I'll help you move her over there. Under that tree."

Neil and Jerry moved Meghan's body with as much care as possible. It wasn't very sensible to allow the corpse to continue to wear its boots, coat, and any other usable item, but that was exactly what they did.

The two men stood there under the tree for a few minutes. There was no one near to them; therefore, there was no one near enough to hear the two of them speak. He asked quietly, "Do you think there is a chance that any of us are going to survive this?"

Jerry conjured up his best day time talk show host voice, "That's just the grief talking."

"Maybe, but it's an honest question. Death has a way of cutting away all the layers that don't matter so that we can talk about what does. We can wonder about things going back to the way they were or maybe even being better somehow. We can talk about the lessons that we could learn so that we can be better prepared for something like this in the future. But really, the only question that matters right now is whether or not we can survive. And by we, I'm talking about us...right here. The most important people to me in the whole world now are standing right here on this road and their survival and mine is really all that matters to me. So, what do you think? Can any of us make it through?"

Jerry glanced around at the sad looking trees and the gray sky. He looked over his shoulder at the rest of the group and at the devastation evident with all of the abandoned cars and trucks sitting idle on the road. Finally, he looked down at Meghan, who was in peaceful repose at his feet. After taking all of that in, Jerry said only, "Neil, I got nothing for ya. I can't somehow give meaning to any of this and to think anyone can is just naive. It's also something that you should know can't be done. Neil, man, I can't begin to tell you how sorry we all are and not just for you. We all lost Meghan. Have you thought how Jules feels? Meghan had become a bit of a mother to her. I wish I could make it all stop hurting, but we both know that just isn't possible.

"What I can say with certainty is that we need you and your judgment so that we don't all end up the same. Think about how much you needed Meghan and then multiply that by all of us and that's how much we need you. I'm sorry that I have to say this to you, but you really don't have the luxury of being selfish and feeling sorry for yourself. And after something like this happens, we'll likely need you all the more."

Neil allowed a defeated chuckle to creep from his chest. He said with a smile, "You might want to stay away from Hallmark my friend. They don't typically like their cards to be so damned honest."

"Just trying to do my part."

As he turned to walk back up to the truck and the others still waiting, Neil said, "Getting past this will be a little easier with your help my friend. Thanks."

Neil said it, but he didn't feel it. Other than nauseous, Neil wasn't quite certain what he was feeling. He was still reeling from Dr. Caldwell's death and now this.

Standing alone now, Neil knelt next to Meghan. He pulled away the jacket he and Jerry had laid across her peaceful face. He lowered his forehead to her chin and let the tears, as powerful and sudden as a flash flood, spill onto her neck. The warm, salty droplets breathed steam as they coursed down her cold skin. He pressed his cheek to hers and whispered, "Good night, sweetheart. Pleasant dreams."

Before he pulled away from her, he confessed, "I'm gonna miss you."

27

He counted the tick marks on his pocket-sized notepad and then looked through the binoculars again. He took his time, doing his level best to count everyone. Each time, he came up with the same number; five adults and at least five children. He was unable to see clearly into the tinted windows of the big silver truck, but he was fairly certain there could only be five kids. There was only so much room in the truck's back seat. He was satisfied that his count was accurate. His keen eyes had never failed him

He returned the lightweight but powerful binoculars to the hard case attached to his belt. He was draped in a single piece camouflaged zippered hunting suit that resembled a woodland colored snowsuit. Across his waist, chest, and back, he wore military-style web gear holding a two-way radio, combat knife, sidearm, and other odds and ends needed to complete his mission. Over his shoulder hung his vintage but well maintained Armalite AR15 assault rifle which was the original design copied by the mass produced M16 for the United States military. The assault rifle, which he had obtained many years ago, was a source of pride for him. It was a well-maintained and perfectly functioning weapon from yesteryear and it was his.

He had watched from his hiding spot quite some distance down the road as the woman standing beside the truck had been attacked and killed by a pair of the skins, the name he had given to the undead. His first instinct was to use the scope on his rifle to site and then take down the two monsters before they struck, but he was under strict orders not to reveal himself.

A couple of months prior, he would probably have not thought twice about helping that girl. He had plenty of time. It wasn't like the things were stealthy at all. Stupid skins weren't even as smart as bugs or spiders. He'd seen cows that acted with more intelligence as they were being led to slaughter. They would have been a pair of easy kills but it wasn't to be.

The two things must have been further off the road than the large group that formed on the pavement. Watching that big silver truck plow into and through the gathering crowd was great. He liked watching that a lot. It was like demolition derby or some other loud, destructive, and fun activity about which all the liberal sissies complained. But they had missed those two, who just walked down the road after those other folks decided to venture into the traffic jam. He couldn't figure out for the life of him why they had done that. They should never split their forces in unknown territory. It was just common, military sense. It was sad that something so apparent to him and not by these other people could result in such a tragic result.

He couldn't figure out how they were able get to the pretty redhead so easily. How is it that he could see them and she couldn't? Did she not know to keep her guard up at all times? He kept waiting for her to turn around or for someone else in the truck to see them. They just got closer and closer until it was too late.

He watched her get pulled away from the truck and onto the ground. Watching through the binoculars made it almost feel like he was watching it all unfold on his television or on a computer screen. It wasn't easy but it helped that it felt as if it was like he wasn't really there or something. The sensory disconnect likely made it much easier for him to be a passive spectator and stick to his job and his orders.

His job was very simple. He was to seek out anything on the road, gather intelligence, and then report that information back to the Colonel or, in this case, the Colonel's lieutenant Carter, who decided what to do about it. He wasn't on a seek and destroy mission; nor was he on a mercy mission to help folks in trouble. That point was made very clearly to him before he left on any of his excursions. Their enclave had limited resources as it was, which was the primary reason for his current foray.

And so he watched as the woman was caught off guard and brought down by the beasts. He also watched the furious response by the large black woman. She was vicious if a little slow and not to be taken lightly. She kicked the hell out of the two skins in no time at all.

When the other folks started to show up, he used that as his opportunity to count everyone. Nothing like a little tragedy to bring everyone out and make them oblivious to his watching. He'd seen it all before and knew that such an event would have all of them letting their guard down a little. It was a dangerous time for groups like the one he was currently tracking, but that wasn't his concern. No. He was primarily focused on watching, counting, and recording.

His name was Melton "Mel" Taranto. He was a corporal in the Alaska Freedom Militia formed and stationed on the Kenai Peninsula. He was chosen for this mission because he was good at it and could be trusted to follow the Colonel's explicit orders. He was a hunter and a tracker, both of which he loved but he had always preferred the tracking part of it. It really had nothing to do with killing animals or anything else for that matter. He craved the challenge; immersing himself in the nominally foreign environment and outwitting thousands of years of survival instincts. He conceded to some that it was as much about ego as anything else. The admission to which did nothing to diminish his joy in the hunt.

He was finishing his reconnaissance when a sound behind him caught his attention. He thought it sounded like footsteps, uncoordinated and sloppy. As he spun around swinging his razor sharp hand-axe, he thought to himself, *fucking skins never learn not to fuck with me.* The axe's silver tipped blade cut the air as easily as it did the hungry beast's skull.

Mel barely took the time to register the creature's features. He didn't pause to see if it was once a man or a woman. He didn't care that its frame was bone thin and that most of its clothes had been shredded and torn from its body. None of this mattered to him because it wasn't part of his mission. He kept himself focused on the task at hand, which was, at present, to get himself and the information he had collected back to the base on the Kenai.

He needed to regroup with the rest of the long range patrol. Quickly scanning all around himself for any other flesh eaters, Mel ran down the slope and got onto his mountain bike. He rode away silently, leaving the grieving group behind without a clue that they had been watched in the first place. Their not knowing, Mel hoped, would be their undoing.

28

The grief was so overwhelming that Neil was finding it difficult to feel anything at all. He was surprisingly unemotional, although neither he nor anyone else felt his lack of expression was a good thing. The only thing Neil was missing was a burning fuse or a ticking timer counting down to the inevitable explosion.

He was scaring even himself. Search as he might, there was no remorse, no regret, and surprisingly no tears to be found. Just steps away from her still cooling body, he was already missing Meghan, but his longing did not produce the anticipated sorrow. He just continued to walk, putting more and more distance from the only person he had allowed himself to love in a very long time.

They had no choice but to abandon the truck temporarily as they picked their way through the tangle of automobiles. Emma and DB led them over the route they had scouted. There were fewer larger vehicles along the path and, having been checked and scouted already, everyone appeared to be a little calmer.

Jerry was helping Claire, who was struggling to both walk and breathe. Danny and Alec were walking with their rifles at the ready, looking almost like a pair of boys playing war. Jules, meanwhile, was becoming quite the "little mother" to Nikki and Paul. She led the two of them and warned them not to get too close to the cars on either side and to watch in the windows in case of *them*. She didn't want anything to happen to either of them after all.

Jules appeared to be coming out of a shell and re-engaging with all of them. Many of them had caught Jules smiling and even giggling recently, both of which were welcome changes. Since Alec had reappeared, her mood change seemed to be accelerating more. She seemed much more comfortable and secure. She spoke more and always had a story to tell to the younger kids. Jules was clearly in her element and thriving in it.

Meghan's death had quieted her somewhat, but she was still mothering and protecting the younger kids. She was careful to keep all of them well behind Neil. She knew Neil was sad. She was sad too. She really liked Meghan, who always made certain she and Danny were warm on cold nights and had plenty to eat. She was a very nice lady and awfully special to Neil. Jules wished there was something she could do but no ideas were forthcoming. Instead, she just thought it was best that she and the other kids stay out of Neil's way. It's probably what her mother would have told her if her father was having a bad day. And thinking like that only made her miss her mom and dad.

She was teased with a little guilt about not having cried for the loss of her parents. She missed them terribly and was sad that she would never see them again, but the true revelation of their fates over a long stretch of time being largely pieced together by what others said around her had softened the news of their deaths. She sighed heavily and looked over at her brother and Danny.

What a pair. Two boys trying their utmost to be young men. Even to young Jules, the disparity between their perception of themselves and reality was evident. Of course, this wasn't unique to Alec and Danny. The circumstances, however, made the transformation much more necessary. Jules too was being expected to abandon much of what it was to be a child. Most of this was lost on Jules and the boys; the new expectations of them were simply the consequences of their new reality. When Jules looked at her brother and Danny, she still saw two boys with whom she liked to play. It just seemed they didn't have many opportunities to play these days.

Further up the road, a large Gray Line tour bus was partially in and partially out of a ditch. The behemoth was not quite on its side, but it was listing badly due to its position and threatening to capsize at any moment. In losing control, the driver had laid its weight across the road, effectively blocking anything but travel by foot to both the Begich Boggs Visitor Center and the tunnel leading to Whittier. The long ago accident involved several cars and a panel truck as well, all of which were snarled both in front of and behind the stuck mass transit vehicle in a tangled impasse. Hence the reason for all the vehicles packed so tightly together on the road behind them.

Several cars had attempted to drive around the roadblock, but had become stuck in the soft, damp earth to either side of the road. There they sat in frozen mud up to and above in some instances the vehicles' wheel wells, extending the obstruction for several feet and apparently ending any other attempts by motorists to skirt the blockage.

The bus was like a great barrier wall separating one world from the next. Anything...absolutely anything could have been on the other side and there was only one painfully obvious way to find out what awaited them. And given the extraordinary times through which they were all living, the possibilities were simply frightening to all of them.

The paralyzing fear stopped their progress dead in its tracks. No one was willing to commit to taking the plunge. There were no heroes standing on that seemingly deserted, cold highway in the middle of nowhere Alaska. They were just tired and hungry people flirting with helplessness and hopelessness.

They looked each to the other, searching for willing eyes waiting for someone to propel them forward. There was no such will amongst them. This revelation to Neil elicited a weary and defeated smile. He muttered to no one in particular, "I guess I'll go have a look. If anything..." He cut short his directive. It was unnecessary and understood. It was also just as likely to be ignored as followed, so there was little point.

"Can...uh...someone help me up onto the side of the bus? The slant seems like it's maybe climbable. Probably a little safer from there in case... Well, can someone give me a lift?"

Jerry lowered Claire to the ground, using the side of a car against which to prop her. He and DB knelt with intertwined fingers each making a stirrup for Neil to step up, and they would lift him even further.

From his perch, Neil took just a moment to survey the area immediately in front of them. He said after a few seconds, "Yeah. I think it's safe." And that was all he said, but he smiled, indicating that it was at least, as he said, safe.

Cautiously, they rounded the bus and picked their way over the now frozen, deep, muddy ruts around the bus' front end. Feeling like astronauts about to behold the dark side of the moon, they didn't know entirely what to expect. One could almost hear their collective breath being held in anticipation.

On the blind side there was...nothing. Well, nothing was a bit of an exaggeration. There were more empty parking spots than there were cars. There was garbage, some of which was stirring in the gathering breeze. There were also what appeared to be two empty buildings.

Closer to where they were standing sat a small retail shop doing its best to resemble a residential home and not a business. There was an unlit and silent neon *Open* sign in the window next to the door and a bygone *Daily Specials* sign lying on its side.

It was in front of the nearer building where most of the refuse was amassed: empty cardboard boxes, swirling plastic shopping bags, discarded Styrofoam coffee cups, and some odd and end scraps of cloth from blankets or clothing. There was ample evidence of people having been there, but no people currently. Nor were there any zekes or evidence of them; except, of course, the empty desolation left in their consuming wake.

A little further away was the Begich Boggs building. It sat there with its modern, efficient design and looked out over the frigid Portage Lake. The building's lines were rigid and straight, with no frivolous angles or superfluous shapes. The gray stone facade resisted all mirthful attempts by its silver metal trim, electing to instead drape the silver with a muted matte finish. The building was not ugly, but was instead a vision of engineered efficiency.

The only zombie they could see in the entire area was near the larger building. It was a man in a former life. He was wearing casual clothes, a green Alaska sweatshirt and blue jeans. His skin, like the other undead they had encountered, was fast becoming a deathly gray pallor and blending into the dark hue of Portage Lake behind him. He wasn't moving or exhibiting any other signs that there was a suggestion of life to his limbs. He appeared to be as animated as a stone monument dedicated to days gone by, just waiting outside the main entrance to the visitor center as if his party would join him in the parking lot at any moment. He seemed to be oblivious to the fact that he was being watched.

To Neil, the creature was pitiful. He couldn't imagine being any more alone. Like a dog waiting in vain at the door for its deceased master to return home from work, it merely stood and watched and waited. Neil found himself feeling conflicted.

Perhaps it was Meghan's death or Dr. Caldwell's death or...there were just so many deaths for which he felt at least partially responsible and indelibly connected. His sadness ran very deep; so deep that he was barely able to sense it. With all the death that seemed to hover around him and his thoughts, he couldn't help but succumb to the existential acceptance of his plight. And that acceptance only made him feel pity for the beast that stood so close to the building and yet so far from his stolen humanity. Neil wondered, as he looked at the pitiful creature who had once been a son, a husband, a father, and perhaps more, if there was any more hope for him to hold onto his fading humanity than there was for an infected victim. He was seriously beginning to doubt his fate.

And up on the side of the bus still, Neil finally began to cry for Meghan. He realized that he was likely crying as much for himself as he was for her, but his silent tears felt refreshing...felt human. The salty drops filled his eyes as he thought back on the weeks he had spent with Meghan. He remembered that hectic first morning at the Fred Meyer and seeing her for the first time. He didn't think about the reason for his being there or the terror from which he was running. He only thought about talking to her and remembered how glad he was that it was Meghan who had drawn the short straw and was working the early shift that morning. He envisioned the long nights of talking and sharing their lives with one another in the house in South Anchorage, but he couldn't hear the moaning from the undead outside or their horrific smell anymore. Neil was tortured with the memory of their first kiss and how sweet and perfect it was despite its awkwardness.

This last remembrance brought a smile to his face. He removed his glove and touched his chapped lips softly with his cold finger as if doing so might somehow help the memory to become more real. He exhaled a long, cleansing breath and wiped the tears from his eyes. He knew that the pain would not recede; not yet anyway. Like the tides, the waters of his grief would ebb when it was time to do so and not before. Anyone who claimed to have control over those powerful emotions was kidding himself and had never actually felt true sorrow.

Neil whistled quietly to get Jerry's attention. "There is one zeke over by the visitor center. I think he's alone, but let's keep sharp just in case."

Jerry was no fool. He could see Neil's struggle. He asked, "You okay my friend?"

Neil smiled and looked up at the morose sky but said nothing.

29

The fading afternoon light yielded to the mixed advances of evening and a gathering drizzle. By morning, the rain had become a blowing and growing snowstorm. It was obvious to all of them that winter was set to pounce.

Though the cold was pervasive, it was somewhat mitigated by the four walls and solid roof of the shop, in which they had elected to stay for the night. Those base comforts, unfortunately, were all that remained to be had. All of the food, including even condiments, had been eaten, the furniture had all been broken down and burned for heat, and the toilet, much to Emma's disappointment, yielded no toilet paper and a mess so aggressive that none of them dared to go inside. They were, however, mostly dry and not nearly as cold as they would be if they had been forced to sleep outside.

That first morning, as early as they dared, Emma and Jerry wandered out into the gusting white. They had decided the need to eliminate the ghoul stalking near them was enough of a priority to justify venturing out into the storm.

As they were leaving, Neil, sitting silently and motionless in a dark corner, caught both of their eyes. He rasped from the shadows, "Make it quick. Okay?"

Emma smiled and Jerry nodded, but neither spoke.

Once outside, Jerry said to Emma, "I'm real worried about Neil. He's taking this awfully hard. I mean, I get it but..."

Wincing against the blowing wind and snow, Emma said, "I think you should be worried. We all should be. We've all expected so much from Neil and he's always delivered and been willing to step up for us when no one else was. But losing Meghan is gonna take a lot out of him. Believe me when I say that I know where he's coming from."

"Yeah, I know." Jerry was going to ask how Emma was doing considering Dr. Caldwell's death was still only a handful of days in the past, but Emma spoke first.

"No. I don't think you do. Meghan wasn't just a girlfriend to Neil. I'm not sure what you would call her after all the changes to what we call a normal life. No. Neil had been kicked so hard by life in the past that all he knew was how to be down...how to be depressed and lower his expectations for what life had to offer. He had given up on himself and his world. Meghan changed all that. Meghan gave him a reason to care and to want to be alive when it probably would have been just as easy to not be. For Neil, Meghan was his renewed belief. And with her gone now, that belief has been rocked once again. I don't know if Neil is going to be able to find a new reason to keep going and if we keep leaning on him the way we have, well...I just don't know that we'll still be able to, I guess."

Their discussion came to an abrupt end when they beheld the ghoul. It appeared as if he hadn't even moved from where he stood the previous day. The weather didn't seem to have the slightest effect on him. He was still waiting for whatever had stood him in that position in the first place.

As opposed to Neil who saw sadness and loneliness when he looked at this particular creature, Jerry saw only a monster. He understood Neil's current sentimentality given his recent loss, but Jerry was not equally affected. He didn't hesitate. He hefted his trusted rifle to his shoulder, took aim through his scope at his target's head, and fired.

The echoing report surprised Neil. He reached over for the shotgun leaned in the corner next to him. He hadn't expected Jerry and Emma to shoot the zeke, so the gunshot did raise an alarm in his head. When the first shot was not followed by a second, his concern retreated. Given the weather conditions outside, it may have just been a prudent decision by Emma and Jerry to not approach the monster and give it an opportunity to surprise them.

Obviously, the gunshot caught others' attention as well. DB hurried to the front door and looked out, confused, into the empty parking lot in front of the building. Duke was right there alongside him as usual. The dog's hearing was weak enough that he likely did not hear the thunderclap from the rifle, but DB's urgent movement had caught his attention. Duke stood at the door as ready as any senior citizen might be for whatever was on the other side which had caught his owner's ear.

Neil said softly, scarcely more than a whisper, "It's Emma and Jerry doing some house cleaning near the lake."

Without looking back, DB asked, "They gettin' that thing over by that big building then?"

"Yeah."

"Prob'ly a good idea. Can't have it sneakin' up on us. We seen any more of 'em?"

Neil was slow to respond, perhaps a product of DB's meandering and unhurried speech pattern. Finally Neil said, "He's the only one so far, but we all know how that goes. Kind of like finding a shrew running along the floorboards in your house. Where there's one, there's bound to be others."

DB asked, "So, what's the plan now?"

Confused, Neil said, "I'm not following you."

DB shifted his position so he could see out the window into other parts of the empty lot in front of him. He said, again without looking at Neil or increasing the speed of his diction, "We still goin' to try for Whittier?"

"I don't see why not. What's to stop us now? It's just on the other side of the mountain."

DB, his eyes never looking away from the outside, said, "On the other sides of the snow too now. And what about all them folks on the road that you ran down with that big Ram? You think that's gonna be all of them? Besides, why those people out on the road instead of the other side of the tunnel?"

Curious about DB's reasoning, Neil asked, "I still don't think I'm following you. Doesn't that mean the tunnel is probably closed? Isn't that a good thing? Whittier could be clear. It may actually be what we hoped for. Something might finally work out for us. What could be wrong with that?"

When DB answered, he finally turned to face Neil. "Don't you see? If that tunnel is closed to them, it's closed to us too."

To this, Neil rose to his feet. He grabbed his shotgun, checked his pockets for more shells, but then thought better of it and grabbed his still full and heavy backpack. He zipped his heavy coat tight, and donned his black, tight-fitting stocking cap. As he readied himself, he muttered with concern, "Jesus. You may be right. What the hell are we gonna...?"

Neil started to exit the same back door through which Jerry and Emma had gone. "Danny!"

They boy appeared from another room still yawning and stretching his arms above his head. Looking Danny firmly in the eyes, Neil said to him, "Keep an eye on things for me, will ya?"

Danny smiled and nodded with his entire body, enthusiastically agreeing despite the sleep that still clung to his eyes. "You can count on me."

Danny glanced at DB wondering if he and Duke might be a part of the command but quickly deduced that the directive was strictly meant for him. DB and Duke wandered off, returning from where they had come without another word. Neil and Danny watched the two older "gentlemen" as they plodded out of sight.

"I know, Danny. I just wanted to.... watch out for Jules. Okay?" Neil didn't wait for an answer. He was out the door and into the weather without another word.

Danny was confused by Neil's display and his disposition. Regardless, he was going to do whatever Neil asked of him. Seeking a source to center his focus, he laid his hands across the small pistol in his zippered jacket pocket and gave his awareness a jolt of energy. And like the first swallow from a strong energy drink or even stronger cup of coffee, he felt his eyes open wide and his senses become alert.

He looked at the closed door a bit longer for no reason other than savoring the moment. He broke his trance and floated into the room where Claire, Jules, Nikki, and Paul were all still sleeping. Della was there too, humming a quiet tune and working her hands rhythmically in front of her. If she had yarn and needles, she would have been knitting. As it was, she was simply turning and twisting her hands into a swirling vortex of fingers and palms.

Danny surveyed the room itself, measuring any vulnerabilities the way he assumed Neil would do. In so doing, he realized Alec was absent, though he had been in the room the night before. He whispered to himself, "Where's Alec?"

Without looking up, Della answered, either unaware of or disinterested in the rhetorical nature of the query. "Steve? He like to sleep alone when he can. He probably found a closet or somethin' to sleep in. I guess he just got used to bein' alone 'fore he found Steve out on the road. Some people get into those kinda' habits and they just can't shake 'em. You know?"

Della's using the moniker Steve as a name for every male she encountered forced a level of confusion into every interaction with her. Having heard Alec's story though, Danny figured Della meant that Alec probably got accustomed to sleeping alone in the tight spaces for security before he encountered DB and Duke. He acknowledged Della's comment and then quietly sat next to her below the window that was providing a stark, dull glow in the room.

Della, her eyes ever fixed on her twisting hands, asked calmly, "You worried 'bout Steve goin' out by hisself?"

"Yeah," was all Danny could manage. It suddenly felt like he was talking to his Sunday school teacher, who was a very proper and strict man at his church. Whether Danny had more to say or not was immaterial. His brain found itself unwilling to venture into multi-syllabic territory, let alone into multiple word responses. That's not to say that either Della or his teacher were bad or angry or intimidating. Well, intimidating was perhaps a fair description, but it wasn't rooted in fear. Danny simply, in both cases, inferred from their dispositions that short, directed responses were what was needed and expected.

Della adjusted the phantom yarn and began to work her phantom needles into a new pattern. She said without the slightest rise in her inflection or emotion, "That Steve, he a smart one. If, that is, he don't forget where or who he is."

Danny felt like he was talking to Yoda who spoke in riddles. He wanted to ask Della what she meant when she said that Neil needed to remember who he was. However, he didn't sense there was an opportunity to seek clarification from her at the moment. He was finding himself being drawn into her twisting hands.

Watching her dark flesh whirl and spin into and around itself was mesmerizing. Danny watched the undulating vortex and listened to her deep, chesty humming until that was all he could sense. The room was no longer cold, the harsh light was forgotten, and he felt oddly at ease.

Her tune filled his head and then the room with its earthy presence. The gentle purr resonated in his chest in the same way that the idling engine of his father's John Deere lawnmower did when he leaned against it. He felt the buzzing travel south until it was producing pleasant sensations for him in his genitals. He was awash in the pleasant malaise and didn't notice when he fell back into sleep like the others in the room.

Della's song continued to fill the room, hoping to hold the uncertainty and questions of the day's early light at arm's length. She hummed a tune that tempted dawn's early light out from its slumber, beckoning the day to begin.

30

Walking briskly into the blistering wind was tough. Trying to track down two friends in the same gusts while avoiding becoming someone else's hot breakfast was more than Neil had anticipated in his rush to find Emma and Jerry. He was beginning to doubt the wisdom of his snap decision until he spied the two.

They were standing near the entrance to the much larger Begich Boggs Visitor Center as if waiting for something, the same way that the zombie had been the day before. He couldn't discern what they were doing. Truth be told, it looked as if they were merely gawking spectators at the scene of a terrible automobile accident.

Jerry caught sight of Neil and waved him over to them. Neil should have suspected whatever stalled their attention as long as it had was likely breathtaking. There was a shallow hope that what they saw was good news, but Neil quickly dismissed any such expectations. Emma shot Neil a warning look as he approached, stopping Neil cold in his tracks. It wasn't going to be good and, given their recent experiences and the nature of Emma's countenance, Neil tried to brace himself.

In another time and in another life, Emma wouldn't have been able to behold such a grisly scene as casually as she was now. The cruel, heartless world through which they had been struggling as of late had muted her sensibilities such that her disgust was only superficial. She seemed incapable of internalizing anything anymore. She was afraid and perhaps a little relieved that her soul was so far removed that nothing could affect her either positively or negatively. She at once felt stronger and emptier at the same time.

When Neil stepped up next to them, he first looked down at the dispatched fiend on the concrete steps. The creature was much more sympathetic from a distance. Up close, it appeared just as ghastly as Neil remembered them to be. Jerry's single bullet had wrecked about a third of its graying skull, though very little of its coagulated blood had escaped from the typically horrific wound.

Inside, though, was a scene more chilling than any he had seen. The floor was literally so caked with gory mortal remains that it was impossible to determine if the floor was tiled or carpeted or both. It looked like the semi-solid surface of a bog or a swamp; a morass of death. Picked clean of tissue, partial skeletons and miscellaneous bones were stacked one atop the other in a pitiless tableau that would have gagged both Dante and Milton and put to shame their visions of Hell.

Neil half expected the rust-hued skeletons to rise up and move toward them, but there was no movement, not even the slightest flutter, in the large building's wide lobby area. Any clothing that was still on or near the barren corpses had long ago been papier-mâchéd to the floor by pools of sticky, drying blood.

The walls appeared as if they had been spatter-painted by an artist who worked solely in a sanguine medium. The bottom third of the walls was layered so heavily with a combination of blood and gore that the true painted color was impossible to determine unless Neil looked toward the ceiling between the irregular rust-colored splotchy patterns.

The air inside moved slightly as some of the wind from the storm outside found a crack on the far side of the building and forced its way through. It was like a final gasp of rotten breath from a dying animal. To Neil, it smelled of mold and mildew, like an inoperable refrigerator whose contents spoiled long ago. While unpleasant, the smell was not nearly as rank as Neil thought it could be.

Neil was transfixed with the scene. He couldn't tear his eyes away from it. The mixture of self-pity and self-loathing tormenting him had him wondering if that was how his soul and his heart looked if he were to gain a glimpse inside of himself. Bones and blood and rot. Was that all that was left of the person he once had been?

Breaking the silence, Neil said flatly, "I guess it was a good decision that we stayed over there last night."

Jerry and Emma both agreed with silent nods.

"What possibly could have happened here?" Emma asked. "They must have gotten trapped inside somehow. But how? Is there not a backdoor? Why didn't any of them get out?"

"Maybe they just lost the will to run anymore," Jerry suggested. "Maybe they just couldn't do it anymore. A father watched his child die...a wife watched a husband...a brother a sister...a complete stranger. People can only take so much."

Neil finally turned to face the other two. "Not everyone's got what it takes to go on I guess." He paused, inviting the questions and the doubts inhabiting Emma's and Jerry's eyes but none followed. He tried to find some emotion hidden in some forgotten recess in him somewhere, but he was unable. He could feel the pain but it was as elusive as an eel, slipping through his every attempt. He knew that his words would sound more authentic with the emotion he knew he should be feeling, but, again, he came up empty. "You're both right," he continued flatly, "I am having a hard time. No point in trying to deny it. Honestly, I don't think it's hit all the way yet. That's kind of how it was with my divorce too. And when it did finally hit me, I was so far removed from it and numb from the heart up, that I didn't even notice the pain. It just became the background noise of my day-to-day. I guess I had ample distractions then too, so maybe comparing then and now isn't fair...."

Neil continued to speak, like a parishioner confessing his sins to a priest. Emma and Jerry merely let him ramble on, hoping for a miraculous catharsis but realizing as he spoke that it was getting further and further away. He was insulating his emotions with his words.

Finally, Emma said, "It's okay to be hurting right now, Neil. But if you're not ready, well, that's okay too. We can say all those things that we say to each other, like *We're here for you* and *Let us know what we can do to help*, and all the other bullshit that we say because we don't really know what to say. Really, there's nothing that can be said. They're just words, however sincerely they may have been intended. What you really need to know is that you don't have to go through this alone. You should know also that the rest of us are hurting too. It's only been a coupla' months, but I thought of Meghan as a younger sister."

Emma abruptly stopped speaking, surprised by her own comment. The realization was so sudden, so rattling that Emma lost her train of thought and her recent hard-edged expression softened slightly. The acid churning in her stomach reminded Emma that, despite her best efforts to distance herself from her feelings, she wasn't totally immune from them.

She resented the fresh ache in her chest as Meghan's death was piled atop Dr. Caldwell's. Her eyes glistened momentarily as a wave of vulnerability found a seam in her otherwise solid veneer. She looked away from Neil and

Jerry as if surveying the landscape. She drew in a deep breath and held it tightly in her chest.

When she turned back to face them, her hardened exterior had returned. The tears were still there but they were tears once again filled with anger, sorrow having already been forcefully evicted. Finally she asked, "Neil, what brought you out here anyway?"

31

Neil explained his exchange with DB and the sudden worry that prompted him to go out in the storm. And it was indeed becoming quite the storm. They were all thankful for the heavy, down-filled coats, insulated boots, and thick gloves they were wearing. The snow was beginning to collect in the lower lying areas of the road and surrounding open ground. Small drifts were starting to form against curbs and the sides of the buildings. It didn't appear as if this was going to be a dress rehearsal for winter; no, this was the start of the protracted season and all the challenges that it brought with it.

Jerry asked, "So what do you think we should do?"

Neil looked up at the road that lay behind the visitor center and led to the tunnel. "I think we should go check it out."

With the menacing M4 Assault Rifle clutched across her chest, Emma looked the part of a Warrior Babe of the Apocalypse, like she was the hardened but sexy heroine of a marginal B-movie. That was how she pictured herself as she took the lead. With Jerry and Neil in tow, she crossed the slate and stone-covered ground to the main road. Feeling like the wind and snow were conspiring against her exposed cheeks and forehead, Emma winced and grimaced as if she were in the cross-hairs of a maniacal sandblaster.

The road immediately gave way to a long bridge that spanned Portage Creek. The couple of vehicles still on the road were scattered haphazardly across the pavement, having been abandoned suddenly by their former occupants. Neil wondered how it all had happened here. How long was it from the initial chaos erupting at Providence until it had spread its lethal reach to Portage? There were no bodies on the bridge, though if he were to look over the edge of the span, he would have seen at least one bleak corpse lying on the rock strewn bank of the creek below. There were no lifeless bodies but, more importantly, there also seemed to be no ravenous undead either.

Neil wondered if, perhaps, it had been a day or more before the rampage reached them. Danny and Jules had told all of them that they were at a cabin near Seward, which sat quite a ways south of their present location, so maybe the "caveman" they had encountered had wandered north, spreading his pestilence. Maybe these folks had been pinched between two spreading pockets of bad news. He doubted he would ever know.

Ahead of them was a tunnel that punched a hole of a little more than a football field's length through the mountain, allowing the road to continue to the much more substantial tunnel connecting to Whittier. Despite its shorter distance, the tunnel ahead was still very dark and the snow falling all around the opening seemed intent upon further obscuring any perspective deeper into the darkness.

Peering into the gloom, barely able to discern the most rudimentary shapes of abandoned vehicles, Neil began, once again, to doubt their greater plan. If this tunnel was as murky as it appeared, how dark would the Anton Anderson Memorial Tunnel be given its daunting length of over a mile? Would their flashlights do anything at all? If any zekes had gotten in, would he and the others be able to respond and protect one another? The answers to his questions were as shrouded in doubt as was their ultimate destination.

Like a curious eye, the light at the far end of the tunnel stared back at them, beckoning them on their way. And with all the doubt and the fear percolating in their veins, the three took their first tenuous steps into the passageway. Once inside, they immediately noticed the air, while still very cool and slightly damp, was much more calm than outside on the road. Amplified slightly by the walls, their footsteps echoed all around them.

His mouth as dry as the Sahara, Neil was finding it difficult to swallow. It seemed as if his eyes and nose had stolen all the moisture to be had, as both sense organs pooled and spilled fluid ceaselessly. With their flashlights lit, they could see fairly well ahead and around them, which helped immensely in curbing their anxiety. As they neared the end of the tunnel, the light coming in from the exit helped to further ease their fears, though the wind and the weather once again increased their wrath.

Jerry wondered aloud, "Where the hell are all of them?"

Emma asked with a sarcastic tone in her voice, "You feelin' lonely all of a sudden?"

"No, but, I mean, don't you wonder about that? We haven't been able to take three steps without runnin' into them and now they're nowhere to be seen. Where are they?"

"We can only see so far in front of us because of the turn in the road," Neil suggested soberly. "Careful for what you wish for, my friend. Ya never know what's on the other side of the bend."

Again with her wit, Emma spat, "Very philosophical, Neil. You thinkin' about puttin' on a toga and spendin' too much alone time with young boys?"

"Emma!" Neil exclaimed.

"Just sayin', is all. Those Greek philosophers had a reputation for a few things."

"Well stop!"

"Touchy, touchy. I musta' hit a nerve or something."

The humor in his voice returning though with a touch of melancholy, Neil said, "I'm in mourning, remember? Can you cut me a little slack?"

Emma shot a knowing and equally mournful smile in Neil's direction. "You win."

Jerry said, "Finally! I thought maybe it was gonna get ugly."

"It may still," warned Neil, pointing down the road in front of them. There on the highway were three staggering, stumbling ghouls slowly making their way toward Emma, Jerry, and Neil.

Neil was surprised by the rush of uncontrolled rage in his brain. He didn't hear Jerry ask what they should do. Instead, Neil had already dropped his heavy backpack and shotgun on the road and was running toward the trio with his aluminum bat poised and ready to swing.

Surprised by Neil's sudden surge forward, Emma and Jerry were both motionless and speechless. Neil was moving so forcefully, there was no hope that either of them could possibly catch up with him. Jerry, instead, spotted another truck to his right and elected to climb into its open bed for a better vantage over Neil's shoulder. Emma released the safety on the military firearm in her hands and walked confidently behind and to the left of her berserking friend who was even then converging on his targets.

Neil plowed into them with all the fury of a tempest, striking all three at once. The bat hit the lone female zeke, pulverizing her jaw and spinning her head around so that it was facing the opposite direction of her body. She tripped and fell to her knees, unable to stand on her own anymore. Neil laid the other two onto the ground by the driving force behind his shoulders, much the same way that a running back might cut through a line of tacklers on the gridiron.

Spinning on his heels, Neil brought the bat down so hard onto one of the supine monster's skulls that it produced a ringing peal as it struck the pavement also. Ignoring the resulting vibrating buzz in his hands, Neil arced the bat down onto the remaining creature's head with a less noisy but equally damaging thud.

The female creature, her head still twisted around awkwardly, was still on her knees, her tenuous balance lost due to her offset perspective. She padded the ground in front of her uselessly like a stunned animal while her wrong-facing head sagged and bobbed on her broken neck.

Neil, apparently unaffected by the horrible display, nudged the thing onto her side and finished her off with another violent swing. He wiped the crusty gore from his aluminum weapon onto the dirty rags wrapped around the dispatched zeke that were once a colorful, thigh length cardigan sweater.

His chest heaving with both exertion and emotion, Neil turned to see Emma and Jerry pointing excitedly beyond him. He wiped the sweat from his brow and turned slowly to see another pack of abominations appearing through the curtain of snow still raging around them. He counted at least eight, but there were multiple ranks so he wasn't certain how many there actually were approaching him.

Jerry wasn't willing to wait. He sighted the first head moving languidly forward through his scope and pulled the trigger without hesitating. He didn't wait to see if the bullet had found its mark, choosing instead to trust his aim and chamber another round.

Emma fanned out further to the left, nearing the natural looking rock formations forming the border along the mountain side of the road. She wanted to get a better angle from which to shoot around Neil. She was ready to shoot, but Neil was still in the line of fire. She thought to herself, *Fucking move! I can't get a shot!*

Neil was, however, already going to work with the automatic pistol taken from a dead police officer some time ago. He fired three quick shots, bringing down two of the oncoming wretches, though one was able to regain his footing and start forward again. The recoil from the powerful handgun rekindled the pulsing vibrations in Neil's hand that were just beginning to fade. It wasn't a comfortable sensation, but it was a comforting sense of power to have the loud pistol continue to bark and growl. Regardless of the pistol's capable fury, feeling pressured as they continued to close on where he was standing, Neil began to give ground, which is what Emma needed him to do.

Emma positioned her feet the way Dr. Caldwell had instructed her and then began to pull the trigger on the M4. That firearm's snarl was much more metallic and industrial sounding than Jerry's hunting rifle. It was an instrument of war and produced music commensurate with its role.

Flinching slightly and wincing her eyes with each pull of the trigger, Emma's initial few bursts were rushed and uncontrolled, the bullets missing their targets as much as hitting.

It occurred to her that she was holding her breath and tensing up in exactly the manner about which Dr. Caldwell had warned her. Hearing his voice and his admonishments, she let out her breath slowly, reset her firing stance, and then started again. The bucking rifle created a rhythmic beat against her shoulder that helped her to concentrate. With more control, her shooting became more accurate and more conservative. She was using fewer bullets but bringing down more targets. She allowed herself to drift into a mental zone not unlike that to which she would wander when she did transcription at Providence Hospital before the world had come to an end. She had found her groove.

Soon, the roadway began to fill with motionless carrion remains. Neil backed away until he was next to the truck in which Jerry was standing. Neil had stopped discharging his pistol as the distance between him and the thinning herd in front of him continued to grow. Jerry reloaded his rifle at least twice while Emma continued to pound shells at the beasts. The effort and time she expended in reloading her rifle was much quicker so she was able to keep up a more consistent rate of fire.

Neil took that time to return to his backpack and retrieve it and, more importantly, his trusty shotgun. By the time he walked back up to Jerry's position, the shooting had ceased. It was all over, at least for the moment.

32

Standing amidst the carnage they had wrought, Emma, Jerry, and Neil took a moment to survey their surroundings. The tunnel behind them seemed like a portal to some other place...some other time. The other side was so much quieter and peaceful. There wasn't a coinciding pile of bodies starting to collect miniature snowdrifts in the twisted angles formed by lifeless limbs and torsos. There wasn't the stubborn acrid aroma of spent gunpowder lingering despite the wind and weather.

Looking over his shoulder while still standing in the truck bed, Jerry took note of how close the Begich Boggs Visitor Center appeared. It was a short distance away over the cold, deep Portage Lake. He could see the surrounding parking lots and short, narrow lanes that led to and from the small shop where the others awaited their return. He couldn't see the shop itself due to a screen of trees and other landscaping, but the proximity at which the three of them had fought their most recent battle to their refuge was startling. He peered through his scope for a better view, scanning the area in a fruitless attempt to see anyone.

Jerry wondered if the undead that had just come at them were already in motion and heading toward the visitor center area before he and his two cohorts had ventured onto the Portage Glacier Highway. Was it his lone gunshot down near the visitor center that had prompted their movement or were they already in motion, searching for their next meal that had wandered so close? He wondered how different things would have been had he and the others in their group been caught unaware by the predators. It likely would have been a much different battle.

Jerry was distracted from his musings by Emma's question, "So now what?"

"We go forward," Neil said, all business, "but we also stay ready. Emma, how is the load on that machine-gun there?"

Authoritatively, she corrected, "It's an assault rifle and I've got plenty." She patted her own backpack and an ugly orange fanny pack stretched tightly and bulging slightly across her hip.

Neil asked Jerry, "You good?"

"Yeah. I've got a few boxes of shells in my pack and both pockets are full. If we don't run into too many more of them, I should be good for days."

Jerry continued, "Hey, Neil? How about if you're gonna do something like that again, you let us know first, huh?"

Smiling, Neil said, "I can't promise anything but I'll try. I just saw those three and all I could think about was—"

Emma interrupted him, "It's okay, Neil. We get it. Remember that it ain't just you that's got a score to settle with those fuckers. Save some for the rest of us. Alright?"

Nodding, Neil pointed down the road with his shotgun. "Shall we?"

When they rounded the bend, the visitor center fell out of sight, but in the distance they could finally see the Bear Valley Staging Area where cars, buses, and all manner of vehicles gathered to await their turn to pass through the substantial Anton Anderson Memorial Tunnel to Whittier and beyond.

There were no more undead to be seen. In fact, the sense of desolation and loss couldn't have been more acute. Of course there were more idle vehicles waiting in vain for their drivers' return. Suitcases and other pieces of luggage and travel packs, some still closed and full but most having spilled their contents on the road, were discarded randomly all along the route. Here and there were also the eviscerated and mostly devoured corpses of past victims, some adult sized piles of bones but many seeming more likely to be those of children who met their gruesome fate many days earlier.

The snow thinned somewhat but the wind, cold and biting, found renewed resolve, whipping itself into a determined frenzy. It blew straight out from the lake, originating from the icy Portage Glacier some five miles distant from them and out of view. The cold cut right through their light gloves and even found passage through the multiple layers covering their legs. Exposed ear lobes, chins, and noses all struggled against the unforgiving arctic chill.

"It's fucking cold!" Emma groused. "Remind me again why I live here."

Neil agreed and sympathized with a silent nod, but chose not to speak and allow the cold air into his mouth and lungs. The frigid gust seemed to blow without end, threatening to chill them all to the bone. Without a word, Neil started to walk, turning his back to the wind as much as possible without losing sight of what lay ahead. Emma and Jerry joined him in his slow, determined trek.

The cold and the quiet forced Neil to retreat inward with his thoughts. Such introspection was not always the most comfortable set of circumstances for Neil. He wasn't entirely comfortable with his own thoughts under the best of conditions, and this was decidedly not the best of conditions.

He felt depressed and more than a little resentful, but he had a hard time in finding a target for his resentment, which led him to spin that resentment on its head and direct it back at himself as well. He stung with loss and disappointment, despite its familiar bitterness. None of that was surprising. In fact, most of that was fairly predictable. He was, however, growing concerned with his own detachment to everything.

That's not to say that he didn't care about Meghan's death or about the others' lives. Quite the contrary, he did care, but his caring seemed to be trumped and bested at every moment by the predictably bad turns that life seemed to throw at him.

Neil didn't hold himself responsible for Meghan's death. Well, maybe he did, but that wasn't the big issue...it wasn't the suspicion that had Neil once again doubting the wisdom of keeping him their de facto leader. Neil was actually merely concerned that perhaps he was just unlucky and that maybe his own luck figured into the fates of everyone else.

He once saw a movie with William H. Macy playing a worker at a Vegas casino. He didn't deal cards or spin roulette wheels or even mix drinks; he was a "cooler". He was so unlucky that his mere presence at a table cooled everyone else's luck the moment he appeared. If there was a gambler on a streak, Macy would walk up and put the streak to an end with doing nothing more than just being himself.

Neil wondered if he was their cooler. Were they all doomed to failure because of the same luck that he seemed to have been dealt in every other pivotal moment in his life?

Emma saw Neil's distant expression and said, "Hey, Gloomy Gus! Stop enjoying your misery all to yourself. Why don't you share a little?"

"You don't want any of what I got. Believe me."

"I wouldn't've asked if I didn't want to know. Give me a little credit, would ya?"

"Can't we just drop it? I promise to stop persecuting myself if we don't have to have this conversation."

With her smile and trademark humor in her voice, Emma said with more than a little condescension, "Did that work for you in your marriage? With Meghan? With your mom?"

Neil lifted his head and asked of the heavens, "What is it with you women?"

"It's not our fault that men are so much less complex and more predictable than women. It's just the way things are and the reason why I still want you to talk."

"Still doesn't make it right."

Emma was wise to Neil's continued stall tactics and said as much, but they had drawn close enough to their destination and possible danger that she let the moment pass. Instead, she checked the load on her firearm and let it settle into a better firing response position rather than the much more casual manner in which she had been carrying it.

They crossed another bridge, this one much shorter than the initial bridge before the first tunnel. The shallow creek below was barely deeper than the rocks that formed its bed. Its lazy waters rippled with each wind gust, but otherwise seemed content to merely sit and wait to freeze. On the creek banks below, there was more luggage which had been tossed aside in an obvious rush. The unnaturally bright colors of the bags and some of their spilled contents contrasted against the pristine location obscenely.

On either side of the road much closer to the entrance of the tunnel sat buildings of various sizes and of various operational roles. All of them shared similar rustic construction themes, trying their utmost to blend in with and accentuate the surroundings. Whatever intended function these buildings may have once had, they had more recently become the failed final refuge of desperate souls. And like every other refuge before, this one had failed to shield its occupants from the newly awoken undead terror stalking the fading remnants of humanity.

The largest building, an official looking A frame structure, appeared to have been frozen in partial birth. An emergency vehicle had been caught halfway in and halfway out of the large garage which had closed violently and suddenly onto the large yellow truck's roof. Apparently trapped in the wreckage, the passengers became easy targets for the ghouls who had been hunting them. Hellish streaks of crusty human remains streaked the yellow doors and sides of the vehicle around the shattered windows through which the undead had feasted upon the helpless victims inside. Shredded bits of clothing, likely discarded by gnashing teeth, twisted and curled on the pavement in colorful patterns. The many pieces of fabric not attached to the ground by the hellish glue of blood and tissue moved to and fro like unfettered leaves caught in the wind.

When Neil saw up close the gargantuan metal garage door sealing off the entrance of the Anton Anderson Tunnel, he was struck with a confusing mix of relief, gloom and wonderment. The door, after all, was closed which led him to be hopeful that it had been shut in time to preserve the town and the people beyond.

However, DB's question and warning about access echoed loudly in Neil's mind. He wondered how exactly to gain entry to the other side. His hope and pessimism were at odds with one another again.

There would be no time for any such conflict however. As they marveled at the engineering feat in front of them, the quiet was interrupted by a not too distant echoing pop, followed by another, and then a flurry more.

"Gunshots?" Jerry said.

Already running, Neil said fearfully, "We gotta get back! They need us!"

Jerry's eyes, as wide as the tunnel in front of them, looked beyond Neil toward the sound of the gunfire. The possibilities chilled him from inside out. He thought about Claire and felt his blood pressure skyrocket until his pulse echoed in his ears. His empty stomach did a single somersault, twisting itself around the churning acid inside.

Both the lurking terror and the unforgiving cold were forgotten as the three of them broke into a full sprint. They ran hard for a few minutes, the only sound besides the gunfire their heavy footfalls and labored breathing.

Then Neil stopped abruptly, resisting the urge to double over for lack of oxygen in his lungs. The burn in his chest was torturous but his growing suspicion was even more so. He paused while Emma and Jerry looked at him doubtfully. They wondered why they were stopping. Neil merely listened and confirmed his suspicion.

The shooting had stopped. It appeared that whatever battle had been fought had come to an end. The torturous quiet fueled their fear and angst all the more.

They flew through the shorter tunnel and found themselves in a better position to see the building the others had been occupying. The first thing seen was a thick trail of smoke, like a beam of light announcing a midnight madness sale, rising from the structure. It was not a promising sign at all.

Jerry was the first to resume the marathon. Neil could feel the other man's fears and knew that there was no stopping him. Neil looked over at the still gasping Emma. "We gotta stick together. We can't let him go down there by himself. No tellin' what he'll find or what will find him."

"Let's stop wastin' oxygen then." And Emma was running again.

Neil, too, was passing a trot pace back toward a sprint again. He didn't see the horde of zombies that he expected to be standing around the parking lots and lanes. In fact, he didn't see any of the undead at all. Why had they been shooting?

The three of them ran across the road and then hesitated next to the visitor center. Emma and Jerry were realizing the same thing that had already occurred to Neil.

Through her struggling breaths, Emma asked, "What's the deal?" She bent over with her hands on her knees and tried to slow her lungs and her mind.

Pointing, Jerry asked, "Who's that out in the open?"

"If that's Duke over near those trees, then the man is probably DB," Neil said.

Emma asked again, "What does that mean? What happened?"

33

It was DB lying in the parking lot. There was blood pooling around him and mixing into a dirty crimson soup with the gravel and dust under him. From in front of the building, Neil could see that the doorframe was smoldering slightly while white smoke was billowing out the shattered front window.

Neil knelt beside DB and touched the man lightly on his shoulder blade. DB was still breathing, but it was shallow. Neil cautiously rolled the man onto his back and hoped for the best.

To Neil's surprise and relief, DB opened his eyes. He started to speak but a blood choked cough stifled his efforts. Neil used the sleeve of his coat to wipe away the blood from DB's lips and cheek, the bright red fluid nearly shone against DB's pale skin. Neil looked down upon the man and felt a frustratingly familiar sense of helplessness.

DB finally managed, "...fucking militia. Think...think they got everyone else. Duke needed to go outside and I think we ran into—"

"Save your strength DB. You're gonna need it. Hang in there." Neil could almost feel the fear in DB's eyes. He knew the reality of his situation even if Neil wasn't willing to admit it to him. His wounds were mortal. The multiple bullets in his chest and abdomen had destroyed many of his internal organs and blood was beginning to pool in his insides.

Emma surveyed all around them while Jerry had gone into the burning building, emerging with only three largely empty backpacks and a couple of smaller caliber rifles that he had stood in the corner of a pantry closet. He shook his head to answer the question the others wanted to ask.

DB said again, "Fucking militia. Took the others. Kenai. Go to Kenai and find them."

Neil offered DB some water, but the other man refused. "I'm bleeding out,

Neil. I can almost feel it. My legs are numb. I don't think I can feel anything but cold below my waist." DB drew in another breath, this one much deeper, and held it, then let it out slowly. "Take care of Duke for me. He's a good dog and always been loyal. You're a good man and I know I can count on you. Watch out for him."

Emma looked over at the dead dog lying near some trees and couldn't contain the tears any longer. She stepped away and tried to regain control, but it was pointless. She could only suppress so much grief for so long until, like a mug filled to overflowing, it just spilled out.

Neil said gently, "You and Duke can count on me. He is a good dog and you're a good man. You deserve one another my friend."

DB, meanwhile, began to whisper into Neil's ear. The dying man's voice was fading fast, as was the life in his eyes. Just above a whisper, DB spoke to Neil who listened intently, trying to hear every word. In mid-sentence, the words simply stopped.

Neil looked down into the other man's vacant eyes, which still glistened with a gloss of tears. With the palm of his hand, Neil closed the other man's eyes and stood up.

Emma asked, "Is he...?"

"Yeah."

"What was he saying to you?"

"He told us to go get those fuckers! Can you guys give me a hand here?"

The three of them moved DB's body over to where Duke's was lying. They laid the two "old men" next to one another as respectfully as they could and paused for just a reverent moment. There wasn't time for words, and grieving was to be done on the run.

There was not time to be spent on anything other than the hunt. They needed to track down the others in their group, and they needed to make up lost ground as quickly as possible. The unfortunate reality was that sudden, violent death and loss had become such a prevalent component of their lives that pausing to observe another person's passing was easily forgotten.

34

They darted between the vehicles on the choked Portage Glacier Highway, throwing caution to the wind, dodging in and out of tight spaces without a thought of the dangers that might be waiting for them.

They were fighting against their struggling lungs and heavy feet, but none of them slackened their pace one bit. They were running so blindly that, when Della emerged dragging behind her a kicking and struggling young man dressed in camouflaged military fatigues, all three nearly tripped into one another.

Gaining his balance, Jerry said with quite a bit of relief in his voice, "Della! Christ, it's good to see you."

Without a smile on her stone cold visage, Della said, "Now that ain't no reason to take the Good Lord's name in vain, Steve."

Neil asked curiously, "Whatcha' got there?"

"I gots me a man who had a mind to do some evil but is havin' second thoughts now. Ain't he?"

The terrified and hurt militiaman pleaded, "She broke my fucking arm."

Della smiled and dangled her tire iron proudly in front of herself. Not satisfied in the least, Jerry kicked the man hard in the back. He would have liked to have been sated with the sound of the other man's air suddenly evacuating his lungs, but he wasn't. So he kicked him again. This time, Neil pulled Jerry away.

He leaned down next to the scared and hurt man much the way he had with DB, but there was neither sympathy nor sorrow in his eyes. He asked, "Hurt?"

The other man, still breathless, nodded. Neil smiled and punched him in the face hard. The punch hurt Neil's fingers despite wearing gloves, but seeing the other man's nose explode in a spatter of red across his cheeks helped him forget the pain.

"That's as good as it's gonna get," Neil snapped. "You're gonna lead us to our friends or it's gonna get a lot worse. Understand me?"

The other man's crying suddenly stopped. His expression became very serious and even a little defiant. Neil could rightly read the fact that the man was going to be anything but compliant.

Neil swallowed, and smiled his understanding of the unspoken message he'd received. "Don't worry little man. You'll tell us everything we need to know because, you see, we got nothing left to lose. And you, well, you've got ten fingers and ten toes to start with. Do you understand that?"

The militiaman understood clearly what he was being told and was fearful of the pain, but he had been trained and knew what to expect if he was broken. The officers back at their base in Soldotna had warned all of them of the interlopers they would encounter and their evil godless ways. He knew if he betrayed them, there would be hell to pay...literally.

And so, with wide eyes and sealed lips, he waited for the worst.

[PART III]

35

Claire awoke, bound and gagged, lying across the back seat of what appeared to be a squad car. Disoriented, she wondered for a moment, hoping actually, if maybe the past several months had just been a rufie-fueled nightmare. Through the pounding pressure in her temples, she fantasized that perhaps the world was how she remembered it before the apocalypse. When she forced a blood and snot filled breath through her nose though, she remembered how she had gotten there in the first place.

Earlier that morning, she was just waking and wondered where Jerry had gone. He was normally right next to her while she slept. He'd been there when she had drifted off to sleep but was absent when she awoke. Yawning and stretching from her uncomfortable spot on the floor, she looked up to see DB standing at the front door. He was looking out at first, but caught sight of her movement and turned to see her. He muttered something under his breath that Claire didn't fully comprehend but she understood his meaning all the same. Duke needed to take a leak, so he and his dog were going out for a quick walk.

Claire rubbed her eyes and smacked her lips together. She was lying on the floor of a small dining area of the coffee shop. No amount of blankets or extra clothing piled under her was capable of making the floor comfortable under normal conditions, but the pain in her back from her fall contributed to her extra stiffness. Danny, Jules, and the other two kids whose names she never seemed to be able to remember were still sleeping near her, but other than them, there was no one to be seen.

Jerry, Neil, Emma, and Della were all out of sight. She thought that maybe they were just in other areas of the shop. She stretched her arms high above her head and felt the pain in her back and shoulder again. They still hurt like hell, but at the moment she didn't feel like just going back to sleep to escape the pain. She winced her eyes as she shifted her spine one way very slowly and then the other to try and loosen her tense and bruised muscles.

She was just starting to get her wits about her when she heard a pop outside. It took her just a second or so to realize she had heard a gunshot that sounded like it was just outside the front door. She shook her head, thinking she must have just imagined it, and then she heard another shot which sounded almost like a very large firecracker.

Danny woke to this latest noise and looked over at Claire for any hint as to what it was. The two were still looking at one another when a shadow passed in front of the window on the room's front wall. Still a little confused about what to do, Danny allowed instinct to take over. He pulled the small pistol from his pocket and pulled the slide back to ready the firearm.

Suddenly the front door burst open and a man wearing a military uniform burst through. At first, Danny and Claire hoped that the man was there to save them. Maybe the Army had finally come back to Alaska to set things right again. When they saw his grizzled face and menacing expression, however, they both realized his intent was anything but to save them. He wasn't a zombie, but he was likely just as dangerous.

Danny didn't hesitate. He pulled the trigger on the pistol, which kicked three quick times against his palm. All three bullets found their marks in the camouflage-clad man's upper chest, neck, and face. He fell to the ground writhing for a moment in pain and then suddenly he was still.

Claire grabbed the pistol from Danny just as a trio of similarly dressed men rushed through the doorway. One of them was quick to run toward Claire, who hesitated momentarily. He kicked the pistol from her hand and then cracked her on the head with the butt of his rifle. The lights went out immediately for her and stayed that way until now.

In addition to the pain in her back, she was now contending with a new pain in her jaw and left side of her face. She tried to sit up but was finding that exceptionally difficult. Every move she made, she could feel the crusty scabs on her back split and ooze fresh blood. Her shirt was already pretty well plastered to the wound and her movements, however slight, were pulling the fabric away with bits of flesh still attached. She whimpered involuntarily at the sensation.

From in front of the steel screen separating the front and back seats, she heard a gruff male voice say, "Is someone waking up back there? Don't worry. I know you can't speak. You can just listen instead. You shot Sullivan's cousin back there and he ain't gonna like that one bit. You're just lucky he ain't with us on this scouting run or you'd really be hurtin' right now. Don't worry though. He'll be waiting for you back at camp. He's gonna be real happy that we brought you back. Pretty little thing like you gonna help keep us all warm."

The gravity of her situation sinking in, Claire's fear took hold. She wondered about the others. Where was everyone else? Was Jerry still alive? Where was she being taken? She started to wrestle with the binding on her wrists but to no avail. Her ankles were also too tightly bound for her to free them.

And then her thoughts focused and she wanted to demand where the kids had been taken. Why were they not with her in the car? She tried to force the handkerchief gag from her mouth, creating a bit of a ruckus. She tried using her teeth to saw through the fabric, but had no more luck with that than she did with freeing her hands.

Grinding a toothpick between his teeth, the driver looked in the rearview mirror and smiled. His words oozed out of him like poison, "Feisty little thing, aren't you? You're gonna be real popular. You just wait and see." He produced a guttural grunt on the heels of speaking and then smiled another toxic, toothy smile.

His smile, so full of hostility, melted all the defiance out of her. Claire wanted to be tough like all heroines from action movies...Jolie in *Salt* or Arquette in *True Romance*. Try as she might, however, she couldn't quiet the paralyzing fear in her chest. She did the only thing that came to mind. She emptied a night's worth of waiting from her bladder onto the seat.

She knew she would eventually regret it when her wet underwear and pants begin to chafe and rub her bottom, but she appreciated the soaking she gave to the cloth seats nonetheless. The smell would take a hell of a lot of scrubbing to remove. And judging by the terrain that passed by the windows, she easily presumed where they were on the highway. It was still quite a distance before they would be arriving anywhere, so she reveled in her quiet rebellion and waited until she was able to urinate again.

While Claire was measuring her fate, Danny was also trying to be strong in the back of a yellow and green Vend Alaska panel truck. He looked around at the other three pairs of wondering, scared eyes and knew that they were all looking to him. The other children needed for him to be their rock. He was expected to be the strength to help them survive this latest encounter. Unfortunately, Danny's distraction was palpable in the dimly lit truck interior, as if it were another passenger along for the ride.

To say that Danny was conflicted in his feelings toward Neil at the moment would earn a nomination to the Understatement Hall of Fame. He understood that Neil, if he was indeed still alive, was the best hope that any of them had to survive their abduction. Danny forced himself to expel any thoughts that Neil, Jerry, and Emma had already met their demise. If Neil was dead, then so was his hope that things were going to work out for any of them.

At the same time, however, he couldn't deny the resentment he felt toward Neil for having left in the first place. If he had still been there, maybe things wouldn't have gone as badly as they did.

Danny envisioned himself defending their new home alongside Neil. He imagined standing at the window, with his rifle in hand. They had stopped *Them*; he had stopped *Them*, whoever *Them* happened to be. The battle was won and they were all safe again, and he had helped. He was no longer a burden or an afterthought. He mattered. But it was Neil's approving look that made the fantasy complete. It wasn't about the killing or the saving for Danny. He just wanted to make Neil proud of him and that was really enough at the present.

As it was, Danny was unfortunately forced to focus on his reality and not on his fantasy. He couldn't stop rewinding and reliving those fateful moments in the coffee shop. He didn't remember taking the pistol from his pocket; it was simply in his hand at the right moment. In his memory, the pistol glimmered like the finely honed steel of a hero's sword. He pointed the gun and then the man was down. He couldn't be certain that he had even pulled the trigger. Other than the man's body on the floor in front of him and the pulsing sensation in his palm, he had no way to know for sure what he had done. He couldn't remember the man's face. Hell, he may not have had time to look. Everything had happened so fast.

And now...now, he couldn't help the reverberating echo in his mind of the words, *I killed a man*. Like an explosion of fireworks, the words flashed in blinding patterns, until the echo found the back of his throat and he whispered, "I killed a man."

Giving the thought voice made it all the more real. He hadn't denied his memory before, but now he couldn't possibly do it. He uttered the simple words as quietly as the flutter of a bird's wing. His voice barely tickled the air.

Jules could tell something was different with Danny. He should have been scared or at least worried, but all he appeared to be was distracted. She needed Danny to be there with them instead of wherever his thoughts had taken him. Didn't he know that? She looked at him, trying to see more of his face in the sparse illumination. She cocked her head this way and then that, but the shadows were too powerful.

Finally giving up, Jules chose to lean against Danny's chest again and hope the security his presence had brought in the past would return. She was feeling a new fear this time but it was just as real and just as terrorizing.

The only other thoughts to which she was able to retreat were wondering where those mean, scary men had taken Alec. They had grabbed Claire and pulled her away by her arms, dragging her behind them like she was already dead. Alec was led away on his feet like the other children, but he had been separated from Jules and the other kids when they had gotten through the cars on the highway. When he protested, one of the men hit him in the face and on his back and on his.... The image of Alec's beating was too painful for Jules to consider. The end result had seen Alec thrown into one car while Jules, Danny, Nikki, and Paul were all led to the truck in which they were riding.

Jules just couldn't figure out what she and the others had done that was so wrong. Why were those men so mad at them? She thought that maybe the building in which they had been sleeping was the army men's house and they were just angry that she and the others were there, kind of like the Three Bears. She couldn't remember what had been Goldilocks' fate, but she was pretty certain she got away. That was the solitary shred of comfort and hope to which she clung; *Goldilocks got away.*

Alec, meanwhile, was sitting in the back seat of a Humvee between two large, malodorous men. His left eye was swollen almost completely shut and was becoming the color of eggplant. The blood had stopped oozing from his nose, and a fair amount had dried and crusted above his upper lip, forming what appeared to be a rust-colored mustache. His hands were bound in his lap but his ankles, unlike Claire's, were free. No one spoke to him. In fact, no one spoke in the vehicle at all. On occasion, the static from the CB radio in the dashboard would crack with distant voices, but none of it made any sense to Alec.

He stared at his lap, afraid that any wandering his eyes might do would solicit another pounding to his temple or the back of his head. He wondered where DB and Della were. He thought he saw a body near their building as he was being pulled and dragged away, but wasn't certain if perhaps that was another person Claire might have shot.

Alec retreated into the shell from which he had only recently started to emerge. The retreat didn't require any real effort on his part. His will obligingly ceded ground until he had none at all. He merely retreated beyond the depth of his skin, turning down the volume on all of his senses as he did. His withdrawal was hastened when one of his abductors struck him on the back of his head. He leaned forward slightly until all that he could see was the dark, wiry carpeted Humvee floor. He stared so long and so intently that his eyes strayed from focus and threatened not to return, which Alec did nothing to discourage. When he did finally look up, his vision had become blurred and dark.

He was detached enough that he didn't feel the next handful of random blows to his skull. The final, an elbow to the bridge of his nose, had started anew the gush of blood from both nostrils, which coursed down across and around his lips and dripped in long, gooey strings of dark crimson from his chin. He made no attempts to stop the flow of red.

36

Neil was learning that the problem with bluffing about torture is that sometimes, when your bluff has been called, you have to be willing to torture to keep the bluff going. Neil was contemplating this unfortunate reality as he drove them all south on the Seward Highway.

The silver Dodge Ram truck had been thankfully left unmolested by the fleeing militiamen. It sat with the keys still in the ignition, seemingly waiting for their return. Neil cast a single, longing look toward the pile of stones covering Meghan's body off the road a bit, but wouldn't spare the time to run over to her. He needed to ask her for advice. He had been robbed of both her and Dr. Caldwell's point of view in just a handful of days and he was beginning to feel a little blind and disoriented, like a boat without a rudder.

There wasn't time to contemplate next steps however. The sustained shooting had obviously attracted the unwanted attention of the herd of zombies that had been wandering back and forth along the Seward Highway. They were starting to appear in small and large groups along the Portage Glacier Highway and were threatening to overrun the road and restrict any attempts to escape. There was no time to dawdle.

Neil, Emma, and Jerry climbed into the front seats while Della and their terrified and bound prisoner took their seats in the back. They had plenty of gas and daylight, so Neil was confident they could get to where they needed to be. The only problem was that Neil didn't know ultimately know where they were going. He had a fair idea about the general area but it didn't go any further or deeper than that. He was going to need some more specific directions eventually, and that's where his problems really began.

It was fairly evident their young, scared prisoner would not willingly share the location of the militia camp. He hadn't said a word since his little exchange with Neil and didn't appear as if he was going to be talking any time soon. They were at a stalemate of sorts, but there were other distractions, like getting on the trail of their kidnaped friends.

They found themselves on the run again; this time toward something rather than away from it. It was running, but it felt different. This kind of running was agitated and aggressive. With the growl of the truck all around them, they began to feel like predators, perhaps a pack or a pride, on the hunt.

Lucky for Neil, the rhythm of the road passing under his tires had always had an enchanting effect upon him. Today's drive was no exception.

The gentle vibrating buzz touched him from his toes to his eyeballs, massaging and relaxing the tension that seemed to plague all of his joints and muscles at once. Like a boa constrictor coiling itself tighter and tighter around its prey, Neil's tension was a formidable force. It resisted its utmost, but the soothing sensation subdued the constricting energy and banish it to his memory. The reprieve was welcomed with a quiet satisfaction across Neil's face.

And lacking any road music to accompany the drive, their soundtrack was the persistent but understated chorus of rubber on pavement. The warm refrains were distant kin to the mesmerizing words of a hypnotist.

Under such conditions was the closest thing Neil ever came to experiencing Zen. His mind wandered without scope or direction. He merely *was*. There were very few other times in which he could so totally lose himself in such empty but complete existence. He was an empty vessel for thought and experience during those brief moments. Neil's thoughts were as untamed and free as a Joyce novel diving headlong into stream of consciousness.

There was really no point in his trying to control or direct his musings. His thoughts quickly became a raging and unpredictable surge which gradually became a parade of faces: Grandma and Grandpa Jordan, his boyhood friend Doug, Dr. Caldwell, a random zombie with its weathered gray skin and hungry snarl, Danny, his mom and dad, his boss sitting in his enormous leather office chair as if it were a throne, and between each random image he caught glimpses of Meghan. Her smile held no judgment or accusation. She was as lovely and as missed as spring.

Along with Neil in the front seat sat Jerry and Emma, who seemed to share in Neil's quiet reverence. No one spoke. Words, for all of them, seemed so intrusive and out of place, like trespassers.

In fact, the only sound that any of them made, with the exception of the occasional deep breath or throat clearing cough, was Della and her soul piercing humming. Her songs never had lyrics but they all seemed so full of meaning and purpose. Next to her, seemingly lost in the drifting melodies of Della's tune, the militiaman, restrained with duct tape and cable ties, sat and awaited his fate.

Neil chanced a glance at him in the rearview mirror and was struck with how young he seemed. He was no militiaman; he was a militia boy, scared and alone. For Neil, the boy was his only link to Danny, Jules, and Claire. Their prisoner was unable to hide the fear lurking in his eyes. It has been said that the eyes are the windows to the soul and in the soul emotions are pure and deep. And it was quite obvious to Neil that, despite the boy's resolute but calm facade, the prisoner was terrified about his immediate future.

Neil couldn't remember a time when he had ever been feared. He was always the likable guy, even in sports. His friends and co-workers all considered him an affable fellow. His wife might have had a different description for him, but her opinion was tainted to say the least. Neil was worried that perhaps he wasn't the best person to be playing the hardened tough guy. It just wasn't in his nature to be that guy. He tried to think of ways to get the information from him, but his grasp on his thoughts drifted again with the overwhelming din of their movement on the road.

Emma knew why Neil looked worried and distracted. She could see that he was contemplating his next move. She could almost see him torturing himself the way that Meghan always said he did when he made decisions. He wasn't really a tough guy to figure out; perpetually dissatisfied with himself and still trying to prove to himself that he was capable.

Emma had known other guys like that in her life. They were usually the nicest men but also the least likely to be attractive to her. She didn't much care for the melancholy, but she accepted it. It was just part of the package. When all was said and done, she knew that she and everyone else could count on him. She knew that Neil would, if asked, step up and use every means possible to get the information they needed.

It was because she knew that they could rely upon Neil's willingness to be the "Man for all Seasons", that she decided she was going to do the dirty work. She started thinking of little tortures with which she could start. She could beat the man with one of their bats. She could break his fingers. Cut him; burn him. If they let her, she was pretty certain she was capable of all of this because she could envision it in the first place. There was a time, not too long ago, that she abhorred violence on television or in movies. Violence was just something that she didn't feel necessary to make a part of her entertainment lineup. She didn't sign petitions to ban violent video games nor did she tell others what to watch, but she didn't typically see those kinds of movies either.

Times had definitely changed and so had Emma. And it wasn't just that she was considering torturing another living being. The problem was that she was considering ways in which to torture another living being to maximum effect, and no objection was forthcoming from her psyche. Emma hadn't become psychopathic; she wasn't looking forward to hurting the kid sitting in the back seat with Della. It was just something that needed to be done and she was perfectly willing to do it. At least that was what she was trying to convince herself to believe it.

Emma pivoted in her seat and took a long look at her quarry. She wondered if it would escalate to include shooting him. Where should she shoot him so as to hurt and possibly maim, but not kill? She thought to herself that she shouldn't shoot him in the leg or foot in case they needed him to be able to walk. Of course, if she shot him in the foot, he wouldn't be able to run away. She looked the scared kid in the eyes and he immediately looked away, sending his gaze to the passing trees along the side of the road.

But Della caught Emma's eyes. The big black woman seemed to fill the entire back of the truck, but still looked comfortable. Della cast her big yellow eyes to the left and then the right, looking at the backs of Neil's and Jerry's heads. Like a tennis serve suddenly hitting the net, her eyes dropped when they came back to the middle and stared back into Emma's eyes. It was clear to both of them what Emma's intentions were, to which Della started to hum another low, soulful song that sounded as if it had first been sung by Nefertiti's head priestess on a pyramid somewhere near Giza and Della had been there to hear it.

Satisfied but a little unsettled, Emma turned back around. If it came to it, she was certain that she could do whatever was necessary to learn where her friends had been taken. She looked back out at the road and let Della's song wash over her.

37

The car lurching to a stop was preceded by an agitated series of chirps on the radio. Despite this early warning, Claire, apparently unprepared, rolled from her supine position on the back seat onto the floor. Without the use of her hands, Claire's tumble was painful and solicited a grunt.

The car's driver, Howard, heard her discomfort and said, "Serves ya right. What the hell were you think' pissin' in my car! Dumb bitch!"

Under her breath, Claire muttered, "Fuck you, redneck!" She'd do more if she could, but wet underpants was her current limit. It was the discomfort of having wet undergarments that had prompted her to lie down in the first place. She was hoping her clothes would dry but the smell would persist.

Instead, Howard, upon noticing the rising pungency, had simply opened the front windows and permitted the cold air outside to fill the car's cabin. He'd turned on the heat, which warmed and comforted him but did nothing for her. Regardless, Claire knew that the foul odor would be hard to dispel from the seat's fabric for some time to come.

She had heard the voice on the radio, but was unable to decipher what had been said. With the passenger window still open now that they had stopped, she could detect a distinctly burnt aroma coming from outside. It wasn't the inviting smell of wood burning as in a campfire though. The acrid air was much more industrial, like perhaps plastic or rubber from some internal part of an engine melting.

Car problems.

Car problems had sidelined their slavers' caravan. Talk about falling victim to the mundane.

Claire climbed from the floor and did her best to right herself on the bench seat. She looked around and saw a wafting cloud of whitish smoke seeping like a last breath from the green and yellow panel truck's grill.

It appeared they were on the Sterling Highway but still well outside of the first large, by Alaska standards, community on the highway when headed south, Cooper Landing. On the left side of the vehicle were trees and a flowing river. She guessed it to be the Russian River but geography and place names were never her strength. They were parked in a small, paved parking area that ran alongside the road. From the tiny lot, the river was easily accessible, allowing hip wader-wearing fisherman to crowd themselves onto the river banks and into the waters themselves in the contest to land any of the plentiful salmon who swam and spawned in its waters.

She wished she could somehow use this respite to her own advantage, but the bindings on her wrists and ankles were constraining her thoughts as well as her activity. She felt helpless and hoped that the delay didn't lead to.... She just hoped that she wouldn't become entertainment for the road. Howard had alluded on a number of times to her upcoming role when they got her back to the encampment...base...whatever.

Burly and disagreeable, Howard pulled himself from the car with some exertion and walked over to the expiring truck. He spit dark, tobacco filled wads of fluid as he and the other drivers debated their next moves. Claire wasn't able to follow all of it, but she did surmise that the convoy was transporting more than just her and her companions. Supplies had been gathered in addition to captives and so they argued which should be carried back and which should be abandoned, even temporarily.

Finally, another man dressed in all black military fatigues, held up his hands to end the discussion. He spoke calmly and quietly enough that Claire could not hear what he was saying. His composed disposition commanded everyone's attention and settled their collective anxiety. Claire wished she could hear what he was saying but the odd thing she noticed was that she felt calmed as well. She sat back, adjusted her little behind on her mostly dry underpants, and awaited her fate. What more could she do?

She sat in total silence for a few moments, contemplating all that she couldn't do. She couldn't run. She couldn't fight. Yelling and screaming was pointless. There was no reasoning with her captors, not yet at least. Claire thought about all of this, barely noticing a low level vibration that was tickling her chest, disguising itself as a cough that was threatening to pounce. She tried to clear her throat to no effect.

And then, all at once, it suddenly dawned on her what she was feeling: the walking dead. They were near and getting closer. She tried to crane her neck around so that she could see them. Nothing, but the buzz was getting stronger.

Was she safe? Could they get in? She'd have no chance to defend herself. She finally knew how live bait felt just before it was hooked on the line or tethered to a stake. Blending themselves into a noxious cocktail in her stomach, Claire's anxiety eagerly mixed with the growing vibrations. She pulled harder and harder on the straps securing her wrists, desperate to get her hands free. She was nearly in a frenzy, her forehead and cheeks glazed with cold sweat and her breath forming a growing cloud in the car's cool interior. *Cool interior?* It occurred to her that the front windows were both down. She looked around for anything she could use to free her hands. If she could reach them, she was almost convinced she would willingly gnaw her hands free by chewing through her own bones if necessary. When she realized she was shaking the whole car and drawing attention to herself, she froze.

Claire finally saw the movement, slow and stilted, to her left and on a depression of inclined ground that separated their parking spot from the river. She turned her head slowly, like a merry-go-round on its final, rapidly deteriorating rotation. She wanted to avoid detection at all costs; she didn't want them to know she was there.

She counted at least five of the ghoulish figures. She contemplated alerting her abductors to the threat but then thought better of it. Let the fuckers die! Maybe she'd get lucky and the zombies and the rednecks would kill each other. She'd be willing to sit and watch that happen; only thing missing would be some popcorn. She was trying her best to be flippant about her situation, but it was no use. She was scared shitless; there was no point denying it.

She heard one of the men standing in the circle say, "Oh shit. More skins."

The undead, or skins as they were known by the militiamen, ascended the gentle slope leading up to the road where the cars and trucks were parked. Claire had seen five of the creatures but in reality there were closer to ten of them. This close to their prey, the rotting abominations were much more vocal and excited. They emitted a collective wet, hungry groan as they approached, their hands reaching out in front of them desperate to close the distance to their next meal.

Spilling around the front and rear of the squad car, the zombies didn't seem to notice Claire sitting in the car's back seat. Watching them, Claire could not control the shaking fit gripping her. It felt like she was suffering a feverish shiver without the fever.

SEAN SCHUBERT

The crowd of undead was an eclectic group to say the least. There were fishermen still wearing hip waders, a businesswoman in a shredded skirt suit, tourists and locals wearing casual tee shirts and jeans, and even a couple of police officers, one of whom had been eviscerated and now had an empty, festering pit where his torso had once held his internal organs. The monsters' skin was not much lighter than the road upon which they were sauntering. And like any corpse, their fingernails had continued to grow, causing their emaciated, bony fingers to resemble small daggers.

One of the police officer ghouls was pinched against the front of the squad car by the press of undead around him. His right hand, more of a claw really, dragged itself across the car's metal hood with an ear shattering and teeth chattering scraping sound. He stopped and looked at the vehicle, a semblance of remembrance in his dark eyes.

Fear, cold and bitter, gripped Claire as she realized it wasn't the car he was seeing. He was looking right at her. He circled around the car and came to the open passenger side window. Luckily, it wasn't down all the way, but it was down far enough that he could reach in toward her. She screamed when his face appeared in the opening, his rancid breath filled the car's interior with its foulness.

She shifted to the far side of the seat and pressed herself against the locked door, trying to make herself as small as possible. The fiend's wiry, gray arm found its way into the partially opened window, reaching toward her fiercely. Its fingers opened and closed, grasping at the space between it and Claire like a hungry, chomping mouth. Claire's terrified scream seemed to go on and on, echoing around her as if she was in a cave. She screamed until her ears rang and her throat ached. But really, screaming was all she could do.

She couldn't hear the shooting over her own shrieks. The militiamen had overcome their own hesitation and were fighting back. There were sixteen militiamen who were drivers and passengers in the convoy. Of the sixteen, several were strictly drivers and retreated in fear toward the vehicles. The problem was that a couple of zombies were coming from the other direction and had found their way undetected into the mix of parked vehicles.

A young man of perhaps twenty was trying to get back to the pickup truck he had been driving when he ran unsuspecting into one of the zombies behind them. He cried out in terror when the gnashing jaws sank themselves into his neck just below his ear. The creature, quite literally quaking with delight at the taste of warm flesh, pulled away a merciless mouthful of bloody skin and, still chewing, dived down for another bite. With his carotid artery now severed and both his vision and his balance fading, the young man fell to his knees and succumbed to the attack.

Another of the militiamen, while firing his shotgun from his hip and backing away calmly, lost his footing when he stepped from the pavement onto the shoulder of the road and did not anticipate the change in height of the ground beneath his feet. He fell backward, discharging the shotgun into the air. One of the zombies took the opportunity to pounce. One of its knife-like fingers burrowed itself into his calf right through his pant leg. The militiaman pulled a pistol from his belt and fired four rounds into the top of the beast's skull, spreading bone fragments and teeth all over the man's legs and feet.

Already on his back and wounded, the man made an easy target for two more of the undead, who fell upon him like hyenas on a wounded gazelle. He shot his pistol a couple more times but to no effect.

The other men were faring a little better. They discharged their rifles, shotguns, and pistols in a furious storm of smoke and death. There was little to no discipline in their fighting, but it was effective. Soon, all of the zombies were dispatched and the shooting ceased.

Claire's screams were still erupting from the squad car. The zombie preoccupied with devouring her was still trying to get enough of himself into the car to be able to pick that seemingly low hanging fruit. He jostled and wrestled with his body to be able to get in a better position to be able to reach her. No matter what he did seemed to matter and his limited reasoning ability did not allow him to fully comprehend the futility of his efforts. He simply continued to reach and stretch, unaware and apparently not caring that he was tearing and splitting his deteriorating skin and leaving dark streaking patches of bodily fluid on the vehicle's partially raised window and door.

Many of the militiamen had recovered from the skirmish and watched Claire's predicament with amusement. They snickered and giggled to one another and dropped comments about Claire bringing this on herself.

After watching for several moments, Howard decided that it was prudent to end the game. He stepped forward and tried to pull the beast away by using its collar as a lever. Its clothing was damp and mildewy to the touch and seemed to hang on its frame, like a soft exoskeleton. He thought to himself that it would be much easier if he could shoot the damned thing, but he didn't want to do any damage to his car. He was proud of his car and didn't want anything to happen to it. And so, he pulled even harder on the fiend who was lodged in the passenger side window of his car.

On the third tug, the zombie shifted position and poured out of the window. He landed awkwardly on top of Howard but then turned with the agility of a predatory cat and found himself face to face with Howard. Cracked and dirty teeth, he lunged at Howard, who barely held his attacker at bay. This all was happening so fast that no one else had been able to react. The other men had been caught unaware and were stunned at the sudden turn of events.

The man in black stepped forward and kicked the brutish creature in the side of the head. It was enough to upset the balance of power that was rapidly tipping away from Howard. The two scrambled again and Howard was getting the better of the thing this time. Howard laid his hand against its leathery cheek and began to force its head into the side of the car repeatedly. Fissures began to form in the thing's forehead as its skull began to crack.

Howard looked at the man in black and smiled. He was pulling back his hand for one final bruising pummeling when the ghoul shifted its head slightly and Howard's hand slid right off its face, leaving Howard defenseless. The zombie didn't hesitate. Its thrashing, jagged teeth and black, rotting gums fell onto Howard's forehead above his right eye. It gnawed skin and eyebrow away from bone and chewed it hungrily.

There wasn't time given for a second bite as the man in black had drawn his pistol from its hip holster. He pulled the trigger and pressed the gun's barrel to the zombie's skull. Though much of the fluid in the zombie's body had long since dried, there was enough to create a sickly Rorschach spatter design on the dirty door of the squad car.

Howard pushed the thing off of him and sat up, pressing his palm against the gushing wound above his eye. He took a handkerchief from an inside jacket pocket and used that to wipe away some of the blood and then held the stained cloth to the ghastly injury. Much of the flowing blood ignored the cloth and continued to pour down the bridge of his nose and onto his lap.

Howard said through clenched jaws, "Sorry. Sorry. I guess he just.... Sorry. Do you think I could go back with you fellas? You can do whatever you need to back there. I'd just like to say good-bye."

The man in black waited for Howard to look up and then nodded slowly. He said, "Yeah, Howard. Whatever you need."

Looking back down, Howard said, "Thanks. That means—"

The heavy revolver in the man in black's hand barked, ending both Howard's sentence and his life. His blood mixed with the coagulated fluids of the zombie already spread across the car's door.

One of the other militiamen looked at the man in black. "Kind of cold, wasn't it, Carter?"

With no compassion whatsoever, the man in black known as Carter said, "You get bitten you can expect the same. Let's get the truck fixed. Someone needs to siphon the gas outta this piece of shit."

The same militiaman asked, "We leaving Howard's car here?"

Again with ice in his words, Carter answered, "Yeah. You wanna stay too?"

There was no answer needed to that rhetorical question. No one was willing to challenge Carter or his judgments. He was more than merely intimidating. There was a ruthless disregard burning behind his cold eyes that set everyone on edge. When it came to terror, zombies had nothing on this guy.

"Kyle, Will, get that damned truck fixed and back on the road. Pete, move that murderin' bitch into the truck with those kids. The rest of you, this ain't no leisure trip. We got a job to do. I want pickets to stand watch. Any more skins show up, I don't want to be surprised again. Now, everyone's got somethin' to do, so let's get to it."

The group of onlookers were frozen in their steps and staring at Howard's warm corpse, seemingly unable to tear themselves away. Of course, their lack of action solicited anger from Carter who shouted, "Get your fucking asses moving! Now!"

From the back seat of the car, Claire watched all of this unfold. The threat of the undead had been mitigated for the time being, but she was more worried now than she had been before. Carter was the scariest person she had ever seen and the authority he wielded had the effect of making everything he did or said okay.

38

When their truck came to the junction where the Seward Highway split between continuing south to Seward or becoming the Sterling Highway and heading toward the Kenai area, Neil took his foot from the gas and let them come to a rolling stop. He wasn't certain what he was going to do at this point, but knew something needed to be done. He needed to know where to take them and the only one in the vehicle who had that information was their captive.

He said calmly, but his voice cracked slightly, "Well, we've got some decisions to be made about where we are headed." He turned in his seat and spoke directly to the young man sitting next to Della. "Are you going to make this easy or hard on yourself? I've been thinking about this since we got in the truck and I'll be honest, I have no interest in torturing you. I do need information though, and if you're not willing to share it with me, then I don't think I have a choice in the matter."

Neil was quiet for a second or two, hoping that the answers to his questions would somehow materialize magically. Emma seized upon the delay to say, "Neil may not be willing to torture you, but I am. You see, I don't really care. You may think that a woman wouldn't be capable of.... Well, let's just say you don't know what I am capable of and neither do I."

Della looked at both Neil and Emma and quieted them with her caramel-colored eyes. Her expression held something that approached contempt or possibly shame. She couldn't believe these nice people could think that way. She had seen some pretty ugly things committed by some even uglier people in her days; abuse, beatings, and some killings. When she looked at Steve in the driver's seat and at that nutty woman next to him, she didn't see the kind of crazy that would drive someone to such extreme behavior. Although, to be fair, the woman seemed like she may be headed for the deep end. Pushed much farther and she might just be capable of...well, Della didn't want to have to explore those possibilities.

Steve, the boy sitting next to the passenger door, he hadn't said a word...not a peep. Della knew when them other fellas took that pretty young girl that Steve would be hurting, but his silent suffering had Della a little concerned. Was he gonna hold all that pain inside and let it build like in an old time pressure cooker? When that boy did finally blow his top, it was gonna be messy for everyone around him. She didn't think he would do anything to this boy next to her, but she couldn't be certain. When a person makes all their decisions from a hurting heart rather than his head, surprises were bound to ensue. So Della had been keeping a careful eye on him, lest Steve turn around and slit this boy's throat as he sat there.

That would be a damned shame, especially given what she had learned. While Neil was lost in his thoughts and Jerry and Emma were drifting in Della's resonant tune, Della had also been talking with the boy. They spoke with voices just short of a whisper. They exchanged Bible verses at first. Steve, their captive, knew his Bible, almost as well as she did. She was impressed with his knowledge of the book. She believed he had somehow forgotten its meaning and its messages throughout, but he knew the words. They talked about God and His Plan and that the suffering around them all fit into that grand scheme. She didn't intimidate and she didn't threaten, but she also neither placated nor absolved. She talked about the greater good and how she thought people should treat one another. She shared details of her life. With her words, she painted images of a rundown, poor existence. Della's life had been full of deprivation and loss. She had seen death early in her days when her father died with his head in Della's lap. She was a young girl then and his death triggered a cascade of hunger, displacement, neglect, and finally solitude. And despite all of that or, perhaps, because of it, she never lost her faith. She held onto it while everything else in her life faded and disappeared.

The boy listened to her intently. Her voice was so deep and so quiet, it was like listening to the echo of someone else's thoughts. But listen he did. On more than one occasion, his chest tightened and he had to control his breathing to stifle a building sob. At first he tried to justify what he had done to others. He tried to suggest that, ultimately, the people they took were much better off after they came back to the camp. They had food and safety. They were given warm, dry housing.

To that, Della said, "That's what they said to the slaves all them years ago. Do you think they better off? They come and go as they please? Do you make them do the work that none of you is willing to do? When the women say no, do you stop?"

Della's last words created a pool of glistening water in the corners of his eyes. He nodded his head and let the tears fall and then he shook his head from side to side. He pleaded, "I didn't want to. Them other fellas made me or they said they would do the same to me. I was scared...too scared to say anything. Too scared to do anything. That's why I go out foraging all the time. I don't want to be back at the camp. I can't—"

"Steve, you know what you have to do," Della said.

"How'd you know my name was Steve?"

"Because that's what it is, Steve."

Looking at her in bewilderment, he said that he would tell them where they needed to go. He couldn't be a part of what they were doing any more. His conscience wouldn't let him. He told her some of what she needed to know and would tell her the rest as they got closer.

And now, as they sat at the Sterling Highway turn off, Della smiled her flashing white teeth. "Steve here said we needed to turn off here and head toward Soldotna. He said he'd show us how to find that girl and them kids. He knows them other boys that was with him are up to no good and he don't want no part of that no more. Ain't that right, Steve?"

The boy militiaman who really was named Steve looked up and choked back the fading tears. He nodded. "I'll show you where to go but I won't help none of you kill no one. They may not be the best people, but until right now they was the only thing I thought well enough of to call family. I don't think it'd be right if I was pullin' the trigger. If you do it right, you may not have to kill anyone no how."

Sensing the questions and the doubts, Della said finally, "You can trust Steve now. He found his way back to God. Didn't you?"

Emma was about to explode about that last comment, as if that was supposed to make her trust the little snake sitting behind her. Emma's disdain for all things religious carried a very short fuse and when it was lit, the explosion was typically immediate. Neil sensed her agitation, likely through her noticeably clenched jaw, and laid his hand upon hers. He threaded his fingers between hers and squeezed. Her jaw loosened slightly but she pulled her hand away.

She realized it was just a gesture of friendship, but she wasn't interested. A friend could be lost just as easily as a lover and, again, she wasn't interested. She cared about Neil and Jerry and Claire and all of them, but she refused to get so inextricably wrapped in her feelings for another person to ever again have to suffer the pain she felt when she lost Dr. Caldwell. She was surprised Neil didn't have the same cautious, guarded instincts.

Putting both of his hands on the steering wheel, Neil said to all of them, "Soldotna it is then." And into the mirror, he said to both Della and Steve, "Thank you."

39

In a matter of minutes the truck was fixed and new fluids had been added to replace those already lost. To Claire, it was quite apparent this wasn't the first time for this kind of repair. It was so commonplace as to have an exercised system in place to correct it.

During that time, another curious and hungry ghoul appeared. By then, their responses seemed rehearsed. They corralled the *skin* and then used a six foot pole with a lariat at the end to snare its neck. Partially subdued and constrained, the zombie was unable to turn and ward off the militiaman who approached from behind to plunge a combat knife into the base of its skull. It seemed almost methodical for them.

The truck fixed, two of the men came for Claire, who was still bound and in the back of the car. They opened the door and pulled her out by grabbing a combination of her hair and her shirt, which ended up around her head. The whistles and catcalls were enough to chill Claire's blood. She thought to herself that it was already beginning and this was nothing. She loathed considering her fate and the ugliness that would likely accompany it. She tried to wiggle her shirt back down, but her movements only created more of a stir for the men. She decided to stop and let herself be dragged by her arms to the truck. She steeled herself to the comments and the pats on her backside as she passed some of the militiamen.

She was literally thrown into the back of the panel truck, her exposed back slapping hard against the cold metal floor. She once again found herself winded and struggling to find her breath. There were more hands on her but these were soft and warm. They weren't grabbing and pinching her skin or tugging on her bra or pants. The hands eased her shirt back down to where it belonged.

When she was finally able to see again, her vision was filled with the familiar faces of four children. Seeing the relief in her eyes, Danny carefully hugged himself against Claire giving as well as receiving comfort. Jules then spilled herself across both of them in a warm wave of damp happiness. The three hugged and sniffled all over one another for several long, emotional moments.

"I didn't know if I'd ever see any of you again," Claire said. "Do you know where they are taking us?" They both shook their heads but said nothing.

"Have you heard them say anything? Maybe what they plan to do with us?" Again her question was met with apologetic stares and shaking heads.

The other two children joined them, huddling together to share their warmth and gather their strength. Danny produced a pocket knife he had hidden in his shoe and cut Claire's bindings. Although her arms welcomed the freedom and comfort, Claire was concerned Danny may have to answer for the concealed weapon eventually. For the time being, however, she was too busy massaging her cramping arm muscles to place much concern for what might happen sometime in the future. She figured they had some time to come up with an explanation for her freedom, which might allow Danny to conceal the knife again.

Before they climbed back onto the road to finish the trip back to their base, one of the men hopped from the GMC truck in which he was riding. The other vehicles were merging onto the road, the lead Humvee already out of sight. The lanky man ran over to the squad car, reached onto the car's dash, and turned on the red and blue flashing lights on the car's top. Like the expanding ripples of waves from a stone dropped in a pool, the red and blue pulses spread out across the road and trees in mesmerizing strobes.

The man ran back to the opened passenger side door and climbed in saying, "Howard woulda' liked that I think. The pain in the ass deserved better."

His sentiment was answered with a quiet but approving nod from the truck's driver. They kicked up a cloud of dust and gravel as their tires spun and they sped back onto the highway at the tail end of their caravan. Behind them, the dazzling lights continued to burn their enthusiastic funeral dirge for Howard and the other members of the militia recently lost.

40

The Sterling Highway was a winding, looping road that cut its track through a dense forest and along an often-roiling river. Its beauty was typically overlooked by its past commuters who were so preoccupied with getting to the fishing hole, the river, the campground, or any combination of leisure pursuits. Its charm was also systematically overwhelmed by the sheer volume of traffic and the large recreational vehicles which comprised the many long lines of slow moving vehicles.

Without the distractions, Neil would have been in a better position to appreciate the fading but resolute beauty along the highway. The trees were still holding on to a handful of their leaves in bold defiance to the season. The green, however slight, was a welcome sign of the persistence of life. The flowing river to their left seemed to cut its course without care or concern, another reminder of how things had once been.

This all passed without registering for Neil. He didn't take his eyes from the road passing under them at dizzying speeds. With the information he had been given by Steve, he felt empowered again and on track. At every tight corner, he downshifted to help him control the vehicle but quickly pushed it forward as soon as the road straightened again.

It was on a particularly wide turn that Neil, Emma and Jerry first noticed the flashing red and blue lights ahead. Neil let the truck slow considerably as he considered the possibilities. Was there an accident ahead? Was someone pulled over for speeding? What could those lights possibly mean?

After two more bends, they were upon the scene. In a small parking lot with access to the river beyond, a Soldotna police car sat with its signal lights spinning absently. Around the car and the parking area were the bodies of several decomposing ghouls and two or three fresh corpses whose dark blood rested in gathering pools near their bodies.

"This is all new," Neil remarked. "Like it just happened a little bit ago."

Steve, his hands still tied, peeked over the seat in front of him and nodded his head. "That's Howard's car and I bet that's Howard on the ground next to it. He was with us on our supply run."

Jerry broke his silence by asking angrily, "Is that what you call it? A supply run? Where does kidnapping figure into that? I mean, what 'supplies' were you looking for that you could've gotten confused with taking someone against her will?"

Neil didn't interrupt or redirect. Jerry's questions filled the interior of their truck and looked squarely at Steve for an answer. Steve, for his part, didn't shy away nor did he conceal the shame he felt for having to answer it. "I was just looking for food and fuel and maybe survivors that needed our help. I didn't mean for...we were..." Steve felt the knot of guilt tightening itself around his windpipe. "I was wrong and I knew what we were doing was wrong but I was too scared to say so. I want to help you find your friends. I wanna help. They can't be that far off now. I'm surprised Carter let them turn on those lights. He's usually more careful than that."

Jerry, his anger still stoked and burning bright, shook his head and looked out the window again. Off the road slightly and obviously drawn to the pulsating lights like a moth to a flame, a zombie, with his shredded clothes and discolored skin, was meandering awkwardly toward them. Jerry said, "We got company on this side."

"Yeah. We've got a couple over here too," Neil said. "I guess we should get going. Huh? Those lights will be drawing them in."

Emma said, "Maybe we should take these fools first. There are only three of them. We could—"

Neil interrupted her by putting the truck back into gear and saying, "No time. We have to catch up to Claire and the others."

They sped away, leaving the gathering menace behind them. They felt like they were getting closer. For that reason, Neil drove with a little more caution. While still pushing the truck's speed above the posted limit, he knew that he needed to be mindful of running them into a trap. This Steve kid seemed to be on the level, but he could have been just as easily leading them into an ambush.

41

When the truck came to a sudden stop, Claire and the children gripped one another in the darkness. They heard more voices, including some that sounded distinctly feminine. Claire tried to get a sense of where they had arrived. It sounded like a bustling center of activity. It sounded like the recent past. It sounded roughly like a fair or a market.

It seemed like an age before the truck's back door finally rolled up. The din of voices quieted at the sight of the newcomers. Standing exposed and seemingly on display like animals in a menagerie, Claire and the kids hiding behind her gazed back at the scores of eyes looking up at them. There was a loud pause while everyone considered what would happen next.

The steel gray skies overhead were eagerly yielding to the forceful advances of evening. It would be dark soon which meant that nearly a day had passed since they had been taken. A lot had happened but Claire was more concerned about what was still to come. Darkness and the night had long been associated with misdeeds and evil. Perhaps it was the anonymity of darkness that encouraged the evil deeds of men. There was little to no accountability beneath a concealing shroud.

If torment was one of Claire's concerns, she needn't bother with her worries. She stood in the back of the truck for a handful of moments before she was dragged out by a tangle of grabbing hands. She heard someone say gruffly, "She killed Slade?" and then, "Yeah. Shot him full o'holes." And finally, "Sullivan's gonna be pissed." The last comment made by several different voices was met with a concerned hush.

The kids were all pulled away from her and led somewhere out of her sight. She was being carried away by her outstretched arms and legs. Countless hands found their way under her loose shirt, pinching at her skin and roughly rubbing the feminine curves held beneath her cotton bra. Claire tried to ignore the gruffness of the touching. She was in a loading bay of some sort at the back of a building. In the area around the bay, the other cars of the convoy had joined still other cars and trucks all parked in a fenced parking lot. That was all she was able to see before she was carried through two sets of double doors.

Claire was carried through a series of doors and hallways, lined with lockers and other doors, and came to the realization that she was in a school. She wondered to which school she had been taken but ultimately it didn't matter. Her scared eyes scanned the walls and doorways for any recognizable banners or names which might give her a clue. Her wondering was cut short, however, when she was stopped and handcuffed to a hospital gurney in a room with a single panel of working overhead fluorescent lights illuminated faintly by a lone bulb. The scant light buzzed and flickered as the failing exposed bulb resisted burning itself out like all of the others which sat around it like lifeless glass skeletons. To her right, was a counter with a couple of sinks and to her left was a series of large, heavy workbench-like stations. It looked like a shop room or some other technical classroom.

She felt alone and scared, but her sense of isolation was short-lived. She heard someone clearing his throat from over in a dark corner just out of her sight. She tried to angle her head so that she could see better, but it was for naught. He was in a blind spot intentionally.

He spoke with a quiet menace. "I hear you killed my cousin. Damned shame really. He was always braver than he was smart. Me, I woulda' sent in someone else to take the first bullets. I understand it was at least quick for him. I guess I could judge that as a kindness...but I won't. You see, Slade was the only family I had left in the whole world. He wasn't much, but he was mine. Sounds kinda like a bumper sticker. Doesn't it? Well, I promised his mother that I'd take care of her boy. Aunt Lilly was always my favorite, so I meant it when I promised it to her. And it didn't change my mind or my promise when I drove the business end of a ball-peen hammer into her skull and left her to gurgle and spit her last filthy breaths in the middle of her fucking kitchen either."

She heard him take a drag from a cigarette and then fill the small partitioned room with smoke. He said in the same, disturbingly calm voice, "Now you're wondering if I killed her before or after the shit hit the fan. To me, it doesn't really matter. Never really did." He paused and took a drag from his cigarette. The smoke twisting in lazy circles above her head was the only evidence, other than the icy voice, that she wasn't alone.

His voice, playing in the shadows like the dark echoes of a cave, whispered, "People say that tragedy...war and such...can bring out the best and the worst in people. I like to think that maybe all that's happened is that I can just be me finally."

Claire wanted to crane her neck around so that she could see better, but decided against it. She was afraid that such a position might look too compromised and might invite unwanted attention. A moment later, she realized the attention was coming her way whether she wanted it or not.

She didn't hear him approach and had no way to expect it when her cheek, just below her eye, began to sizzle and burn from a cigarette cherry pressed against it. Her surprise came close to suppressing the pain; but when the momentary adrenaline surge subsided, Claire's skin screamed in pain. She tried to withhold her shriek, but it forced its way out anyway.

Through the pain and her terror, Claire heard and glimpsed a flame sparking to life from a Zippo lighter. She heard a long pull from another cigarette and waited for his next move.

42

On the far side of the fenced area at the back of the school, Danny shielded Jules, Nikki, and Paul from a voracious, growling, gray-skinned beast. The chain links separating the zekes from the four of them didn't seem nearly strong enough as it sagged and bowed like a sheet of sail in the wind. But as they backed away from the one fence, they only drew closer to the one behind them, which had more of the hungry ghouls waiting on the other side.

The children had been placed in the center kennel of a block of dog kennels atop a cold slab of wet concrete which had once been basketball courts. Sitting at the epicenter of the demons' attention, Danny's stomach was churning and turning as the undeads' sonic buzz became unbearable.

Just short of whimpering, Jules said softly, "I'm real scared, Danny."

"Me too."

"What are we gonna do?"

Danny didn't hesitate a second before he answered with as much reassurance as possible, "Neil will come for us. You just wait and see. Neil will get us outta here."

The tears coming now, Jules asked, "But what if he doesn't?"

"He'll come," Danny promised her. "He always comes. You'll see."

By that time, they had all started crying as they moved by inches forward and back, staying just out of reach of the snapping, snarling jaws only so many inches from their own faces. A particularly nasty wet, guttural groan that reeked of waste and decay oozed through the fence behind them, making them all jump nervously.

In their terror, none of the children could hear the wicked laughter coming from a scattered few spectators enjoying the sport. They also couldn't see the handful of people, mostly women and old, demoralized men, who walked aimlessly around the loading bay area. They didn't appear to be prisoners, but they were anything but free. They appeared to be moving and stacking stores of supplies in cardboard boxes, wooden crates, and aluminum tins which were unloaded from a series of trucks. It wasn't necessarily back breaking labor, but it was enough to keep them occupied and gave them purpose.

If Danny and Jules had been able to see Alec, they might have been jealous, but there was really no need. Alec was at least inside and away from immediate harm, but he was far from safe from his own anguish.

He was first tied down to a hard, wooden bench and was subjected to a form of water boarding by a man everyone called Carter, whom Alec had seen in charge of the operation in which he had been abducted. Carter would alternate between administering the torture himself and directing others in the proper method. Carter was a tall, dark man with black hair and eyes to match. He always wore a black tee shirt and snug, black Levi's. His arms were thick and wiry, the many tendons and veins throughout showing through his skin in many places. The mint scented chewing tobacco forever tucked in his front lip preceded his presence. Alec began to dread the aroma because when it became stronger he knew that a new level of suffering was about to be introduced.

This went on for hours, during which he was denied rest or even reprieve from his suffering. Later he was beaten with bamboo sticks while wildly loud music was played directly into his ears from ear buds which were held in place by tightly wrapped layers of duct tape. The water, the music, the pain, and the deprivation all took their toll on him until he was completely pliable.

Alec was bruised and bloodied, but Carter was always careful not to actually hurt the boy. They needed more loyal troops and someone like Alec was a very good potential recruit. It was all about applying the right amount of pressure and then offering a seemingly generous and protective hand.

The time it took for Carter to turn Alec's allegiance was amazingly short. The boy's exhaustion and hunger contributed in no small part to the easy success in making him join with his new brothers. Of course, under the conditions in which Alec had been kept, time lost its distinction. It became soft and doubtful.

Poor Alec's already fragile soul was incapable of resisting such torture and so he did the only thing his broken mind could think to do. He became one of them in a matter of hours, but Alec Houser had actually fled, never to return again. Alec Houser ceased to exist.

43

The place to which Claire and the children had been taken was indeed a school. It was once Skyview High School, although it would barely be recognized as that now. Once a place of learning and community, it was now a bunkered fortress...a redoubt in the wilderness.

As a structure, it was as far removed from its original purpose as it possibly could be. The people, too, were different. At first, they were just frightened souls hiding from the gathering threats of doom.

They hid behind locked doors and closed windows, hoping such simple measures would suffice. That's how it was all over the area. No one knew what was happening or how to prepare for it.

When people from Kenai and Soldotna began to flee from the undead uprising which seemed to be spreading from Anchorage like a swarm of locusts threatening to consume anything and everything in its path, some people flocked to the local schools and government agencies. That was just what people did. When trouble began to percolate and build, local police stations, firehouses, borough and city government offices, and schools saw their parking lots begin to fill with concerned, scared people who sought protection and answers.

As the plague spread its evil fingers into Soldotna and then Kenai, those sites became ghoul magnets. All of the people seeking protection and all the public servants trying to find answers became fodder for the slaughter.

Skyview High School, just south of Soldotna's city center, saw a few desperate souls make their way there as well, though its location led to far fewer people congregating there. In fact, most people, once they were on the highway heading south, drove right past the high school and continued toward

Homer, which sat at the far end of the road more than an hour away. What none of the people who sought refuge at the school could have known was that it was the sparse numbers of people hiding there which helped keep them largely off of the proverbial butcher's block.

The couple dozen people who did come to Skyview waited for a short while and watched the news from televisions or the numerous computers throughout the school. When the news feeds from Anchorage stopped broadcasting, they all rightly feared the worst. Some decided to venture south while others decided to weather the hard times in the sanctuary they had found.

Some had barely survived encounters with the undead, escaping with just their lives while others close to them hadn't been so lucky. They shared their stories and their sorrow. The talking and story-telling also motivated all of them. They knew their safety would require some work on their parts.

Taking it upon themselves to protect their location, a few of the men and women at the school wandered out into the back parking lot where several full sized school buses were parked. Luckily, the keys had been left in the ignitions, so the buses were moved to make a horseshoe shaped enclosure around the front doors. Outward facing windows on the first floor were fortified with whatever materials could be found. They all did their best to prepare themselves and their new, temporary home for the storm that was headed their way. They had food and water for the time being and felt somewhat secure, though the weapons they had were minimal at best.

With the handful of hunting rifles and various caliber pistols they had, a few felt comfortable enough to venture out into the abandoned edges of Soldotna. They grabbed some lumber and other building materials from a home improvement store on the far side of the river. Some close encounters with the aggressive living dead had all of them second guessing the purpose and the efficacy of the excursions, though their needs seemed to be increasing by the day.

Survivors traveling the treacherous roads found the oasis and hope in the middle of the Alaskan wilderness on the highway between Soldotna and Homer. The handful of lost souls grew to a sizeable group of more than two dozen and their secured compound continued to grow. They found generators to power refrigerators and electric heaters. A Community Health Aide established a clinic of sorts in the school nurse's office and kept it stocked with supplies pillaged from a local clinic and nearby drug stores. While it would be a stretch to call it a thriving community, the little village was stable and relatively safe.

Of course, their activity attracted the attention of a zombie or two on several occasions but those few threats were dealt with and disposed of immediately. The first couple stumbled down the long drive connecting Skyview with the highway and looked simply confused at first. The two horrific ghouls, watched by a group of survivors sitting on top of one of the buses, appeared less and less normal the closer they got. Some folks thought that perhaps the creatures would lose interest when they realized they couldn't breach their defenses and then wander off. Others entertained ideas of possibly helping the poor souls. The debate continued for quite some time.

After listening to the pair of fiends pound their fists and heads into bloody messes against one of the buses and showing no signs of slowing or realizing anything for a few hours, several men armed with baseball bats taken from a gymnasium equipment room ventured outside their wall. The men formed an arc around the still focused attackers and then waited for the creatures to turn. When the beasts did finally turn about, there was no hesitation on their part. The ghouls leapt at the men fearlessly. Their charge was unexpected and caused panic in a couple of the men. The rabid, thrashing devils fell upon one of the unfortunate men and immediately began to bite and claw at his arms, neck, and face.

The other men started to pummel the two attackers with their bats, but nothing seemed to discourage them. Finally, one of the men hit one of the zombies atop his skull and all of its fighting and biting fury stopped. The other creature was dispatched similarly, but not before the man beneath him had stopped struggling. Upon closer inspection, it was discovered that the brutalized man had also expired.

While the men discussed how to discard the bodies, their comrade who had fallen stood back on his feet. The other men took several steps back in surprise. At first, there was a pause during which no one knew what to do. When the recently dead man lifted his head and looked at the others, every shred of humanity had faded from his eyes, having been usurped by primal hunger. He lunged but was met with a flurry of aluminum and wood as the men swung their bats furiously, their arms fueled with adrenaline and fear. They swung and swung until every bone in the dead man's body was broken, including his skull, which had been pounded nearly flat. Looking at him afterward, they realized they would need snow shovels or some other tool to scoop up the remains.

Fear was still an issue for all of them, but they did their best to hold it outside of their walls, like a fairytale castle of good holding its ground in a dark forest of evil. Knowing how to deal with the monsters emboldened everyone, but when they ventured outside the relative safety of the walls, no one felt anything other than anxious, exposed, and vulnerable.

When Colonel Braxton Edwin Arlen Ross, or Colonel Bear as he preferred, arrived with his organized militia in their military vehicles, with their military look, and, perhaps most strikingly, their military firearms, things began to change quickly. The little community became much more ordered and more secure. Their perimeter expanded with the adding of a fenced area around the loading bay and part of the basketball courts nearby and their numbers continued to grow. Actual building projects, requiring raw building materials, began to emerge. Their growing needs meant additional trips into town, which meant more danger and a greater reliance upon the militiamen or, more to the point, their firearms and other military equipment.

Other changes were taking place too. When the community first emerged, it was an organic group with each doing his or her part based upon the skills and experience that each brought to the collective. Everyone had an equal voice, because everyone had an equal share of the risk. Of course there was friction when personalities or opinions clashed, but compromise helped all of them to survive despite all the odds against it.

The stratification that occurred after the militia's arrival was fairly subtle at first but very steady. It didn't take long before Colonel Bear was calling all the shots. Sometimes, decisions seemed to be made strictly on his whim, without an apparent care to the possible outcomes. For instance, when the Colonel decided that the civilians would be better protected if they were all moved from the individual classrooms they had claimed early during the crisis and into the library, he didn't ask and no one put up much of a public objection. It wasn't that the library was any more or less uncomfortable than the classrooms, but there didn't seem to be any reasonable purpose other than to give the militiamen a greater range of options for their own accommodations. Put quite simply, there were those with guns and the willingness to use them and then there was everyone else.

Still reeling from the dramatic and terrifying shifts in their world, the original residents of the bastion were hard pressed to find their voice of protest. For the most part, they simply nodded their heads and consented to the Colonel's directives. Safety, after all, was foremost on their minds at the time.

The biggest challenge for most of the civilians was moving from the second floor, perceived as slightly more secure, to the ground floor for their living quarters. The library's windows were covered over with heavy wooden tables and lumber, but those measures only went so far to calm frayed nerves. The library, now illuminated with the sparing light of a handful of fluorescent tubes and a smattering of battery-powered lanterns, began to resemble a prison for refugees.

Without showers and no water to clean their clothes, rising body odor permeated the walls of books which had been moved and adjusted to afford some level of privacy for those forced to live in such conditions. All of this was done and endured in the name of survival, despite the fact that the militiamen were not subject to the same conditions or deprivations.

Those men lived in the classrooms primarily on the second floor. Many of them had private rooms all to themselves and enjoyed such basic comforts as beds and working electrical outlets. The divide between the haves and the have-nots was stark and troubling.

And troubles certainly followed. Such disparity cannot persist indefinitely. Things would first go from bad to worse for one segment within that arrangement.

A few young women moved upstairs, seeking comfort and security. They were willing to become *wives* of some of the militiamen, some even having mock ceremonies with vows and as much pomp and circumstance as could be mustered. The wives would clean clothes, maintain living quarters, and, of course, avail themselves of their new husbands' every nocturnal whim.

The first handful of wives came somewhat willingly. They were recent widows nearly paralyzed with fear or orphaned daughters or sisters who dreaded the agonizing solitude. Those with husbands or boyfriends or family of any sort stayed in the library...at first.

When a pair of covetous militia eyes spied the soft feminine form of a wife, the status quo changed. It was no longer a matter of choice. The woman was taken against her will and the protesting husband was beaten within an inch of his life by a beer-plied group of militiamen. The next to suffer the same fate was a father of a late teenage girl.

Other complaints were met with more intimidation and more threats. Food supplies and other materials gathered in trips were stockpiled in the militia-controlled kitchen and doled out to the others after the Colonel deemed that his men and women had been properly fed and equipped first. It was largely his men, after all, who risked their lives on the excursions and supply runs. Because they shouldered the greater risk, they were entitled to more of the spoils.

Continued objections by the "civvies", as the Colonel referred to all those outside of his militia circle, led to mandatory duty rosters for all civilian residents. These duties included emptying latrine buckets, building projects, and any other job the Colonel could imagine.

No one in the little community realized that their home, once a school, was now an ad hoc military installation under the official command of the Colonel. But looking around after a few short weeks, most recognized their little refuge had changed dramatically. They all felt safer. But at what cost?

The sinister reality of their situation was finally apparent to all of them when another woman was being forcibly taken. Her brother, seething with contempt and rage, flew at her abductors. He swung his fist as hard as he could and struck one of them. The militiaman's large, gin blossomed nose was crushed, spurting jets of thick, red blood. The other two uniformed men conducting the raid each plunged their long combat knives into the brother's chest again and again, finally standing up and shooting him several times for good measure.

This all took place in the hall, just outside the library entrance. The young girl, barely a teenager, was dragged away as her brother's life drained away onto the floor. Everyone still in the library watched all of this grisly scene play out without any apparent way to stop it. They cowered and waited and watched.

If it wasn't before, the dark costs of their decision to allow the militia to join and then gain control of their lives became apparent to all of them...and still no one acted.

44

Looking down as he spoke so that his words were barely audible, the old man with a grizzly, gray beard and an equally grizzled and gray suit said, "We should be ashamed of ourselves. What are their plans for those kids?"

The old man was among a group of people reinforcing the fence barricade with sheets of pilfered plywood and lumber. They had already covered any exposed first floor windows similarly. The fence they were trying to fortify was something which had been added by the militia and was, therefore, not completely fastened and secured to the building. In order for the fence to truly do its job, work needed to be done to it.

The other benefit to the work was that it produced a distraction for the people residing at the school. And the people who needed the distraction were all those without guns, which was everybody who wasn't part of the militia.

From their elevated position on the loading dock, a few of the militiamen watched as the work progressed. Ostensibly, they were there to provide security if any skins decided to show their faces. Everyone knew better though. The men and women with guns were as much or perhaps more about watching the workers as anything else. They were the eyes and the ears of the Colonel.

Other projects had also been implemented to improve their situation over the past weeks. When all was said and done, all the projects simply served to pass the time. And that was exactly what it felt like they were doing again.

A woman to his left, her head held up recklessly, said, "They had a woman and another person too."

Another man, this one younger but appearing just as beaten as the older man, said, "I heard one of those bastards got shot. I mean one of our "Protectors" that is. Got killed too." He looked back to the wall he was helping to construct and returned to hammering nails into the wood.

The old man answered, "Good. I hope the son of a bitch suffered. I figure it wasn't the Colonel. How about Carter or Sullivan? Either of them maybe?" Defiantly, he dropped his hammer and stood back from the wooden palisade which was rapidly reaching completion.

The younger man shook his head apologetically.

Sighing, the old man shook his own head and spat. "Seems like a bad time to find ourselves stuck in a rut of bad luck."

Her anger flushing her cheeks, the woman, her hair a storm of knotted blonde locks, bristled. "Well, I'm not going to sit here and just let them turn that poor girl into..." She paused, out of breath and wishing for a cigarette, but then continued, "That's just not gonna happen! Not again!"

The younger man paused his own hammering. "Keep your voice down," he warned. "Christ, I don't want them killing any more of us. I don't think I can take anymore butchering. I can't stop thinking about that day and then every day since. It's bad but it could be a whole lot worse."

Fed up, the woman snapped, "That's bullshit Daniel and you know it."

"Would you rather we were all dead?" asked Daniel.

The woman fired back, "That's bullshit too."

Pulling her further down the wall and away from watching eyes and listening ears, Daniel hissed at her, "Are you saying that they won't shoot one of us next? They've already shown us what they are capable of. The only difference between those militia assholes and the skins on the other side of the wall is that the militia boys don't eat us after they kill us. What do you want us to do? I mean, what do you think we really *can* do? Jess, I agree with you. But Christ, what can we do about any of it? They'd probably do the same to you that they're planning with that other girl just like all the others and I'd be shot or thrown in with those things in the dog kennels or—"

"I know, I know," Jess, the blonde woman, interrupted him. "It's still bullshit. Royce is right. We should be ashamed. And I am." She thought back on those days that led her to this place filled with fear and regret. That day so long ago seemed more like the images from a long forgotten movie that was on in the background during one of her many naps than memories from her past. In disjointed bits and pieces, the images presented themselves at unpredictable times.

The only truly clear memory she had was when they first learned that something horrible had set upon Anchorage and was ravaging the city and its population like a voracious blaze. She had been in her cubicle at work trying to force herself through the endless bureaucratic processes of the modern office when a breathless co-worker burst in and demanded that they all go online to see what was happening. Each of the six of them went to different web based news sources and saw for themselves the chaos erupting in Alaska's largest city, which lay just so many hours up the only road from where they were. Most of them simply stood up from their desks and departed, not certain if they would ever see the office or their co-workers again. A few quiet, tearful farewells were shared, but fear muted all of their thoughts. There was no reporting to supervisors or asking permission. In point of fact, most of the supervisors had already gone.

Jess sat at her workstation for several minutes after everyone else had gone. She had never felt so alone in the office in all her many years of working there. She was very nearly stunned into a stupor, thinking about all those souls she knew in Anchorage and wondering if each was safe. Her first actual thought was of her daughter.

She dialed first from her office phone and then from her cell phone but continually encountered that nauseating series of beeps and then the condescending voice informing her that her call could not be completed as dialed...all circuits were busy...or simply the fast busy signal which was the death knell of a failing communique. She was directed to voice mail time and again, which she filled with increasingly desperate messages.

Her boyfriend Bob had taken her teenaged daughter, Syd, with him in their boat on a late season fishing trip. Jess had burned through all of her leave on prior excursions and was unable to join the two of them for this last trip. She had been talked out of calling in sick to be able to join them, and presently regretted it. She would feel much more comfortable if she could somehow talk to them to ensure that her daughter was safe.

Leaving one final message on Bob's phone, she got up from her desk and went out to her car, which sat in a now empty parking lot in the old Carrs Mall in Kenai. She made it back to her house before the roads filled with desperate motorists trying to flee the city. By the time she had arrived to her largely undeveloped neighborhood, which was closer in kinship to the collective prairie homesteads of America's past, full blown panic was starting to take hold. Cars and trucks of all sizes and varieties started to crowd the highway, desperate to put every inch of pavement as possible in their rearview mirrors. Most towed either fishing boats or, in some cases, small aircraft. Like the frustrated line at the Division of Motor Vehicles, the traffic forced its way in frustrating fits and starts down the highway.

Her first instinct was to get back on the road and head south to the boat launch in Ninilchik. She was, however, wise enough to realize that she wouldn't be driving anywhere any time soon. There was very little point in contributing to the growing mess on the main road on the opposite side of the trees.

She sat there at the window for the better part of the afternoon and evening, sipping a beer absently as she watched the nearly motionless line of headlights on the highway. She listened to a chorus of honking horns and revving engines. The television blathered in the background for some time until a test pattern appeared on the screen. The signal, which originated in Anchorage, had been lost but it was of little interest to her. The Pope could have passed by outside and she would have been oblivious to it. She worried about her daughter. She was at once thankful that she was away from whatever horrible thing might be coming down the road and fretful that Syd was out of her sight and therefore away from her protective maternal sensibilities.

When her cell phone began to vibrate excitedly on the end table next to her, Jess nearly leapt clear of her pants trying to answer it. It was a text from Bob. He said that he'd heard what was happening in Anchorage, that Syd was safe with him, but he was trying to figure out how to come for her. He'd heard the National Guard or Coast Guard or someone had closed the roads to try and contain the problem. He wasn't sure how he was going to get to her but he was going to try.

Crying as she punched letters on the tiny keypad, she explained to him in her best text speak that keeping her daughter safe was much more important than his coming to get her. She said that she would try and make it to them instead. He protested, but she held her ground and made him understand that he needed to protect her daughter.

He, of course, promised but also said that he would find a way back to her. In mid-text, the signal bars on her phone disappeared and the words 'No Service' appeared on her screen. Jess remembered wanting to throw the phone across the room but couldn't part herself from the only thing which still might lead to a connection to Bob and Syd. She collapsed on the floor, holding the warm phone against her cheek, the phone's bright lights reflecting in the tears coursing down her cheeks. She hadn't cried with that much abandon in years; she really hadn't any cause.

She remained on the floor for quite some time. The evening gave way to night, which seemed so much darker than usual. The test pattern on the television behind her was the only light she had on in her house.

Jess gathered herself enough to stand on her feet again. Her neck, a constant source of pain and irritation, was throbbing due to the angle at which she had been lying on the floor. She didn't much care for pharmaceuticals in dealing with anything, but she was thankful she let her doctor talk her into having a supply of pain medication on hand just in case.

With the main road in front of her house still full of traffic and the air stirring with the buzz of gears shifting and horns blaring, she realized that her options for leaving at present were fairly limited. She couldn't get on the road and she didn't particularly want to start walking, not knowing what was waiting at the other end of the road. Instead, she swallowed two pain pills, curled up under a blanket on the couch, and fell into a deep slumber.

Sleep was Jess' secret weapon with which she fought stress. Actually, it wasn't that much of a secret and it really wasn't much of a weapon either. When she awoke, the stress was still there but then she also had to deal with the guilt she assessed herself for running from her troubles. Under the present circumstances, it seemed like sleep was as good of an option as any for her to take.

The next morning, Jess woke suddenly, startled. She sat bolt upright from her position on the couch and looked around in the fading darkness. Autumn mornings were crisp and reluctant. The sun, having been on nearly round the clock duty for the past few months, seemed as tired and hungover as she was.

Jess didn't see anything out of place in her house or in the slice of yard she could see through her window. Still, something seemed amiss. She draped the blanket around herself so that it resembled a Roman toga. She wasn't quite sure any respectable Romans would have Hello Kitty as their traditional attire, but she was comfortable with it. She drifted from the living room to the kitchen to turn on the coffee pot and was headed to the bathroom when she heard a sharp, echoing crack outside. It was down the road a bit, but near enough to draw her back to her window to investigate.

She couldn't see clearly due to the angle, but she detected a bit of a commotion up the road. A handful more of the pops convinced her that it was gunshots she was hearing and that she should get herself ready to leave.

Her thinking limited to taking the next step in front of her, she grabbed her car keys, the couple of bottles of water on the top shelf of the refrigerator, and her cell phone and ran out to her car parked in the driveway. She shot a cautious glance over her shoulder as she dropped into her front seat.

There were still people down the road. She thought she recognized one of the men carrying a rifle of some sort across his shoulders, but from that distance it was hard to be certain. Maybe she had seen him at the liquor store or maybe at the Carrs grocery store. He might have been a client of some different component of her office for all she knew. Regardless, with the man were a handful more, all of whom appeared to be armed.

Jess paused in her car, worried that perhaps she didn't want to draw their attention toward her. The keys were already in the ignition, but she seemed incapable of turning the key. She waited and watched, trying to decide what to do next. The air outside was cool but not yet cold, but her breath generated enough warmth to fog the windows and cloud her vision.

From the road and the gathered young men, raised voices and sudden movement caught her attention. Jess wiped a clear but streaked spot on the windshield but was confused by what she thought she was seeing. The four or five men were shouting at something out of sight, but their shouts very quickly gave way to shooting.

They were shooting at someone! *Shooting!*

Jess' hands were shaking uncontrollably as she reached for the key and turned over the car's engine. Thankfully, her car cooperated and started effortlessly. She turned on the defrost which quickly cleared the windows. Feeling trapped, she didn't know what to do next. To her right was the unfinished side of what would eventually become a neighborhood. The paved road gave way to a muddy gravel road which came to an abrupt end in an as of yet incomplete cul de sac. It was a dead end. And if she were to turn left, she would drive straight for the shooting and the insanity that seemed to be taking hold in her neighborhood. There would be no avoiding the armed men standing guard behind the trucks.

Not seeing any feasible options, she put her car into drive and slowly crept out of her driveway. She felt the worried tears burning her eyes and blurring her vision. Jess had no idea what she was going to do once she was spotted by the men, but she had few other options. The men had two trucks sitting nose to nose across the road in the fashion of a police roadblock.

When one of the men spotted her and signaled with his hand as much, Jess felt her heart sink into her stomach and start to boil in her digestive acids. Much to her surprise and relief, he didn't turn the gun on her. He waved to her with a friendly but shaking hand. He didn't appear to pose any immediate threat, despite the gun in his hands.

She stopped her car short of their position. From the angle her car was sitting, she was able to see somewhat under and beyond the two trucks. Jess dismissed the thought as soon as it occurred to her, but she could have sworn she could see bodies lying in the street on the other side of the trucks. *It couldn't be*, she told herself. *It's probably something else entirely.* Bob always told her she had an overactive imagination. She invited his calming demeanor into her memory, trying to soothe the disquieting thoughts to which she was prone.

She was so distracted with what she thought she was seeing that she didn't see one of the young men walking over to her driver side window. He waved to her and started to speak which of course she could not hear through the still closed window. She rolled the window down a bit. "Sorry, what were you saying?"

His eyes may have been able to disguise his fear, but his voice cracked with distress. He asked politely, a slight hint of Texas curling cozily around his words, "You doin' okay?"

She nodded but couldn't find any words with which to answer.

"You hear 'bout what's been happenin'?" Again she nodded.

"You know where you're headed?"

She shrugged, still distracted with the apparent body lying in the road and the disregard with which it was being treated by everyone else.

The man, his face still evincing signs of adolescence, turned his eyes in the same direction as hers. "You...you don't w-want to go that way unless you hafta'," he stammered. "I don't know what's happenin' to them folks, but somethin's makin' em all crazy."

Jess moved her eyes and then her head so that she was facing him again. Her mouth stood partially agape but produced no words.

He looked away. "They just keep comin', no matter what we do. They just don't stop. One of em bit Trey on the hand before he shot it in the face. It was just an old lady who was mad as a dog. She came at em and he pushed her away, but she didn't stop. So he pushed her down but she got back up. Ain't nothin' he could do. The craziest thing was that she just kept bitin' at him like she ain't eaten in a week and he was a big ole T-bone or somethin'. When she bit em, I guess he had enough and shot her. We been shootin' all the others ever since."

She was finally able to ask, "Others?"

He gestured with his chin. "You can see 'em. We ain't murderers. They was...just not right."

Jess put her car into park and removed her foot from the brake. She sat back in her seat and let his revelation settle into her mind. *An old woman.*

Shooting people. Crazy. Dead bodies. Terror.

One of the other men nearer the trucks said with some distress, "I think Trey is gettin' worse."

She got out of the car and walked over to the other man standing beside the truck's open door. With both concern and fear in his eyes, he asked her, "What's wrong with him? It didn't seem like much of a bite, but it just keeps bleeding. It won't stop."

Jess leaned into the truck, the interior of which was heavy with the scent and moisture of perspiration. She could smell something else too. It was a different kind of salty, warm odor which she immediately realized was the aroma of blood. The man was breathing in quick, labored, shallow breaths; his chest barely rising enough to allow air into his lungs. His clothes and the seat in which he was sitting were both streaked with drying patterns of red.

"How long ago did he get bitten?"

The first man with whom the young man had spoken said, "It happened early this mornin'. Just before dawn. She was walking down the street but when she saw us, she started to run at us. We thought maybe she needed help or somethin' but when we could see her face... I ain't never seen no one looked so...mad, I guess. I been around some real mean drunks in my day, but ain't none of them ever look as bad as her. After she bit 'im, we drove outta town and headed down this way. We stopped to pick up Hank over there but Trey looked too sick to do much travelin'. We decided to hole up for a bit, but he just keeps gettin' worse."

Jess realized that Hank was the man she recognized and then remembered that she had indeed seen him in her office. He was standing close to the tail end of the other truck. He looked up, realizing she was still processing his face. "Me and Geraldine ain't workin' out so I was over here visitin' a friend."

She surmised he was admitting to some possible infidelity from the woman with whom he had visited her office. His face was riddled with guilt, but her memory of the woman was hazy at best so there was no need for his blushing cheeks. She nodded, trying her best to absolve him of whatever affront he had committed.

Jess met the rest of the guys as they discussed what to do. The first young man was named Allen. There was a darkly tanned Native man named Simeon. She couldn't decide if he was young or old, but he was certainly weathered. His hands looked like leather work gloves and his cheeks looked as tough as rawhide, and his dark eyes were serious. The final man in the group was Justin, a thin, wiry man in his early thirties whose metabolism had obviously not marched much beyond his adolescence. His arms, while nothing but sinewy muscle, weren't much bigger around than a mop handle. He was the only man not armed with a rifle of some sort. Instead, tucked in the waistband of his Carhartt pants like some suburban gangsta was a semi-automatic pistol. His boxers rising slightly above his sagging pants helped to complete the look in Jess' opinion.

They debated whether to stay or to go, and then they debated which direction to go if they were to leave. Every discussion, however, returned to what to do about Trey, who was still languishing in the growing pool of his own blood. Trey wasn't involved in any of the discussions. Of course, he hadn't been conscious in some time, but he likely would have been excluded anyway. In his last moments of consciousness, he had been delirious and his speech unintelligible. No one wanted to admit it, but it had occurred to all of them at one point or another that Trey was likely dying.

Jess finally asked, "Where the hell were you guys headed when you stopped here in the first place?"

In a jumbled, out of tune chorus, they all answered, "Homer."

She shook her head and huffed. "Then why the fuck don't we just go to Homer?" Jess knew that Bob and Syd would be somewhere near Ninilchik which was just outside of Homer, so heading in that direction would get her closer to them.

Allen said, "Last we heard, the Guard had closed the road between here and there and weren't lettin' no one through."

Undeterred, she answered, "And?"

Hank, the oldest in the group, said, "There's probably a line of cars a mile long down that way. What we gonna do when we get stuck in that?"

Simeon ended the discussion with, "We walk."

Jess seconded his motion with a nod and an approving, "We walk."

45

Jess pulled her car in behind the two trucks and they started on their way out of the neighborhood and down to Homer. As they steered around the dead bodies in the road, Jess refused to look down at them for fear that they might be people she had known. She still didn't know what was happening, but she had to trust that these men, even the slightly off Justin, were not ruthless, cold-blooded killers. There had to be a reason for it.

She was alone in her car and was thankful that none of the men had wanted to ride with her. She wasn't certain how she would have handled such a request. After all, she didn't really know any of them and, desperation or no, she would have felt very compromised.

In the black Chevy in front of her was Justin and Hank with the suffering Trey across the back seat in the full sized cab. His breathing had become raspy and sounded as if his throat and lungs were filling with fluid. Attempts to position his head in such a manner as to allow it to drain had been unfruitful. His condition was critical and was worsening by the minute.

The smaller black GMC, with Simeon at the wheel and Allen sitting next to him, was in the lead. They drove with dire intention, whipping their vehicles into a growling, gravel-spitting frenzy.

The three vehicle convoy was quickly out on the highway heading south. While she could feel herself starting to calm down a bit, Jess was still very much on edge. She was glad to be on the move, but her questions and her concern lingered, but guilt was looming larger for her than any other emotion. She felt guilty for not trying to flee Soldotna sooner. She should have left as soon as she got the news like everyone else. She could have and maybe she would be with Syd at that very moment. But what would she have done if, after she had fled with the rest of Soldotna, Syd and Bob had returned? She would never have forgiven herself if her daughter had come home and not found her mother. At the very least, she had a fair idea of where to find her daughter now and that was exactly what she was going to do. She wiped the misting tears from her eyes with her sleeve and focused on the road.

It was a good thing she did. Through the black Chevy's rear window, she saw Trey suddenly sit straight up in his seat. Though she couldn't see his face clearly, he seemed to have shaken the debilitating sickness which had laid him low, as evidenced by his more alert posture. A rush of activity followed in which it appeared Trey was reaching into the front of the truck.

The next few immediate moments were some of the most intense and frightening of Jess' life. The big black truck, like a pinball bouncing its chaotic way down the table, careened from one side of the road to the other. The truck's brake lights protested suddenly, forcing Jess to bring her car to an abrupt stop. She watched motionless as the truck then sped forward out of control and struck the back of the lead truck. Like the booming voice of thunder, the collision's impact created a sound that rattled Jess' teeth and made her jump in her seat.

Both trucks lost control and toppled violently end over end off the road and into the trees. Shattered pieces of fenders, windows, and mirrors exploded into a tornado of swirling plastic, metal, and fiberglass that was strewn across the road. A thin cloud of smoke and dust kicked up by the collision settled over the debris and the still clicking and ticking but motionless trucks.

Simeon's truck came to rest on its tires, though it had rolled on its top at least once. Sitting in her car, Jess was stunned speechless. For a long time, she merely stared and waited. There didn't seem to be any movement in either vehicle.

Leaving her car door open and the engine running, Jess climbed from her car to investigate. The nearer of the two vehicles was Simeon's. By the time she stood next to the passenger side window now devoid of glass, Allen was sitting upright again. His forehead was cut and bleeding quite profusely, coursing rivulets of crimson having been forged around both sides of his right eye, his eyebrow forming a temporary but rapidly saturating barrier around which the blood was forced to flow. His cornea was splotchy from burst capillaries, producing a spreading patch of red.

When Jess looked in upon all of this, she let out a tiny, surprised sound resembling a kitten's mewling. Allen looked at her with his other eye and asked with some humor still in his voice, "Do I really look that bad? I guess either I'm in shock or it looks a helluva lot worse than it feels."

She asked quickly, "Do you think you can get out?"

"I don't feel broken, if that's what you're askin', but I think the door may be. I might need a second or two before I'm up for that though."

She hadn't seen Simeon move yet. He was draped over his steering wheel, which seemed to be twisted into an unusual angle. She was about to ask if he was alright when he leaned back into his seat, removed from his pocket a pack of cigarettes, and lit one, though doing so with his shaking hands, proved quite a task.

He looked over at Jess and Allen. "Ya miss one insurance payment and that's when you get into an accident."

Jess responded, "I think Allstate gonna cut you a break on this one. You okay?"

He looked down at his waist and then at his legs. Everything seemed to be in proper order, though his chest hurt from impacting upon the steering wheel. He could feel the deep bruises with every breath. He nodded and leaned hard into his door until it opened. Had he not been still wearing his seatbelt, he likely would have landed squarely on his face due to the dizzying disorientation that swept him as a result of his exertion. He was also introduced to the throbbing ache in his neck which had avoided detection.

Jess hurried around to the opposite side of the truck and stood next to Simeon. She suggested, "Maybe you should take it easy like Allen."

Simeon asked, "What about the others? Hank? Justin? Trey?"

"I'll go check. It looked like Trey had gotten better just before they crashed. I thought I saw him sit up maybe."

Simeon looked over at Allen and cocked an eyebrow. She started to walk away when Simeon said with some urgency, "Here take this. Just in case." He took a small revolver from an inside pocket in his jacket and put it in her hand.

"And what the hell would I need this for?"

"Just take it."

Guns didn't solicit any specific response from Jess; she could take or leave them really. Having grown up in Soldotna, she had always been around firearms, so seeing one was of little consequence to her. She was neither a gun enthusiast nor an opponent of the right to bear arms, but fell somewhere in between. The small pistol Simeon gave to her was only different in that she was holding it now rather than just looking at it or listening to someone else discharge it. She slipped the pistol into the front pocket of the blue kuspuk she was wearing and walked over to the other truck.

The Chevy was resting on its driver's side. Steam from the engine was

MITIGATION: ALASKAN UNDEAD APOCALYPSE III

creating a malodorous cloud that clung to the truck and the area around it. She could hear movement in the truck, although from this angle all she could see was the vehicle's suspension, transmission, and axles. She walked through the noxious vapor, using her hands in a fruitless attempt to fan it from her face.

Hank's head was partially visible through a shattered opening in the front windshield. His skin was torn and his skull was partially broken. His blood was spilling down the glass in efficient streams which spread into web-like tributaries the further it got from the source. A small dark puddle was forming on the ground just below the leaning truck. Despite the grievous wound, Jess saw that he was moving. Perhaps he was still alive but stuck and unable to extricate himself.

"Hold on, Hank," she said aloud. "I think I need to get some help. Just hold on. I'll go get Simeon and Allen." Hank said nothing, though his head came forward a little further into the jagged gap in the glass. "I'll be right back."

As she ran back, she thought she heard a grunt or possibly a groan. She knew she needed to hurry. She also knew that she couldn't help the men alone. She needed help. Jess' life didn't demand a level of fitness above the most rudimentary level and if the rescue was going to require significant physical exertion, she wanted to make sure that it wouldn't be up to her solely. She would get the job done, but it wouldn't be pretty or efficient. With a little assistance, she knew she could get those guys out of the truck.

Simeon was already on his feet as she emerged from the cloud.

"They need help. Hank looks hurt real bad," Jess said to him.

Simeon leaned his head back trying to stretch his injured neck. "Did you see anyone else?"

"No. I saw Hank's head through the windshield and came back to get you. I didn't even take the time to look. Sorry, guess I should've."

He shook his head and followed her back. A concealing shadow hung over the truck and obscured their view in. They approached and, from just above the glass, peered inside. Jess was confused by what she saw. Someone was moving inside but she was having a hard time discerning what he was doing. Whoever it was, he seemed to be rooting around looking for something.

Pressing her face against the window, Jess was finally able to see in clearly. Trey was the one who was moving. He was digging into the side of the passenger seat but she could not make out what he was trying to get. When his hands re-emerged from their errand, he was holding what appeared to be

Hank's slick, dripping innards. Trey shoveled the oozing bits of flesh into his chomping maw and swallowed them down only half chewed before he forced in more.

Jess was frozen in utter terror, incapable of processing what she was witnessing. Her brain didn't seem to want to register or acknowledge what she was seeing. She also couldn't look away or even blink. She finally flinched, blinking rapidly when a geyser of blood sprayed from a newly punctured pocket of flesh between Trey's teeth. Her sudden movement caught Trey's attention, and he paused momentarily, his mouth still full of Hank's skin and organs.

Seeing her, he lunged straight for her, slamming his face into and further shattering the windshield. Jess retreated, falling backward as she did. Simeon caught her by the arm and steadied her before she completely lost her balance. They shared a look between one another as the growling and rustling on the other side of the glass rose in pitch and intensity.

With her terror filled blue eyes darting between Simeon and the windshield, Jess asked, "What is going on? It looked like Trey was...was eating Hank. I think that's what I saw."

Pressing the inside, Trey began to force the shattered glass from its frame. Hank's head fell from the opening in the windshield and disappeared from sight. When the glass finally fell away, Trey spilled out of the vehicle's cab. His back obviously broken and his legs not working for him, Trey flopped around on the ground in the horrific soup of blood, organs, and human detritus. His face was spattered with blood and small pieces of tissue from Hank and possibly Justin, both of whom were still strapped into their seats by their seatbelts.

Jess screamed and stepped back behind Simeon, who pulled another, larger pistol from a concealed shoulder holster under his jacket. He pulled the trigger three times, unleashing a storm of nine millimeter bullets which seemed to do little to discourage Trey's rage.

He squirmed around like a predatory lizard, his legs resembling a long trailing tail. Simeon and Jess retreated a few steps as Simeon discharged a handful more shots, none of which had any more effect than their predecessors. When Trey managed to turn himself around so that he was again facing the two of them, Simeon finally raised the pistol barrel and sent a bullet through Trey's forehead, producing the desired result. With a single bubbling gurgle, Trey's head dropped to the ground and ceased moving.

By that time, Hank had started to move as well, though he no longer appeared to be himself. His dilated pupils burned with ravenous aggression while his face was twisted into an animalistic snarl. He reached out toward them, but his seat restraints held him in place. He stretched his arms to their fullest length and worked his fingers desperately, hoping that his manipulation would help close the distance between him and them. A frustrated quake rippled through his body. He was so close to his prey, but just out of reach.

Simeon raised his pistol but Jess touched his arm in order to forestall his action. She said, "Shoot him in the chest. Shoot him in the heart."

"Why?"

"Just do it. I want to see something."

Thinking that perhaps this cute blonde girl wasn't nearly as innocent or as helpless as she originally seemed, Simeon followed her directive and shot his friend squarely in the chest. To his surprise, the gunshot seemed to have no effect whatsoever.

Jess demanded over the horrible moan coming from Hank, "Shoot him again."

Simeon again listened to her and shot Hank in the chest. The second bullet passed all the way through Hank's body and struck some metal piece on the truck behind him. Regardless of the mortal wounds inflicted upon him, Hank seemed not to notice. If anything, he became more excited and animated in his efforts, straining against the seatbelt but to no avail.

Simeon looked back at Jess, who was as incredulous as he was. He wanted to ask her something, but couldn't form the words of his elusive question. He just didn't know what to think.

She finally said to him, "Now shoot him in the head just like you did Trey."

Simeon raised the pistol and squeezed off a single round. The bullet struck the squirming Hank just above his left eye, scattering the gray matter inside his skull upon the seat behind him. With this final bullet, Hank or, more precisely, the beast who was once Hank, fell limp against his restraints and struggled no more.

When Justin started to squirm similarly, Jess simply said to Simeon, "We need to get outta here."

They ran over to Allen, who had just gotten the bleeding from the cut above his eye under control, collected the rifles and ammunition from the back of Simeon's wrecked truck, and climbed into Jess' car. The three of them sped away with Justin still hungrily fighting to free himself from his simple but seemingly effective prison. They drove south and couldn't put enough distance between themselves and the horrible revelations behind them fast enough.

Simeon kept looking over his shoulder, afraid of what might be following them. He wasn't much for believing in fairy tales or ghost stories, but the things he had seen over the past day or so was changing the way in which he thought about the world.

46

Not too long thereafter, the three of them riding in Jess' little blue sedan came upon the tail end of a solid wall of cars and trucks all stopped end to end and packed tightly asshole to elbow as her father used to say. There was no driving through it and no driving around it. It may as well have been a brick wall. But all of the cars were empty; there wasn't a soul to see in any direction.

Allen wondered aloud for all of them, "I wonder what happened to all the people. Where the hell is everyone?"

Simeon suggested, "Back up the car a bit and maybe turn around."

Jess looked over at him, her face screwed into a question. "What the hell will that accomplish? Homer's that way...in front of us...not behind."

"But what else is in front of us?"

Frustrated at having become no closer to Syd and possibly putting more distance between the two of them again, Jess had to grudgingly admit that it was probably a good idea. If they had to get out of there quickly, doing so in reverse could prove both difficult and dangerous.

While she turned the car around, Simeon climbed out with his hunting rifle, which looked as weathered as he did everywhere but in its metallic action. Those parts that were the truly functioning pieces of the rifle looked immaculate and well kept. He walked cautiously over to the first truck he encountered which happened to be a couple of ranks of cars into the mess. He checked in the rear windows of every car he passed, hoping not to encounter another creature as terrifying as what Trey and Hank had become.

Simeon walked like a hunter on the prowl. Jess watched him in her rearview mirror as he picked his way through and finally leapt into the bed of the truck. It was a big Ford that sat well above all of the cars immediately around it. Simeon hoisted the rifle to his shoulder and peered through the powerful scope. He stood as still as possible, letting his eye adjust to the incredible magnification produced by the optic device.

He was able to see well down this open, straight stretch of road. There were dips and slight rises, but overall the road ahead was a fairly direct path forward. He saw cars and trucks and dozens and dozens of boats that had never made their way to water.

Some of the boats more than others caught his eye. He admired some of the amazing water craft to which he would never have access. Of course, he had proven time and time again that he didn't need a fancy boat or expensive equipment to catch fish or to hunt moose or any other outdoor pursuit he chose. His father had often told him that being a hunter was in his blood and having those expensive gadgets wouldn't make him a better hunter, always warning him not to become a slave to modern devices because they were fleeting and would only thin his blood and make him forget his way. Looking out at all the vehicles sitting uselessly on the road, he couldn't help but think about his father's wise words. His father wasn't a mystical shaman, but he did understand nature and man's place in it. Simeon wondered what his father would have had to say about what was happening.

Satisfied that he had seen all that there was to see, he hopped back down and trotted back to Jess' car. He sat down heavily and handed his rifle back to Allen, who instinctively checked the rifle for live rounds in the firing chamber. Seeing nothing there, Allen leaned the rifle next to his on the floor of the back seat.

Simeon said without much inflection in his voice, "Cars and cars. Miles of cars. But no people."

Shaking his head, Allen asked, "Where could they all be? It's not like they just disappeared or somethin'. Did they?"

Overwhelmed, Jess gushed emotionally, "My daughter is down there somewhere and I'll be damned if I'm just gonna—"

"D'you guys hear that?" asked Allen suddenly.

Jess answered, "Hear what?"

"That. It kinda sounds like a buzzing, but I'm feelin' it all over."

Jess admitted, "I don't hear or feel anything. You're just distracting me. I need to find a way to get to my..."

Allen was looking over his shoulder by then and could see some movement amongst the cars that were now behind them. He was seeing it in the narrow spaces between the vehicles. He quickly surmised that the noise was coming from whatever was moving. He rolled down his window just a crack and the buzzing became louder but it was accompanied by something more.

They could all hear a screeching groan that sounded almost human. It was definitely coming from somewhere within the traffic jam and was getting closer by the moment.

Simeon said to Jess, "I think we need to be moving."

"But Syd is down that way goddamnit!"

Simeon's face became very serious, and he said again, "I think we should get moving."

Jess put the car into gear and reluctantly let it inch forward. Moments later, three and then four enraged, terrifying people, who all shared common characteristics with Trey and Hank, emerged from the jam and started to sprint toward Jess' car.

"Please get movin'!" Allen said, agreeing with Simeon.

Jess, still watching in her rearview mirror as the people got closer and closer, could see that all of them were either painters working with shades of red or that each was spattered to differing degrees with blood. She could also see, even from the rapidly declining distance between her and them, that their eyes were as steeped in fury as Trey's and Hank's had been.

She pressed the accelerator and asked over and over, "What is happening? What is happening? What is happening?" As she repeated the phrase, Jess' words found themselves steeped more fully in desperate sorrow and agonizing, like a bitter tea that left a sour taste in the back of her mouth. She needed to get to her daughter, but there didn't seem to be an immediate way to make that happen.

Her car gained speed and put their pursuers firmly in the distance but it didn't seem to be deterring them from the pursuit. Glancing in the rearview mirror often, she saw Allen visibly shiver, the prickly goose bumps rising on his neck. She completely agreed with his sentiment, whether it was spoken or not.

They drove hard back toward Soldotna, noticing for the first time there appeared to be people wandering aimlessly in the open spaces off the side of the road. They all knew, despite the distance between their car and those souls on foot, that there was something different about the other people. Sometimes they were wearing torn or otherwise tattered clothing. On one occasion, they saw a woman dressed in a nursing uniform who appeared to have seeping, lethal wounds on her neck and face. Part of her cheek had been peeled back, exposing teeth and gums to little black gnats and flies who hungrily swarmed the open and inviting wound.

As they neared Soldotna, on their left hand side was Skyview High School. From the highway, they weren't able to see the school itself, but they knew that it was there just the same. Jess pulled into the parking lot, surprised to see a series of school buses parked end to end to form a kind of a barrier. The great yellow and black wall cordoned off the front entrance of the school and part of the parking lot in front of the building.

Jess stopped her car and waited expectantly. Sure enough, one of the buses slowly began to reverse itself, making room for her to drive her car into the enclosure. She, Simeon, and Allen were relieved, but Jess still felt sick over the distance separating her from her daughter.

47

The first pair of zombies found the school on the second day after Jess and her companions arrived. Simeon was alongside the other men swinging his bat like a club. There was no denying its rudimentary effectiveness. It wasn't as loud as one of their guns and it still got the job done.

As it was, Jess, Simeon, and Allen were among the few people at the school to have firearms with ammunition at their disposal. The three of them were immediate celebrities as a result. At least two of them accompanied every excursion outside the wall. They were rarely called upon to use their guns for fear that the sound would attract more of the ghouls, but the reassurance of having the guns along eased many worried minds.

On more than one occasion, however, especially the further they were from the first day, their guns were the difference between everyone returning to the school and none of them returning. Jess was a capable shot with her pistol and put it to good use. Both Simeon and Allen toted powerful hunting rifles. Though the rifles were slower to shoot than the pistols that several people carried, the large caliber bullets which hurtled from their barrels were quite capable of dispatching more than one of the devils at a time so long as the angle was right. Simeon learned this fact very early during a trip to the gas station.

They had a couple of very efficient generators to run a limited number of appliances and some lights, but the generators required gasoline. A recent survivor who had found his way to the school told everyone about a tanker which was parked partially in and partially out of the road at the Chevron station near the juncture of the Sterling and Kenai Spur Highways. He told all of them that it looked like the driver had just left it there.

The gas station was only a little further than they had been already. They could take Jess' car and as many gas cans as they could carry. If they were lucky, the truck would still have its keys in it. A woman named Francine, a pretty, young Native girl, had experience driving heavy equipment, so she agreed to come along. Simeon and Jess were in the front seat, while Francine and another older man named Royce rode in the back. They had four large jerry cans, each capable of holding five gallons of gasoline, loaded into the trunk. There was room for more, but at their disposal they only had the four empty cans. There were two other cans which still had gasoline in them at the school. The hope was that they would lay their hands on more gas cans at the gas station or on the truck.

Jess sped them across the bridge and into Soldotna. Every time she found herself back in the city, she felt more and more like an interloper. This wasn't her home anymore. This wasn't the town that she had always called home. It was still, painfully familiar however.

Having been out on more than one occasion, all the grim reminders of their current circumstances were also becoming horribly familiar. The empty buildings, the abandoned cars, and the bodies...always the bodies. She wondered about each and every nameless, faceless corpse. She likely knew more than a few of them. Like Dante's torments in his Inferno, the sorrow she felt each time she saw the decomposing piles of bones was as if it were the first time. The bitter burning acid scorched her stomach and her heart simultaneously, taking her breath away. She couldn't deny the distraction that it threatened to be every time she drove them near any of the bodies she had spotted.

Of course, the bodies that were still moving around gave her equal pause and they lacked predictability. The threat of their unpredictability had her and all of her fellow pillagers on edge from the moment they drove away.

Luckily, on that day, they didn't see any of the walking dead lurking about. They could see the stalled tanker truck as they passed the Carrs grocery store and they all became anxious. The furthest any of them had ventured into town was to go to the Spenard Builder Supply store which sat just across the river. Had any of them gone the slightest bit more, they would have seen the tanker clearly. It didn't matter. They were on their way now.

Francine hopped from Jess' car and into the cab of the big rig while barely touching feet to ground. Royce got out, opened the trunk and took one of the cans with him. In his other hand was his bat. Simeon too was up and out. He still carried the bat he had used during his first close encounter with the undead at Skyview but over his shoulder was slung his rifle.

Simeon circled Jess' car, looking at their surroundings from different angles. When Francine tried to start the big truck, the diesel engine choked loudly, causing everyone to jump. She leaned out of the cab and said with an embarrassed laugh, "Sorry, I should have warned everyone. My bad."

The loud, mechanical bark echoed through the quiet morning air. Simeon knew they were there on borrowed time as soon as she did that. Royce hurried over to a valve on the tanker trailer but was puzzled how to proceed. The wrong move and he would be doused with fuel and become a walking fire bomb. Maybe Francine would know. He walked back over toward the cab but was stunned to see one of the walking corpses pull itself from the wheel hub of the truck. It had obviously been run over by the truck's driver and assumed dead. Stuck and immobile, the zombie must have been dislodged by the sudden lurch caused by the engine. It slithered out of its lodgment, pulling itself along by its hands, its legs largely missing from about mid-thigh down.

From the distance at which he was standing, there was no way he could arrive in time to save Francine, who was unaware of the danger and concentrating on getting the truck started. He shouted and finally got Jess' attention. Royce pointed excitedly. It didn't take another look.

Jess was already holding her pistol in her hand. She took a few steps to narrow the distance between her target and herself, but was already in the process of raising the revolver and siting down its barrel. She took a couple of final steps, steadied her arm the way her boyfriend Bob had shown her, and squeezed the trigger.

Jess shot the slinking abomination in the back of the head, its congealed gray matter spattering all over Francine's legs. Francine's terrified expression froze on her face, her eyes and mouth wide with surprise. Deciding that the truck was beyond starting, she gave up on trying.

Luckily, she did know how to get gas from the tanker's out spout, but there didn't appear to be time to do so. The sound of their car had apparently drawn the attention of several of the undead loitering in some of the surrounding parking lots. The truck engine's bark and the gunshot had piqued their interest and set them on a course toward the four human beings.

Simeon saw the first one as it appeared around the far side of the truck. He dangled the bat at his side expectantly and started toward the thing, however, he stopped dead in his tracks when the second and then the third creature joined the original one. Seeing their quarry, the zombies became agitated and excited. Their unwieldy, slow gait became much more focused and fast, their quickened steps rapidly propelling them forward. Dropping his bat, Simeon pulled his rifle into his hands and quickly chambered a round. He took one quick look and fired. The bullet punched its way through the closest devil's eye and exited the back of his head. The bullet then continued into the forehead of the woman following closely behind. Both slumped backward without any fanfare, their brains having been scrambled.

The third ghoul continued forward without missing a step. Simeon calmly chambered another round. By that time, Jess had joined him and was raising her own gun. Simeon waved her off and finished the third attacker with a single bullet.

Royce shouted, "There are more over there!" He was pointing toward the Mexican restaurant which was behind them on the south side of the road.

Francine added, "More from back that way too!" And from around the nearby gas station, more of the abominations were emerging. Simeon knew their position was quickly becoming untenable.

"We need to go! Now!" After which Simeon aimed his rifle and brought down another one.

Jess jumped into her car and realized there wasn't room for her to be able to maneuver their way out. She hadn't parked in such a manner as to be able to speed away quickly which she presently regretted. The car wouldn't be getting them out this time. She got back out and looked apologetically at the others. In shutting her door behind her, they all instantly knew they wouldn't be driving back to their refuge. Francine leapt back into the truck cab and then leaned out to say, "C'mon, this way! We can cut through the cab. They're thinner on that side."

Francine was through the cab and on the other side very quickly, with the others following quickly on her heels. Scurrying like the scared prey she was, Jess held her breath involuntarily as she tried to keep pace with the others. She was behind Royce but just ahead of Simeon, who had stalled to protect the rear. Simeon had to use his rifle butt like a club into the forehead of their closest pursuer, sending him head over tail into the next closest, who ran into the next. The resulting knot of tangled bodies bought Simeon and the others enough time to emerge on the other side of the truck and close the door behind them.

Francine was right. There were fewer of the undead on the far side of the truck, but there were still quite a few of them coming. The four of them paused, feeling overwhelmed by the odds that were building against them. The street, parking lots, and open spaces in front of them were starting to fill with the staggering, rotting wretches.

Jess uttered, "Oh God!"

"Later," Royce said. "We gotta get away right now." He pointed to a fairly broad seam between two larger bodies of oncoming walking undead, which were threatening to merge into one contiguous mass of rotting aggression.

Francine, confused, asked, "But doesn't that take us away from where we want to be? Are you sure?"

Simeon was the first to start moving. He said over his shoulder, "We just want to be away from here right now. There's too many of those things. C'mon!" With that said, Simeon dropped another target with his rifle. Truth be told, he was trying to line the creatures up in such a way as to hit multiple targets with single bullets. Deciding that he needed quicker shooting to deal with the threat of their avenue of escape getting cut, Simeon shouldered the rifle and pulled his automatic pistol from his shoulder holster.

Repeating "Shit!" over and over again in quick bursts like a revving two-stroke motor, Jess was struggling to load her pistol with some of her few remaining shells and run at the same time. She ran square into Royce's back and nearly knocked the both of them off their feet. She did end up dropping several precious bullets. Out of habit, she stopped to retrieve the fallen deadly necessities, not realizing there were hands a scant few steps away from grabbing her.

Luckily, Simeon had seen her predicament. He was making his way toward her and firing the pistol at the same time. Royce too had pivoted and was swinging his bat feverishly, hitting everything in its path. Francine, terrified and screaming, had continued to run, oblivious to the others' plight. It wasn't personal and she hadn't intended to ditch everyone. She was simply being driven by her fear, which had taken control of all of her judgment. She watched breathlessly as the envelopment of ghouls around her friends threatened to close.

Royce grabbed Jess' collar and pulled her upright. She had gotten her hands on four of six dropped bullets. The other two brass colored beauties eluded capture and had to be left in the street. Jess jammed the four bullets into the revolver and had it back ready to fire just as Simeon emptied the magazine on his own pistol.

Firing those four bullets in quick succession, Jess, Simeon, and Royce got themselves extracted from the tightening pocket, sprinting toward Francine. She had stopped running near a small car dealership and was currently fighting to catch her breath. Bent at the waist and looking up from that position, Francine saw the horde of ghastly nightmares, their expressions burning with a single collective ravenous rage, chasing her friends. The four of them accelerated away from their hunters, but it was a pace that none of them could maintain. They were all heaving and wheezing, their lungs protesting their overexertion.

They were running through the loading areas and back parking lots of the businesses that sat along the main highway. Their trek luckily took them clear of any more of the menacing wraiths. The activity at the tanker had apparently attracted every ghoul in the vicinity to the street.

In no time, they were back at the river. Exhausted, with muscles aching and lungs struggling, Jess looked toward the bridge and was disgusted to see a small pack of the creatures standing, waiting in the middle of the road. She counted four zombies who were even then starting to put their noses to the air, and that's when she realized those things could smell them.

There was no time to hesitate and she knew full well that none of them really had any reserves on which to draw to have another battle. She looked at Simeon, who was already checking the load on his pistol. She had six more shots and six beyond that in her pocket.

They nodded at one another and charged out from behind their cover. It took a moment or two before their movement was detected, which allowed them to get closer and ensure that their bullets hit their marks.

Simeon shot first when he pulled his trigger twice quickly. Both bullets hit the nearest zombie above the shoulders. The first struck the thing in the neck and the second hit it on the side of the head just above the ear. It collapsed into another of the beasts which righted itself only to take a bullet to its forehead.

Jess fired as well, but the sharp cracks from Simeon's pistol made her wince, and her first shot went wild. The second hit its chosen target, though it only punched a small hole in the ghoul's Carrs apron. She fired again and was finally able to produce the tiniest of holes in the fiend's forehead. It appeared to be enough, as the beast shuddered and then slowly fell forward, all of its fire having faded from its upturned eyes.

Simeon finished off the final monster and they all started to run again. The renewed shooting had reawakened the percolating hunger of the zombies still searching for their prey back near the truck.

There was a fair amount of distance between them and the zombies, but there was no time to dawdle. They needed to get back to the school as quickly as possible. They would be coming back empty-handed but at least all of them would be returning.

That was the last time Jess had wandered outside the school or its protective walls. She'd seen enough of what lay beyond. She realized that it could just as easily have gone much differently, much worse for all of them. Not an optimist by nature, Jess could only imagine around which corner she could have met a violent end.

And then there was the guilt, a gnawing, relentless, ulcerous feeling that chewed her insides whether her eyes were opened or closed. She found that she couldn't close her eyes anymore without seeing Syd's face. In the quiet solitary moments of night, she could hear her daughter's voice and her warm laugh in her thoughts.

Jess' actions never went beyond chastising herself though. During those dreamy moments that hovered between sleep and awake, she could imagine herself sneaking away to head south. The first few steps would be exhilarating. When she started to imagine picking her way alone in the dark, through the string of bumper to bumper cars on the highway, Jess would be jarred back awake, having to attempt her descent to sleep all over again. On some nights she found it impossible to sleep. Instead, she wept silent, painful tears all night long until the glow of morning signified it was time to rise again.

48

A handful of days later, when the shock of that day still resonated with all of them, the militia arrived. Hauling their own small tanker filled with gasoline, they drove up to the line of school buses. Seeing the military-looking vehicles and the military-looking uniforms and, perhaps most importantly, the military-looking weapons, the gate was opened and the militia was allowed to take over.

While Jess grew closer to Royce, she felt herself drifting further away from both Simeon and Allen over the days that followed. Allen was immediately drawn to the militia's authority and perceived power. It started with simple curiosity and conversations. Soon though, he was eating his meals with them and standing watch with them.

When Allen showed up one morning wearing a uniform, Jess couldn't claim to be surprised. It was just a matter of time really. To herself, she wondered what kind of initiation rite he had to endure. With the new black eyes, he looked a little like a raccoon, but he wore those battle scars with pride. It was not unlike joining a fraternity and with his affiliation with the group, he could and would enjoy all the benefits granted. He received better sleeping accommodations and slightly better rations. He was also given one of the much coveted assault rifles to have on his person at all times.

Allen believed it when he was told that sometimes they had to appear cruel in order to maintain both security and order. Of course, those terms were dictated and practiced by those in power who had the luxury of deciding how to provide security and what was the accepted definition of order. And as a very smart man once said, when there is a miscommunication or a misunderstanding, the party under the thumb is always the party that suffers.

Allen didn't consider this, nor would he have considered it. He simply didn't think that way. It wasn't a matter of intelligence or critical thinking; he was just not inclined to consider issues that deeply. He actually thought that his position with the militia might benefit Jess and Simeon as well as everyone else at the refuge. He was a good man and would act accordingly. He hoped that he would be able to make a difference for all of them at their sanctuary.

Simeon, on the other hand, continued to go out on every excursion outside the wall. He ran himself ragged, like he was running from something or possibly atoning for something. He rarely spoke, and when he did he didn't waste words on such musings. For him, things were simply the way they were.

At first, he chose to sleep outside, near a large metal trash can which he used as a burn barrel. He went into the woods surrounding the school and retrieved pieces of wood to burn and generally kept to himself. When he was out in the town, he engaged no one in conversation and shared few words. He always stepped up to help anyone in need and refused to allow anyone to be left behind, regardless of the danger.

As the temperature continued to edge its way down, he allowed Jess to talk him into sleeping inside. She had to convince him that it wasn't for his sake but for the sake of those people, likely herself, who would have to care for him if he became ill. He grudgingly consented but then chose to sleep near one of the numerous exits.

Every morning, Jess would go to Simeon's area to wake him and spend some largely silent moments with him. His quiet nature and flat disposition made her feel lonely. If she was lucky enough to have something warm to bring him to eat or to drink, she would but often she came to him empty-handed. He would smile up at her from his bed of newspapers and discarded towels as she touched his shoulder lightly to wake him. This went on for days and days. It became a bit of a ritual.

One morning she came down to his little nest and found that her tortured bird had flown. Sometime during the night, he'd gathered his newspapers into one tidy stack and his towels in another and departed. It pained her to think that she was the only one who would miss him more than his guns or his nerve. He was gone and she rightly doubted he would ever return.

Despite the growing number of people at the school, Jess felt more and more isolated. Royce was the only one with whom she really spoke and he was a bitter curmudgeon most of the time, which made it difficult to be around him.

And through all of this, her overwhelming fear battled with her overwhelming guilt to determine her daily torment. Her daughter was still out there. She could feel it. Syd was alive and safe. Jess had to find her. But how? There was a world of walking death separating the two of them. She also doubted that her daughter would still be in Ninilchik or Kasilof or anywhere else on the Kenai Peninsula. Jess had to hope that Bob would have taken her as far from this place as was possible. Again, Jess had to ask herself to where they would go. The world had changed and nowhere was safe any longer.

She was nearing the limit of her resolve when the idiot militia guys brought in the captives. When she saw them drag that girl down into the darker end of the hall toward the "secured" portion of the school, she suspected the worst. And when they led those four kids over to the fenced kennels they'd put some of those things in out on the basketball court, she knew there was no limit to their cruelty or depravity.

Jess had reached the end of her rope and wished that Simeon was still around to help her take action. The problem she had...well, actually, she had several problems, but the first problem she had to overcome was resolving herself to do something. She'd gotten so comfortable in her complacency. She, like many of the people at the school, simply needed a catalyst to set her into motion.

49

Coming closer to Soldotna, Neil let his foot off the gas a bit. He needed to be careful and pay better attention to the gas gauge. He didn't want to run out of fuel too soon. The truck would make a very handy vehicle in which to make their escape.

Emma asked, "So where the hell is Skyview?"

Della answered flatly, "On the other side of town. Just down the road a bit."

Confirming, Neil asked, "On the other side of the river?'"

Della again responded without emotion or inflection in her voice. "On the other side of the river."

Ahead, in the road, Neil spied some movement. There were a couple zekes, looking lost but frightful, wandering aimlessly on the lanes of the highway. He tightened his grip on the steering wheel and pressed the gas pedal a little more. With a clenched jaw, he braced himself for the coming impact.

The silver truck growled like an armored war elephant and surged forward. It was almost too late when Neil realized that it wasn't just two zekes in the road. With their V-8 Hemi engine steadily building steam, they crested a last rise in the road and saw a large crowd of the creatures milling about expectantly on the highway in front of the looted Fred Meyer store. Just beyond the mass of walking dead, was a large, shiny silver tanker truck. It blocked most of the road and what the tanker didn't block, the zombies did.

Holding his breath and barely controlling his fear, Neil was forced to veer right and continue north on the highway or risk becoming enveloped by the mob.

"It's that way? Right?" Jerry asked.

Frustrated and a little on edge, Neil snapped, "I'm working on it, okay?"

"Just checkin'."

In his rearview mirror, Neil watched the terrifying mob become much more animated as they gave chase. The lethargy of the grave was shaken away by their flailing arms and groaning mouths. Like an amorphous plague culture devouring the contents of a petri dish, the pursuing horde filled the road and median behind them. Jerry rubbed his temples and his chest trying to ease the discomfort from the increased density of the undead subsonic buzz.

Steve, their militia hostage, was also massaging his head, suffering from the strain, his eyes widened with surprise. "Where the hell did all these come from?"

"You never seen a big group of zekes before?" Emma asked.

"Zekes, huh? We call 'em skins. But yeah, I seen 'em thick and heavy, but...the Colonel...he told us they'd killed or chased all of 'em off. He said that Soldotna was mostly clear and that maybe we'd be able to go home soon."

Emma summed up what everyone else was thinking when she said, "Nobody's ever gonna be able to go home. There's just no such thing anymore."

"Well, maybe we can make a new home then," Steve said hopefully. "I didn't have much of one before anyway. Anything would be better than what I had."

Emma warned, "Careful for what you wish for."

"What do you mean by that?"

"It can always get worse than it is," Jerry said, "and sometimes you don't even notice until it's too late and you're boxed in."

Sensing the conversation was headed for a decidedly dark philosophical place, Neil punched the accelerator with a very heavy foot. He was trying to ignore all the talk but finally determined his efforts were futile. "This Colonel. Who is he? Is he really military? Does he have any answers?"

"No, he ain't military or connected to the government at all. He just organized us. He and Carter and Sullivan all lived out on a homestead near Kasilof. They been collecting supplies and preparing for the collapse of civilization. They knew it was comin'. They could see all the signs. They bought guns and ammo and other military equipment. I don't know how they got what they did. The Colonel was a lawyer and had lots of money, so he could afford to buy all kinds of things and in lots of different ways."

Neil asked for clarification, "Meaning?"

"Meaning, he had his own contacts in the black market arms trade. Let's just say where there's the will and the cash, there's a way. When it did finally happen, the fall I mean, he gathered all his people out on his property and closed the gate behind them. He had lots of land and a barbed wire fence around all of it. I went along with a friend when my mom and dad decided to go south and leave me a note. They didn't bother to even look for me. They just took my younger sister and headed out of town without me. They probably were hopin' to find a place on someone's boat down in Homer. Maybe they made it. To be honest, I don't really give a shit one way or the other. I guess I cared about them as much as they cared about me."

Steve breathed heavily and paused with that realization. "On the Colonel's property, they gave me some food, this uniform, and a gun. They invited me in and made me one of 'em. I don't remember a time when I felt like I belonged as much as I did with those folks."

Skeptical, Emma asked, "So what's different? Why the change of heart? If they are your new family, why are you helping us?"

Steve looked at Della. "I was raised a Christian."

Emma rolled her eyes and allowed a disparaging, silent chuckle. Steve ignored it and said, "I was raised a Christian, that much of my upbringing stuck with me. And Christians don't kidnap folks. They don't steal and they don't kill."

Under her breath, Emma hissed, "That's not been my experience."

"Well, maybe you ain't never met any real Christians. It takes more than just goin' to church."

Neil, sensing the anger rising in Emma, touched her on the arm and extinguished her burning fuse. He did so because he didn't want Emma to embarrass herself. He knew and had seen Emma's disdain for religion, but he also recognized the wisdom of Steve's words. He was right, Emma had simply had nothing but bad experiences in her recent memory and her opinion had been formed as a result of those bad memories.

Emma bit back her comments, but seethed with resentment. She didn't like someone else telling her what to say or how to say it. She knew Neil's intention was good, but it didn't make it any easier to take. She had a lifetime of feeling like she had to take it and she had no intention with whatever little time she had left to go back to that kind of a life. Hell, even her old job as a medical transcriptionist was built around someone dictating in her ear what to type. She breathed deeply and stared ahead.

Neil wanted to get away from these things, but he also came to the conclusion that to approach the high school in the truck would alert the militia to their plans. They needed to be able to get to the school much more stealthily. Of that he was certain, but beyond that the plan became very hazy.

The zombie roadblock likely saved all their lives. Had they not been in the road, Neil would have probably driven them straight into the waiting guns of the militia or whatever they were. Neil wasn't too impressed from what he had heard thus far from Steve. They sounded like a bunch of assholes who no longer had the constraints of civilization to keep their behavior in check. But if they had automatic weapons and God knows what else at their disposal and the willingness to use that equipment on anyone deemed a threat, he was rightly concerned for their well-being.

He remembered a different way to get them to the road that ran along this side of the river separating them from Skyview High School. He just needed to get them far enough ahead of the zekes chasing them and then double back. That would be the easy part. Zombies were nothing if not predictable. Dealing with the militia would be a different thing entirely.

50

Claire couldn't contain her tears or her pain any longer. She had tried to be strong; she had tried to resist, but it was all for naught. She couldn't kid herself. The agonizing scream leapt from her unexpectedly. She didn't even recognize the voice as her own. It filled the room and then came crashing back down upon her.

She searched her mind feverishly, trying to remember if there was a question that she had failed to answer. What could she say to make the pain stop? What did he want from her?

Suddenly, a man's face was filling her vision. Spread across the breadth of the face was a menacing, toothy grin. The man said with playful terror in his words, "This little piggy went to the market..." he dropped the toe he was holding between his fingers and flashed the blood-glistening garden trimmers, "How many more piggies do we have?"

She couldn't remember. Was that the answer he needed to make him stop? Claire knew that it wasn't the first toe he had cut from her feet, but she had lost count of how many he had removed. The first one had been her second toe from her right foot; the one with her silver toe ring on it. He was currently wearing that ring on the first knuckle of his pinky finger.

"I hope we don't run out of piggies any time soon. I'm having so much fun with you. I didn't know you could scream so loud. Did you?"

When no answer was forthcoming, Sullivan said, "Tsk, tsk, tsk," and disappeared from view again. When she felt the blade brush against her skin and slowly close around her next digit, she didn't wait for the pain to let fly a reverberating wail. She thought maybe she could hear an evil snicker as the sharpened blades came together again and slashed through another toe, which fell to the floor. He once again used the flat surface of a glowing red butter knife to cauterize the wound. He didn't want her to bleed to death; not yet anyway. Where was the fun in that?

Sullivan had both of her feet held firmly between the ruthless jaws of a pair of table vises mounted to the workbench on which she had been strapped. Her struggling and frantic movement had left her ankles bruised and bloodied. As he picked up the toe and repositioned himself on the stool next to her, he said quietly while he stroked her hair, "The Colonel, he said he didn't want you dead, at least not right away. But he didn't say I couldn't have a little fun before he talked to you. Are you having as much fun as I am?"

Again, Claire couldn't find an answer that she thought might lead to the end of the torture session. Instead, she simply surrendered herself to her tears which came hot and heavy. She tried to blubber out an answer, but her words were as filled with tears as were her eyes.

Sullivan said with all the warmth of a serpent, "Your silence must mean that you *are* having fun. What should we do next?"

Claire closed her eyes and begged for any kind of delivery from this madness. She pleaded with the world to stop the pain. She hoped and prayed that Jerry would somehow make all of this go away. She needed him to come and save her. In her lucid moments, she tried to guess how long she had been a prisoner. It had certainly been hours. But had it exceeded days? She wasn't sure.

Through her fear and despite her pain, she thought of the children. She was fearful for their fates. Her crazy torturer had never mentioned them. In fact, he had never said anything about anyone. He went on and on about nothing; telling stories about people whom she didn't know who had done him wrong in some way.

When her wrist was moved and her clenched fingers separated somewhat, she could only dread what was coming next and her expectation wasn't far from reality. Sullivan started with her pinky on her right hand and snipped it off one knuckle at a time, using the same heated knife each time to close the wound and stifle the blood flow. It was a routine he had either practiced to perfection or had been considering for a long time. The putrid odor of her own melting skin and singed hair filled her nostrils. Over the past few hours, she had smelled it so many times that it no longer solicited the same nausea.

Her mind flooded her senses with endorphins and helped her retreat from the agony. At one point she blacked out. Though her eyes were still open, her consciousness had thankfully fled.

When she awoke again, she was alone. Her hands and feet throbbed so intensely, it felt as if they buzzed. She was loath to look at the damage done to her body but she couldn't resist. Slowly, her vision inched across the ceiling above as she forced her eyes down toward her extremities.

She couldn't help the gasp that escaped her. She knew it was coming but it surprised her just the same. She was not able to recognize the mangled flesh as her own. The pinky fingers on both hands were largely gone. The pinky on her left hand still had a lone knuckle but her right one was gone. The ring finger on her right hand was gone down to the last knuckle too, the ring her parents had given her was gone as well.

Claire couldn't see her feet, but she couldn't imagine they looked any better. The swelling in both feet made wiggling her toes out of the question. For all she knew, all of her toes had been hacked from her feet.

She wondered about her respite and how long it would last. She was fairly certain she could wriggle her wrists free, but she realized she would not be able to make an escape. Her feet would be of no use to her. Claire would be forced to crawl away on her hands and knees and she had no illusions about her chances under those circumstances. Still, she had to try.

Moments later, she was pulling herself along the cold tile floor of the shop classroom. Once, long ago, she remembered her mind in such a hazy state and crawling on the floor, but that time had involved an entire bottle of cheap vodka and a gallon of orange juice.

Likely resulting from the shock her system was experiencing, she shivered and quaked with each labored breath. With willpower and adrenaline, she forced herself to keep moving through her teeth-chattering fever. It took her several agonizing minutes to cross the room to the closed classroom door where she stopped and wept. There was no way she would be able to stand to open the door.

Her torturer would return and find her on the floor. She knew she would pay a terrible price, but she was terrified of the possibilities, and she had no choice but to wait for him to return and deliver her punishment. That was her last thought as she thankfully fell into unconsciousness.

51

Sullivan walked slowly through the empty, barely lit school hallway, enjoying the echo of his heavy footfalls. He had been summoned by Colonel Bear and was dutifully reporting. He didn't like being taken away from his work, but he rightly figured his guest wasn't going anywhere anytime in the near future.

He walked into the school office and was greeted immediately by Sherry and Terry. They were two pretty-ish young women who played the part of the Colonel's secretaries. Neither of them really did anything, but they were willing to carry on the charade. It wasn't like the phones were ringing or visitors were coming in to see the principal or anything, but it added a level of normalcy for those who needed it. The Colonel liked having the pretty girls jumping at his voice and doing his bidding. Sherry and Terry weren't their real names but he couldn't think of anything else to call them and he didn't care enough to actually learn their names.

He smiled as he rounded the corner and stepped into the office. Sherry—or was it Terry?—smiled back and said, "He's expecting you."

Sullivan stifled the urge to say, *No shit? He's expecting me? Is that because he sent for me?* He simply nodded and walked into the Colonel's office, shutting the door behind him. Sometimes he hated people and their simple minds.

Once the door was shut, Sullivan said, "You rang?"

The Colonel was a big man, with an ego and voice to match. His larger than average head and thick neck appeared to be amorphously spilling outward from his overly tight-fitting military colored golf shirt. There was no definition between the soft, pink flesh of his neck and his head. His jaw line barely distinguished itself. There were no rolls however. His abundant skin was distended just enough to give him the appearance of a close relative of human beings, but something that still seemed otherworldly. If he were a comic book character, his name would probably have been *Blob Man* or something like that.

His size and weight, of course, turned him into a perspiration machine. Typically, the Colonel's forehead would be adorned with beads of glistening sweat and his shirt would have damp patches in all the typical places. The air in his office was heavy with moisture and the not-too-subtle aroma of body odor.

While everyone else bitched about the smell, Sullivan, an idea man, had learned tricks to help him deal with it. For instance, on that day, he popped in a fresh piece of Big Red chewing gum as he walked into the office. The strong cinnamon scent, discouraged to venture far from its source, hovered around his nose and warded off the assault the Colonel's limited sense of hygiene might try to mount.

Sullivan sat in the large, plush, leather chair in front of the Colonel's desk and smiled. Sullivan hadn't realized his forehead and left cheek bore the evidence of his time with Claire. Both were speckled with drying blood. The Colonel noticed his second in command's adornment and handed Sullivan a towel. The large man said, his breath shallow and labored, "Ya might want to clean up before you go wandering around. No point in inciting the civvies."

His voice dry and humorless, Sullivan replied, "If you say so, sir, but what's the point? No disrespect intended, you understand."

"Sullivan, you may not know it, but we will need those people eventually. If we get them all up in arms, we may be forced to make certain adjustments which probably won't sit too well with them. At least not yet. We need to ease them into totally accepting everything we say or there'll always be someone willing to stand up to us. If they think they can't get by without us, well.... life could be real easy for all of us then."

Sullivan hadn't bought into the Colonel's bullshit about establishing a new world order. He didn't see how one world order was any different than the next. He wasn't any more interested in telling someone else what to do that he was in letting someone else do the same to him. He'd lived his entire life having to pretend to care about what others thought and said and did, and now wasn't any different. The Colonel, though, pretty much let him do what he wanted, and Sullivan could appreciate that kind of management.

"So what's the plan then?" he asked.

The Colonel sat back in his chair which creaked and popped due to his excessive weight. He laced his fingers together behind his head and neck, which didn't seem to have a defining line separating the one from the other, and exhaled a long, satisfied deep breath. "Tell me about the teenager you brought in. Any chances he might become a new recruit?"

Sullivan smiled. "Carter's already working on it. He's pretty good at those things. I'm sure he can get it done."

"Good. And the woman?"

By that time, Sullivan caught scent of the Colonel's ripe breath. He stood up and walked over to the window, so as to subtly escape the hovering odor.

"Sullivan..."

With a sinister slant to both his eyes and his voice, Sullivan said, "For what we want of her, she doesn't need to be on board with your...vision. She just needs to be...well plied. Believe me, she won't have any fight left in her when I get done."

"She's no good to us dead, Sullivan," The Colonel admonished.

"She's no good to us at all. She's just another liability. Ya might as well let me have my fun for once. I listen to you and I follow your orders. Don't I deserve a little R-n-R? Haven't I earned it?"

The colonel wrinkled his face into a question. He asked with his head tilting slightly, "Earned what? What are you plannin' to do?"

Sullivan smiled a grin that still had idiomatic canary feathers fluttering around it. "I earned you not asking any questions on this one. I earned no interference. And afterward, you can tell me what to do and when to do it, but let me be right now. Like I said, I earned it."

The Colonel leaned farther into his chair and somehow projected enough of his musk to fill Sullivan's nose. The gum was failing him, and he was becoming bored with this discussion. He needed to go back up to his room for a few minutes. There was a bottle of Johnny Walker that was calling out his name. And then it hit him. The bottle. He could be real creative with that bottle. And if it broke, he could use the pieces. His creativity pleased him immensely.

Leaving the room slowly, Sullivan said over his shoulder so the two women could hear him as well as the Colonel, "I got it covered boss. The woman will know her place at our feet...just like all women should know." He shot the two women in the front office a smile, from which they cowered and looked away.

52

Neil slammed his hand against the steering wheel in frustration. He continued to wait for some revelation. They needed a plan and he'd be damned if he could think of one. He knew they were both outnumbered and outgunned. He wondered if the militiamen were expecting them. He also wondered about the discipline of the militia forces. Would they have pickets on watch outside their defenses or would they simply hide behind their walls and wait?

Really, zekes weren't tactically creative. Neil and his group had used that against them many times over the past several weeks. They didn't use subterfuge or stealth. Zombies were nothing if not predictable. They simply came at their quarry relentlessly, overwhelming any resistance through sheer hunger and rage.

If he knew that, then maybe this Colonel guy knew that too. There really wasn't much need to have people outside the walls so long as there were diligent lookouts atop the walls. Neil needed to think of a way to use that against them.

In the road ahead, shuffling along the pavement like a stray dog, a lanky, bony wraith saw the shiny, silver truck barreling toward it. The zombie raised its ashen arms and started to head on a collision course with the truck. The ghoul, which had once been a woman, perhaps a housewife, a mother, a neighbor, was showing the advancing signs of decay through the tattered shreds of clothing that still clung to her emaciated frame and trailed behind her like a fluttering war banner. Her teeth were fully exposed, the skin around her mouth having curled away. Her cheekbones protruded through gaps in her skin, as did some of her ribs and part of her right shoulder. Some of the bones peeking through were the result of the wounds which had claimed her life in the first place. The closer she drew to the truck, the more fearsome she became.

Neil looked over at Emma, expecting to see an approving nod, as he edged the truck into a more direct path toward the thing in the road. She wasn't even acknowledging that Neil was looking at her. She was too busy looking at the zombie too, at least that was what she wanted Neil to think.

Of course Emma saw him look over at her and she knew exactly what he needed, but she also knew that he was also expecting to look over and see Meghan giving that nod. Emma wasn't willing to be that person; she just didn't have it in her anymore. Her affection for Dr. Caldwell had caught her by surprise, almost as much as his affection for her did. She hadn't found much luck in love in her life.

She'd been in love and had been loved, but it never seemed to last. And after each, she had always sworn she would never love again. This particular time was no different, other than perhaps her resolve and resignation.

It wasn't that Emma was trying to be heartless. She cared deeply for Neil, respected him, and appreciated him, but it was simply not enough to encourage her to let down her guard and make herself vulnerable again. She wasn't willing to go down that path another time. Some people might feel compelled to seek mates and relationships, but Emma wasn't one of those people. All the warmth and security and whatever else one derived from romance did not come close to balancing with all the misery, loss, and whatever else she would suffer when the relationship eventually failed.

Jerry was instead the one who commented on Neil's apparent decision. "Uh, Neil, have you thought that maybe hitting it with the truck might not be a great idea?"

"Why not?"

"I mean, I'm the damned teenager here. Why am I the only one who might be worried her head or other body part might come through the windshield or my window? I like being warm and dry for a change. Oh yeah, and my legs not always feeling tired is pretty freaking cool, too, by the way. So, I think it might be a good idea to take care of this truck so maybe it'll take care of us."

Neil corrected their course and steered them away from the zombie who turned slowly as they passed and hissed at them its disappointment. "Sorry. I guess I just let myself get distracted."

As if answering a question that hadn't been asked, Della said, "Maybe that's the key. Maybe them monsters distract everyone. Maybe they can help us. Maybe they can be our distraction."

Emma shook her head and asked, "What in the hell are you talking about?"

"No, Della's right," Neil said. "I was trying to figure out how to get Claire and those kids back. I was comin' up empty to be honest. Steve, you said the Colonel had more than twenty men and a bunch of guns?"

Steve, watching a trio of wretched ghouls loitering in a parking lot of a looted and burned business, answered, "Yeah quite a few more'n twenty I guess. That is unless Carter's convinced any more of the other men in the group to join his men and then who knows how many? When you caught me, I'd been out with them boys for a few days lookin' for supplies and scouting around in general. Carter's real persuasive, I'd guess you'd say. They got a couple of honest to God machine-guns and a bunch of guns that might be what you'd call cousins of military hardware. They got some other odds and ends too but I don't know what all of it did."

"Twenty guns is enough," Neil remarked. "That's more than we can deal with. We need some kind of an edge if we're gonna have any hope at all." Neil slowed the vehicle and turned left. He asked, "So how are we gonna do this then?"

53

Royce, his hair as white and stormy as a cloud, stood in the doorway of the small conference room of the Skyview school library. He looked over his shoulder to make certain no one was within earshot. Satisfied, he said, "I don't trust no one here. No one gives a rat's ass about no one else."

Jess nodded her head in agreement. She was about to say something, when Royce continued, "No one except you that is. I need help and you're the only one here that I can ask."

Jess was caught off guard by his candor and by the compliment. She looked up at him this time and nodded much more slowly. She was agreeing without having first heard what was being asked of her. She would have agreed regardless. She had been missing something for quite a while and she suddenly realized what it was: purpose. She no longer went on outside excursions and her duties as a laundress were less than fulfilling.

Royce, almost with a whisper, said calmly, "I'm gonna go get those kids out and then get them away from here. And I can't do it alone."

"I'm in."

Royce smiled as much as he ever did, revealing his perfect teeth which were as white as his hair. "I was hopin' you'd say that. I really didn't know how I was gonna do it alone."

"How do you plan on getting them out?"

"I don't know yet, but I'm gonna go do it now."

Jess leaned forward and whispered, "Well hold on just a second. I might have something that will help."

Just outside the doors of the conference room was a bookshelf that housed, among other things, Toni Morrison's *Song of Solomon*. Jess walked up to that section, touched the book lightly and then pulled it from the shelf.

She reached in quickly, as if she was thrusting her hand into boiling water, and then pulled it back out with something small, wrapped in a scrap of cloth. She held the item in her hand as if weighing it for authenticity, and then rolled it out of the cloth.

It was the revolver Simeon had given her. There was a small handful of shiny bullets lying in the cloth next to it. The little gun seemed almost a child's plaything but the bullets added to the toy a sense of purpose and gravitas.

Royce, his eyes wide with wonderment, asked in disbelief, "How the hell did you hide that?"

"Girl's gotta have her secrets."

More than a little pleased, Royce gushed, "Well hallelujah for that, sister. I think you just made all this a lot easier."

"Royce, what about that woman?" Jess asked with concern. "Are we gonna try and help her? We can't just leave her."

"One thing at a time. We gotta get those kids outta that hell those bastards put them in. If we can actually get that done, then we can talk. Well, get it done without..."

Jess finished for him, "...getting us both killed."

Royce said, "I figure either way, something gets resolved tonight."

54

Jess opened the back door where Simeon had slept all those weeks ago. The outside air was crisp and dry against her cheeks as she entered the dark evening. While the short days of winter were still some time off in the future, the nights were starting to become much darker much quicker. Due to the absence of any artificial light from street lamps, vehicle headlights, or neon store marquees, the darkness seemed so much more absolute in the dead of night. Luckily, there was still some lingering purple tinted light when she stepped outside.

She looked over and could make out the contours of the cages sitting like an isolated archipelago in a concrete sea. There was something else too. A swirling twist of air with a little more than just air to it. Snow. It was faint, not much more than frost that spread wet kisses on the cold air, but it was definitely there. Jess stopped and breathed in the cold moisture which crowded out all the warmth in her lungs. The chill swept through her from the inside out.

Almost at once, she could hear the snarling, snorting foulness of the undead who had been caged in kennels surrounding the children. Luckily, the loading bay and car lot were both empty.

Jess had been concerned that her resolve might fade a bit when actually facing the task. She was pleasantly surprised to find that hearing the creatures steeled her nerves and set her on her path. There were at least three of the militiamen patrolling along the wall perimeter but still some distance away. All three walked with the enthusiasm of a mall cop on beat after hours.

Jess looked at Royce, who hadn't taken his eyes off of the cages. He was carrying a mop handle that he had sharpened and honed into a very lethal point. He was also carrying an equally sharp but much shorter filleting knife.

Ignoring any looks thrown their direction by the armed men, the two of them walked up to the nearest cage. Jess said over the grunts of the ghoul separating her from the children on the other side, "Hold tight, kids. We're here to get you out."

Danny, who had neither slept nor sat since he had been locked inside, sighed and started to cry tears of relief. He knew someone would come for them. He just thought it would have been Neil. He didn't care at the moment though. He just wanted to be able to rest his legs and his eyes. He'd been fighting both the cold and sleep all day and into the night. He knew that if he was to surrender to sleep, he would have ended up in the clutches of one of those things that was almost close enough to touch him as it was.

The frigid air would have made sleep difficult as well. He and the three other children were pressed as tightly together as possible due to more than just fear of the zombies. They were freezing, their teeth chattering uncontrollably and shivers running the lengths of their bodies every few seconds. Danny tried to hug all of them against him through most of the day, but he was starting to get so tired. For a moment, he was afraid the voice he was hearing was merely a hallucination.

Royce said gruffly, "C'mon you bastard. Come on over and see what ol' Royce has got for ya."

The beast in the cage became even more agitated with the introduction of more prey. It pressed its face against the fence, trying to get closer to Royce who was standing just out of reach. The stench of rot, though faded with time and the elements, was much thicker from this proximity. The odor was kin with raw sewage, animal feces, and mothballs. It was hard to remember that these things were once human.

Royce smiled at Jess and then plunged the sharpened stick into the demon's empty eye socket. A small stream of heavy, dark, syrupy fluid spilled from the new wound as the abomination convulsed momentarily and then slid down the chain link fence. It curled itself into a twisted heap and was no more.

There was a padlock hanging on the fence, but it hadn't been locked because no one could find the key. Royce pulled the lock out and hurled it across the basketball court. He flung open the gate which whistled and creaked like old bones. In a flash, he was through the next barrier and face to face with four very scared faces. He nodded and motioned to them with his hands.

The four children needed no more encouragement. They scurried out of the enclosure and sprinted across the basketball court to the back of the school without saying a word. Against the school wall and as far from their prison as they were able to be, they turned and huddled into a ball of scared, shivering bodies.

Looking at the children, Royce was feeling pretty good about himself and his decision. The hurried footsteps approaching from behind threatened to change all that. Ignoring the sound, he started to walk away toward the kids and Jess who was already making her way toward them as well.

The voice that caused Royce to stop dead in his tracks was that of Mel, one of the Colonel's loyal henchmen. Mel was a believer in the Colonel's madness which made him extremely dangerous. Royce breathed in deeply and pulled the knife from his jacket pocket. He hoped the darkness was enough to conceal his intent. He didn't know if he was ready to do what he resolved to do or not, but he would soon.

The footsteps behind him grew ever closer, as did the volume of the questions. Royce had his eyes closed when he turned to face the much younger man. The confrontation was interrupted with frantic shouting and thunderous gunshots arising from the front of the school.

The younger Mel looked away from Royce and watched the shadowy silhouettes of his fellow soldiers head away toward the ruckus at the front of the school. Royce took the opportunity to pounce. He stabbed at Mel with the knife, hitting the young man in his stomach and chest. The blade, cutting through the man's jacket and shirts underneath, produced a long gash across Mel's torso. Unfortunately for Royce, the knife struck one of Mel's ribs and was deflected away from doing any significant damage.

Regardless, Mel fell backward clutching the bleeding wound, the warm fluid spilling between his fingers in dark, flowing trails. Royce looked triumphantly over at Jess and smiled. He didn't see Mel take the pistol from his holster and aim it at Royce's back. There was, of course, no hesitation from the wounded warrior. From this distance, he needn't even take aim. He simply pointed the deadly instrument at Royce and let it do its work. The crack echoed off of the school's outer walls as Mel pulled the trigger and sent a nine millimeter bullet through Royce's back.

Royce felt the bullet enter and exit his body. It was a sharp, hot pain that sent an uncomfortable buzz from his toes to his eyes. Like he had been punched in the gut, his breath burst forth like a storm cloud from deep within his chest. Gasping, he reached for the little hole in his belly, pulling his hand away with a dark sheen of blood covering his fingers. He tried to recapture his breath but was jolted when Mel pulled the trigger again, sending another bullet into his back.

Royce let the knife, still held in his right hand, fall to the ground. The second bullet hurt far more than the first, hitting him higher on his back and exiting this time through his chest. Jess screamed and started to run toward him but Royce held up his hand to stop her. He smiled at her, though he doubted she could see his expression in the still gathering darkness. His focus lost and his balance faltering, he began to swoon slightly.

Jess ignored Royce's gesture and ran over to him. She caught him just as he was falling forward, his eyes rolling up into their sockets. She was sobbing and begging Royce to keep breathing, but her effort fell on deaf ears. In a blood-sputtering, violent convulsion, Royce died in Jess' arms.

Still on the ground and holding his sliced flesh, Mel demanded, "Get me some help! I'm going to bleed to death!"

"You won't get the chance," Jess said defiantly and shot him in the neck twice from close range with the pistol she pulled from her pocket. Mel dropped his own pistol and brought both of his hands up to his throat in a futile attempt to stem the flow of blood from the two mortal wounds. His windpipe shredded, when he tried to speak, all that emerged was a gurgling, blood wet sound that was not unlike Royce's final utterance. She would have shot him again, but the violent shaking in her hands made pulling the trigger nearly impossible.

Jess gently set Royce's head on the pavement and touched his cheek. She couldn't stop the tears, though she knew time was of the essence. She needed to get moving, but first she found Mel's pistol on the ground next to his still struggling, kicking body. As he watched her grab his discarded firearm, Mel's eyes filled with rage. He felt betrayed by one of the very people he had been, in his mind, protecting from the evil that had fallen upon the world. He couldn't believe she had shot him. He wanted to strike out at her, but was afraid that if he took his hands away from the spurting wounds on his neck that he would certainly bleed to death. Jess met his stare with equal ire but she chose to say nothing. She shook her head and backed away from him, his own pistol pointed at him as a precaution.

She looked around again and saw the other gun he'd been carrying when Royce surprised him. When she hefted it from the pavement, she was expecting it to be much heavier. She thought to herself how much difference having a gun like that with her might make. She didn't know how many bullets it held, but just the feel of it in her hands made her feel a little more secure.

By then, Mel was barely breathing and his hands had fallen away from his neck. Jess cursed him as she walked away. She had all but forgotten about the zombies in the cages when she heard one of them moan slightly. It was as if they had been watching the violence like a spectacle of blood in a Roman arena. Caught in their ravenous gaze, Jess couldn't help the shiver that stopped her in her tracks. She had to fight her rising fear to convince her legs to move again.

She ran to the children, shouting, "We've only got a few minutes. We gotta get outta here."

Danny nodded to her. "Where should we go?"

Jess didn't know for sure where to go, but knew that they needed to get themselves away from the school which had become a prison. Another series of gunshots from the front of the school distracted both of them from their conversation. She weighed the small pistol in her right hand against the larger pistol in her left. She looked at the silver revolver and thought of Simeon for a moment. The thought was there and gone in a flash. She handed Danny the revolver and fished out the extra shells from her pocket.

She asked the boy, "Do you know how to handle one of these?"

Danny nodded and held out his hand. "Yeah, I had to learn to be able to help."

This time Jess nodded. She said to him, "You gotta be careful with this. Okay?"

Danny knew the drill. He looked her in the eyes and nodded another reassurance to her. He slipped the pistol into his pocket and put the extra bullets in his other jacket pocket. The revolver was much bigger and heavier than the pistol Neil had entrusted to him.

Jess asked the air, "What is going on out there?"

55

Prior to Royce's gallant but ultimately fateful decision, Emma and Jerry were sprinting at full steam across the bridge spanning the Kenai River. Jerry looked over his shoulder against his better judgment and lost whatever breath he had been able to retain. Fast on the heels of his retreating breath, his will melted away, wilting like a fading flower. He almost lost his balance and had to consciously guide his foot back to the ground so as not to trip. He was worried that if he did fall, he wouldn't be able to get himself back to his feet in time to escape being today's dinner special.

Jerry trusted Neil's judgment, which had served them all well so far. Regardless, through Jerry's mind paraded a stream of obscenities all directed at Neil and his mother for having had him in the first place. When he looked over at Emma he didn't see fear or distress or even extreme exertion. She seemed preoccupied by some mundane distraction; nothing more, nothing less. Of course, it could have been a matter of concentration, but he couldn't tell for sure.

Emma, however, was anything but distracted. She just happened to be focusing on what lay ahead instead of what was pursuing them from behind. Having those things close on their tails had become a simple fact of life. If she were to dwell on that unfortunate circumstance, she doubted she would be able to function. A waking nightmare from which she couldn't escape by simply opening her eyes would possibly have been enough to stop her cold.

She was carrying the M4 assault rifle and was ready to use it at the first sign of danger to appear in front of them. She concentrated on the road ahead. She didn't want to miss anything...one of those things or one of those militiamen. It didn't matter to her. She and her rifle would deal with either in the same manner.

That thought was passing through her mind when out stepped an unsuspecting man armed with another of the assault rifles like the one she was carrying. He stopped and hesitated, his mouth opening and closing in disbelief. He hadn't seen a group of skins this size in weeks. There were hundreds of them, all in various stages of rot. In front of the oncoming horde by a fair margin was what appeared to be two people. It dawned on him too late that one of the people, a woman, was even then aiming a gun at him. He was incapable of doing anything other than waiting to see what happened.

Emma, upon seeing the man emerge, stopped, raised the rifle, and fired. The first burst and resulting clap of sound caused her to wince reflexively. Those first few shots always did that to her; seemed to be no way to grow accustomed to it. Even so, she aimed carefully and hit her target. She wasn't sure where the bullets struck him, but it was enough to send the sentry sprawling to his belly, yelping with surprise and fear.

Jerry had continued to run and was upon the man only heartbeats later. He grabbed the man's dropped assault rifle and stepped back. Emma was with him by then. She took the gun, extracted the magazine, and discarded the firearm. Jerry looked at her confused.

"We need the bullets more than we need the gun," she said. "It's just dead weight."

Already running again, Jerry said, "Okay. Whatever. But let's go."

The hurt, scared sentry begged, "You can't leave me here. You gotta help me." His voice trailed off as Jerry and Emma put distance between him and them. He was trying to get to his feet, but both of his legs had taken bullets. A desperate sound filled with terror emerged from his throat as he struggled to get away. He was wounded prey without any hope of escape.

The guard pulled himself painfully along on the pavement, but he was doomed from the moment Emma pulled the trigger. A crowd of perhaps twenty zombies set upon him. The first grabbed hold of his trailing legs and pulled him backward. The man kicked at his attacker, but another one only laid its hands upon his other foot. With the two of them pulling at him, his forward movement ceased. He tried to fight but it was utterly and ultimately futile.

Soon, dozens of hands were reaching, clawing, tearing at first his clothes and then his flesh. Several jagged-clawed fingers began to pull at his face, the nails gouging his skin and producing seeping, oozing wounds. When the hands found the corners of his mouth, the gruesome results defied description. Flesh, torn and bloody, was ripped from his bones and fed into hungry mouths. His tongue and eyes were literally gnawed from his skull while he still struggled.

The feast on the sentry did not distract the entire stampeding herd following Emma and Jerry, but enough of the first rank of zombies detoured to create a little more comfort for the man and woman. Emma's shooting had alerted the defenders at the school who pierced the night with both bright lights and bullets. They shot wildly at shadows, but the bullets, coming fast and furious, were a growing danger for Emma and Jerry.

The commotion also distracted all the zombies' attention from Emma and Jerry as well. The two of them continued to run in a wide arc around the school until they were rounding the building toward its rear. They saw the semi-circle of fortified buses transformed into battlements around the school's main entrance, just as Steve had described. Against the sweeping arcs of floodlights and flashlights, the two spied the frantic silhouettes of militia defenders moving to and fro, both atop and inside the buses. From random points all across the rounded wall, little sparks and flashes of light erupted as guns were fired.

The parking lot in which they were running seemed to stretch on forever, like some first time marathoner's paved nightmare. Eventually, Emma and Jerry came upon a cordon of concrete traffic barricades. As they hopped the chest high wall, Jerry looked back over his shoulder. A few of the ragged creatures continued their pursuit, but the vast majority seemed to have taken the bait. With any luck, the wall across the parking lot would end the chase for the rest of them as well, leaving Jerry and Emma to find their way into the school without that threat at their backs.

It was apparent the concrete traffic barrier had been placed prior to the emergence of Armageddon. On this side of the lot, the pavement was largely broken and, in some places, had been stripped back completely down to bare earth. Distracted while he looked around, Jerry nearly turned his ankle on the uneven surface.

Looking up, Jerry saw that they were in a gathering lot of cars, truck, vans, and all manner of small commercial vehicles. Most appeared very used and definitely abandoned, probably utilized by some of the survivors to get there and then discarded. Through the middle of the motor pool was a clearly marked path that led from an opening in the concrete wall and to a closed fenced gate.

He pointed. "That's our way in."

Emma nodded and kept pumping her legs, forcing herself to run despite her growing fatigue. The plan. They needed to stick to the plan. The plan

SEAN SCHUBERT

would keep them all alive.

56

They didn't have much going for them. Neil estimated that the only real thing they did have was the element of surprise. So, when they devised a plan, there weren't a whole lot of moving parts to it. They needed to lead as many zombies as they could to the walls of the fortified school, use the diversion to get inside, rescue their cohorts, and then get away.

The emerging weather might also play a part. The closer they came to the river, the more flakes they began to see in the dim light afforded their eyes. The thin, icy fog had definitely given way to a light flurry. It wasn't diminishing his vision yet, but it was threatening to do so. Maybe they could ride in behind it and never get noticed.

It was the best Neil and the others could do with little to no time and even fewer resources at their disposal. Neil, Della, and Steve rode in the truck at a safe distance behind the attacking mob of frenzied fiends. It was their job to ride in following the chaos and collect the others while the fight still occupied the defenders.

It was important that revenge didn't preoccupy their intentions. They needed to be quick and stealthy. Revenge would only compromise their efforts. Neil tried to explain and then emphasize this to Jerry, who had demanded to be one of the runners. Neil was worried about what Jerry might find and was even more worried that he might go looking for those responsible.

When Steve heard the shooting, his breathing changed. Each exhaled breath held a little doubt and a little guilt. He shifted uncomfortably several times in his seat next to Della in the back of the truck. His regret hung as heavy in the air as did the smell of everyone's body odor.

Neil sensed the shift in his disposition almost immediately, and spent as much time watching Steve in the rearview mirror as he did watching the road. "You doin' alright back there, Steve?" When Steve made no response, and only peered over Neil's shoulder out the front windshield, Neil said reassuringly, "If they're as good as you said, then they'll be okay. I've got no interest in killing anyone. I just want our people back. We're gonna get in and out as quick as we can."

When Steve looked away, Neil shot a glance at Della. Her expression rarely changed and this time was no exception. She wore a constant mask of serious consideration which could be mistaken for belligerence or hostility. Looking at her eyes, Neil felt calm again and knew that he had nothing to fear from Steve. Della, as DB had said many times, was not a woman with which to trifle. His concerns temporarily allayed, Neil paid closer attention to the road ahead.

The lingering evening had yielded to the press of night. The darkness, as absolute as Neil had ever seen, made him feel claustrophobic so overwhelming was its presence. He was driving with only the parking lights to show the way for fear that he would compromise their plan. Even the moon had pulled a heavy, gray cloud around itself as a means to shield it from the unrelenting night and the gathering wintry winds.

They crossed the bridge slowly so as not to distract the undead army from its siege. Below, the river had begun to embrace its winter ebb, its depths as shallow as they would be all year. Neil strained to try and see better what lay ahead but it was of little use. He was as blind as the proverbial bat but he lacked the sonic radar system for navigation.

Across the bridge, the road and the area to either side widened, adding a new depth and dimension to the darkness. It felt like they were driving down a well. Neil couldn't take it any longer.

"I don't think I can drive any farther without lights. I can't see a goddamned thing."

Both Della and Steve nodded, but Neil had already made up his mind. He flipped on the lights and revealed only a few yards in front a slow moving procession with its back to them. "Holy shit!" he exclaimed.

"There's hundreds of 'em!" Steve gasped. Steve was correct. There *were* hundreds of the ghouls immediately in front of them and hundreds more over at the battle at the school. Slowly, like a many-headed serpent of gray stone, the slithering parade of death wheeled about to face this fast approaching new opportunity. Only man made his own light and it was only man that the infection craved.

The hunger fueled the rage that coursed through the creatures' black coagulated veins. Their hands, as thick as branches, clawed at the night. From their open mouths spilled a vile chorus that engorged the black all around them and produced a rising nausea in Neil's, Della's, and Steve's stomachs.

Through the tight forest of reaching, decaying dark arms, Neil pressed the truck forward. He pulled the large silver vehicle hard to the left, trying to escape the cul-de-sac forming in front of them, and found a little space into which he could continue their forward momentum.

Neil hadn't anticipated this many of the foul creatures, based upon the isolated pockets they had encountered thus far in and around Soldotna. He had been concerned that Jerry and Emma wouldn't have been successful in attracting enough of the undead to create the diversion needed to liberate their abducted friends.

Apparently, his concerns were not well founded. Sensing that perhaps he needed to change his own role in their scheme, Neil said over his shoulder, "When I get us a little breathing room, Steve I want you to come up here and drive. You probably know the lay of the land around the school better than I do anyway."

Steve asked doubtfully, "What do you plan on doing?"

"We might need some protection, so I'm gonna climb into the bed of the truck and be ready with my shotgun. If we hit another big pocket of 'em, I'll try and clear us a path."

Steve nodded his understanding, but the nod also held a little doubt about Neil's judgment. Steve had no interest in being out amongst those things, even if it only meant in the back of their truck. He didn't want to be any closer to those things than he had to be. When Neil stopped the truck, Steve threw open the door, leapt out, and then quickly hopped into the driver's side door. He didn't even pause to breathe. Once back inside, he locked the door and finally exhaled.

Neil deftly climbed into the bed of the truck and lifted a backpack full of handguns and ammunition onto his back. At his feet lay another backpack holding more ammunition for his shotgun as well as his trusty aluminum bat. He grabbed hold of the truck's decorative roll bar and slapped his hand twice on the roof of the cab to signal he was ready. Della had also taken the opportunity to climb into the front seat and was preparing herself, though her demeanor was much calmer than that of her male counterparts. Across her lap she was holding a dangerous looking blade that most resembled a machete. Once seated, she began to hum quietly to herself.

Steve pressed the gas, spinning the tires slightly in the gravel. Neil held tightly as they lurched forward, getting away just as a large group of zombies was closing around them. Steve drove over two of the beasts who fell from sight beneath the grill and were crushed by the truck's heavy wheels.

Neil hoped they could trust Steve. He, Della, Jerry and Emma were all placing a lot of faith in the young man. Della didn't seem to be as hesitant as Neil, but that only went so far in alleviating Neil's worry.

There was more shooting coming from the school and now they could hear shouting as well. There was no discerning individual voices, but the sound was clearly that of desperation. Perhaps the wall was not as solid as they had thought or had hoped. They never were.

The battle was fully engaged, the outcome very much in doubt. The militia was killing scores of the undead, but there always seemed to be more to fill the gaps that opened. Lacking the discipline of fully and professionally trained soldiers, the militia expended large quantities of ammunition needlessly. Their shooting was erratic, and oftentimes ineffective.

From the tops of the buses, several militia members threw flaming Molotov cocktails into the masses of decomposing but still animated flesh. The fires lit the killing ground somewhat but did little else. Several of the fiery ghouls pressed themselves against the sides of the buses, threatening to torch those sections of the wall and its hapless defenders.

It was one of the bursting firebombs that caught Steve's attention. He looked over for just a second but that was enough. When he looked back, he saw too late the concrete barricade which separated the old parking lot from the new expanded lot which was still under construction. It was a wall that shouldn't have been there and caught poor Steve completely unaware. He had no time to react other than to gasp and close his eyes.

The truck ran headlong into the concrete wall with a sound that rivaled all the shooting combined. Pieces of steel, shards of glass, and splinters of plastic and fiberglass exploded into the air. Smoke seeped and steam hissed. The truck was dead after a series of exasperated and fruitless clicks and pops from the engine.

Neil was thrown like a flailing ragdoll over the top of the tuck and onto the other side of the barrier. Landing on his back with a jarring thud which robbed him of both his senses and his breath momentarily, Neil was thankful for the padding the full backpack over his shoulders provided him. The pack's contents, lumpy and hard as they were, inflicted some significant bruising and aching pains, but he was thankful for being alive. He allowed a few precious seconds to pass as he appreciated his first struggling breath into his starving lungs. His vision was still absent which allowed his mind to struggle to process what had just happened.

Neil saw the barricade before Steve did and had time to prepare. Neil thought for sure that Steve had seen the obstacle, but when the truck neither changed course nor speed, Neil had braced for the impact. Now, his moment of reflection and gratitude behind him, Neil got his feet under him and looked around. One of the headlights from the truck was still functioning, as was a single yellow hazard light which flashed on and off in rhythmic clicks. All of which cast a haunting, pulsating glow over the accident scene.

The truck's demise was not lost on the army of zombies who had already dispatched contingents to attack, overwhelm, and devour whomever was involved in the crash. The monsters shuffled hungrily, their bile-fouled voices rushing forward and preceding them like the tide. Neil could make out their silhouettes as they approached.

"Della? Della?" he shouted. "Steve? Anyone?" Looking around desperately for anything he might use, Neil thought he recognized something on the pavement. Excited, he tried to run, but his legs and especially his back were hurting worse than he had originally thought. Instead, he stumbled forward and fell painfully.

Breathless and suffering, Neil managed to pull himself along the ground until he had laid his hands on the object. It was his shotgun and its oily, cool, metal surface instantly helped him to feel more confident. At least with the gun, he had a fighting chance.

Time was working against him. It was working against all of them. Neil didn't know if either Della or Steve was still alive but he needed to get back up so he could help them. He gritted his teeth and stood up on his hurt leg, which sent currents of pain shooting up from his bruised and bleeding knee as well as his aching tail bone. When he straightened his back, his tail bone shifted uncomfortably like the unoiled hinge joints of a door that hadn't been opened in a millennium. He could almost hear the grinding of bone against bone. Neil was in need of a good oiling more so than Oz's Tin Man ever had been.

Once up, Neil could see that Della was starting to move again. She shook her head, the blood on her brow glistening in the faint glow from the lone working headlight. She looked over at Steve who was still unconscious behind the steering wheel. From Della's reaction when she touched Steve's forehead,

Neil could deduce that Steve was still breathing.

Della looked up and finally saw Neil. She could see the fear in his eyes despite the sparse light. She followed his gaze over her shoulder and saw the oncoming ranks of death. Excited by the prospect of a meal of flesh, the ghouls moved with a ravenous purpose toward their prey. Rotting arms lashed out in anticipation and heads the color of granite rippled with tics. She looked at her approaching fate and knew her time was limited.

Della locked her yellow eyes on Neil's and said calmly, "You need to be goin' on now. Me and Steve, we'll keep 'em busy. You go get the others. Protect 'em as best you can."

"No, Della. You don't know what you're saying. We can..." but Neil's protests fell on deaf ears. Della had already started to hum to herself.

She forced open her partially crushed door, which creaked and popped loudly. Grabbing a baseball bat that was on the floor of the truck, Della climbed out and faced the predators who were mere feet away by then.

"Go," Della demanded over her shoulder, "before it's too late. You gotta go now. Here," she said as she quickly reached down and tossed him the other backpack. He watched it sail through the air and roll to a clanging stop some yards away from him. And the last thing Neil heard her say was, "God bless and keep you, Neil."

Hearing his name from her lips was enough to shake Neil from his stupor. He fired the shotgun several times into the horde. Della, for her part, swung the bat high above her head in lethal, swooping circles that struck head after head. In her left hand, she brandished the machete, which sliced off reaching hands that drew too close to her.

Della's hum became a grunt which quickly transformed into an animalistic growl, but it was of no use; there were simply too many of them for her to be able to hold at bay indefinitely. She flinched slightly when a few of them made their way around the other side of the truck and began to gnaw on the slowly reawakening Steve.

Poor Steve didn't scream, but instead only whimpered, his consciousness thankfully not completely revived. By the time his arm had been pulled ruthlessly from his body, his eyes had again closed and his breathing had stopped. Gnashing teeth rived flesh from bone, creating great red rupturing geysers which coated the inside windshield of the truck.

With both backpacks tossed over one shoulder, Neil did as he was told and left Della while she was still fighting. The concrete barricade, if he was lucky, would help to stall his pursuers indefinitely. Of course, there was always that possibility that some of the infected souls had already found their way around or over the low wall, but he would simply have to deal with those possibilities as they arose. For the time being, he needed to find Jerry and Emma and get the kids out of harm's way.

Neil snaked in and out of a maze of parked vehicles, afraid for a few moments that he had been thrown into an adjoining salvation yard or something. He couldn't fathom why they'd been parked so precisely otherwise. Should he be wary of some lingering, bitter, but determined junkyard dog waiting to pounce from the shadows? Could there be more than just the undead to fear in the dark?

Neil stumbled and fumbled his way clumsily through the narrow spaces between doors and fenders. His eyes wide, Neil was nearly blind in the dark. There may have been a flashlight in one of his backpacks, but he didn't feel like he had the time to stop and search. He had to keep moving. He needed to get back to the school. They were all counting on him and now he only had bad news to bear.

After several painful strides, Neil found himself standing in what appeared to be an open lane. To his right, he saw a gate and maybe a building on the other side. Maybe he'd get lucky. Maybe he could get his bearings and then find his way back to the others in time to be of assistance.

His legs and back aching more with each step, Neil forced himself forward. The backpacks on his shoulder felt as if they weighed a ton and the gun in his hands weighed another. He would simply have to carry the weight. They would likely need the guns and definitely the ammunition in the future.

57

For all the talk and the swagger shown over the past few weeks, the militiamen seemed pushed to their limit from the outset of the assault. There just seemed to be so many of the skins attacking all at once. They'd never seen anything so frightening.

The citizen soldiers watched from atop the school buses as a sea of festering soulless beasts spread out before them in undulating waves. The creatures pelted the buses with their fists and their heads, shaking the large yellow vehicles until they were no longer safe to be used as platforms. Getting down from the vehicles proved no simple task.

One young man with hopeful blue eyes and shaggy, fair hair lost his balance and had the misfortune of toppling forward amidst the hungry ghouls. His screams lasted only a few brief moments but the sheer terror of them shook all within earshot. And then another unfortunate person, this one a young woman, fell to the same fate. If Jess had been there to witness it, she would have been horrified to see that it was Francine, the pretty Native girl, who had been lost.

With the deaths, fear and doubt began to intrude into the rudimentary discipline which had been imposed upon the defenders. Cohesive and mutually supporting gunfire was exchanged for wild shots fired in manic bursts. Orders from composed group leaders were ignored and met with wild, fear-filled screams. It appeared as if their redoubt was doomed to be overrun and suffer the same fate as every other bastion, large and small, which had been created in the apocalypse.

One voice rose up above the fury to calm frayed nerves and regain control of the dispirited militia. Carter walked up and down the line of defenders, shouting orders and directing traffic. He watched the buses as they teetered on their deflated tires and threatened to fall onto their sides. Carter knew that it was time to act before he was unable to do so.

When the militia had first arrived with all of their military equipment all those days ago, several of them, Carter included, had set about preparing their defenses using some of those tools. On the outsides of three of the buses and at about shoulder height, they had taped a curious item that had the words *Front Toward Enemy* embossed upon it. From the curious items ran wires which were connected to small, olive colored devices not much larger than cell phones but with a working part that looked like the grip of a hole puncher. The three pieces of equipment, thought to be merely detection tools, were then nearly forgotten by everyone else in the compound.

Carter went to a small wooden box into which the wires had been led and removed the three small olive colored devices. He shouted for everyone to cover their ears and then calmly triggered the devices.

Following World War II, governments and industry devoted much of their collective attention to developing and producing new and innovative ways of conducting warfare. The approach of total war mobilized a new way of thinking, which gave birth to entire new industries and opportunities. Antipersonnel mines, too, went through an evolution of sorts with the discovery and application of shaped charges. While land mines had seen widespread use during World War II as a means to create defensive perimeters, their random nature and uncontrolled detonations proved to be somewhat problematic.

A shaped charge was simply an explosive device whose destructive force could be directed through the proper application of a solid base or backing surface typically made of steel. The blast couldn't go through the metal surface, so it was forced to direct itself away from that surface, spreading in a controlled arc a hail of deadly shrapnel produced by the explosion. Such charges could also be controlled through command detonation or, more simply put, a soldier could wait until the device would have the most optimum effect and then trigger it manually. The design was quite simple and very innovative.

From this development arose a new type of killing tool called a Claymore mine, which saw mass production beginning in the 1950s. The mine was used in limited numbers during the Korean War but improvements in design and effectiveness increased its use in subsequent conflicts.

And, as with all things mass produced, the Claymore found its way into the black market, which was where Colonel Bear was obtained several for his own use. The olive green mines sat for years in specially designed cases in the Colonel's storage shed waiting for their opportunity to do what they did best.

Carter had always wanted to use the Claymores and was all the more eager to detonate the explosives that night. With his head down, he touched off the mines. In three great, horrific flashes of fire, smoke, and steel, the bombs belched death out away from the defenders. An arc of death and dismemberment roughly the size of half a football field opened in three large cones spreading out from the buses.

Entire bodies of zombies simply disintegrated while others were decapitated or similarly disfigured. Decomposing limbs and torsos were tossed into the air over the ranks of the undead further back. The lull that followed swept through both the living and the living dead. No one, not even Carter, had anticipated such a raging torrent of sound and fury.

With his ears ringing and his chest still pounding from the concussion of the explosions, Carter stood up and began to shout orders. He directed some of the defenders to climb onto the buses while others were sent into the buses to shoot through the windows. Much of this was done in pantomime with the aid of a flashlight because everyone else's ears were still ringing as well.

He looked for a specific face, and finding it, he shouted, "You! Fucking New Guy, get your ass into the bus and make yourself useful."

Alec, his eyes distant and nearly empty despite the battle in full throttle, nodded and climbed onto the bus. He was now toting a twenty gauge shotgun, which carried quite a bit more kick than the small caliber rifle he had carried with him from his family's cabin all those weeks ago.

None of the militia had found the courage to enter the buses before, but with Carter ordering them to do so and that new kid jumping in so readily, none of them hesitated for very long. They took advantage of the lull to reestablish themselves into better positions. Thankfully, the explosive devices had worked exactly as designed, leaving the buses only scorched from the blasts but seemingly still very much intact.

The bus Alec stepped up into was filled with blinding, choking smoke, which made walking down the narrow, off kilter aisle very difficult. Alec and the others found their way onto the bus and into firing positions through the bus' shattered windows. With the tires of the bus having been flattened, the militiamen didn't seem to be nearly high enough for comfort any longer. In front of them was a sea of bobbing heads appearing out of the darkness and these heads were just inches below the muzzles of their guns.

Gnarled fingers reached into and around the militiamen brave enough to set about their tasks. At first Alec hesitated, his courage melting with his first choking fit as he made his way to the end of the bus. Alec's position next to the emergency exit was more than he had anticipated. He had essentially two walls of partially broken windows to defend and a single gun with a handful of shells with which to do it.

Alec's hands were lead weights hanging at the bottoms of his arms. He could barely feel the gun in his quivering hands. He missed his mom and his dad. Hell, he even missed his little brother. He missed being a kid without any worries beyond looking and acting cool, which seemed to be as far from his mother's and father's grasp as he could imagine. He missed that guns were something that he used only in video games. His head filled with all that he missed and threatened to burst at any moment. He couldn't possibly be expected to fight.

A loud rap on the outside of the bus drew his attention. He turned and saw Carter there with a big smile and a menacing bat. Carter shouted above the din, "Don't think! Just shoot! Remember, this is for your sister."

Alec shook all over as his resolve struggled against his terror. With the will of a titan, he raised his shotgun, held his breath, and pulled the trigger. Nothing happened. Again, he heard the loud crack behind him against the bus.

"Turn the safety off, dipshit," Alec heard Carter chastise.

Alec found the switch with his thumb and fired a quick, nervous blast which sailed well over all of his possible targets' heads.

"Remember your sister," Carter said. "She's counting on you."

With the shotgun at his shoulder this time, Alec aimed better and fired a slug which plowed a furrow through the nearest head in front of him. He looked back over his shoulder but found that Carter had already moved away.

There wasn't time to consider the departure. Alec looked to his right at the others on the bus-turned-redoubt and wasn't filled with comfort. They all looked as ill-prepared and as terrified as he was. He couldn't see all the men on the bus but he was fairly certain he was the youngest. The man closest to him looked to be at least his father's age if not older. The smoke was starting to disperse, but the darkness again resumed its overwhelming crush all around them.

Firing his shotgun, Alec turned to face the advancing ghouls pressed against the bus' metal skin. Their nails, like steel claws, raked across the painted metal, removing scorched bits of paint while seeking soft bits of clothing or flesh. He screamed as he shot the next several blasts from his shotgun. He fired until there were no more shells to discharge.

He looked to his right again in time to see another young man make the mistake of following his gun out the window as he fought to keep hold of it. As soon as the young man started out the window, his legs went vertical and then he was gone. Alec thought he could hear the man's screams, but they may have been his own.

Alec reloaded quickly but with clumsy fingers. It wasn't fast enough to save another from the party on the bus. There were only three of them left including Alec when they decided it was time to abandon the bus. The first man, an older guy wearing an orange hunting vest over a business suit coat, looked down toward Alec and simply turned and ran off the bus. As he fled, he ran into another militiaman and knocked him onto his back. When the second man regained his footing, he too decided it was time to depart and followed the lead from the other man. Alec, feeling very alone and all but surrounded, ran too.

He emerged from the position, fully expecting to be berated by a violently disappointed Carter, but there was no sign of him. The defense was starting to unravel, despite all the carefully scripted plans. Alec's wasn't the only position which had been compromised.

On another of the buses from which a Claymore mine had been detonated, the side of the vehicle had started to give way. At first, the windows fell from their frames and then seams began to open as rivets loosened and welds separated. Leaning across the larger window apertures, the unfortunate souls in that bus forced the weakened side of the vehicle free. It didn't collapse fully like an opening drawbridge but it opened enough to spook the men and women fighting within it. They panicked and tried to withdraw, which only invited more disaster.

The storm of death around them began to rage and intensify, the dark clouds swirling uncontrollably. Scared and desperate people ran in both directions screaming and pointing and shooting mostly blindly. They shot at every shadow while from behind the shadows, the undead continued their assault.

Like frightened eyes, searchlights and flashlights scanned the ground and the heavens but found only more and more ugliness emerging from the night. Carter walked from defensive pocket to defensive pocket trying to calm his troops, but he was finding it hard to compete with the chaos.

Pulling out all the tricks at his disposal, Carter began handing out Molotov cocktails to those standing around him. "Light 'em up! Light 'em up!" he kept shouting.

Carter knew the battle was not going well, but also that it was far from lost. There just seemed to be so many of the undead. There simply weren't enough bullets. They needed to get creative in dealing with them. If only he had a handful more Claymore mines. There *were* some more, but the Colonel had other intentions for them.

58

There was no use trying to ignore the battle raging in the front of the school. The horrific sound, filled with terrified screams and echoing gunshots, defied Jerry's and Emma's best efforts. The locked gate stood between them and another smaller car lot situated around the school's receiving area. The gate was secured with a heavy, intimidating lock and an equally imposing chain. Neither Jerry nor Emma had on them a tool capable of dealing with either the lock or the chain.

"Now what?" Jerry whispered. "Do we shoot it off?"

The shooting on the opposite side of the building might mask their own gunshot, but there was no guarantee. If a guard had been posted to cover this entrance, shooting might just alert them to Emma's and Jerry's presence. They could ill afford finding themselves in a firefight. They needed to get in and get out as quietly as possible. That was their only chance.

Thinking all of this in an instant, Emma answered, "No, we climb."

Jerry, desperate to find Claire, slung his rifle over his shoulder and started to climb. The gate sagged and swayed too much, so they ascended a section of chain link fence with what appeared to be a wooden fence of sorts behind it. He hooked his fingers and forced the toe of his boots into the crisscrossed openings in the stiff, twisted wires comprising the fence. He pulled and pushed himself up.

Once atop the wall, Jerry paused momentarily to survey the area. He appeared to be looking down at basketball courts but there was something else toward the middle. It looked like dog kennels or something. He couldn't be sure but he thought that perhaps there was something or someone in the cages.

Emma, feeling exposed and vulnerable while she climbed, pulled herself up next to Jerry. She looked back over her shoulder to prove to herself that her fears were unfounded and saw nothing but empty space. They hadn't been followed after all.

She whispered, "C'mon, let's go find your girl."

They climbed down carefully, though the presence of the wooden fence posed new challenges. On Jerry's second step, his foot slipped and he fell painfully to the ground below.

"Fuck!" he screeched as the pain from his ankle and the bottoms of his feet crept up the length of his spine to his brain.

"You okay?" Emma called to him.

Shaking his head and rubbing his ankle, he answered, "Yeah, but watch that last step. It's a bitch."

It was darker down below the height of the wall, as if the moonlight dared not venture so deep. It felt as if Jerry had fallen into a well of shadows. He stepped tentatively through the dark hoping for dear life that he wouldn't run into something.

Emma leapt down behind Jerry, startling him and causing him to jump. "Sorry," she partly giggled the word in a rare moment of levity. More seriously, she asked, "Where's your flashlight?"

Jerry felt like a fool. With the flashlight in hand, he clicked it on and pointed its beam into the gloom. The light reached out and found the kennels they had spied from the top of the wall. Both Jerry and Emma recoiled slightly when the festering, rage-filled faced suddenly filled the light. It snapped its jaws closed hungrily and aggressively several times, pressing its face roughly against the bowing fence, which gouged darkening troughs in its skin.

"What the hell?" Emma's gasped.

Jerry wondered aloud, "Pets?"

Panning the light left, they saw a recently dead body with a still spreading pool of blood around it. Jerry looked at Emma and cocked his eyebrows. The dead man looked like a soldier, probably one of those militiamen. He didn't look like a zeke to Jerry, so he found himself very curious about what had happened to the man.

Emma approached the dead body cautiously. Leaning over him, she began to search him. From a deep pouch attached to his belt, she pulled a pair of ammunition magazines. They weren't the same size as her rifle's but the bullets looked to be the same caliber. Ammunition was ammunition. She stuffed the clips into her backpack and continued her search. He had cigarettes, a lighter, a small flask with what smelled like whiskey in it, an MRE ration kit, and some other odds and ends. The search took her a mere moment, but their proximity to the zeke kennels were making both of them uncomfortable.

They needed to get in the school and find Claire and the kids.

59

When Jess burst into the library, her breathless entry caused a gathering crowd at the door to scurry into dark corners like roaches fleeing the light. They uttered weak, surprised gasps as they retreated deeper into the bookshelves. Many had survived similar, if slightly scaled back versions of the battle outside and the desperate sounds were reviving suppressed fears. Their collective psyche was largely broken, as was their morale. They were a scared herd of prey, corralled into a trap and waiting to die. The sad truth was that most of the people hiding in the library were well aware of that fact and their probable fate but they were paralyzed with fear.

Jess, standing alone in the entryway, scanned the library for anyone who might help but not a single soul looked at her. They avoided her gaze as much as they avoided the reality of the struggle happening outside the school. They were detached and dispirited. Not a one of them was willing to engage her. No one was even willing to acknowledge her.

That wasn't good enough for her and she didn't have time for subtlety. Unfortunately, as she started to speak, she was overcome with emotion and began to sob, drenching her words and the fire of her passion. She said to everyone, "I'm taking those kids outta here. I could use some help. Those kids could use some help. This is our chance. They killed Royce and any of us might be next!"

Her plea was met with silence, other than an embarrassed sniffle or a throat clearing cough. To which she continued, "This is no way to live. We're all prisoners here. This is our chance to get away." Still nothing.

Jess waited for a second or two, hoping that guilt would work its magic. She was a mother and was adept at using her daughter's sense of guilt to influence her decisions and actions. She was pulling out all her tricks to encourage someone to step forward. She was more than a little concerned about taking those kids out beyond the walls, especially at night and even more so without the aid of another adult pair of eyes and arms.

She waited until she was certain that no one was willing to be that person. Something in her belly turned and crawled up into her chest and then into her throat. "No one? Not one of you? You all make me sick! Fucking cowardly pieces of shit! Every one of you. You *deserve* to be prey. You deserve what you get."

She was again only met with breathing and the staccato pops of gunfire outside. Jess allowed a disgusted, single, silent laugh to find its way to the surface. She shook her head in frustration and walked back out.

The children had been waiting in the hallway all that time. The littlest boy was standing near the wall and messing with a small rectangular object which appeared to have been taped there by someone. The wires which led away from the device had also been taped to the wall. Little Paul seemed to be tracing some raised letters on the object with his tiny index finger. Jess signaled to all the children to gather around her so they could get on their way. They needed to use the distraction, whatever it was, to their benefit.

"What about Claire?" Danny asked.

"Claire?"

"She's the woman who was with us. She needs your help too. We can't just leave her here."

"You're right...?"

"Danny. My name is Danny and this is Jules and Paul and Nikki."

Jess nodded to each in turn and then continued, "Danny, you're right. We need to get her outta here too. We need to go find her but I don't think we have much time."

Lucky for both of them, Jess was very familiar with the school. Her daughter had already attended two years of high school at Skyview, which had afforded Jess opportunities to be in the school. She knew of some shop classrooms on the far side of the cafeteria. They were somewhat removed and in a blind corner away from the more trafficked areas of the building. It would likely be a good place to hide someone. She thought that maybe some other folks who had been brought to the school under similar circumstances had started out there.

Jess' footsteps echoed in the dark, cavernous room as she ran toward the shop corner. She rounded the corner and was surprised when the fist came out of the gloom and struck her squarely in the face, hitting her with all the fury and force of Thor's Hammer, drawing blood from her nose and tears from her eyes. She was instantly unbalanced and thrown backward, gliding awkwardly across the slick tiled floor. The rifle she had taken from Mel clattered away from her, sounding like a squad of tin soldiers wearing plastic boots running across the floor. It came to rest well out of sight, not that she could see anything at the moment anyway.

With her eyes filled with fearful tears and her chest empty of breath, Jess began to panic. Try as she might though, she couldn't get herself back to her feet. When she heard the chillingly calm voice emerge from behind her disorientation, her panic nearly climbed to full blown attack.

With icebergs chilling his speech, Sullivan said coolly, "Yeah, I don't think so bitch. It's way past visiting hours." Apparently pleased with his creativity, Sullivan produced a poisonous snicker. Despite the bludgeoning he had just dealt to Jess, Sullivan's breathing had never changed and his heart rate never fluctuated. He was as cool as frostbite and just as hospitable.

Danny recoiled from the terrifying man and tried to shield the other children at the same time. They all retreated clumsily, tripping over one another as they did, inextricably knotted together like a basket of crabs.

Sullivan smiled and said to them, "I was always good with kids too. They always learned to respect me or pay the price. You kids not like your kiddy kennel outside? I guess I'll just have to come up with something better next time, huh?"

Danny found enough courage to demand, "Where's Claire? What'd you do with her?"

Sullivan took out a large hunting knife from a scabbard hidden under his jacket and acted as if he was picking his teeth with the enormous blade. He asked absently, "Was that her name? We never got around to formal introductions I guess. Tell you the truth, I wasn't that interested. No, I was curious about a completely different side of her. And let me tell you; she was remarkable."

Sullivan looked at Danny, who was barely visible in the darkness. "You want to see her? Or what's left of her, I should say. Help yourself. She's inside."

Danny wanted to run into Claire and get her out, but Sullivan's grin froze him in his tracks, with a slight sensation of vertigo and nausea. It held all of Medusa's menace with the power to change men to stone.

Sullivan laughed and leaned forward so that he was towering over the still huddling group of children. He hovered like a vulture awaiting the fateful moment of its carrion promise. Sullivan relished those moments and the accompanying sense of power that surged in his veins. There was no narcotic he had ever tried which produced the same effect.

"Is she...?"

Sullivan again laughed a toxic chuckle. "D'you wanna know if she is okay? Or just alive? There's a big difference, ya know. The Colonel...he ordered me to keep her alive and I guess I did my best, but I kinda lost track of her in all my fun."

The man's laughing did not return, but the sneer had never left. It was still painted across his face like a grim splash of dark graffiti.

Jess was still not recovered enough to get back to her feet, but her mouth was well on its way. "Such a tough man, torturing a woman. She was probably tied down too."

Sullivan's smiled barely receded but something happened to his eyes. They narrowed and filled with anger. Whatever calm had been a part of his facade evaporated as his fury formed into threatening storms of emotion promising to burst at any moment.

Jess, her eyes still not in focus, wouldn't have paused even if she could see the homicidal urge in Sullivan's eyes. "She was, wasn't she? My hero. Hey, maybe as an encore, you could take one of those kids and—"

Starting across the cafeteria, his hands balling into angry, tight fists, Sullivan's acidic voice cut her off, "You better watch what you say bitch, 'cause you're next."

From the entrance to the cafeteria, one of the Colonel's girls, he couldn't be sure if it was Sherry or Terry, screamed, "What are you doing? You've got to stop! They're just children for God's sake!"

Sullivan was once again hearing someone tell him what he could and what he could not do, and he had just about heard enough of that for one day. He especially didn't like to be given orders by a woman. He'd never worked for a woman and couldn't imagine having done so. With a murderous scowl, he looked at the woman standing in the middle of the hallway and thought about what to do for a moment.

With no other ideas surfacing immediately, Sullivan leaned back on his heels and hurled his large knife at her. The blade rocketed across the cafeteria, turning end over end as it cut through the air. Having practiced such a throw for countless hours on the Colonel's ranch, Sullivan had gotten quite adept at throwing knives and axes over the years. This distance, however, was several more yards than that to which he had grown accustomed. The blade struck its target, but instead of sinking itself into her flesh, the silver metal only cut her. A wound opened up on her arm and her abdomen which spilled a torrent of blood from cut arteries.

The woman screamed and fell over backward. Out of Sullivan's sight but viewing all of this was the other of Colonel Bear's *secretaries* who had just emerged from the Colonel's office. She saw her friend fall, scattering blood on the floor and walls. Both women were now screaming, though the one still standing took off running down the hall toward the library.

Flanked by two of his more loyal men, Colonel Bear was by then standing behind the counter separating the office from the hallway. He watched the young woman, who only moments before had been pleasuring him to his delight, run toward the library, screaming.

He looked at the two men and with his chin gestured down the hallway toward the library. His obedient men did his bidding without question. They marched down the hall and out of sight. Colonel Bear sighed heavily, already regretting what he suspected he would be forced to do. Teaching lessons to these people was something in which he had no interest. Carter, and especially Sullivan, were thankfully more willing to put forth the effort necessary to rein in people's wills.

Seconds after his guards disappeared into the doors, the Colonel could hear the doors open again. There was commotion erupting; voices filled with anger and devoid of fear filled the echoing hallway. Jess had relit the pilot lights of their resolve and the other woman's hysterical shouting had added fuel to the fire.

The two militiamen did their best to quiet the agitated civilians. Unfortunately, their efforts were limited to pointing their rifles and shouting at everyone to "get the fuck back!" When the two men felt like they had exhausted all their options, they started to pull their triggers.

Already excited, the civilians did not shrink away from the shooting. They surged forward, a mob with a single purpose, and quickly overwhelmed the men, who were bludgeoned to death with boot heels, fists, and the butts of their own rifles turned against them.

A new voice found its way above the others in the hallway. It was one of the men who had refused to join his militia; Daniel maybe. He was trying to get them organized. The Colonel could tell by their frantic voices that they had guns and were now trying to decide how best to use them. There were only a few brief moments before the uprising would likely begin. It would likely be messy and the Colonel didn't have the resources to be able to fight a battle outside against the skins and one inside against...his slaves.

The Colonel shook his head and sighed a disappointed chest full of air. The hallway was now bubbling with new voices and with questions. There was doubt where there had only been fear and control before. Again the Colonel sighed. He had so hoped his efforts could lead to a new beginning. Apparently it wasn't going to be this time. He would simply have to try again. He was going to miss his little mistresses, but he had to do what he had to do. He had to have control, especially now. He couldn't allow this moment to slip away from him.

Colonel Bear took a small contraption from a wooden box on the counter. The olive colored device wasn't much larger than a cell phone but looked kind of like a hole puncher. He clicked off the safety and then detonated the claymore mines which lined the hallway walls outside the library.

The explosion shook the school to its core. The shrapnel, without anywhere else to go, careened seemingly endlessly off the walls, wreaking a bloody vengeance upon flesh with utter abandon. The intensity of the blast forced a rush of hot, fiery air to surge through the hallways, knocking the Colonel, who hadn't anticipated the fury of the explosion, onto his large posterior. The gush of wind along with the concussion of the explosion also set Sullivan off balance, sending him to the floor as well.

Taking the opportunity to get around him, Danny stood up and tried to run into the back rooms to find Claire. He took one step and was tackled by the big, scary man. Danny kicked and struggled, but the man was just too big, too strong, and too willing to be mean. Very quickly, the man had his hands around Danny's throat and was squeezing until Danny's eyes felt like they would burst from the pressure.

Danny was fairly certain the man was going to kill him until Jess intervened with a kick to Sullivan's side. The man let up his grip slightly, but didn't release Danny. When Jess reared back to deliver another kick, Sullivan rolled and grabbed her leg. He pulled her to the floor, punching her between the shoulder blades.

Luckily, Danny was able to extricate himself from the fray. He retreated to the wall and pulled his legs up to his chest. He'd never been so afraid in all his life. Trying to draw him out from his stupor, Jules yelled, "Danny! Do something! He'll kill 'er!"

Sullivan had finally gotten his hand onto the back of Jess' head and was in the process of forcing it down violently onto the floor. Danny shook and in so doing, he felt that familiar weight in his jacket pocket.

Danny stood and pulled the revolver from his pocket. He screamed at the top of his voice, "Leavvvvve her aloooooone!"

Sullivan stopped and smiled up at Danny. If the man was afraid at all, he was doing an amazing job hiding it. Danny immediately felt like the man was more in control of the situation than he was, despite the fact that it was Danny who was holding the firearm.

Sullivan sneered, "Kid, unless you're ready to use that thing, you better not make a habit of pointing it at people."

Danny wilted. The gun began to sag and droop in front of him, like a lifeless tree branch ready to be pruned. The pistol felt so heavy and the trigger seemed so impossible. Sullivan was probably right. The image of the other man Danny had inadvertently shot flashed into his mind. It had happened so quickly. There had been no thinking on Danny's part; he only reacted and then the man was dead. This felt so different; so premeditated and vengeful. It felt so much more real and calculated.

Danny was crying frustrated and fearful tears by then, which Sullivan saw and relished. The man's smile grew until it filled the entire room. He laughed. "I knew you didn't have it in you. You're no killer."

From behind and to the side of Danny, Emma shouted, "No, but I am!" She fired two three-round bursts from close range, all the bullets striking Sullivan in the torso and legs. He tried to move as the bullets punched holes into and through his body, breaking bones and laying waste to internal organs. His right lung, pierced completely through from front to back, filled with blood and collapsed. Another bullet shattered his torso. Still another found its way to his groin, emasculating him violently. Sullivan fell backward with an ugly, startling thud.

Jerry was already running over to Danny, who was still pointing his gun at the dead or dying Sullivan. Danny was still crying. He was ashamed. He needed to be strong and he was unable. He felt like he'd let down Jules, Nikki, and Paul; not to mention Jess who was very nearly beaten to death.

Jerry stepped next to Danny and slowly lowered Danny's arm back to his side, removing the pistol from his hand. Sensing Danny's frustration, he said reassuringly, "I'm proud of you, buddy."

Danny looked up at Jerry questioningly. He couldn't possibly guess the source of Jerry's pride. He didn't need an explanation though. He just wanted to get away from the school. He wanted to be away from the zombies. He wanted to feel safe again. At the moment, burrowing himself into Jerry's jacket and chest would suffice. He hugged himself to Jerry and felt Jules' little arms when she joined the embrace.

Jerry whispered to both of them, "I'm so sorry. I promised I'd protect both of you."

"You came for us, Jerry," Jules said. "You kept your promise."

There was no time to discuss any of it at the moment. They needed to get away while the zekes were still threatening but not yet overrunning the base. Emma asked, "Where's Claire? Where's Alec?"

Danny turned to look toward the rooms in the dark corner. "I think Claire may be back there."

Jules said, "We haven't seen Alec since we got here."

Jerry ran by her toward the doors to which Danny had referred. Jerry opened one but immediately ran across the hall to the next. He paused in the doorway, his breath taken away by what he saw.

Emma watched Jerry's posture sink, his shoulders rolling forward sadly as if he was trying to wrap himself in a warm, protective cocoon. His whole body shook as he was swept by a sudden emotional wave. He didn't seem capable of moving into the room on his own accord.

Emma stood up from the kids and walked over to where Jerry was standing. She touched his shoulder gently and stepped up next to him. The room was lit with a single, flickering incandescent bulb. The rank stench of body odor and human waste punctuated the already heavy, moist air hanging in the room.

Lying motionless atop a workshop classroom bench was the seemingly lifeless body of Claire. The gray-green tabletop surface was spattered and smeared with drops and streaks of blood, her blood.

Emma swallowed her gasp and whispered, "Do you want me to...?"

Jerry stepped into the room and slowly approached Claire. She was neither moving nor breathing. His hand shaking fearfully, Jerry reached out and touched Claire's bruised and bloodied face. Her skin was cold and somewhat spongy, the result of the beating she had received. Jerry wasn't entirely sure about what he was feeling.

The air was warm and sticky, like a small weight room where all the heat and smells from the lifters is trapped upon itself, and yet his skin crawled with goose bumps. His feet and hands hung so heavily at his side, but his head felt light and dizzy like a balloon threatening to drift away.

Emma, mindful of the fact that they had limited time with which to work, pivoted around Jerry. She stepped lightly, almost on her tiptoes, toward Claire. Even from this distance, she could see that Claire's life had already fled.

Seeing Claire's mangled hands and feet on the table drew a gasp from Emma. She hoped Jerry hadn't seen them yet. Emma knew she needed to get Jerry out of that room. She had precious little time and needed to act.

Emma grabbed Jerry's arm and tried to pull him away but he was immovable; a statue with a vacant, pale face staring forever at his doom. Emma was suddenly gripped with fear. *What if she couldn't get Jerry on the move again? Could she keep everyone going by herself?* And the fact that kept rearing its head through her doubt and indecision was that there was no time for any of it. The shooting and screaming and fighting outside was still loud and raging, but it couldn't last. There were only so many bullets and a finite number of targets. When the shooting stopped, she would know that the clock had stopped ticking for them.

"Jerry, we need to go." The words came without Emma's knowledge or conscious intent. It was as if her thoughts became self-aware and took to flight of their own will. When she repeated them, she was less surprised, but in both instances Jerry either willfully ignored her or was unable to respond. Either way, her message did little to alleviate her anxiety or spur Jerry to action.

Jerry finally said, his eyes moving no more than his feet, "Go on without me. I'm gonna stay here with her. She shouldn't be left her alone like this. She... I mean I...." His thoughts were as muddled as his speech. He was having a hard time understanding what had happened, let alone why.

Emma pleaded, "Jerry, she's gone. I'm sorry but there's nothing we can do for her." She grabbed his arms and forced him around to look her in the eyes. "I need your help. Those kids...they need your help. Please." By the time her final word emerged Emma was crying, which made her angry. She hated to cry. She resented her loss of control as a result of crying...the sniffling, the blubbering, the hyperventilating. She hated all of it.

She hated it so much that when the tears started, her mood immediately soured. Her bottom lip twitched with anger as the tears rounded her down turned mouth. She was nearing a total emotional explosion, when a familiar voice echoed from the other side of the cafeteria.

"Jerry? Emma? Where are you guys?" It was Neil and he couldn't have arrived at a better time.

60

Neil had neither the patience nor the immediate dexterity to hoist himself over the wall the way Emma and Jerry had done. He just didn't have it in him at the moment.

When his bat failed to unfasten the lock or its chain counterpart, Neil held the barrel of his shotgun inches away and fired. The twelve gauge slug was more than effective; the gate flung open effortlessly after the blast.

He walked into the enclosed compound and looked around. Deciding it was prudent to use his flashlight now, he swept left and right with the beam. The left side of the yard had more cars, all of which appeared to be still serviceable and recently used. Neil wandered over to the nearest vehicle, a dark Chevy truck. He smiled when he looked in the window and saw keys on the dashboard.

He found a beat up Suburban in the front rank a little further down. Again, the keys were there. Neil propped open the doors in anticipation of a hasty exit. Under their typical circumstances, a little preparation typically went a long way and that Suburban would make a great ride out of town.

Satisfied, Neil looked the other direction only to see the kenneled zekes on the far side of the enclosure. The moaning creature in the nearest cage became much more animated when the light fell upon it.

Having had enough, Neil again raised his shotgun and fired two quick successive slugs into the beast. He was fairly certain he hadn't dispatched it, but he had momentarily quieted it which was good enough for him.

Indeed, both of Neil's shots had struck the creature in its upper chest; two very lethal pulls of a trigger under normal circumstances. Unfortunately, his first shot had also hit and destroyed the gate's latching mechanism. By the time the zombie had gotten back to its balance-challenged feet, Neil was gone. The decomposing ghoul leaned forward ever so slightly and the gate gave way. It swung open slowly, uttering the creak of a long closed coffin as it did.

With unsteady but capable steps, the zombie began to make its way into the building following in Neil's footsteps.

Meanwhile, in the cafeteria now, Neil limped across the largely dark room and thankfully found himself amongst his family. He could sense the grief before he had crossed the full distance. Seeing the children scared but safe, meant that it could only have been either Claire or Alec. Neil was about to ask as much when Danny leapt to his feet and ran full into Neil, wrapping his small arms around Neil's waist.

Neil touched Danny on the back gently and then leaned down to return his embrace.

"I knew you'd come for us," Danny said quietly. "I just knew it."

Neil smiled but was unable to combat the thankful tears and so didn't bother to try. Jules joined their hug eagerly, getting her even smaller arms intertwined tightly between Neil's and Danny's. The hug could have lasted longer, but an unfamiliar voice said, "I don't think we have much time. We should be gettin' outta here."

Neil reluctantly pulled himself free of Danny's and Jules' arms. He didn't recognize the voice any more than he did the face, but it was of little consequence at the moment. He nodded in agreement.

Emma emerged from around the corner. "Jerry needs your help," she said. "Now."

Neil ran to her and knew what to expect when Emma grabbed his arm as he passed and squeezed it forcefully. He stopped and looked her in the eyes to see the warning that she shared. He slowed his pace as he entered a room which reeked of loss and tears. When he touched Jerry's shoulder, he could feel a soft, steady, but building vibration through his layers of clothing and jackets. It was an unfortunately all too familiar sensation, and one that they didn't seem capable of escaping.

Jerry appreciated Neil's sudden and unexpected appearance as much as Emma did; maybe even more so. Jerry didn't want to have an emotional breakdown at all, but he especially didn't want to in front of Neil, who seemed to have accepted Meghan's death with a stoic resolve that surprised all of them. Jerry wasn't a machismo-driven person, but he also didn't want to appear weak when all those around needed him to be strong. He felt like he was caught in a trap

How the hell did Neil do it all the time? Jerry had seen all the telling signs of his responsibilities in Neil's face and in the tired way in which he carried himself on occasion, but that was really as bad as it got. Neil always seemed so composed and reliable. Jerry didn't want to be another burden to Neil.

If they were to just leave him behind, then he wouldn't be anyone's burden to bear. He could just stay with Claire until...well, until whatever happened next. As he thought it, Jerry recognized how ridiculous it was but that was what he wanted. He wanted to be with Claire and if that meant death or any other options, well so be it. His own internal struggle and the hard realizations of their reality finally sent him over the edge.

He doubled forward and produced a loud, long, deep wail at the tail of which the single word question stretched on and on. "Whyyyyyyyyyyyyyyyyyyyy?"

Neil stood with Jerry and didn't say a word. He didn't know how to help and that is likely the reason that he had appeared so stoic to Jerry and everyone else. He'd never really had to deal with loss and suddenly it was all around him, haunting his every step and every thought.

Meghan's face, which he had yearned to see in all of his waking hours, was already starting to fade from his memory. It was drifting away on a growing, surging torrent of other faces lost to the infection and all of its destructive wrath.

And now, Jerry was suffering the same pain that Neil had somehow absorbed and, at least temporarily, avoided. He didn't envy Jerry's suffering but he envied Jerry's ability to at least feel it. Hating to do it, Neil was forced to interrupt Jerry's grieving with another reality.

"Jerry, I know that you're going to ask to be left with Claire. And I also know that you know that isn't gonna happen. We have to leave in one minute. You've got a minute with her and then we have to go, and you're comin' with us. I'm hurt and need your help more than ever."

Neil waited for Jerry to stand back up, which happened slowly. When he was righted again, Jerry looked away from Neil but nodded his understanding. He held up a hand and waved Neil into the other room.

Neil complied but did not leave Jerry out of his sight, mindful of the fact that grief can sometimes cloud judgment. Neil didn't want Jerry to try anything he or any of them would regret. He got Emma's attention and had her stand in the doorway. Neil then went over to Jess to introduce himself.

Before Neil had a chance to speak, she said, "I'm Jess. I get that you're Neil, but we don't really have time for formal introductions. We really need to be getting outta here, and I mean now. Pretty soon things are gonna change out there and either them militia assholes or the skins are gonna get the upper hand and then—"

Neil nodded. "You're right. Emma, can you help Jerry? Kids, we need to get going."

Jules asked again, "What about Alec? He's here somewhere too."

61

Alec was still carrying the shotgun he had been given despite having no bullets for it. He was dragging it absently behind him by its strap. He resembled a tired boy at the end of a long day of playing. His steps held no enthusiasm and his stare, struggling to see in the inadequate lighting produced by waving flashlights and random fires, was distant and vacant.

Alec's surroundings were unfamiliar and chaotic. People were running to and fro, shouting and crying. He didn't know any of them and didn't care to get to know them. It felt like his first day in junior high school when all that he knew seemed so far away. He looked around for Carter, the one person whose name he knew, but didn't see his face anywhere.

He kept waiting for someone to tell him what to do. He didn't much care for feeling lost and a little direction would have been very welcome. He started to walk back toward the main school entrance when the screams behind him grew much louder.

He thought he heard a woman shouting some kind of a warning but then her shrill cries were suddenly quiet. When the first ghoul emerged from inside the bus, it was as if everything stopped. Time itself paused to see what would happen next.

Luckily, not everyone was frozen in panic. One man stepped up to deal with the danger, swinging his rifle like a club, striking the beast just above its eyebrows. The creature fell backward against the bus as the man continued his attack. With his rifle butt, he crushed bone and brain matter until it was smeared hideously on the vehicle's yellow side.

Unfortunately, the man was so engrossed in destroying his foe that he didn't see the next one lumbering down the narrow steps. It turned abruptly and grabbed the man's shoulders, forcing him to the ground. The two struggled as Alec watched, not able to muster the courage to step forward and help the endangered man.

Another man joined the close quarters melee just as two more zombies climbed out of the bus. And then a steady stream of the fiends began to appear. Alec heard someone scream, "They've broken through! They're through!"

The chaotic battle that ensued was only manageable because the appearance of the creatures was limited to a trickle at first. As one was dispatched, another was there to take its place. The first several were teetering wretches without much dexterity or flexibility, but then some of the recently deceased militiamen and women began to join the fray.

They moved much more lithely, like fearsome predators on the prowl. Unable to discern friend from foe, many of the militia began to shoot indiscriminately at the dark shadows that ran about. Many living militiamen fell prey to the bullets of militia guns.

Alec was still backing away from the growing fight, when a stray bullet careened from the pavement and struck him in the right knee. His knee cap shattered and the attending ligaments and tendons shredded, Alec was swept from his feet. Unable to get up from the ground, he tried to crawl to safety.

His efforts were doomed from the start. In mere moments, three ghouls saw the crawling figure as hapless and helpless as a wounded bird. Excited by the prospect of young flesh, the trio stumbled toward Alec and fell upon him.

One set of jagged teeth sank themselves into the nape of Alec's neck, biting through both hair and skin. Alec swung his hand around trying to fend off his attacker, but this only invited another of the beasts to grab hold of Alec's exposed arm. The zombie pulled back on the limb, dislocating Alec's upper arm from his shoulder joint. It forced Alec's fingers into its mouth and chomped down on the digits with its gnashing jaws.

The third demon sat upon Alec's back and, pulling the boy's jacket up to expose his skin, began to gnaw on the tender flesh just above the boy's waist. His breath stolen away by both the weight on his back and the currents of pain filling his brain, Alec was unable to either fight off his attackers or call for help.

For several more seconds, Alec flailed uselessly with his one good arm until his life faded and he fell limp. The fiends chomped and chewed his young flesh between their blood dripping lips. Turning his lifeless body onto its back, they began to harvest his delectable organs, devouring the delicious internal tissues and sweet juices in greedy, succulent mouthfuls.

More and more of the militia fell under similar circumstances. Carter, still holding ground near one of the buses, directed the defense of what little territory he could. Finally, sensing he needed to face reality, he ordered a full retreat back to the school. The few disciplined soldiers he had at his side fought a moving retreat as they collapsed toward the school's entrance.

Despite the frantic disposition of the majority of the little bastion, Carter's withdrawal to the school was fairly orderly and successful. A dozen or so of the militia had repositioned themselves in second-story windows overlooking the bastion's courtyard. These troops began to lay down very effective covering fire, allowing many more of the defenders to extricate themselves from their positions.

The trickle of undead coming through the breached bus were handled one at a time as they appeared. Of course, the unattended corpses of many of the recently deceased militia began to reanimate, adding more confusion to the mix.

So far, however, none had been able to gain access to the school. The second line of defense was holding for the moment.

62

Neil didn't know what to do. Jules was right. Alec was still out there, as far as all of them were concerned. He needed their help as much as anyone. The seconds ticked away without any action taken. Neil knew they needed to be leaving but he couldn't bring himself to do it.

Fortunately for Neil, or possibly unfortunately, he wasn't forced to make a decision. In the seconds that followed their reunion, two fateful events propelled circumstances beyond Neil's control.

Colonel Bear, having recovered from the Claymore's detonation, wandered down the hall. Strapped to his hip, like General George Patton, were a pair of pearl handled Colt revolvers. Moving his large body with the agility of a Sherman tank, the Colonel plodded toward the sound of the shooting in the cafeteria. The gunfire, unexpected and close, startled him to purpose.

Sitting on the floor and propped against the wall, his young secretary, cut terribly by Sullivan's knife, was whimpering pitifully. The Colonel stood over her, looking down at her with as much empathy as he could muster. He tried to soothe her with a few comforting words which held all the emotion of Stephen Hawking's voice modulator. It was of no consequence, she wasn't listening to him anyway. The reality of her situation had finally become starkly clear when she saw her blood course out of her body in heavy spurts and fall to the floor. She couldn't bring herself to look up at the disgusting, smelly man with whom she had compromised herself and her self-respect so completely in the name of security. She wished him dead.

The Colonel heard voices...voices of strangers. With one of his polished silver Colts in his hand, he headed toward the intruders. He was like a man moving to confront a trespasser in his house. His was a short trip. On the far side of the cafeteria, near a hallway which cut off to the left, some movement caught his eye. His breath stalled in his throat and his finger squeezed the trigger twice quickly. The bullets careened off the walls creating an echoing series of off-key notes which chased the shadows deeper into the darkness.

In response to the shots fired in their direction, first Emma and then everyone else dropped to their bellies. It was sheer luck both bullets missed all of them, but they did.

Losing no time, Neil forced himself back onto his bruised and sore legs. He peeked around the corner but was unable to pick out any figures in the black. There was an echo of some light from other corners in the school, but not enough to pierce the darkness.

Neil didn't look for long. He said, "Jerry. Emma. We gotta go now."

Emma looked seriously but apologetically at Jules. "Honey, we have to go. We can try and come back for Alec later. Okay?"

The seriousness in Emma's eyes and in her voice stole the fight away from Jules, who merely nodded her understanding and wiped away her tears. She'd just gotten Alec back and now he was being taken away from her again. She was unable to understand, let alone express the devastating loss her emotions were experiencing.

A deep voice from around the corner surprised all of them almost as much as the bullets had, "Sullivan? You over there?"

Jess whispered, "That's the Colonel."

Again the voice boomed, "Who the hell is over there? *Royce*, is that you? Where's Sullivan?"

After hearing her friend's name said with such disdain, Jess felt her anger rise. She spit back at the Colonel, "Sullivan's dead and you're next!"

"Who the hell is that?" demanded the Colonel.

Without any fear, Jess hollered back, "This is Jess."

"Jess?"

After having spent several weeks of very close living, Jess was aggravated that he didn't even know her name or her voice. "Yeah, Jess, you piece of shit."

With her new assault rifle taken from Mel, Jess leaned around the edge of the wall and shot back at the Colonel. Her bullets were no more effective than the Colonel's, but it felt good to be shooting back for a change.

Everything seemed to be on hold, as if waiting, until Emma broke the stalemate. "Neil, we don't really have the time to spare. We need to go and you know it. If we stay any longer, we might not be able to get away at all."

There was no more time for discussion. The front doors of the school suddenly burst forth and several militia people entered the school. Shouting and scared, they ran in, without acknowledging the standoff between the Colonel and the hidden group of strangers in the cafeteria. They were simply too scared and too loud. Some of them fell to their knees once inside the school. There were six of them in total, five men and a woman. None of them were carrying their firearms, which had been discarded hastily in their retreat.

Ignoring the menace in the cafeteria as a lesser threat, the Colonel turned to face his troops and met their scared gazes with his own reproachful eyes. He barked, "Get up off yer knees! Fucking cowards! Where the hell is Carter?"

A young man not much older than Alec answered, "He's still out there, sir."

"Then why the hell are all of you in here? And where the hell are your guns?"

There were no immediate answers forthcoming to these largely rhetorical questions. Not waiting, the Colonel bellowed, "Find yer backbones! We're goin' back out there!"

His command was met with surprised expressions and no action, which only served to raise the Colonel's ire all the more. He started to storm forward toward them, his feet stomping thunder with each step.

One of the men, more afraid of the Colonel's wrath than the threat of the undead outside, threw himself into the reinforced doors. The heavy door swung slowly on its hinges and there in the entrance waited a trio of walking corpses, one of which was a recently deceased militiaman.

The freshest ghoul was the first to pounce, grabbing hold of the man at the door. He easily overpowered the unsuspecting man, biting his cheek first and then his neck just below his jaw line. The militiaman zombie's attack was relentless and merciless, silencing its victim's woeful cries into gurgling, blood-filled gags.

The Colonel hesitated only a second or two while he assessed his surroundings. He fired his revolver two more times, one of the bullets striking the distracted zombie in the back of the head. The bullet continued its trajectory through the fiend's forehead and lodged itself into the now expired man's chest.

By this time, three militiamen, actually militia women, came downstairs to assist at the front doors. All three were armed with pistols and immediately set upon the two remaining zombies who fell in a flurry of nine millimeter and thirty-eight caliber bullets.

The Colonel, in a rare change of heart, ordered the still unarmed and largely motionless militia in front of him to close and barricade the doors. One of the newly arrived militia women told the Colonel that Carter and three or four of his men had retreated into one of the school buses. They were surrounded and under siege, but holding out so far. She also told him that there were still eight people, mostly women, upstairs providing cover fire for Carter and anyone else still out front.

The Colonel's little fortress was being pressed to its limits. He wasn't sure how much longer they would be able to hold but was also certain that they would. There was no other viable option. He ordered those without guns to either find some or get some other weapons in order to continue the defense.

One of the men seeking a weapon headed toward the office and looked further down the hall. The lingering smoke and smell of spent explosives cast a concealing veil over some new piles of soft debris on which he was walking. As he got closer and the air got clearer, he realized the piles of debris were actually dismembered and disfigured bodies, the grisly remains of the Colonel's Claymore mine detonation.

The man heard a scant few hushed sobs coming from deep inside the library. In walking toward the room's entrance, the man nearly stumbled over a discarded assault rifle. He picked up the oily firearm only to discover what he thought was oil was actually blood and gore. Seeing the blood on his hands, he nearly dropped the rifle. His resolve, however, was gone. He walked tentatively into the library to offer whatever assistance he could. He couldn't be a part of this any longer, regardless of the consequences. He would figure a way to make a run for it and get on his way at first light. That is, of course, if he was still alive come the morning.

During all of that, Neil decided that it was high time for him and his group to also make their escape. The latest distraction was what they needed. While the Colonel dealt with the developing situation at the school's threatened main entrance, Neil got them on the move.

Neil scooped Jules up in his arms and started to run. Emma was pulling Jerry by the arm while Jess herded the other children in the same direction. Neil led them back through a series of hallways to the loading bay exit. It was still dark on this side of the school, though he could discern the kennels and the silhouette of the wall and fence against the night sky.

Jules still struggled in his arms, though much of her fight was giving way to tears and grief. Neil was afraid that if he set her down, she would try and run back into the school. And so, with his back and his leg still screaming at him in pain, he forced himself to continue to run forward.

Emma asked, "Where the hell's the truck? Where are Della and Steve?

Neil shook his head, though he was fairly certain Emma couldn't see his gesture. "I'm the only one who made it."

"What about the truck?"

"It's gone too." His words were heavy with apology.

Emma stopped in her tracks and demanded, "Well, how the fuck are we going to get away then?"

"We'll have to improvise, like we always have. We just have to keep on going. Besides, I have a plan."

Emma asked doubtfully, "Another plan? Do you think this one is going to work out any better?"

"Emma, Christ, I'm doin' the best I can. You got any better ideas? I'm all up for hearing them. I found us a ride. It's out back."

Jess had Danny, Nikki, and Paul in tow. They were still approaching the others who had stalled near the exit, when an errant, disfigured hand reached from the darkness and clutched Paul's little arm. The gnarled and knobby fingers curled around the boy's flesh and started to pull him away.

When the creature emerged from the deep shadows and into the dim light coming through the doorway, Danny felt his bladder empty in his pants. It had on a tattered business coat, but whatever shirt he had worn in his previous life had been worn away, exposing its bone thin chest. The throat had been ripped asunder, the ravaged internal flesh exposed and suffering from exposure to the elements. He was barely recognizable as having once been human but Danny recognized him as one of his tormentors from out in the kennels.

Danny recoiled but tried to keep hold of little Paul, who seemed to be going limp with fear like a baby gazelle caught in the jaws of an attacking lioness. He didn't struggle; he didn't fight. With terror filled eyes, all Paul could do was simply look back at Danny.

Jess' and Danny's screams were enough to get the others' attention, but it was not enough to save little Paul. The ghoul snatched away the little boy who struggled to hold Danny's moist hand. Victoriously, the staggering ghoul turned about, already starting to bite and chew into Paul's bony shoulder and upper arm. Jess was too afraid to shoot for fear of hitting little Paul in the process and then it didn't matter. And just like that, Paul disappeared into the veil of night as if being pulled into a sea of dark, enveloping tar.

Danny looked at his now empty hand in disbelief and then looked back at Neil who was as stunned as everyone else. They didn't hear any painful cries or pleas for help from the little boy. He was simply gone.

Neil shouted, "C'mon! We have to get outta here!"

Seeing Paul carried away into the dark, Jules let the fight fade from her limbs. She got her feet back to the pavement and, still holding Neil's hand, started to run toward the wall. Without a word, everyone was running again.

Their haste was quickly justified as more of the undead began to appear, their preternatural groans overwhelming the roar and blasts from the battle on the other side of the school. Neil's mouth dried while Emma's palms moistened. The creatures must have found the opening in the concrete barricade wall and followed the path toward the now open gate. They surged down the lane with growing excitement as they spotted the humans exiting the building.

Neil ordered all of them, "Gooooooo! Godamnit! Goooooo! The big Suburban with all the doors open! Keys are on the dash."

Despite his limp and his pain, Neil led them to the big vehicle. They piled in quickly and breathed a collective sigh of relief when the engine fired to life with the turn of the key. Emma was at the helm and wasted no time in building speed. The big engine in the Chevy Suburban revved higher and higher as Emma pushed the accelerator to the floor.

She shouted, "Keep your heads down!" just as she Suburban's heavy duty bumper plowed into the first thin ranks of living dead. As their desiccated bodies, light and brittle with decay, crumpled beneath the vehicle's weight and force, they made a sound that resembled sleet and hail striking the lower half of their transport.

Emma kept their ride going forward at full tilt. She couldn't afford to let them slow lest they get bogged down and trapped in the thickening but still manageable crowd of demons around them. There was no maneuvering, so they just had to wade through it.

With each new thud, another surprised gasp escaped from a different person. In the headlights, Emma could see an end to the rushing horde. She took a deep breath and held it, willing the big truck to continue forward at all costs.

She almost lost control when they broke free. They were thankfully beyond the barricade, though none of them knew it. The truck fishtailed violently as it emerged into the open space. Emma let out her breath finally and righted the steering wheel with a deft motion.

The battle in front of the school was largely over. Random shots still rang out in the darkness and a few handfuls of zekes still waited their turn to feast, but the majority of the action had passed. Each of them wondered about the results of the engagement, but not enough to investigate. Who had won? And was there such a thing as winning anymore?

None wondered more than Jess. She knew most of the people back at the school, and there were still some she cared about. A couple of small fires burned here and there, providing a ghostly, flickering light by which to behold the ghastly tableau. It looked like the fires of Hell lighting the procession of the dead. Jess swallowed hard as the lost oasis faded behind them.

Jerry, on the other hand, was quiet and largely absent, not much more animated than the undead. He couldn't force the images of Claire's tortured and disfigured body from his mind. The guilt of his failure defied purging.

Emma turned to Neil and asked, "So what happened to Della and that guy? I mean, besides the obvious."

Neil shook his head and looked back at the kids, saying only, "Later."

They sped out of the parking lot and almost immediately, their truck began to sputter and struggle. Emma looked at the gas gauge. "Uh, Neil. I think we've got a problem."

"What?"

Jess spoke up from the back seat. "Shit. I'm sorry. You couldn't have known. The Colonel never left fuel in the vehicles out back in case someone tried to steal one to get away. When you said you had a ride waiting, I just assumed it was one you brought with you."

Neil allowed a defeated laugh to escape. "No fucking gas. Great. How far can we make it?"

The Suburban answered for itself when its engine choked again, gasping for fuel to fire its engine. The vehicle shuddered twice and then the engine went quiet. They coasted for a few more yards and then they were still again.

There wasn't time to lament their worries however. They had to keep moving. The bridge was just up ahead and beyond it was Soldotna.

63

Straggling well behind the main body of shuffling ghouls, a dozen or so undead were still making their way across the expanse to join the battle already engaged at the former high school. These wraiths moved slower due to their advanced decay or the severity of the fatal injuries which had originally claimed their lives. These were the first zombies they saw after abandoning their stalled Suburban on the highway just out of sight of both the school and the bridge.

Emma and Jerry, at the front of the emerging line of survivors, had a hard time in seeing clearly all the threats that lurked, but there appeared to be enough room to be able to continue their exodus. Unfortunately, the zekes immediately sensed the emergence of new prey and began to wander closer and closer, their collective moans steadily rising in volume.

Jerry, whose grief become anger, hefted his hunting rifle to his shoulder and squeezed off a round which took all of them by surprise. The high caliber bullet struck its target in the dark but it wasn't an effective kill shot and the beast was back on its feet in seconds. Neil wanted to stop him but whatever potential damage could have been wrought by the decision was already done. The undead knew that they were there. There was no need to chide his friend, not that it would have done any good anyway.

Neil looked at Jess and ordered her to stick close to them and keep the children between them. He looked at Danny and was both surprised and pleased to see the boy take a small revolver from his own pocket. The boy was quickly becoming a much needed asset to their survival. Danny caught Neil's stare and nodded to the man that he was ready.

They walked out together, with Emma, Jerry, and Neil forming an arc like an umbrella in front and the others with Jess at the rear falling under the protective screen. The seven of them walked briskly but didn't run.

An abandoned Ford Explorer approximately halfway across the bridge served as a way point around which they gathered their nerves and their breath for the rest of the bridge crossing. They waited for just a handful of heartbeats but it was enough.

From around the front of the sport utility vehicle appeared a frail ghoul still wearing a dressing gown. Jules and Nikki both let slip a small, surprised squeal as the old woman's emaciated, skull-like face became visible. Neil fired a deafening blast from his shotgun which splintered the woman's sternum and opened a hole clean through her chest. She was thrown backward several yards and ended up on her back. Lying there still for a few seconds, she started to struggle to her feet again.

Dispatching the zombie was less important than getting away, so they continued their retreat with a little more speed in their steps. Another of the demons, this one a teenager still wearing a bright colored drawstring backpack, approached them with a little more dexterity than the old woman. Emma shot this time, sending a single bullet through his head just below his right eye. First its head and then its whole body was flung backward and landed with a chilling thump on the pavement out of sight.

Emma hadn't intended to fire only one shot, but apparently the magazine on her assault rifle was empty. She knew how to reload her weapon, but in the dark she was afraid she might do something wrong. Instead, she slung the rifle over her shoulder and put a pistol in her hand.

They continued forward with a growing band of undead drawing closer and closer. Neil said to all of them, "We have to keep moving. No stopping. Just keep moving."

For some strange reason, Emma, upon hearing Neil's command, remembered a line from Pixar's *Finding Nemo*. She began to repeat over and over in her head, *Just keep swimming. Just keep swimming.* Ellen DeGeneres' voice immediately brought a very surprising smile to her face.

The words repeated as she spotted another target which she quickly brought down with a pair of shots that split its ossified skull. Ellen's silly voice filled her head as she continued forward alongside Neil and Jerry.

She had never felt so much an equal as she did at that moment. The real difference that she could sense in the moment is that she felt justified in judging her peers as equal to herself rather than the other way around. She had never before possessed the confidence to find herself in that position. And so with her chest filled with a swagger and her head brimming with a Disney fish's voice, Emma set about clearing a path through which they could pass to...

To where? To what really? To safety? Was it even possible to find such a lofty possibility? Emma would just be happy to not be on her feet any longer. She was really going to miss that truck.

It was then, as they stepped from the bridge onto the main roadway, that Jess said curiously, "I think I have an idea. We need to head straight up this road."

"What's up there?" Neil asked.

Jess was still a little guarded and didn't want to reveal her secret, so she only said, "At the main intersection. Right before the Fred Meyer."

Neil remembered that a fuel truck was parked at the intersection. Did Jess know something about that truck that perhaps they didn't? And why the hell wouldn't she just say? He wanted to ask her, but there were other pressing concerns at hand.

The more they fired their weapons and the more noise they made, the more attention they drew to themselves. The numbers of flesh eaters beginning to shuffle hungrily in the shadows was beginning to grow. They moved slowly but their sheer numbers were beginning to worry all of them.

Neil forgot his pains and Jerry forgot his suffering. They worked like the team that they had become. When Jerry had fired all the rounds from his rifle, he and Emma switched places so that Jerry was in the middle. He could reload while they moved forward and had Emma and Neil to protect him. They went through the same process when Neil needed to reload his shotgun.

In this way, they were able to cover the ground behind them and their goal some distance away. Using the path in reverse that Jess had used to return to the fortified school on her last excursion, they moved behind the Aspen Hotel and several other businesses. A small drainage ditch combined with their speed and stealthy movements to deliver them without further incident to their destination.

Soon, they were within reach of the intersection and Jess' surprise. Neil looked at the fuel truck and wondered what she had in mind. Was this some kind of revenge ploy? Did she want to drive that truck into the school in some grand suicidal gesture?

Jess, of course, was only using the tanker truck as a point of reference. She was more interested in her car which had been left all those days ago. When she caught sight of its silhouette in the scant light, she almost began to laugh. Not much had worked out for her recently. Jess had suffered separation's sting and death's remorse far too much.

Jess' daughter and the man she loved were worlds away and hopefully safe and waiting for her. Hell stood between her and them. Finding her car was the one bright spot of hope she'd had in quite some time. These people might be one more. Only time would tell.

She looked at Neil and pointed. Realizing he wasn't seeing the forest for the trees, she said, "That's my car and it's got gas in it."

"Will it start?"

Jess nodded. "That car's a champ. It's never let me down. We just have to get out to it."

Neil nodded his understanding and looked over at Emma and Jerry. "You heard the lady. We got a ride out of here..."

Emma was in the process of loading another thirty-round magazine into her assault rifle and Jerry was checking the load on his hunting rifle. Jess didn't appear nearly as experienced with her own assault rifle, but she followed Emma's lead and prepared her own firearm.

As ready as they would ever be, the group of seven hopeful people stepped from their cover and into a side parking lot of a long dormant business. At first, they neither saw nor heard any of the undead. Jerry stopped abruptly and pointed to the gas station across the street. There were three or four zombies loitering between the pumps and the station building. Jerry raised his rifle to shoot but was interrupted with a swat to his shoulder. Emma was pointing toward the road leading toward the school. There were dozens of rambling specters marching toward the continuing ruckus of the battle. It appeared as if all of the creatures were thankfully moving away from the seven of them.

Emma shook her head from side to side and then put her finger to her lips in the universal *Shhhh* gesture. Jerry nodded and noticed that Neil and Jess were already moving across the street. Danny was doing his part keeping the other kids and himself tight to Neil's tail.

Reaching the car without mishap, Neil found himself standing at the driver side door. Jess whispered, "The keys are on the seat."

Neil started to come around to her side, but Jess chided him with, "Just get in and drive for God's sake."

Neil did as he was told, getting in and putting the keys into the ignition. Unfortunately, when he did so, his door was still open which triggered a series of beeps warning a forgetful motorist the keys were still in the ignition. He cringed and quickly shut the door, which also created more noise than he wanted.

The cluster of sound did alert the zombies in the gas station and a handful of others from the road to their presence. Jerry and Emma slid into the back seat, each placing one of the smaller children upon their laps.

"Okay, let's go," Emma pled from the back seat.

Neil turned the key and to everyone's gleeful surprise, the car started. He flipped on the lights to see a gathering mob coming at them from multiple angles. Neil squealed the tires as he punched the car forward and swung around. He drove them back out toward Sterling and the Seward Highway beyond.

For just a second or so, Jess was tormented to scream at Neil to drive them back south. South was where Syd was...where she might be. South was where Bob was...where he was supposed to be. South was where she needed to be. She reached over and lowered the driver's side visor. Syd smiled back at her from last year's high school photograph. Seeing her daughter's face surprisingly calmed Jess' nerves. She pulled the photograph from the visor clip and said coolly, "The road is blocked to the south. North. Take us north."

Neil nodded and did as he was told, which was his plan all along. The car was already moving, so he pulled hard on the wheel and got them moving back along the Sterling Highway and to the Seward Highway further on.

64

Anyone who has ever suggested that silence was empty couldn't have been more wrong. The silence in Jess' car as they headed north on the Seward Highway was spilling over and splitting at the seams with emotion and tears. Tears of sorrow. Tears of relief. Tears of exhaustion and hunger. And tears of disbelief about all that had happened.

It wasn't bad enough that the world was being overrun by flesh-eating monsters who had once been neighbors and friends. In the midst of that horror, some men continued to prey upon other men, women, and even children.

Neil was feeling very conflicted. They had gotten away...well, most of them. What about Claire? Della? Alec? He felt guilty about inviting disaster upon everyone at the school. There was no pleasure in having wrought destruction upon a bastion such as that. And yet, having safely retrieved Danny and Jules meant more to him than he had imagined.

He thought he had been motivated by a sense of duty to the children, but he now understood that it went much deeper for him. He'd not been granted the opportunity to be a father. In point of fact, he had always doubted his own abilities at parenthood, as had his ex-wife, which was why they never had children.

When Danny wrapped his arms around Neil's legs at the school, Neil had never felt more gratified or paternal in his entire life. Being an uncle was completely different; not that he ever saw his niece or nephew.

It was that sense of responsibility which encouraged him to put his foot to the brake and bring the car to a stop. With the high beam lights of the car, there was little that they couldn't see on the highway, so he felt secure in stopping.

No one asked, so Neil asked calmly, "What are we doing?"

The silence persisted. There was more than one answer to that question. Emma thought that perhaps she understood the nature of Neil's query but she also wanted to avoid the futility of the answers it might generate.

The simple answer was that they were driving north on the Seward Highway looking for sanctuary. They were surviving and little else. They hadn't eaten in two days and the last meal they did have consisted of a partial container of fish food Della found which was poured into a warm pot of water and some green grass; not exactly a feast. They were struggling with little to no hope of reward.

Emma realized all of this but was hesitant to acknowledge it. Instead, she simply said, "We're gettin' by."

Neil asked, "Is that enough?"

To which, Emma responded, "There's not much else we can do. We just have to keep moving. That's what you used to say."

Nodding his head, Neil still couldn't lift his thoughts from his foreboding doubts. Emma didn't hesitate. She said to all of them, "Do we prefer the alternative? Do we just want to give up?"

Emma's question hung heavily in the air of the car's dark interior. It was Danny who first responded, "My dad told me to never give up. When I wanted to quit playing soccer 'cause I didn't like not playing with my friends, he told me that I had to honor my commitments." Danny emphasized the words *honor my commitments* as if he was channeling his father.

Jerry said from behind Jules' blond head, "Your dad was a smart man." Realizing his gaffe, Jerry quickly corrected by saying, "Sorry. Your dad is a smart man. Didn't mean anything by that." The distinction was apparently lost on Danny who simply nodded to Jerry.

Jess asked, "Where were you taking us?"

"Before we headed down to Soldotna, we were trying to go to Whittier. We thought that maybe Whittier was free of all of this. I guess we hoped that we could find a place where we could go to be able to escape," Neil admitted.

Without missing a beat, Jess asked, "Escape to where?"

Neil looked over at Jess to ask for clarification, to which Jess continued, "This infection or whatever it is has spread everywhere. At least that's what we heard before the Colonel's satellite phone stopped working. That was the last outside contact any of us had with the Lower Forty-Eight. I don't know about the rest of the planet, but our side of the globe is pretty quiet."

Emma asked, "But how?"

Jess looked away from them and stared out the window into the dark.

65

"It started on that first day," Jess said in a hushed voice filled with surrender. People all over Anchorage were just trying to get away, or that's what we heard at least. Nobody knew for sure what was happening or what was causing all the chaos. It just seemed like Hell had opened its mouth and was trying to swallow Anchorage whole. Down in Soldotna, all we knew was what CNN or whoever was telling us. The most accepted theory was that it was a terrorist attack. Maybe biological weapons or something. Maybe they were right. Some mad scientist's experiment finding its way out of the lab. I don't know.

"Anyway, people were getting onto planes and boats and whatever was available. Some bribed their way on and others fought their way. Some of the last things I saw online were people at the airport or port or wherever all standing in long lines hoping that maybe they'd be granted passage out. Scared faces, young and old, men and women. And then, on one of the reports, there was some screaming and then a bunch of commotion just outside of the frame. I thought that maybe whatever was happening everywhere else had finally made it to them. And I guess that's kind of what happened. Some folks decided that maybe guns were their ticket out. They started shooting everyone in their path. Policemen, airline people, and just people standing in line. The person with the video camera just kept recording as the massacre unfolded. Kids, women, men, and even dogs...no one was safe from those people. I wonder if it worked for them? I wonder if they got a ride out of town like they wanted?" The last two comments created a pause for Jess, in which she allowed her curiosity to wander a bit.

Finding her way back to her story, Jess continued, "It was like watching some horrible movie. Regardless of how they made it happen, some people found their way out of Anchorage. The problem was that no one knew it was in the bites and that anyone who'd been bitten had been infected.

"I saw more than a few folks pushing their way through who had bloody wounds and dangling bandages. I didn't know what was going on. No one knew. I was as scared for those people as they were for themselves. Christ, they should've left all of them behind, but, like I said, nobody knew.

"The first plane to land was in Fairbanks. Someone on board had been bitten and must've died en route and then you know what happened. Could you imagine dealing with one or some of those things at thirty thousand feet? Talk about a fucking nightmare. Jesus, that must've been awful." Jess visibly shuddered as that possibility played out in her mind.

"Well, the plane landed but the pilots didn't know what was happening in the cabin. Their door was bolted and so they were protected from whatever they'd heard was happening on the other side. When they came to a stop on the tarmac, police and firefighters were waiting, but they didn't know what to expect either. And when the doors opened, dozens of those things came spilling out, killing everything in their paths. And then the cycle started all over again. Some of that was caught by independent reporters at the airport too. When I saw that happen on the television, I thought...maybe I hoped that I was dreaming, but it was too real.

"Fairbanks only lasted a few hours...less than a day. I guess a lot of people got out of town and headed to the Bush, but most of the population was stuck just like in Anchorage. Eielson and Wainwright held out for a bit, but pretty soon connections were lost with the military up there too. It was like a light going out suddenly. The reporting from up there just stopped.

"That was about the time that I left my house. When I got to the school back there, some other folks told me that planes loaded with those things landed in Seattle and Vancouver and a coupla' other places too. It was like we were invading ourselves or something; our own worst enemies." Again Jess paused. She seemed to be lost in a swirl of memories

No one in the car could have known she was thinking about her daughter, though they could all sense her concern and her drifting thoughts. She had been operating under the, now she suspected false, assumptions that Syd was somewhere safe and removed from this tragedy. Hearing her own voice recount those early days and the quick spread of the cataclysm was rekindling her doubts. She tried to picture her daughter's face but couldn't dispel the visions of a hundred snarling, decomposing, ghouls which wouldn't allow her to have peace. She closed her eyes tight but they could never feel as tight as the growing lump in her throat and chest. Tears, scorching her from the inside out, found their way through the tiny cracks between her eyelids. She held the picture of Syd to her chest and cuddled it as if it were a baby.

Not wanting to acknowledge but unable to ignore the probable truth, Jess said in disgust, "I don't think there is anywhere to run. As soon as this thing got out of Anchorage, I don't think there was any way to stop it. Nobody's comin' for us because there's no one left able to. We're on our own whether we like it or not."

Neil asked, "Are you sure?"

Jess held up her daughter's picture. "She has been the only reason why I found the courage to wake up most days and go to a job that was slowly killing me from the inside out. She was my world. I had hoped to get away from all of this and find her. I wanted to get to her and make sure that she was safe and..." Jess' emotion caused her to bite back a sob and stop speaking or lose all control. She breathed deeply, trying to hold back the tsunami of emotion. "Like I said, the same thing that happened in Fairbanks happened in Seattle and Vancouver. Maybe in other cities too. Everywhere a plane went, that plague went with it. There were boats and ships and yachts and who knows what else on the sea too. A whole fleet of death set to sea. Some of them started to make landfall a few days later and the problem just got worse. Sure enough though, most people wanted the military to sink the drifting cruise ships and tankers still on the ocean, but corporate lobbyists forced a discussion in Congress that delayed action until it was too late." Jess paused again, this time in anger, and continued more sarcastically, "Those big ships represent a huge investment in capital after all."

Quieter, with a funeral voice, Jess finished with, "The last thing I heard was them talking about bombing our own cities and using whatever force necessary to contain the threat. The voice reporting the plan...reporter...general...spokesperson...whatever...was, I don't know, a little less than convincing. Probably because he was a little less than convinced. I don't think they got this thing figured out and I don't know that they will."

Jerry, quiet up to this point, asked, "So what does that mean?"

Jess didn't have an answer to that question. She both wished to have one and dreaded what it might be. Instead, she said, "That means that I need to find a way to find my daughter. We gotta find a place where we can rest tonight and eat tomorrow." She took a deep breath and summed up for them, "I guess it means we go to Whittier."

Neil repeated, "*Whittier*. That's where *we've* been headin' all along. It's seems so far away."

Still looking at the picture of her daughter, Jess said softly, "Everything does. We just gotta keep on trying."

[EPILOGUE]

Shangri-La. El Dorado. Camelot. Whittier, Alaska. Each of these places held mythic properties during its time. Well, three out of four did anyway. Whittier was at least real, an attribute the other cities couldn't claim, though Whittier's shine was much less shimmering. Each, however, attracted the attentions and affections of some very enthusiastic seekers during its day.

Whittier, again as opposed to its municipal brethren, was also in a position to be able to deliver on its purported promises. This was primarily due to the proverbial expectations bar having been set so low because of the track record of the others. None seemed to ever be able to deliver.

El Dorado was the lost city of gold sought out by Conquistadors from the Sixteenth and Seventeenth Centuries. The lucky soul or souls who happened upon its storied halls was rewarded with untold riches and a lifetime of spending without any care given to earning. Entire fortunes were spent pursuing the elusive city and yet no one was ever able to lay hands on the mythic and epic treasure.

Shangri-La was a peaceful utopia, free of want and aging in a turbulent world full of suffering and loss. A cast of seekers ranging from Tibetan Monks to wayward adventurers sought the undying lands which always managed to stay just one step away despite entire lifetimes devoted to searching.

On the other hand, there was Whittier, Alaska. It wasn't a bad place, nor did it always deserve the playful moniker "Shittier" to which it was referred by regional locals. The weather was typically lousy but the fishing was most often good. Truth be told, there really wasn't much Whittier to Whittier.

It was a nice community, once upon a time, but that wasn't the present draw for Neil and his companions. They sought neither gold nor other treasure. They weren't even on the hunt for an epic fishing trip as promised by many a charter fishing brochure. Neil, Jerry, Emma, and the others were looking for the peace of Shangri-La without the utopian visions. They wanted to find a place where they could just stop running and let some moss begin to grow.

With Whittier so close but still separated from them by a door of titan proportions, they couldn't know if the town was a sanctuary waiting on the other side or a Pandora's Box of suffering waiting to be cracked open. There was no way of knowing, short of finding a way beyond the barrier.

There was nowhere left for them to run.

And so the final leg of the *Alaskan Undead Apocalypse* will play out in Whittier in *Resolution.*

14
BY PETER CLINES

Padlocked doors. Strange light fixtures. Mutant cockroaches. There are some odd things about Nate's new apartment. Every room in this old brownstone has a mystery. Mysteries that stretch back over a hundred years. Some of them are in plain sight. Some are behind locked doors. And all together these mysteries could mean the end of Nate and his friends. Or the end of everything...

"A riveting apocalyptic mystery in the style of LOST."
—Craig DiLouie, author of *The Infection*

14
PETER CLINES

PERMUTEDPRESS.COM

DAY BY DAY ARMAGEDDON
GREY FOX
BY J.L. BOURNE

Time is a very fluid thing, no one really has a grasp on it other than maybe how to measure it. As the maestro of the Day by Day Armageddon Universe, I have the latitude of being in control of that time. You have again stumbled upon a ticket with service through the apocalyptic wastes, but this time the train is a little bit older, a little more beat up, and maybe a little wiser.

DAY BY DAY ARMAGEDDON
GREY FOX
J.L. BOURNE

DEAD TIDE
BY STEPHEN A. NORTH

THE WORLD IS ENDING. BUT THERE ARE SURVIVORS. Nick Talaski is a hard-bitten, angry cop. Graham is a newly divorced cab driver. Bronte is a Gulf War veteran hunting his brother's killer. Janicea is a woman consumed by unflinching hate. Trish is a gentleman's club dancer. Morgan is a morgue janitor. The dead have risen and the citizens of St. Petersburg and Pinellas Park are trapped. The survivors are scattered, and options are few. And not all monsters are created by a bite. Some still have a mind of their own...

PERMUTEDPRESS.COM

DEAD TIDE RISING
BY STEPHEN A. NORTH

The sequel to Dead Tide continues the carnage in Pinellas Park near St. Pete, Florida. Follow all of the characters from the first book, Dead Tide, as they fight for survival in a world destroyed by the zombie apocalypse.

BREW
BY BILL BRADDOCK

Ever been to a big college town on a football Saturday night? Loud drunks glut the streets, swaggering about in roaring, leering, laughing packs, like sailors on shore leave. These nights crackle with a dark energy born of incongruity; for beneath all that smiling and singing sprawls a bedrock of malice.

PERMUTEDPRESS.COM

TANKBREAD
BY PAUL MANNERING

Ten years ago humanity lost the war for survival. Now intelligent zombies rule the world. Feeding the undead of a steady diet of cloned people called Tankbread, the survivors live in a dangerous world on the brink of final extinction.

THE ROAD TO NOWHERE
BY BILL BRADDOCK

Welcome to the city of Las Vegas. Gone are the days of tourist filled streets. After waking up alone in a hospital bed, everyone seems to have fled, leaving me behind. Survival becomes my only driving force. Nothing was as it should have been. Things seemed to lurk in the buildings and darkest shadows. I didn't know what they were, but I could always feel their eyes on me.

ZOMBIE ATTACK: RISE OF THE HORDE
BY PAUL MANNERING

Voted best Zombie/ Horror E-books of 2012 on Goodreads. When 16 year old Xander's older brother Moto left him at Vandenberg Airforce Base he only had one request - don't leave no matter what. But there was no way he could have known that one day zombies would gather into groups big enough to knock down walls and take out entire buildings full of people. That was before the rise of the horde!

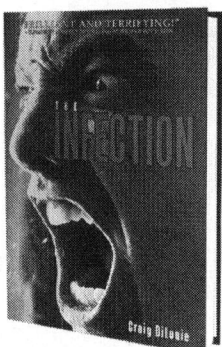
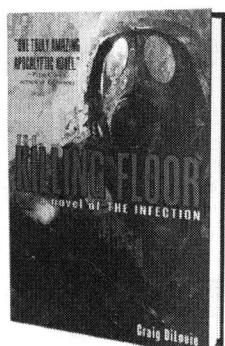

THE BECOMING
BY JESSICA MEIGS

The Michaluk Virus has escaped the CDC, and its effects are widespread and devastating. Most of the population of the southeastern United States have become homicidal cannibals. As society rapidly crumbles under the hordes of infected, three people--Ethan, a Memphis police officer; Cade, his best friend; and Brandt, a lieutenant in the US Marines--band together against the oncoming crush of death.

THE BECOMING:
GROUND ZERO (BOOK 2)
BY JESSICA MEIGS

After the Michaluk Virus decimated the southeast, Ethan and his companions became like family. But the arrival of a mysterious woman forces them to flee from the infected, and the cohesion the group cultivated is shattered. As members of the group succumb to the escalating dangers on their path, new alliances form, new loves develop, and old friendships crumble.

THE BECOMING:
REVELATIONS (BOOK 3)
BY JESSICA MEIGS

In a world ruled by the dead, Brandt Evans is floundering. Leadership of their dysfunctional group wasn't something he asked for or wanted. Their problems are numerous: Remy Angellette is grief-stricken and suicidal, Gray Carter is distant and reclusive, and Cade Alton is near death. And things only get worse.

DOMAIN OF THE DEAD
BY IAIN MCKINNON

The world is dead, devoured by a plague of reanimated corpses. Barricaded inside a warehouse with dwindling food, a group of survivors faces two possible deaths: creeping starvation, or the undead outside. In their darkest hour hope appears in the form of a helicopter approaching the city... but is it the salvation the survivors have been waiting for?

PERMUTEDPRESS.COM

REMAINS OF THE DEAD
BY IAIN MCKINNON

The world is dead. Cahz and his squad of veteran soldiers are tasked with flying into abandoned cities and retrieving zombies for scientific study. Then the unbelievable happens. After years of encountering nothing but the undead, the team discovers a handful of survivors in a fortified warehouse with dwindling supplies.

PERMUTEDPRESS.COM

DEMISE OF THE LIVING
BY IAIN MCKINNON

The world is infected. The dead are reanimating and attacking the living. In a city being overrun with zombies a disparate group of strangers seek sanctuary in an office block. But for how long can the barricades hold back the undead? How long will the food last? How long before those who were bitten succumb turn? And how long before they realise the dead outside are the least of their fears?

ROADS LESS TRAVELED: THE PLAN
BY C. DULANEY

Ask yourself this: If the dead rise tomorrow, are you ready? Do you have a plan? Kasey, a strong-willed loner, has something she calls The Zombie Plan. But every plan has its weaknesses, and a freight train of tragedy is bearing down on Kasey and her friends. In the darkness that follows, Kasey's Plan slowly unravels: friends lost, family taken, their stronghold reduced to ashes.

PERMUTEDPRESS.COM

MURPHY'S LAW
(ROADS LESS TRAVELED BOOK 2)
BY C. DULANEY

Kasey and the gang were held together by a set of rules, their Zombie Plan. It kept them alive through the beginning of the End. But when the chaos faded, they became careless, and Murphy's Law decided to pay a long-overdue visit. Now the group is broken and scattered with no refuge in sight. Those remaining must make their way across West Virginia in search of those who were stolen from them.

PERMUTEDPRESS.COM

SHADES OF GRAY
(ROADS LESS TRAVELED BOOK 3)
BY C. DULANEY

Kasey and the gang have come full circle through the crumbling world. Working for the National Guard, they realize old friends and fellow survivors are disappearing. When the missing start to reappear as walking corpses, the group sets out on another journey to discover the truth. Their answers wait in the West Virginia Command Center.

PAVLOV'S DOGS
BY D.L. SNELL & THOM BRANNAN

WEREWOLVES Dr. Crispin has engineered the saviors of mankind: soldiers capable of transforming into beasts. ZOMBIES Ken and Jorge get caught in a traffic jam on their way home from work. It's the first sign of a major outbreak. ARMAGEDDON Should Dr. Crisping send the Dogs out into the zombie apocalypse to rescue survivors? Or should they hoard their resources and post the Dogs as island guards?

PERMUTEDPRESS.COM

THE OMEGA DOG
BY D.L. SNELL & THOM BRANNAN

Twisting and turning through hordes of zombies, cartel territory, Mayan ruins, and the things that now inhabit them, a group of survivors must travel to save one man's family from a nightmarish third world gone to hell. But this time, even best friends have deadly secrets, and even allies can't be trusted - as a father's only hope of getting his kids out alive is the very thing that's hunting him down.

DEAD LIVING
BY GLENN BULLION

It didn't take long for the world to die. And it didn't take long, either, for the dead to rise. Aaron was born on the day the world ended. Kept in seclusion, his family teaches him the basics. How to read and write. How to survive. Then Aaron makes a shocking discovery. The undead, who desire nothing but flesh, ignore him. It's as if he's invisible to them.

——— PERMUTEDPRESS.COM ———

AUTOBIOGRAPHY of a WEREWOLF HUNTER
BY BRIAN P. EASTON

After his mother is butchered by a werewolf, Sylvester James is taken in by a Cheyenne mystic. The boy trains to be a werewolf hunter, learning to block out pain, stalk, fight, and kill. As Sylvester sacrifices himself to the hunt, his hatred has become a monster all its own. As he follows his vendetta into the outlands of the occult, he learns it takes more than silver bullets to kill a werewolf.

PALE GODS
BY KIM PAFFENROTH

In a world where the undead rule the continents and the few remaining survivors inhabit only island outposts, six men make the dangerous journey to the mainland to hunt for supplies amid the ruins. But on this trip, the dead act stranger and smarter than ever before and the living must adjust or die.

PERMUTEDPRESS.COM

THE JUNKIE QUATRAIN
BY PETER CLINES

Six months ago, the world ended. The Baugh Contagion swept across the planet. Its victims were left twitching, adrenalized cannibals that quickly became know as Junkies. THE JUNKIE QUATRAIN is four tales of survival, and four types of post-apocalypse story. Because the end of the world means different things for different people. Loss. Opportunity. Hope. Or maybe just another day on the job.

BLOOD SOAKED & CONTAGIOUS
BY JAMES CRAWFORD

I am not going to complain to you about my life.

We've got zombies. They are not the brainless, rotting creatures we'd been led to expect. Unfortunately for us, they're just as smart as they were before they died, very fast, much stronger than you or me, and possess no internal editor at all.

Claws. Did I mention claws?

PERMUTEDPRESS.COM

BLOOD SOAKED & INVADED
BY JAMES CRAWFORD

Zombies were bad enough, but now we're being invaded from all sides. Up to our necks in blood, body parts, and unanswerable questions...

...As soon as the realization hit me, I lost my cool. I curled into the fetal position in a pile of blood, offal, and body parts, and froze there. What in the Hell was I becoming that killing was entertaining and satisfying?

THE KING OF CLAYFIELD
BY SHANE GREGORY

On a cold February day in the small town of Clayfield, Kentucky, an unsuspecting and unprepared museum director he finds himself in the middle of hell on Earth. A pandemic is spreading around the globe, and it's turning most of the residents of Clayfield into murderous zombies. Having no safe haven to which he can flee, the director decides to stick it out near his hometown and wait for the government to send help.

PERMUTEDPRESS.COM

THE KING OF CLAYFIELD 2
ALL THAT I SEE
BY SHANE GREGORY

It has been more than a month since the Canton B virus turned the people of the world into hungry zombies. The survivors of Clayfield, Kentucky attempt to carve out new lives for themselves in this harsh new world. Those who remain have been hardened by their environment and their choices over the previous weeks, but their optimism has not been extinguished. There is hope that eventually Clayfield can be secured, but first, the undead must be eliminated and law and order must be restored. Unfortunately, the group might not ever get to implement their plan.

PERMUTEDPRESS.COM

THE KING OF CLAYFIELD 3
FIRE BIRDS
BY SHANE GREGORY

For weeks, he has fought the undead and believed that he was Clayfield's sole survivor. But when odd things begin to happen in the town, it becomes clear that other healthy people are around. A friend returns full of trouble and secrets, and they are not alone.

Something bad is coming to Clayfield, and there could be nowhere to hide.

INFECTION:
ALASKAN UNDEAD APOCALYPSE
BY SEAN SCHUBERT

Anchorage, Alaska: gateway to serene wilderness of The Last Frontier. No stranger to struggle, the city on the edge of the world is about to become even more isolated. When a plague strikes, Anchorage becomes a deadly trap for its citizens. The only two land routes out of the city are cut, forcing people to fight or die as the infection spreads.

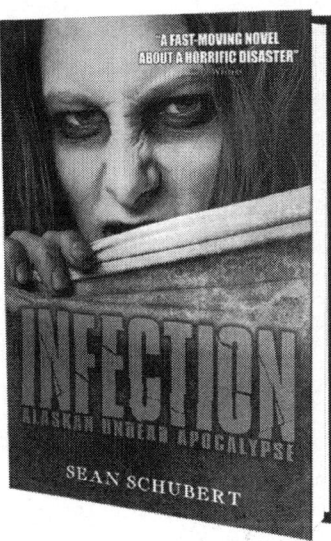

PERMUTEDPRESS.COM

CONTAINMENT
(ALASKAN UNDEAD APOCALYPSE BOOK 2)
BY SEAN SCHUBERT

Running. Hiding. Surviving. Anchorage, once Alaska's largest city, has fallen. Now a threatening maze of death, the city is firmly in the cold grip of a growing zombie horde. Neil Jordan and Dr. Caldwell lead a small band of desperate survivors through the maelstrom. The group has one last hope: that this nightmare has been contained, and there still exists a sane world free of infection.

THE UNDEAD SITUATION
BY ELOISE J. KNAPP

The dead are rising. People are dying. Civilization is collapsing. But Cyrus V. Sinclair couldn't care less; he's a sociopath. Amidst the chaos, Cyrus sits with little more emotion than one of the walking corpses... until he meets up with other inconvenient survivors who cramp his style and force him to re-evaluate his outlook on life. It's Armageddon, and things will definitely get messy.

PERMUTEDPRESS.COM

THE UNDEAD HAZE
(THE UNDEAD SITUATION BOOK 2)
BY ELOISE J. KNAPP

When remorse drives Cyrus to abandon his hidden compound he doesn't realize what new dangers lurk in the undead world. He knows he must wade through the vilest remains of humanity and hordes of zombies to settle scores and find the one person who might understand him. But this time, it won't be so easy. Zombies and unpleasant survivors aren't the only thing Cyrus has to worry about.

MAD SWINE: THE BEGINNING
BY STEVEN PAJAK

People refer to the infected as "zombies," but that's not what they really are. Zombie implies the infected have died and reanimated. The thing is, they didn't die. They're just not human anymore. As the infection spreads and crazed hordes--dubbed "Mad Swine"--take over the cities, the residents of Randall Oaks find themselves locked in a desperate struggle to survive in the new world.

PERMUTEDPRESS.COM

MAD SWINE: DEAD WINTER
BY STEVEN PAJAK

Three months after the beginning of the Mad Swine outbreak, the residents of Randall Oaks have reached their breaking point. After surviving the initial outbreak and a war waged with their neighboring community, Providence, their supplies are severely close to depletion. With hostile neighbors at their flanks and hordes of infected outside their walls, they have become prisoners within their own community.

RISE
BY GARETH WOOD

Within hours of succumbing to a plague, millions of dead rise to attack the living. Brian Williams flees the city with his sister Sarah. Banded with other survivors, the group remains desperately outnumbered and under-armed. With no food and little fuel, they must fight their way to safety. RISE is the story of the extreme measures a family will take to survive a trek across a country gone mad.

PERMUTEDPRESS.COM

AGE OF THE DEAD
BY GARETH WOOD

A year has passed since the dead rose, and the citizens of Cold Lake are out of hope. Food and weapons are nearly impossible to find, and the dead are everywhere. In desperation Brian Williams leads a salvage team into the mountains. But outside the small safe zones the world is a foreign place. Williams and his team must use all of their skills to survive in the wilderness ruled by the dead.

DEAD MEAT
BY PATRICK & CHRIS WILLIAMS

The city of River's Edge has been quarantined due to a rodent borne rabies outbreak. But it quickly becomes clear to the citizens that the infection is something much, much worse than rabies... The townsfolk are attacked and fed upon by packs of the living dead. Gavin and Benny attempt to survive the chaos in River's Edge while making their way north in search of sanctuary.

ROTTER WORLD
BY SCOTT M. BAKER

Eight months ago vampires released the Revenant Virus on humanity. Both species were nearly wiped out. The creator of the virus claims there is a vaccine that will make humans and vampires immune to the virus, but it's located in a secure underground facility five hundred miles away. To retrieve the vaccine, a raiding party of humans and vampires must travel down the devastated East Coast.

AMONG THE LIVING
BY TIMOTHY W. LONG

The dead walk. Now the real battle for Seattle has begun. Lester has a new clientele, the kind that requires him to deal lead instead of drugs. Mike suspects a conspiracy lies behind the chaos. Kate has a dark secret: she's a budding young serial killer. These survivors, along with others, are drawn together in their quest to find the truth behind the spreading apocalypse.

PERMUTEDPRESS.COM

AMONG THE DEAD
BY TIMOTHY W. LONG

Seattle is under siege by masses of living dead, and the military struggles to prevent the virus from spreading outside the city. Kate is tired of sitting around. When she learns that a rescue mission is heading back into the chaos, she jumps at the chance to tag along and put her unique skill set and, more importantly, swords to use.

LONG VOYAGE BACK
BY LUKE RHINEHART

When the bombs came, only the lucky escaped. In the horror that followed, only the strong would survive. The voyage of the trimaran Vagabond began as a pleasure cruise on the Chesapeake Bay. Then came the War Alert ... the unholy glow on the horizon ... the terrifying reports of nuclear destruction. In the days that followed, it became clear just how much chaos was still to come.

PERMUTEDPRESS.COM

QUARANTINED
BY JOE MCKINNEY

The citizens of San Antonio, Texas are threatened with extermination by a terrifying outbreak of the flu. Quarantined by the military to contain the virus, the city is in a desperate struggle to survive. Inside the quarantine walls, Detective Lily Harris finds herself caught up in a conspiracy intent on hiding the news from the world and fighting a population threatening to boil over into revolt.

PERMUTEDPRESS.COM

THE DESERT
BY BRYON MORRIGAN

Give up trying to leave. There's no way out. Those are the final words in a journal left by the last apparent survivor of a platoon that disappear in Iraq. Years later, two soldiers realize that what happened to the "Lost Platoon" is now happening to them. Now they must confront the horrifying creatures responsible for their misfortune, or risk the same fate as that of the soldiers before them.

Made in the USA
San Bernardino, CA
10 December 2016